Tanker 10

By Jonathan Curelop

Tanker 10

By Jonathan Curelop

Book Case Engine, New York

Tanker 10 Copyright © 2013 by Jonathan Curelop

Library of Congress cataloguing-in-publication data is available

ISBN: Softcover 978-1-62848-032-0

ISBN: MOBI 978-1-62848-030-6

ISBN: EPUB 978-1-62848-031-3

www.bookcasetv.com

This is a work of fiction. Names, characters, places and incidents either are the product of the author's imagination or are used fictitiously, and any resemblance to any actual person, living or dead, events, or locales is entirely coincidental.

Cover Design: by Book Case Engine.

File under: Young Adult - New Adult Fiction

First print published by Book Case Engine and printed in the United State of America

For Pamela

Acknowledgments

I'd like to thank my wife, Pamela, for boundless encouragement and love. *Tanker 10* is about brothers, so I'd like to thank mine—Gary and Mark. I'd like to thank my parents—Edward and Ethel.

For all things baseball, I'd like to thank: Edward T. Joel, Todd Schmucker, Earnest Earl Smith, Jr., Mike Stone and the entire University of Massachusetts/Amherst baseball coaching staff and team, and Luke Winn.

I'd like to thank a few people who read and reread and commented on the manuscript:

Sharon Mattlin, Lisa Pacenza, and Matt Perron.

In this regard, I would particularly like to thank Valerie Cihylik, who generously gave her time, spirit and unique vision during every stage of the manuscript's development.

And I would like to acknowledge a childhood friend, Bobby J.—taken from us much too young.

Table of Contents

wasn't much when it came to school, but reading was different. On Tuesdays and Thursdays, Mrs. Conroy took me out of class and I joined a few other students in a small room on the third floor. It was called the Accelerated Reading Program and required an additional booklist to the one from our regular reading class. Tuesdays and Thursdays were the best.

"Maybe you'll get a skateboard."

"Can you picture me on a skateboard? Look out below!" I looked at Ben but he wasn't laughing. "It's the same every birthday, every Christmas. Boxes of too-tight clothes that I have to try on in front of everyone…" I didn't want to finish the bleak thought. Ben only took so much of my complaining.

"What?"

"I don't know." I picked up a few pebbles from the ground and arranged them in order of size in my palm. "It's like if she buys me smaller clothes then somehow *I'm* smaller, you know, not really as fat as I am. Watch, *she'll* be calling me Tanker soon."

"Cut the cry baby crap. That's Cliff talking and you know it."

**

We walked down Clydemore, a narrow circular road, toward my house. Several other streets emptied onto it so a few of those "Blind Driveway" signs stood up and down the sidewalk. You couldn't walk out the door without someone's mother yelling, "Be careful of the cars" or "look both ways."

Ben pulled my *Pippi Longstocking* out of my back pocket and flipped through the pages. He was a tall broad kid, only a year older than me and heading into the sixth grade, but he could easily have been mistaken for a junior high student. Popular too, never without someone to play with. "Jeez, you even carry them around with you."

"So."

"Isn't this for girls?"

"It's *about* a girl. You don't have to be a girl to read it."

He looked at me questioningly, pointing at Pippi on the cover.

"So what. It's got pirates," I said. "And a monkey!"

"Maybe I'll read it after you," he said, giving back the book.

"Yeah," I joked. "I'll help you get through it."

We noticed my father on his knees by the edge of his cucumber plants.

"Dad," I said as we walked toward the garden.

"Hey kiddo," he said, his attention focused on the soil. Standing over him, I could see his balding head. My uncles always greeted him by kissing his bald spot or rubbing his scalp with their sleeves. They were just kidding and my father laughed right along, but the teasing made me feel bad, as though I should defend him. "How are you, Ben?" he said.

"Fine, thanks."

"How was work?" I said.

"Oh, not too bad. Same old, same old." He worked the counter at the main branch of the post office on Crescent Street. Whenever asked about his day there, it was always the "same old, same old" reply. He preferred talking about gardening. "Careful there, Ben, watch your step."

Ben's sneaker stood on the edge of a massive clear plastic bag, its brown chunky contents spilling out of the opening.

"Is that dirt?" Ben asked.

"Manure," my father said with a smile. "The finest in southern Mass."

Ben stepped away from the bag. Every year after the frost, my father drove to farms and returned with plastic bags of manure that he mixed with the earth throughout the season. He used anything he could get his hands on for fertilizer—eggshells, carrot and potato peels, coffee grounds and apple cores. The garden was enclosed by a makeshift wire fence; the vegetables separated by rows of rocks he had dug up while expanding the garden's boundaries. His tools were a shovel, a spade, the handle of which had broken off years before, a cracked pitchfork and a rake my grandfather had used at his home in Weymouth.

In February of every year the catalogues from Burpee arrived and after supper he pored over them at the kitchen table, deciding what he would plant in the coming months. Mother mostly just shook her head at all the gardening. Once in a while she mentioned how healthy it was to have fresh vegetables, but for the most part she felt it was too much effort. After all, she often said, they sold fresh vegetables down at the Stop & Shop.

"When did you get that?" I pointed to the bag. "I thought we used the rest."

"Picked it up on the way home. I'm thinking of expanding up the side yard." He was on his knees, inspecting a tiny curled bug that he'd plucked from one of the cukes.

"Darn buggers," he said. "Have to spray after supper." He crushed the thing between his thumb and finger and rubbed what was left on his trousers. "So you feel any older today, Jimmy?" he said, standing up.

"Na, no older," I said as we all made our way to the back door.

"Pretty soon you'll be old like me."

"You're not old."

"Want to bet?" He leaned over, grabbed his lower back and slowed his pace. "I'm soooo old," he said in a weak raspy voice. "I need your help, boys. I'm tuckered out. I can't make it another step."

When we reached out to him, he grabbed me first then Ben and tried to wrestle us to the ground. We twisted out of his grip and he chased us around the backyard for a minute before we brushed ourselves off.

Ben got to eat over because it was my birthday. Mother had prepared homemade pizzas and the whole house was filled with the smell of tangy sauce and dough. After supper, she brought out a birthday cake decorated with frosting roses and "Happy Birthday James" across in bright red. "I purchased this at The Better Baker, that new gourmet shop on Baldwin. Everyone goes there." Ten candles glowing, she placed it on the table, flicked off the wall switch and Mother, my dad and Ben sang *Happy Birthday*. Cliff didn't join in the fun. He just sat there, the candles' flames reflecting in his brown eyes, his lips clamped shut.

Song over and candles blown out, Mother bent over to kiss my cheek. She whispered, "Happy birthday, my sweet boy."

I made the initial cut in the cake and Mother took it to the counter to divvy up the slices and plop on the ice cream. When she brought the dishes to the table my portion was noticeably smaller than the others. Not much more than a sliver, the ice cream little more than a tablespoon. I caught Ben's eye, but he lowered his gaze to his dish and slid his spoon into his mound of ice cream. Cliff didn't say a word, but I imagined him to holding in laughter.

Sure, I was embarrassed. Hell, I loved cake and ice cream. It was my favorite combination food; better than chips and dip, peanut butter and jelly, cookies and milk. Besides, it was my birthday. My portion should have been *bigger* than the others. Although the small portion reminded me that in a few minutes I'd be struggling to button and zip my new birthday presents over my belly. I should have been happy that the portion was tiny. I should have been overjoyed that Mother was looking out for my well-being. In the end, I gobbled up what was in front of me in two or three bites, then brought my plate to the sink.

"Cards and presents," Mother shouted merrily as she gathered the other dessert dishes.

"Hey Mom," Cliff said. "I'm gonna take off. I told Todd I'd be over."

"It's Jimmy's birthday, honey. Why don't you wait until we finish with the presents."

"I told them six-thirty. It's already after."

"I think you can spare a few moments for—"

"Come on Ma," he said, his hands pressed down against the table, eager to spring.

"Hey!" My father stood. "Come with me," he said to Cliff as he walked down the steps that led to the playroom. He didn't have to look back to see if Cliff was following.

The three of us waited in silence.

"Supper was delicious, Mrs. LaPlante."

She smiled. "Thank you, Ben."

In another minute Cliff returned to his chair while my father strolled to the counter and pick up an envelope. "From Cliff," he said.

I lifted the flap. The card was brightly colored and full of flowers. The inscription started, "To my Loving Brother." It was hard to keep a straight face thinking Cliff would select such a card.

I skipped down to the signature. The C was sort of legible; the rest was a squiggly line.

"Which should he open first?" Mother asked as she placed her hands on my shoulders. A sensation of heat swirled behind my ears. No clothes, I prayed. No clothes.

"This one first," my father said.

He reached under the table near his feet. Onto the table he set down an awkwardly shaped package. I ripped into it, tearing off several layers of paper, until I held in my hands a baseball glove. Not just any baseball glove. A real glove. Until now, I had only owned cheap plastic mitts. But this one felt and smelled like real leather, its webbing intricately designed. It even had Carl Yastrzemski's signature. My fingers slipped comfortably into the glove, though it appeared enormous on my hand. Playing ball against the house would reach a whole new level. I rubbed it all over—the heel, the fingers, the pocket. I'd wear it always—while I ate, went to school, slept, did homework.

"It's perfect, Dad. I love it."

"Hey, what about me?" Mother said.

"Sorry, Mom. You too."

My father said, "I have some oil downstairs. We'll get it broken in in no time."

When I looked up from the glove a large beautifully wrapped box was on the table. She loved to wrap presents, Mother. Bright colors, frilly bows and ribbons. I wanted to take my glove and run away.

"Are you going to open it, honey?" Mother said as she took her seat at the table.

"Yeah," Cliff said, "hurry it up."

I removed the glove, then reached for the box and slowly slid my fingers under the paper. Anything to prolong the inevitable. Maybe the phone would ring. My grandfather wishing me a happy birthday. Or, better yet, someone for Mother, to take her mind off the proceedings long enough for me to slip out the door.

But the phone didn't ring. I lifted the side flaps and pulled the paper away from where it was perfectly taped down the middle of the box. God, it was quiet. Was I sweating? I broke the tape in the two places and started to lift the cover. Man, this was taking forever. I felt like one of those guys on the cop shows who have to dismantle the bomb. Clip the wrong wire and the whole building blows. Pick the blue one! No, the green one, the GREEN one!

Several items lay under frilly pastel-colored tissue paper. I wasn't sure if I should put the lid back on, say thank you and leave, as though nothing more was expected; or, knowing what was expected, slowly remove the awful pieces one by one, even further delaying the inevitable. In the end, I took them out, shaping my lips into a grin: pants that would cling to my thighs and a tee shirt with a large 10 across the front, among other treasures.

"Thank you." I gathered up the gifts, placed them in the box and started to replace the lid.

"Wait, wait," Mother said. "Don't you want to try them on?"

"I, well . . . I mean, uh . . ."

"Mrs. LaPlante, my folks were hoping to wish Jimmy a happy birthday before they went out tonight," Ben said.

"Oh, that's fine," she said.

Cliff was up and away from the table in seconds.

"Call if you're going to be late," Mother said.

But the only sound from his direction was the slamming of the screen door.

**

We were in the clearing again. We both lay on our backs. My new baseball glove served as my pillow. We talked baseball, as usual. It was already August, but we were still talking about Hank Aaron's 755th homer. Of course we talked about the Red Sox, too—whether we'd be able to put some distance between us and Cleveland, whether we'd be able to catch the Orioles and Yankees. Anything would have been a letdown after last year, except a return to the World Series.

"Thanks for the rescue."

"You think I want to spend the night watching you try on clothes?"

Voices rose from deep in the woods. I rolled onto my stomach and peeked out between the tree trunks and stalks of bamboo. Ben scampered to my side and pushed away some tall wild grass. We watched them swagger: Cliff and his posse of bullies. Tony Langley, practically emaciated, even though he ate everything in sight. That was reason enough to hate him, never mind that he threw rocks at me. He never got me in the head or anything, but whether that was a conscious decision or bad aim I wasn't sure. Reggie Conner walked at the head of the pack with Cliff. His head was surrounded by a humongous reddish afro, but he was still the tallest with or without that thing. Reggie was the quiet one. He didn't bother me that much, but when the others started teasing, his laugh could be heard down the Village. Bringing up the rear was Todd McAffee, the worst of the lot. He always wore the same outfit—a grimy white t-shirt and a pair of those bright blue dungarees they stack in the dollar bin over at King's on North Main Street. I stayed quiet in front of Todd because every time I opened my mouth he mimicked me, extending the vowels loud and shrill. "Shut uuuuuup." "Cut it oooouuuuuut." "Leave me alooooone."

Cliff's stride was quicker than the others. He was tall like our father and I hated that. He looked more like Dad than I did. I hated that too. But something about his head was just plain weird. Like the fact that his forehead was so much larger in proportion than the rest of his head. Freakish. Yes, that was it! I realized as the clan moved toward us, my body becoming totally still. His head was like one of those 1950s black and white movie space creatures.

Ben maneuvered onto his hands and knees and said, "Why don't we—"

I looked up at him with a menacing glare.

"What?" he mouthed.

I put my finger to my lips. I barely breathed until Cliff and the gang were safely past our clearing, probably on their way to sling Coke and beer bottles at the back wall of the Cumberland Farms on East Ashland.

"Want to go inside?" I said while sitting up, my voice still quiet.

"It's plenty light yet." He pointed to my glove. "Let's toss the ball around." I loved the idea of using the glove, but I must have looked panicked at the possibility of being so out in the open, so exposed, because next he said, "Why are you so afraid of them? It's not like they're—"

"Yeah, I know, I know . . ." I stood and started out of the woods towards Ben's house. I turned to find that Ben hadn't budged. "You all right there?" He remained quiet. "It's easy," I said. "You see those things you're standing on? You just move them a little bit, one in front of the other. Like the Winter Warlock." I sang: "*Put one foot in front of the other. And soon you'll be walking out the door . . . oor . . . oor."*

He smiled. But instead of joining me, he said, "I'm not running away from them anymore."

Ben was more like my brother than Cliff. I would have done anything to preserve our friendship. But he didn't understand. He couldn't. He was too popular, too handsome, too athletic. He couldn't understand how it felt when Cliff tortured me with his antics. The sadness. And the need to escape that sadness.

It wasn't the insults. It wasn't even the occasional hits, shoves and punches. What bugged me was that I allowed it to bug me. Sometimes it didn't even take a nasty comment from Cliff, just a quick glance over the supper table while I placed a forkful of food in my mouth. Kids at school frequently taunted me—in lunch line, gym class, on the bus. No problem. Cliff, though. That was another matter.

It might have been right then, face to face with Ben as though we were gunslingers in a movie, that I realized why I allowed the sadness to paralyze me. The son of a bitch was my older brother. He was the one who was supposed to defend me from teasing. He had the power to say, Stop, to say, Come on guys, knock it off. But he never did.

The tears crept up behind my eyes so quickly I didn't have time to flee. I just turned away from Ben and squeezed the tears back down. But the more I squeezed the more they wanted to bust through. Poor Ben didn't know what to do. He just stood there, muttered things like, "You okay?" and "It'll be all right." I wasn't sure he actually saw a tear, but I was still embarrassed.

He apologized. I told him to never mind, it had nothing to do with him. We walked for a few minutes, then sat on a large rock at the edge of the woods. I told him what I was thinking about when I'd started to cry.

"That's goofy," Ben said. "Name two brothers or sisters that get along. I can't."

"This is different. Besides, you don't have brothers or sisters."

"I know, but . . . Don't make too much of it."

It was getting a little darker. The last thing I wanted to do was go home. Cliff would be there soon, Mother was probably waiting for me. I stood up.

"You could get skinny if you wanted."

"Huh?" I said, shocked. "What?"

"Don't freak. I'm just saying."

Ben had never started a conversation about my weight. It had always been the same: I bitched, he listened.

"I better leave." I started to rise from the rock, but before I could fully stand he had scrambled from where he sat and stood over me. My butt fell back onto the rock.

"I didn't mean it like that. I didn't mean anything bad. Hey, all they got on you is the weight. You lose it, they shut up."

"I ain't changing for them."

"For yourself then."

"Not for them. I'd rather stay fat." I thought of Mother's voice in my ear at supper—*my sweet boy*—the beautifully wrapped box. "I'll do it for her. So she won't be ashamed of me anymore." A hot pressure rose in my cheeks and eyes.

"What's wrong?"

This time the tears rolled down. I didn't even try squeezing them away. They trickled down my cheeks at first, then burned. I found myself slipping down the rock until my ass found dirt.

Ben sat on the ground next to me and wrapped an arm around my shoulder. "Oh brother, enough with the crying. Between this and *Pippi Longstocking* I'd swear you were a girl." He pulled my shirt at the neck and tried to look down. "You're not, are ya?"

I pulled myself away, but he grabbed my shoulders and playfully flattened me to the ground. We both ended up sprawled on the dirt laughing. Ben put up with way too much. Most of the kids in the neighborhood were either Cliff's age or much younger than me and Ben, so I wondered sometimes if he felt stuck with me. He got up, extended his arm.

"Swim with us," he said as we glanced up and down the street before crossing. "My dad won't mind." He was referring to the hour or so a day he spent swimming with the AAU team, which his father coached at the Y. Just last month he competed in Memphis at the Junior Olympics and took second place in the 50 freestyle and third place in two other events. A couple of times I'd even heard his father mention Moscow, 1980. Ben brushed it off, saying he would be too young, that his father was just joking, but I wasn't so sure.

Sometimes I felt inadequate when I thought of his accomplishments. The most athletic thing I did was toss the ball against the house, which I could do for hours at a time, but there was no Olympic event for throwing a tennis ball against the back of your house. "Your father would let me?"

"Yeah, definitely."

I thought of having to undress in front of his teammates, peeling off my bathing suit. I thought of sharing swim lanes with future Olympians. "What if I take up all the space in the lane and the other swimmers can't get by?"

"What if you shut up and quit ranking on yourself?"

**

I held one of Mother's birthday shirts in my hand, the tee shirt with the 10. Mother was in the next room laying on her bed above the covers reading one of her fashion magazines. The idea of just shouting that everything fit fine occurred to me, but she would want to see for herself. I shoved my head through the neck of the shirt, pushed my arms through the short sleeves and yanked the material down over my body.

I liked it. It was snug, but not nearly as tight as I thought it would be. The colors were cool, black and gold, like the Bruins. Knowing I would lose weight I decided to keep it. Wear it once a week or so, feel it becoming looser and looser. Next came the pants. One leg in, then the other. I pulled them up. They barely buttoned around the waist. I had to keep my gut sucked in, otherwise the button would surely bust. No, she would have to take them back. I couldn't do it. I lowered the pants to my ankles and sat on the edge of my bed.

Mother's voice rose from her room. "You okay there, Jimmy?" I didn't want to answer her, just wanted to throw the clothes back in the box and slide the damn thing under the bed. The bed next door squeaked. Her feet padded down the hall. I was looking up at her when she appeared in the doorway.

"What are you doing?"

I shrugged and finally said, "Just sitting here."

"Come on," she said, bending down and trying to lift the pants up my legs. "Let's give it a try."

"I did already," I said too loudly.

"You have to stand up. You have to help me."

I did as instructed, but slowly, without enthusiasm, keeping my arms down by my sides. They remained rigid at my hips as she tried to bring the pants over the swell of my ass. I couldn't help being defiant in my own little way.

"You have to move your arms, sweetie. We need to get these buttoned."

I relented only to push out my gut. I kept my eyes on her face as she struggled with the button and fly.

She sat back on her heels and sighed. A light sheen had broken out on her forehead. "They don't button at all, do they?" she said.

"I'm sorry I'm fat." I wasn't sure why I said it. I guess I felt bad about making this difficult, about her having to go to sleep all sweaty and stinky. I sat back on the edge of the bed, letting the pants fall to my ankles.

"What did you say?"

"I said I'm sorry I'm fat." I couldn't look at her, no way. My eyes remained fixed on the bunched material at my feet. "Why do you buy me these clothes? Maybe you don't want your friends seeing you in the Husky Department. Shopping for a fat kid."

Her face crumpled. Her skin became blotchy. Wrinkles puckered around her lips and eyes. She sniffed and mucus made noise in her nostrils. Sitting next to me on the bed, she ran a warm hand through my hair and let it rest on the back of my neck. She kissed my temple.

I wasn't sure if she wanted me to keep talking, but since she didn't say anything I said, "When I put my clothes on and they're tight, sometimes I feel like . . ."

Her hand slid off my neck and down my back. She sniffled again. I looked at her in profile; two tears rolled down her cheek and I knew that I was about to deepen the wound. What scared me and at the same time thrilled me was that I could have stopped but didn't.

" . . . like, you don't like me."

She held my face in her sweaty palms. Her eyes grew large. "That's not true. Never, ever." Watery snot appeared at her nose. She wrapped her arms around my shoulders; every surface of her skin seemed feverish. "You musn't ever think that," she said into my ear. She separated, still holding my arms, and said, "Jimmy, I'm your mother. I will always love you. No matter what. Always always always. You understand?"

I nodded.

"Promise me something," she said. "You have to tell me if I ever upset you."

I nodded again.

"Promise?"

"Yes," I said.

"Say it."

"I promise."

She continued to stare at me, waiting.

"I promise I will tell you if you ever upset me."

She smiled. "You know how I tell you if you do something wrong? Well, you're a big boy now, you can tell me I'm wrong, especially if I do something that hurts you."

She leaned into me and kissed the side of my mouth. I breathed in her nighttime smell, Jergens and butterscotch. Some nights it was spearmint or cinnamon. She liked hard candy before going to bed. Standing up, she gathered the pants at my feet and tossed them in the gift box with the other clothes.

My father's voice drifted up from the kitchen.

Mother opened the door and said, "What's that?"

"You want some tea?"

"Tea would be great." There was no sound of tears or sniffling in her voice. Her coloring had smoothed over, her wrinkles had somehow receded, her hazel eyes were clear and dry. Box in hand, she turned to me in the doorway. She held out her arm and said, "Let's have it," referring to the 10 shirt I was wearing.

"Not this one," I said. "I like this one."

"You sure? It looks tight."

Not for long, I thought. "I want to keep it."

"Okay. Get your jammies on and come down. I'll set up the cribbage board."

She walked downstairs toward the clinking of silverware. Jergens and butterscotch hung in the air.

2. Tanker 10

My father would be late. He was helping a guy from work put together a shed. When they finished, they were going to grab pizzas and beer at Karl's Café. I wondered if they were going to get the curly fries. That place had great curly fries.

For supper that night Mother made Neopolitan Casserole. A great dish for many reasons, one of which was she always prepared it earlier in the day and when I came home from school the house smelled delicious. It was made with hamburger, little pasta shells, spinach, minced vegetables, tons of herbs, spices and seeds. One of the other things I liked about it was that Mother always made it with popovers. I loved popovers.

Mother removed the casserole dish from the counter where it had been cooling and placed it on the table between Cliff and me. She stuck a serving spoon into the casserole, whereupon Cliff heaped some of the food onto his plate.

The phone rang. Cliff stood up and answered it. "Hello . . . Hey Todd, I'll take it upstairs." He put the phone on the counter and took the stairs two at a time to pick up the line in our parents' room. "Got it," he bellowed from above and Mother replaced the kitchen phone.

I spooned some of the casserole onto my plate, about half as much as usual. I tore the top off one of the popovers and watched the steam rise up in a swirl. Loading the pocket of dough with the casserole, I brought it to my mouth. My nose filled with the rich aroma of the dish.

Cliff returned to the table. "Ma, everyone's going to Westgate tonight. John Bucyk and Wayne Cashman are signing autographs."

My heart leaped. "Really? Can I . . .?" Then I recovered my senses.

"You want to go, Jimmy?" Mother said as she finished sponging off the counter near the sink. "Maybe Cliff will take you along."

"Sure," Cliff said jovially so Mother could hear. Then only for my ears, an unsettling whisper: "What do you say, Tanker? Want to come along for the fun? There's a food court."

"That's okay," I said.

"No?" Mother said. "Well maybe Cliff will bring you back an autograph." She looked at Cliff while rinsing dishes at the sink, raising her eyebrows, smiling.

"You bet," he said.

The phone rang again. And again Cliff was quick to answer. "Hello . . . We're eating. He can't come to the phone right now." He hung up and resumed eating.

"Why didn't you let me talk?" I almost yelled.

"We're in the middle of supper."

"Who was it?"

"I don't know," he said matter-of-factly, shoveling food into his mouth as he spoke. "Said he'd call back."

Anger surged in my chest. "Was it Ben?" I yelled.

"I said I don't know," he shouted back.

I barely heard Mother say, "Settle down, boys," something like that.

"Of course it was Ben. Who else would want to talk to you?"

The anger rushed higher now, to my shoulders, up into my neck. "I don't get it. Why didn't you let me talk?"

"That's enough now," Mother interjected.

"We're eating, that's why. How many times do I have to say it? Should I say it slower?" He leaned forward so that his big ugly head floated halfway across the table. He spoke in slow motion, his mouth full of food. "Wweee aaarrre eeeaaatttiiinnnggggggggg."

"We were eating when you went upstairs to talk to Todd."

He spoke slowly again. "Wwwweee aaarrre—"

Fury raged in my head. Barely aware of what I was doing, I sank my hand into the casserole dish, lifted chunks of the hamburger, pasta and vegetables, slammed them against Cliff's face with thick squishing sounds and screamed into his face, "I hate you, you dick. You dick, I hate you."

He leaped over the table and grabbed my shoulders. Before he could hit me, Mother raced across the kitchen and dragged us to the sink. She ran my hand under the faucet and kept a cold washcloth against Cliff's face and neck. But it wouldn't have mattered if I had burned myself. I wouldn't have felt it anyway. I had stood up to him, and it felt sweet.

"What the hell's the matter with you two?" Mother screamed.

"What are ya yelling at me for?" Cliff said, taking off the washcloth. "He slung food all over."

"You started it," I said. "You wouldn't let me talk. You knew what you were doing."

"Well, neither of you are going anywhere until it's cleaned up." She pulled some vegetable bits out of Cliff's hair. A small chunk of meat stuck near a nostril.

"I'm not touching it. Jimmy did it. He should clean it."

"Maybe I'll have your father do it. And when he asks why he needs to clean the kitchen floor I'll be happy to tell him."

Cliff rinsed his washcloth and wrung it dry. Then he unrolled some paper towels from the rack and gave them to me. It only took a few minutes to wipe up the food and dry the floor. Mother then made us finish our meal, which we did quickly and in silence. Afterward, Cliff brought his dish and fork to the sink, said to Mother, "Thanks, it was good, I'll be home early" and gently closed the front door as he left.

He walked into my bedroom when he returned from Westgate. I practically jumped off my bed when I saw him standing in the doorway, but then remembered that Mother was next door watching a re-airing of *Upstairs Downstairs*.

"I brought you something," he said.

He handed me two 5"x7" publicity shots of John Bucyk and Wayne Cashman wearing their black and gold Bruins uniforms. Above the autograph on each picture were the words: "To Tanker—"

When I looked up, the fleshy area between his thumb and index finger was buried in his mouth, stifling laughter. His shoulders shook.

I smiled along with him. I removed two thumbtacks from a desk drawer and pinned the pictures above my desk at eye level, then sat down in the chair and leaned back.

"You can do and say whatever you want," I said.

"Is that right?"

"That's right. See, while Mom was digging hamburger out of your nose I realized something."

"Oh yeah?" he scoffed. "What's that?"

"Me being fat, that's temporary. You being a prick? That's forever."

**

Dad got home about twenty minutes after Cliff. Since we had cleaned the kitchen and everything ended civilly I wasn't too worried about Dad's reaction to the food fight. It had blown over; Mother probably wouldn't even bother to tell him. But she did.

"Are you kidding me?" he hollered, standing over us in his tank top tee shirt. He must have been undressing when Mother told him. A tall white plastic bucket stood at his side. He had called us down from our rooms and made us sit at the kitchen table. I could smell the beer. He sometimes smelled like this at barbeques. "Here's what we're gonna do. Did I say we? Not we. You two. Here's what *you two* are gonna do." He paced as he considered what to say. When he reached the sink he nonchalantly swiped a large serving spoon that had been drying in the dish rack. "You two are going to make this kitchen floor spick and span. Oh yes."

"We already cleaned it," Cliff said.

"Doesn't matter," he said. "Needs to be redone. Re. Done." He emphasized each syllable by pointing the spoon as he laid out the cleaning instructions. Move the table and chairs to the other side of the kitchen. Fill the bucket with hot water from the basement sink. Add detergent. Get the mop. Dry the floor. Polish the floor.

So Cliff and I cleaned the floor for a second time while our parents played crazy eights and drank coffee in the dining room. Toward the end, we were on our hands and knees polishing the floor with rags. We had started at separate sides and met in the middle. My hand brushed Cliff's by accident. He slid his hand into mine hard and I said, "Ouch." Dad was at the kitchen entrance in a second. "We got more rooms that need cleaning." He counted on his fingers. "Basement. Playroom. Bedrooms. Living room. So keep it up."

When it was over we emptied the dirty water and placed the dirty rags in the hamper. Mom and Dad helped us move the furniture back. The floor glistened. "A job well done," my father said as they surveyed the floor. Mother added, "Now no more fighting. Right?"

Cliff and I nodded.

"Right?" she said again.

"Right," Cliff and I said. "Right."

Cliff climbed the stairs ahead of me. When he got to his room he stepped inside and closed the door. A moment later I heard *Won't Get Fooled Again* blaring from inside. Cliff listened to The Who about ten hours a day.

I sat on the edge of my bed. I thought about how Cliff and I had gone about getting the job done. Mixing the water and soap in the bucket and sloshing it around with a wooden paint paddle; taking turns ringing out the mop, not putting it back until it was as dry as possible; washing our hands at the same time in the big basement sink. It seemed goofy, but it made me feel like we'd actually done something as a team. I walked down the hall to see what he thought. Maybe he felt the same way. But I hesitated when I got there. The music blared too loudly to be inviting.

**

It was a Sunday. My parents were at a brunch, a fundraiser for city beaches—Nantasket, Wollaston, the like. I was in my room watching a *Twilight Zone* marathon. Mother wouldn't have been too happy about that, but it wasn't like I was watching *The Night Stalker* or *Night Gallery*. I read during the episodes I had already seen. *Pippi* was long gone; I was now onto *The Dark Is Rising*, a fantasy series about a boy who, on his eleventh birthday, discovers that he is the last of the Old Ones, powerful immortals who exist to protect the Light.

I also ate during the breaks. I hadn't forgotten my plan to lose weight, but Mother just bought a box of Dolly Madison treats for my father's lunches—jelly and cream cheese rolled up in some kind of orange sponge cake—and I knew I wouldn't be able to resist. I mean Dolly Madison. Come on! Don't get me wrong, Hostess was great too. It was hard to beat Twinkies and Ring Dings. And Little Debbie's were top notch, with their signature oatmeal cream pies.

The front door opened. Boisterous voices rose from downstairs. Cliff and Todd. I reached to close my door and heard them scuttle through the front room, the kitchen, toward the stairs.

"Don't be a chicken shit," Cliff was saying, "you hate him as much as I do. This will serve him right."

"A teacher, though? What if we get caught?"

"We won't."

"Let's pick someone else."

"Nope," Cliff said flatly, in charge. "The phone book's in my mother's room."

I closed the door before they reached the stairs. Hopefully, they would think I was out. I lowered the television for good measure. With the volume down, I heard Cliff.

"I'll call him as the Chinese guy. Then we'll let him stew for a while. Then you call as the cop." I could tell Todd was iffy because Cliff kept trying different tactics, like enthusiastic ("It'll be fun!"), then bullying ("What do you gotta be a pussy for?"), then sullen ("What else are we gonna do?"). Something must have worked because the next thing I heard was a hideous Chinese accent. "Hewwo. Is this Missa Charles Duflesne? Hewwo. This is Johnny Wong at Shanghai Dumpring. You muss pick up fiffy dorrar pratter. Why no you pick up pratter?"

I could just imagine Cliff's joy at finding Mr. Dufresne at home. "You muss pick up pratter now. No matter. Fiffy dorrar, fiffy dorrar. Don't want to call porice. You will see. You be sorry."

He banged the phone down so loudly I heard the after-ring. I opened my door, stepped into the hall and took just enough steps to spy into Mother's room. Cliff laughed like a squirrel if a squirrel could laugh; Todd's laugh erupted from deep in his gut.

They sat on the edge of the large bed, causing the bedding to shift and wrinkle. I knew Cliff would smooth the blankets before leaving, fearing Mother's reaction.

Cliff reached for the phone and handed the receiver to his friend, but Todd was still laughing. Cliff grabbed a pillow and tossed it at Todd, who pasted it against his face. Mother would need to change the pillowcases because Todd's face was infamous for its clusters of acne. When he wasn't with the gang, they always talked about Todd's face. They compared the clusters to mountain ranges, the individual pimples to actual mountains. The Himalayas on his cheek, the Rockies along his jaw. And lately the Vesuvius and the Olympus, gruesome twin zits on either side of his forehead, which Todd tried to keep hidden with his greasy black bangs.

When the laughs finally died, Cliff held out the receiver. Todd crossed his arms on his chest and looked down. Cliff pressed the phone into Todd's torso and I feared that the phone, if Todd didn't agree, might be used as a weapon. "Come on, Todd," my brother said, "it's funny as shit, man."

Todd smirked and loosened his arms. He seemed physically the oldest of the crew. His arms were hairier than the others', his muscles more developed. A wispy mustache rested beneath his nose. Todd's thick fingers wrapped around the phone as Cliff redialed.

"Good afternoon, Mr. Dufresne. This is . . . this is, ah, Sergeant Davis from Brockton Police. As I guess you know, Mr. Wong insists that you placed an order at his restaurant . . . uh, establishment." He looked to Cliff for guidance, but soon recovered. Cliff leaned in toward the phone. Their heads connected and remained so, like Siamese twins, until the words on the other end agitated Todd enough to stand up. "All right, settle down now, Mr. Dufresne, I'm just doing my job . . . Yes, I know we all have a job to do, but when I do my job I'm not an asshole like you are when you do your job." Cliff's hands flew to his head, his lips opened wide in amazement. "No, I'm not a cop, you moron. How can such a stupid fuck like you teach anything?" He placed the receiver down. Cliff bounced on the bed. They roared with laughter and slapped each other's hands over their heads.

"Let's do another one," Todd said.

Not for me. Even being in my room was too close. I continued *The Twilight Zone* marathon in the playroom, tiptoeing down the stairs. I had been watching for about ten minutes when a trumpet blasted from above. I hated the trumpet, but the possibility of Todd's pimply lips on my mouthpiece made me want to rescue it. Taking the stairs two at a time, I found Cliff holding the phone out in front of him while Todd delivered another blast into the receiver.

"Cut it out," I screamed. "Stop it."

Todd pressed his thick lips against the silver mouthpiece and blew. I lunged for the horn, but he held it away with one hand while pushing me aside with the other. I lunged again and grabbed the horn's bell. The tug of war lasted a few seconds. Just when I felt I was going to yank it from Todd's grip, he let go, causing me to fall backward. I was able to right myself before falling to the floor, but the bell of the horn glanced against the leg of Mother's dresser.

The bell was dented. I held it out for Todd to see. "Look what you did," I shouted.

"I didn't do it. You pulled it away."

"Look what you did." I couldn't think of anything else to say.

"Look what you did," Todd mimicked, his voice squeaky like a baby's. "Look what you did."

Cliff loved Todd's Tanker impersonations. He sat on the bed clapping his hands, a brainless toy monkey banging cymbals.

I should have just left. I had the trumpet. But as I looked into their faces, I realized that now that the prank call was over, I was their next victim. So I gathered as much saliva in my mouth as possible and let it fly. I wanted it to spray them both. I didn't find out where it landed, though, because I fled as soon as I spit.

One of them was behind me. I heard heavy feet, even their breathing. Then: "I'll get you, you fat Tanker fuck." It was Todd. I flew into the bathroom, but before I could close the door Todd had wedged his foot into the jam. He had me in the tub in a second, my head under the spigot, my legs flailing over the tub's wall. The cold water came on hard. It poured over the back of my head, soaking my shoulders. He pushed my face into the corner of the tub. My nose and cheeks squished against the porcelain. From above, over the running water, I heard Cliff's voice.

"Cut the shit, Todd."

Todd loosened his grip enough for me to look up. Cliff was pulling on Todd's shoulder. He was rescuing me.

"What the fuck?" Todd said. "I'm just getting started."

"We can beat on him anytime," Cliff said. "My parents' room. You too," he said, pointing to me. So much for being rescued. Todd gave me a final shove before getting up, leaving me to turn off the water. I climbed out of the tub and started to follow them, but Cliff stopped me before I was able make it out of the bathroom. He removed a hand towel from the rack, tossed it at my face and told me to dry off. "You don't want to drip all down the hall. Get us in trouble again."

By the time I got to my parents' room they were sitting on the edge of the bed staring silently at the dresser. I joined them; me on one end, Todd in the middle, Cliff on the other end. What transfixed us was a thumbnail sized chip that my trumpet had removed from one of the legs of the bureau.

"She's gonna kill us," Cliff said.

"Let's blame Todd," I said.

He turned and looked down at me. "What the fuck."

"She won't kill *you*," I said.

He said, "You don't know that." Then shoved me hard with his elbow and I slid off the corner of the bed.

Cliff stood up and left the room. Todd followed him. I followed Todd. Cliff led the way to the basement. On a shelf above the washer dryer my father kept an array of furniture stains and varnishes. Cliff chose the darkest, grabbed a couple paper towels from the kitchen on the way back to the bedroom and applied the stain. I had to hand it to him, it looked pretty good. He returned the stain to precisely where he'd found it. He even gave the dirty paper towels to Todd to discard away from our house. A future criminal if ever there was one.

**

"Your new shirt," Mother said with a smile, spreading a small amount of margarine on a piece of toast.

Day number one, I thought. I would wear it again in a week, see how it fit. Then the following week, and the week after that.

"Ben's father stopped by this morning. There's a swim class at the high school that meets on Saturday mornings. It's for . . ." Instead of continuing, she lifted a shiny brochure from the kitchen table. "It's for . . ."

I took the brochure and said, "I know about it." I had seen the brochure before. Lots of pamphlets and papers having to do with extracurricular activities were handed out at school—sports, arts and crafts, performance workshops, martial arts. This one advertised swim classes for students who didn't feel comfortable swimming with other students. A swim class for misfits, for the physically deformed, for freaks. Everyone called it Fat Swim.

I imagined Cliff's reaction when he found out I was enrolled in Fat Swim. Oh, the mileage he would get out of that. Levels of torture never before reached. "I don't know about this, Ma."

"No need to decide now," she said, taking back the brochure. "Only if it's something you want to do. It's an ongoing class, so you could join anytime."

"Where's Cliff?" I wanted to play ball against the house, but not if he were around.

"He said something about going to D.W. Fields Park with friends."

She allowed the matter of Fat Swim to drop and I walked over to the toaster. After breakfast, I grabbed my glove from under my mattress, grabbed a tennis ball from a bucket of them by the back door and jogged out to the back yard as though being introduced onto the Fenway Park outfield by Sherm Feller, my name booming out over the loudspeakers.

I threw the ball against the foundation to field ground balls, against the upper wall for line drives, the roof for pop flies. Wherever the ball came from, my position was always the same—centerfield.

The Yankees were in town. First up Bobby Bonds. I threw the ball lightly against the house for the easy grab. The new glove felt like it was custom made for my hand. Ernie Maddox, who had gone two for three last night with two walks against Baltimore, belted a solid base hit. Roy White batted third. He slashed a double down the leftfield line, caroming around in the corner so I could face Thurman Munson with runners on second and third. He had been held hitless the previous night, but always posed a dangerous threat. I whipped the tennis ball with all my strength. Just as it hit the house, Munson swung and the ball exploded from his bat. If I ran as fast as possible, I would have made the catch standing up, but I slowed down on purpose to make the athletic sprawling diving catch. Roy White tagged up from third, but not to worry, I anticipated it and threw a rope to Carlton Fisk, who crouched at the plate waiting for White to slide into the baseball.

I was about to throw the ball again, make another circus catch when the sound of screeching tires came from up the street. Shouts erupted and I ran to see what happened.

Oh God, they must have changed their minds. They hadn't gone to the park. They were all gathered at the curve near Ben's house, a makeshift hockey net on each side of the street, several sticks and street pucks and balls scattered to the side of the road. A car had obviously stopped short. Todd stood behind it as it pulled way, his arms in the air. "Watch where you're going," he screamed at the car's exhaust.

Cliff saw me first. "Hey Tanker," he said, "bring us the ball." At first I thought he meant my tennis ball, but when he pointed to the side of the road about mid distance between us I saw an orange hockey ball. I didn't want to bring him the ball, but if I walked away he would have had that against me the next time we met. *Hey Tanker, why didn't you bring me the ball? Why do you have to be such a fat asshole?*

So I walked toward the ball. I could have just thrown it to him. But I didn't want to give him the satisfaction of me making the effort to bend over and pick it up. A solid kick, if I smacked it just so, would deliver the ball most of the distance. That way, I was giving him the ball without getting too close. I reared my leg back and flung my foot into the ball. I caught it with the side of my sneaker and it rolled weakly toward the other side of the street. The lame kick provoked giggles. I just wanted out of there now, so I strolled quickly to the ball, picked it up and was about to throw it toward them when Cliff shouted, "Don't throw it. Bring it over."

"You can play with us," Todd said.

I wasn't sure what Todd was up to. Surely he'd had enough when he soaked my head and ground my face into the bathtub. They all waved me enthusiastically in their direction. Cliff picked up his Bauer and started stick-handling around one of the nets. The others followed suit, gathering sticks, passing balls and pucks to one another, taking shots on net. Did they really want me to join them? I wasn't naïve enough to think so, but still, it seemed important to give them another chance, to allow them to include me in their horseplay.

"You're right on time, Tanker," Todd said. "We were just setting up the goals when old Henderson almost took us out. Damn, they'll let anyone behind a wheel." His eyes disappeared into slits when he laughed. "Get in net, Tanker, you're the goalie. We'll see if we can get anything by you."

"Doubt it," one of them I didn't know said. "He'll take up the whole net."

"We got no goalie pads, but that doesn't matter." This from Tony.

"Na, he's got all the padding he needs," said another one I didn't know.

The clan was growing! Weeks from now there'd be dozens, trying to top each other with their witty zingers.

Cliff stood off to the side bouncing a puck off his stick blade, trying to keep it from falling to the street. I remembered the night we got that blade. When we returned home from the store he and Dad held it over the stove flame forming the perfect curve.

He was still balancing the puck when I walked over to him and said softly, "Tell them to stop."

He let the puck fall to the ground.

"You know they will if you tell them."

It seemed he was about to say something but opted instead to deliver a mighty slap shot into the far goal, causing the netting to shudder outward. He did this so quickly I leaped out of the way. He retrieved the puck and continued some fancy stick-handling before saying, "Let's choose sides, let's play."

Turning to leave, I heard Todd say, "Tanker, where you going? You're gonna play net, right?"

"That's kind of tight, ain't it?"

My shirt! I looked down to find it had crawled up my stomach, exposing my lower belly to the street and the wolves who occupied it. I quickly pulled it down, stretching it tightly over my skin.

"He got it for his birthday," Cliff said. "Tanker turned ten the other day." They erupted with a mock cheer. "Tanker 10," he shouted as though he just discovered a brilliant idea. "Tanker 10. Tanker 10." The others joined in. "Tan-ker 10. Tan-ker 10. Tan-ker 10." I watched my brother lead the mantra, watched the joy spread across his face as the nickname took hold. In a few seconds the chant dissolved into laughter. Cliff's laughs almost brought him to his knees. He clutched his hockey stick for balance.

**

The first thing I wanted to do was burn the shirt. The second thing I wanted to do was crawl under my bed and spend the rest of the day alternating between Oreos, Chip Ahoys and 'Nilla Wafers. I did neither. I sat on the patio at the base of the foundation in the backyard and pulled the shirt over my bent knees. No amount of pulling seemed to stretch the shirt. I decided to resume prowling the green Fenway outfield, to work through at least the first round of the Yankees batting order.

After a few minutes it started to rain and I went inside where I read, ate lunch with Mother and read some more. The rain stopped after a while so once again I ran outside to finish off the Yankees. Just outside the back door, I practically banged into Cliff, who was carving large letters into the wooden fence that lined a portion of our patio. He had completed a T and was starting another letter. He was using the broken pitchfork to gnaw out the wood and his jackknife for the finer points. Other tools—rake and shovels among them—lay at Cliff's feet because our father had been digging up this part of the lawn to extend the garden.

"Better be careful, Tanker," he said, our bodies two inches apart; his gaze never wavered from the fence. "You don't want to get an eye poked out, do you?"

"No."

"Bug off then."

"What are you doing?"

"It's so you won't forget your name."

He was carving my nickname into the fence. What was wrong with him? Had he forgotten about having to scrub the kitchen floor? Or the close call with the bureau?

"Why are you doing that?"

"Nothing else to do."

"Dad's gonna be pissed."

Cliff continued his project, maneuvering the pitchfork in the fence.

"Mom will be mad too."

"Shut up." The first line of the A was almost complete.

"You better stop."

I reached for the handle of the pitchfork and tried to grab it away. There was no guarantee my father would take the fence down just because "Tanker" had been carved into it. And I didn't want that name displayed for the world to see. Cliff wrenched the pitchfork from my grip and pushed me away. I slipped on the wet grass, landing on my back. He tossed the pitch fork aside, grabbed the broken spade and was on top of me in seconds with all his weight.

"I'm gonna do you a favor, Tanker, I'm gonna flatten you out." He placed the curved spade over my gut and straddled me, a knee on either side, his ass atop the spade, his arms holding down mine. The steel spade dug into my skin a bit, but it didn't hurt too much. I remained still, hoping he'd grow bored and leave. "No more Tanker 10. You can thank me later."

He lowered his goofy alien head until it hovered inches from mine. God, that thing was big, like his brain wanted no part of his body and was doing its darnedest to push itself free.

"Got a little present for you."

Foamy spit slid from his lips and landed in warm slimy drops on my cheeks and chin. "Todd got you back," he said. "But I never did."

I turned my head to avoid the spit torture. Cliff's weight gave way for a second so I tried to turn on to my side, maybe push him off. No good. He adjusted his position and locked in even tighter. His movements caused the spade to slide from my belly and nestle between my legs. As I twisted under Cliff's weight again, the spade found its way against my balls. Cliff straightened his back and sat up on me, his knee now in the curve of the spade, the spade still over my balls, squashing them like a concrete slab over eggshells. I screamed, my entire body instantly afire with intense pain and slick with sweat. Cliff probably thought I was screaming just to get Mother's attention, to get him in trouble. So to punish me he bounced up and down.

My arms now free, I tried to rock upward like doing a sit up but he just pushed me back down with his long arms. I tried to make the screams form words—*my balls, my nuts, get off*—but my lungs betrayed me.

That was the last thing I was aware of before the blackness. My own screams.

3. Good News, and Bad

Aaaahhhhhhhh.

My whole body roared! Small angry mouths all over my torso and legs, hundreds of them, screeching out in pain. Disjointed images flashed, spurts of memory—pounding footfalls; a heavy mud-coated shoe at the side of my head; a huge man in a dark blue uniform, the Sunoco guy; a vague sense of flying.

My heart pounded. Mother was looking down at me. Some type of low gray ceiling overhead. So close you could touch it. Her hand gently stroked my arm. She was saying something. I tried to speak when a siren exploded.

I needed an ambulance! That's how heart attack victims were taken to hospitals. Dying people. Like me? But what if I pulled through? Oh yeah! I'd be known as the ambulance kid! They'd talk about me at school: There goes Jimmy; he went to the hospital in an ambulance; sirens, lights, everything. And he *survived.*

My heart battered the insides of my chest. Blows climbed upward into my throat. Ahhh, a pothole or something. Oh God, it hurt. Down my thighs and up into my belly.

"You're going to be fine, baby."

"Yes you are." A deep voice from my other side. Didn't even notice him. The Sunoco guy.

He let go of my arm and dropped a needle into a plastic trash bucket on a shelf built into the side of the ambulance. Did he just give me a shot? Why did I need a shot? Wasn't I in enough pain?

How did I get in here? Did the man in blue carry me? Probably a stretcher.

Metal clicking. I heard it. The double doors of the ambulance. They squeaked. Sunlight poured into the back.

Wait. Hadn't it been raining earlier? Was this the same day? I was flying again. Not flying, rolling. Mother kept pace, and there was Cliff, shuffling alongside. He must've ridden in front. Probably got to flick the switch. Lucky. It should have been me up front and him in back.

Inside, upper bodies flashed by my field of vision and voices came in and out of earshot. The cart took a couple of turns, then stopped inside a small room. Someone lowered a monstrous curved metal arm over my groin then disappeared. A nurse laid a blanket on my legs then another over my torso. They weighed a ton.

"Why are they so heavy?" I asked.

"Just protection," she said with a smile.

She left the room in a hurry, but when I twisted my neck to look for her I saw that she was standing near the door. What was this twisted metal arm? I pictured it lowering, pressing against my belly and hips, splintering bone. The machine buzzed. I struggled to get off the stretcher, but my legs were strapped down.

"Keep still," the nurse said sternly from the corridor.

Keep still? I thought. The thing just buzzed, and was about to laser-zap me through the floor.

"That didn't hurt now, did it?"

The transport guys wheeled me away. I zipped along more hallways, turned more corners, but for some reason I wasn't scared. And my pain was gone. When did that happen?

We were in an elevator, me, Mother, Cliff and the two orderlies. Complete quiet, Mother's fingers on my shoulder. I craned my neck to look up at her. I saw tears. I started to say something.

"Try not to talk, Jimmy." A third man was examining my injury. I couldn't see his face. All I saw were curled fists holding up the sheet. How could he see through my pants? I slid my hand under the sheet. My pants were gone! Someone took my pants!

"My name is Dr. Simpson," he said. "You're going to be back on your feet in no time. In a few minutes you'll take a little nap, and while you're sleeping we'll take a closer look at what happened."

He lowered the sheet and looked down at me. A square-faced gentleman with a narrow carefully trimmed mustache, which stood out against the reddish tone of his skin. His smile somehow put everything at ease. I liked the way the skin around his eyes bunched and crinkled. He rested his hand on my chest and I felt its light pressure through the thin sheet. My shirt was gone too. I was completely naked!

"You comfy?" he asked.

I looked up at Mother. "I don't have my clothes," I said. I was going to be in big trouble. Mother had strict rules about losing toys and things, never mind clothes. "I don't know where they are."

"Don't worry." Her fingers pressed against the sheet. "They had to remove them."

Oh no. Not in the yard, I hoped. The ambulance would have attracted neighbors—kids playing ball, adults working in the yard—running from blocks away to see the hubbub.

"No pain?"

People staring down at my fat naked body.

"Jimmy, I said are you in pain?"

"Huh?" I shook my head. "No."

As the elevator doors opened, he said, "You'll be following me through those doors into the operating room. We're going to take good care of you."

"The what room?" But he was gone, pushing through the set of swinging doors.

"What did he say?" My gaze fastened on Mother's face.

The orderlies had started to follow Dr. Simpson, but Mother took hold of the gurney and they stopped. She bent over and kissed my lips. "I'll be right here when you come out."

I grabbed her hand, heard myself scream: "I can't go in there." Tears dripped down the side of my face. "Mommy, they operate in there."

She wiped my tears and held her cheek against mine. "Would I let anything happen to you?" I felt the stretcher move. The foot of it banged up against the swinging doors. As it rolled away I grabbed Mother's arm, but one of the orderlies separated us. I still held one of her fingers, barely grasping her gold ring for a second longer. But the room engulfed me like a dragon's throat. I knew I was dead.

Before the door fully closed behind me I twisted my head back to see Mother. She stood there, crying. But the face I noticed just before the door closed was Cliff's. His eyes wide, his mouth open. He looked terrified. He knew I was going to die, too.

Inside the operating room, I couldn't stop thinking of Cliff's face. Part of me enjoyed it. He'd be grounded for days, maybe weeks. Good. My chest, my whole body, began to settle. But what had he done to me? All of a sudden a couple of orderlies lifted me easily on to the operating table. A nurse placed round white sticky pads on my chest then clipped on tiny cables.

A man examined surgical tools on a metal table. They looked sharp and dangerous. They were about to cut into me, probe, move things around. A nurse tried to place a weird-shaped thing in my mouth.

"What's that?" I said.

"It's a digital thermometer."

She gave me a second to take a peak, then slid it under my tongue. She wrapped a black cuff around my bicep and squeezed a pump the size of a lemon, which tightened the cuff around my arm. "Just checking your blood pressure. It might pinch, but only for a sec." She studied a small dial in her hand. "Okay, good." Then she removed the thermometer, took a glance and showed me the blinking black numbers. "Perfectly normal," she said through her mask.

I turned my head and saw Dr. Simpson wearing a shower cap on his head. A mask pulled down below his chin looked like a scarf. He asked me when I last ate.

"I had lunch a little while ago. My mom said I could eat early."

A woman appeared at his side and said, "Do you know how long ago?"

"An hour?"

"What did you have?" the woman asked. "It will help us determine what anesthesia to use."

"Turkey sandwich."

A man and a woman eased me toward the end of the table until my butt was close to the edge and my legs hung down. The nurse set up a cloth partition above my chest, obstructing my view of everything beyond it.

"Here we go," someone said, placing a cone-shaped breathing device over my nose and mouth. "Just breathe normally now. Count backwards from twenty...Just breathe normally. Just breathe..."

Cliff's ugly mug suddenly came into view, that frightened face, those petrified eyes.

"Just breathe . . . Easy now. Breathe . . ."

**

Only part of me was awake. Most of me was still in la-la land. I tried to remember what time the Sox game was on. 1:00 or 2:00, since it was the weekend. But was it the weekend? Or maybe they were playing on the west coast, in which case they'd play later. Gosh, how could I not know this? I wasn't even sure who was pitching. I heard a rattling noise, probably Mother downstairs putting dishes away.

Another noise, completely unfamiliar this time. A clang, something heavy and metallic. Then strange voices. And then I remembered. Was I alive? I wondered if a handful of doctors were standing over me, studying me. My eyes struggled to open. Had I said anything in my sleep? Something about food or being naked? About wanting to poke Cliff's eyes out?

I heard elevators. When I opened my eyes I found myself in a little room. My father and mother were looking down at me. So yes I was definitely alive! Cliff stood behind them, as if he needed protection. What had the jerk done to me anyway? I still didn't know. He must have busted something down there. I wanted to challenge him, tell him to come out of hiding. But I had to be careful; it was only a matter of time before I'd be back on my feet and he'd be Tanker Tenning me again all over the neighborhood.

"How are you, kiddo?" my father said.

"Good." The room was quiet except for some bustling in the hallway and an occasional announcement over the loudspeaker. "Can we go home now?"

"Sweetie," Mother said, "they need you to stay for a couple of days. Just to make sure everything is okay."

"What? No, I'm fine."

"It's just—"

"Mom, nothing hurts. I'm fine." I didn't want to whine in front of Cliff, but I didn't want to spend the night alone in the hospital either.

"The people are so nice here. And we'll visit all the time. And Ben said he'll come by."

"Ben knows?"

"Of course. I called the Clancys from here."

"What did he say?"

"I spoke to his mother. She said he'll come later."

My family stayed close to me as I was rolled into the elevator. The doors opened to pink and blue and yellow and purple and lime green walls with large lettered blocks and huge paintings of Big Bird, Cookie Monster, Beaker and Oscar the Grouch. *Sesame Street?* Did they think I was a baby?

Both beds were empty. A phone sat on a bedside table. A blank television hung on a metal shelf in a corner by the window. Wow, my own phone. And my own TV! I thought of talking to Ben late at night; watching shows that came on after the news, shows Cliff talked about, like *Benny Hill* and *Love American Style*. This room had a citrus smell, like something my father sprayed after a visit to the bathroom.

The orderlies lined up the litter to the bed next to the window, lowered the metal sides and shifted me onto the bed. The window overlooked the parking lot, which surrounded a small park quartered with trails made of reddish wood chips.

The white round pads were still affixed to my skin and the nurse hooked me up to a monitor below the window. She turned on a switch and before my eyes the beat of my heart appeared in green lines against a black screen. I hadn't thought much about what my heart looked like. I knew it didn't look like the hearts on valentines, but that's all I had to go on, except for this green line that I now imagined spiking and diving in the middle of my chest.

"Once in a while," the nurse said, "you'll hear the printer run.

Don't let it bother you."

"We'll be back," my father said.

"Huh?"

They were putting on their coats! But if they stayed, what would they do? Just look at me probably. They would ask me how I was and I'd say fine. Over and over.

Mother said, "We're going to bring back some of your things. Your slippers, your robe, what else?"

"Uh…" I'd never been away from my family except when I slept over Ben's.

"Book?" Cliff said.

"Oh yes, on my bookcase." I responded to Mother, not to Cliff. "I need a new one. The ones I haven't read yet are on the bottom shelf. They're in order of what I want to read next, left to right."

Mother and Father kissed me and walked toward the door. "We won't be gone long," Mother said from the hall. Cliff walked to my bedside and looked down at me.

"You gonna finish me off?" Maybe I said it to make him feel bad. Or maybe as a joke so he wouldn't feel bad.

He didn't laugh. He opened his mouth to speak. "I . . ." But that was all.

That's when my insides started to shake. He had the same frightened expression I saw from the operating room. I'd forgotten about that expression until now. If he was afraid, something must be wrong. Cliff being nice was proof of that. He remembered that I liked to read! The whole universe was out of whack. I wanted to rewind the clock. Leave him alone at the fence. No shovel, no wrestling on the ground. No ambulance, no hospital. Just him being mean to me. Me avoiding him. End of story. But my parents hadn't said anything was wrong. Then again, what would they have said: Hey Jimmy, you're dying, we'll catch you later?

Cliff's fingers bunched the blanket at the edge of the bed. I placed my hand on top of his. "I'm dying, right?" I whispered. His eyes stayed down. He tried to move his hand, but I held onto it. "Why can't I go home?" He wrenched his hand free and ran out the door.

Shortly after they left a nurse walked in. Her voice sounded official. She didn't bother to pause between sentences and pointed a chubby finger throughout. "The call button is here on the rail, this plastic container here is for your urine if you need to go overnight, you can use the bathroom starting tomorrow, don't ever touch the dressing no matter what, nurses will change it if needed." She took my temperature and blood pressure and started for the door without a word.

"Excuse me," I said.

She turned back and lifted her brow.

"Am I okay?"

She said, "You're going to be just fine" and walked toward the door.

"Am I hurt bad, though?"

"You'll be home in a couple of days." She smiled and left the room.

Despite her warning, I lifted the covers to inspect the damage. I bunched up my little cotton johnny, but discovered that although the tip of my penis poked through, everything down there was a bundle of gauze and bandages.

My hand kept wandering down to my penis. I wasn't doing it on purpose; it just sort of ended up down there. What else was my hand supposed to do? It always ended up down there before the accident so why shouldn't it end up down there after? What was the penis there for if not to play with once in a while? Hell, my father messed with his all the time. Whenever he was on the phone he'd have one hand on the receiver while the other one dug around in his pants like he was searching for the car keys.

There was no clock in the room, but there was still daylight. I wondered how much time had passed since Cliff had used me for a trampoline. I opened my eyes and was greeted by a bone thin woman with a pack of Virginia Slims tucked into the breast pocket of her yellow smock. I recognized it from the ad on the back of the *TV Guide*. Her name was Marcy, the hospital's dietician. It was her job, she instructed, to make sure I received three square meals a day. She gave me a few menus, each one listing several choices for breakfast, lunch and dinner. I was to place an X next to each item I wanted.

I remembered that I was on a diet, but figured, What the hell. I'm in the hospital. I'm probably dying. I chose all the tantalizing selections, things Mother never kept in the house. I handed over the three menus and said, "Am I really going to be here three days?"

"This is usually a good indication," she said with a nod. She looked at the menus, then at me. "You have your appetite, I see." Her lips were thin and chapped. I wondered if she realized she was nibbling her lower lip. "So tomorrow for breakfast you're going with the cinnamon bun and the chocolate milk?"

"No good?"

"It's a lot of sugar. And you checked bacon and eggs too."

"I wanted to cover all the food groups."

"What about fruits and vegetables?"

"Did my mother get to you?"

"How about . . ." she started changing the selections with her pen. " . . . a glass of orange juice, a slice of wheat toast and a bowl of cereal with skim milk and banana?"

"Skim milk is gray."

"It's not gray, it's white."

"It's gray*ish*."

"It's good for you." She continued to study the menus. "I'm going to have to change most of these, I'm afraid. For your own good."

Ridiculous. Why did she tell me to fill out the menus if she was just going to make her own selections anyway? Besides, who was she to preach health? After she was done with me she was probably going to inhale a Virginia Slim.

"We'll have some supper brought in for you tonight." She scribbled something on the bottom of each menu as she left the room.

Not the fruit cup, I wanted to say. If they were anything like the ones at school they were gross. Darn it, I forgot to ask someone to turn on the TV. I started to press the call button but changed my mind. I didn't want to pester people right away. They might report it back to Mother or Dr. Simpson. So I just lay there. Staring at the yellow walls.

The cement walls had all these holes and crannies embedded in them, creating patterns. It reminded me of the puzzles you sometimes see in the Sunday papers where thousands of dots resemble a famous person if you look at it from just the right distance and angle. On the wall in front of me I could make out a prehistoric monster. It had huge wings and a gaping mouth filled with sharp teeth. I imagined it swooping down on a gang of hunters gathering food. The tallest hunter-gatherer was about to lose his head.

I started dozing and awoke thinking about death. I remembered how easily I had fallen asleep in the operating room. I remembered that Dr. Simpson had to select the right anesthesia. What if they had chosen the wrong one? Would I have not woken up? Ben's great uncle woke up in the middle of the night to pee and, while standing at the toilet, lost consciousness. Dead by the time he hit the floor, Ben had heard.

I could drop dead at any moment. No kissing Mom and Dad goodnight. No playing ball against the house, no reading, no playing with Ben. Just gone. Sure, there would be a funeral and people would cry and bring flowers, but the tears and flowers wouldn't last. After a while, the same people that had gathered at my funeral would be singing to their radios on the way to school, watching television, working in the garden, playing street hockey.

I imagined watching my funeral from above. My parents bawling at the graveside. Cliff would probably be in jail for murder, but maybe they'd let him out for the funeral. There'd be lots of people. Kids from school, my dad's co-workers. My brother's goons would be there, feeling bad that they had hounded me.

Ah God, I thought, lay off all the death thoughts. They were driving me nuts. I had more immediate concerns: What was I supposed to do if I had to poop?

I was getting hungry. Hankering for my energy pills. Boy, did I look forward to those when I got home from school. The first thing I did was take out two slices of American cheese from the refrigerator. Then I cut two slices of salami, grabbed some spicy brown mustard and poured a tall glass of soda. I brought all the food downstairs to the playroom and set it up in front of the television to watch Merv Griffin or Mike Douglas. I cut the salami and cheese so that I ended up with eight squares of cheese and eight wedges of salami. Then I built my pills. First the salami, then a dot of mustard, then the cheese.

It would have been something if that lady with the cigarettes came in here at suppertime and dropped off some energy pills. The joy of that possibility came to a thud at the realization that I needed to start my new food plan. Even if she did come into the room with a tray piled high with energy pill fixings and a pitcher of ice cold Coke I would have had to decline and eat a slimy fruit cup.

**

I ate an early supper while watching *F Troop* on channel 56. They had brought me a piece of boneless chicken, mixed vegetables (I picked out the lima beans) and potatoes cut into evenly shaped squares. It was kind of tasteless, but I ate it all, except for the beans. Oh, there was a small portion of butterscotch pudding too. It was a little watery, but I would have eaten six of them.

Ben rushed into the room, right up against the bed. "You okay, what happened?"

"You're dressed up?" I said. He had an oxford shirt tucked into trousers.

"My mother said I had to wear school clothes. So what happened?"

"Cliff tried to kill me."

"Come on. Seriously."

"I don't know. He was bouncing on top of me, then there was all this pain. How'd you get here?"

"My mom dropped me off. She's going to pick me up after she runs an errand." He grabbed a metal stool from the corner of the room and brought it by the side of the bed. Something seemed wrong. His hand danced around the circle of the seat before sitting down. "I'm supposed to be at practice."

"He let you skip?"

He shrugged his shoulders and turned away on the stool. "He gets crazy sometimes. I don't know what to say to him." He leaned forward on the stool so that his elbows rested on his knees. I placed my hand on his knee, not sure what else to do. I felt a tug of pain inside my groin.

"I just wanted to get here, that's all." He hopped off the stool and started talking to the room. "I asked him if I could miss practice. He said no. Looked at me like I was demented. Said I could see you tomorrow."

"What happened?"

"He asked what was more important, Jimmy or the Olympics."

"What did you say?"

"I said Jimmy."

"Why'd you say that?"

"I don't know."

"Then what?"

"It's not like he screamed or anything. It was worse. He just stared at me for a long time. Like he didn't know me. We were in his office at the pool. He just walked out and headed to the blocks."

"You should go to practice."

"Na, too late anyway. Beside, you know something? It felt good." He returned to the stool. "I don't know. I mean, I mean not practicing today was the right move. I knew it was right."

"You might change your mind when you get home."

He laughed again. "I think it'll be okay. I'll go to practice tomorrow, hopefully he'll let it go."

"I'm glad you're here."

"You'd do the same for me, right?" He turned to face the TV. We watched for a while, then he promised he'd be back tomorrow.

**

My parents returned with slippers and a robe, books and a little bathroom bag filled with stuff. Cliff was absent. I wondered if my pleading had freaked him out. If so, didn't that support my fear that something was terribly wrong? The TV was on and everyone's faces gravitated toward it.

"Where's Cliff?"

"He's home." My father reached to the TV and lowered the volume. "He asked if he could stay back. Don't feel bad that he's not here," my father said from the foot of the bed, his hands resting on my blanketed toes. "Look, we know he can be a troublemaker. But you need to know he would never do anything intentionally to harm you. It was an accident."

The talk of Cliff made me think again of the frightened face I had glimpsed from the operating room just before the doors closed. I thought of his reaction to my question, those fingers twisting away from mine.

"Am I sick?"

"No," Mother said, sitting at my side.

"Am I going to die?"

"God no." She placed her hand on the swell of my belly. "Don't talk like that. Don't . . ."

"You had surgery," my father said. "They want to be careful of infection, check out some other things, make sure you're shipshape before sending you home."

"What other things?"

They exchanged a nervous glance. They recovered quickly, but I saw it. My father smiled. It might have been a fake smile. Was that the same as a lie?

"Just the usual. A day or so of observation." He switched the subject, bringing up the Red Sox and our trip next month to visit Uncle Mark in Pennsylvania, the amusement parks, the caves.

They stayed late, watching the TV and reading the paper. Toward the end my dad was working through the *Enterprise* crossword puzzle. When they left I thought about Cliff all guilt-ridden at home and smiled. Good, let the jerk suffer!

The next day was pretty much like the first. The nurses took my temperature and blood pressure (temp. and b.p. as they called them) about a hundred times. They redressed my wound by removing the bandages, dabbing the area with a cloth, then swabbing it with a cool gel. At first I was embarrassed. My hands instinctively covered my groin, but they always placed them firmly on the bed.

Sometimes I was able to sneak a peek down there before the new bandages were applied. The scrotum was definitely swollen and purplish. Once in a while I felt a twinge in my groin or a pull at the underside of my scrotum from the stitches, but I didn't experience severe pain unless I pressed down on the bruised area.

On my last night there, it seemed like during the wee hours, I was awoken by a tall bushy-haired man studying the monitor printouts. I think I smelled him first, an adult smell, cologne. He had laid the papers out at the foot of the bed and was peering down at them through thick plastic-rimmed glasses.

I was scared at first. Did this have something to do with what my parents were holding back? Was this guy going to tell me my fate? In the middle of the night so as few people as possible would hear my cries? I felt myself squirming beneath the blanket. Where were my parents?

He saw that I was awake. "How's life, young fella?"

"Who are you?"

"Dr. Aranofsky."

"Do you know Dr. Simpson?"

"Yes. He's a urologist." He was still staring at the papers, following the spiked lines up and down.

"What kind of doctor are you?"

"Cardiologist."

"Hearts," I said.

He looked up. "You're a smart one."

"We study root words at school. Prefixes. Besides, I read a story once. This guy's heart was too big. They had to call in all kinds of people. Like you."

"What happened?"

"I don't remember. I think he lived."

"That's good. I like when they live."

"Is my heart too big?"

"I doubt it."

"What's wrong with it?"

He gathered the long strips of paper and brought them closer. "Once in a while," he said, "your heart beats erratically. See these squiggles that are close together?"

"Sure."

"Then the squiggles stop and the beats become regular. I wouldn't mind knowing what triggers it. Do you ever experience anything unusual in your chest?"

"It beats fast when I play ball."

"How about when you're watching TV?"

Although I'd never felt anything strange in my chest, I got scared that he was asking the question. I wondered what time it was, when my parents would be arriving. "No."

"There's nothing to worry about," he said, placing the paper on the printer tray. "No two people are the same so why should they have the same heartbeat? We all got a little anxious, because the tachycardia, the rapid heart rate, occurred during surgery. Just being cautious. We'll likely get you out of here tomorrow." He patted my head before leaving. The sound of his hard-heeled shoes against the linoleum floor lasted for many seconds amidst the silence of the hospital.

The next morning, so early the sun was barely out, an unfamiliar nurse came into my room to take my temp and b.p. I was still groggy as she placed the cuff around my forearm. As the cuff tightened she smiled down at me. Dr. Simpson appeared at the door. He was still wearing his coat. Talking to a nurse. His back to me. He entered the room quickly, as though he had only seconds to spare. He rested his coat on the empty bed and walked briskly to the foot of my bed. I noticed for the first time an instruments tray just to the side of where Dr. Simpson stood. He flipped up the sheets and started to remove the dressing.

"It's a good day, Jimmy," he said enthusiastically. "Time to go home." He took in my silence. "What's the matter?" he said. "Aren't you happy?"

"I guess," I said uncertainly. I didn't like the look of those instruments. Nobody said anything about more instruments. Ah, so this was what my parents couldn't tell me the first night I was here. But how bad could it be if I was going home?

The nurse was through with the blood pressure and was holding my hand. The sticky tape pulled against the tiny hairs of my crotch as Dr. Simpson removed the last of the bandages.

"This will only take a second, Jimmy," Dr. Simpson said in a soothing voice. "We just have to remove the stitches."

Remove stitches? People had stitches removed all the time.

Cliff, when he had sliced his hand trying to fix his bike, needed to get stitches removed. I started to relax.

The pain in my balls was vicious, a sudden explosion of fire. I involuntarily clutched the nurse's hand. In an instant it was done. The nurse was wiping perspiration from my face and neck. She gave me some tissues and I pressed them against my forehead. Dr. Simpson bandaged a thin layer of gauze over where the stitches had been. He said that there were more stitches, but they would dissolve on their own. Then he said he would be seeing me later with my parents, grabbed his coat and was out the door.

The nurse smiled at me again. "You did great," she said, touching my arm. Then she left, wheeling away the surgical tray.

**

"Discharge"—an ugly word. When I first heard it I thought of the thick goo that the nurses must have wiped away from my wound when changing my bandages. Whether it was blood or puss or some other horrible fluid I didn't know. Nurses had a way of not talking. But this morning, thankfully, "discharge" meant something completely different: I was going home. The bags were packed and the papers signed. All that was left was to stop by Dr. Simpson's office.

The frayed edges of gauze rubbed against my thighs down the hall. Also, the incisions tugged and I was forced to shorten my stride. I was surprised my father was with us, considering what they said about everything having gone so well. He hardly ever took an unplanned vacation day. But he was at my side, his hand on my shoulder, as we approached the closed door at the end of the hall. A tall thin woman whose hair was worn up in a bun stood from her chair when she saw us approach and opened Dr. Simpson's door. His name was engraved into a gold plate.

Mother had told me many times that my room looked like a tornado had hit it, but it was never as bad as this. A couple of dress shirts and ties lay draped over his chair. The desk was stacked with notebooks, loose papers and colored folders of various sizes. A large easel with human diagrams attached to its crossbar stood next to the desk. The people in the drawings had invisible skin so you could see their body parts, their bones and organs.

Diplomas decorated the walls, but were slightly crooked. A

human skeleton stood long and straight in the corner. On its head was a red knit hat with the emblem of Pat Patriot of the New England Patriots.

And standing in the middle of it all with his arm outstretched was tidy little Dr. Simpson, his hair perfectly combed and moustache neatly trimmed. He welcomed us into the office, easing my father toward a free space on a sofa stacked with hard-cover books, pads and clipboards and Mother toward a stuffed chair. I walked straight for the skeleton.

"Is it real?" I asked.

"No, a replica."

"Can I touch it?"

"Come sit, Jimmy," Mother said.

"But it's a skeleton!"

"Sit right there."

I took a seat on a metal folding chair a few yards from the skeleton. My stitches pinched. When Dr. Simpson closed the door I noticed a dartboard on the back, several red and green darts sticking out of its center.

"You ready to go home, Jimmy?"

"Sure."

"Good, good." He was looking at me now, just me. "I want to tell you a little bit about what's going to happen going forward." He walked over to the easel and flipped some of the diagrams over the top until he came to one called "Male Reproduction." The sheet was divided in two. One side showed a full frontal man; the other showed the same thing in profile.

"First of all, some good news. I consulted with Dr. Aranofsky this morning. We're in agreement that nothing needs to be done at this time regarding the arrhythmia . . ."

I got pieces of what he said next, something about stress tests and treadmills, but I was mostly focused on the skeleton, the way the two sets of ribs curved so evenly toward each other. And the smoothness of the bones. I wanted to touch them.

". . . so there is no real concern there."

He paced in front of his easel. "You suffered some damage,

Jimmy, in your groin." His tone like a weatherman's when discussing an impending blizzard—serious, but not catastrophic.

I looked over to my folks, whose faces were solemn. My father had slid one of his hands under his leg. He was twitchy, ill at ease, which was unusual. I wanted to ask what was wrong. Mother sat on the very edge of her chair, as though if she relaxed backward she would fall into an abyss.

"All us men, boys . . . males, we have our sex organs, genitalia, just like females have their sex organs."

"Penis," I said.

"Right. Penis. Good. But in addition to that we also have a sack, and in that sack are the testicles . . ."

I wasn't sure why he kept saying "sack." He could have said scrotum. I knew what a scrotum was. A sack was what Santa used to lug around Christmas presents.

"You mean scrotum?"

"Scrotum, right, that's right. And as I said, in the scrotum we have the testicles . . . And the testicles are very important because they supply our bodies with hormones that give us our appearance... that make us look like men as we get older. Your father and I, we have hair on our bodies, our muscles are defined, our voices are deep compared to yours, certainly compared to a female's . . ."

He hadn't used the easel yet, which was too bad because there were lots of pictures behind the one that was shown. I wondered if they were close-ups of specific parts of the body, maybe even specific organs. I remembered Dr. Aranofsky and thought for sure there would be one of the heart, with all kinds of veins and tubes going in and out.

". . . and as boys get older, twelve, thirteen years old, they start to develop these traits, secondary sex characteristics they're called. In your case, your testicles . . . Well, they were damaged to the point where we had to remove them."

I looked again at the easel and the male sex poster, its muscles and organs, the red blood coursing through the two-dimensional paper body. And I realized that if there was a "Male Reproduction" chart, then there must be a "Female Reproduction" chart. So if I didn't have these organs, this genitalia, did that mean I was going to be a girl?

But all that worry left me in an instant when I remembered that I did have my testicles. My sack was full! I had seen them while the nurse changed my bandages. I felt them with my own fingers underneath the bandages when I peed before leaving the hospital room. He had it all wrong, I wasn't going to become a girl; my scrotum was full of just the right amount of testicles. I blurted, "I have a sack."

"Well, yes, you have a sack, but you don't have what's inside the sack."

"But I do!" I felt between my legs just to be sure. The stitches hurt again, but I didn't care. I was making my point, conversing with adults. "I felt them." I looked at my parents, but I wasn't winning them over. Mother remained on the edge of the stuffed chair, her hand rubbing the side of her head.

"They're not real," Dr. Simpson said. "They're fake, you see. Prosthetics."

My face must've looked blank.

"You've seen people with fake arms, right? Why, right here in this hospital we have arms made of metal, of plastic, of fiberglass. This is the same thing."

I understood, but something about what he said didn't seem right. I wanted to talk to him about it, this comparison of a metal arm to plastic testicles, or whatever they were made of, but I couldn't keep up.

"The important thing for you to know is that you will still develop from a normal boy to a normal man. No one will be able to tell the difference."

"Why wouldn't I be normal?"

"That's what I'm saying," the doctor said. "You will be."

"But just by saying it . . ." I looked at my father. "Doesn't that mean? . . . I don't know . . ."

"Everything will be fine, Jimmy. When you get older, thirteen or so, you'll visit a different doctor, an endocrinologist. The hormones that would have been provided naturally will simply be provided medically, through a program of injections."

"Will they hurt?"

"That's not something you need to worry about for a couple of years," he said.

Translation: Of course they'll hurt!

"How often will I need shots?"

I felt very alone in the office. My parents hadn't been much help since we stepped into this room. I found myself reaching between my legs again. If they were fake why couldn't I tell the difference?

But this wasn't about appearance. It was deeper than that somehow. I noticed the hollow look in Mother's eyes as she watched me struggle with all this new information that was being piled upon me. Her poor face. It was as though a tiny bomb was going off in her mouth and she was using all of her facial muscles to keep her head from exploding.

My father stood. "Maybe that's enough for now."

"Certainly," Dr. Simpson said. "We'll be seeing you in a couple of weeks anyway to make sure the incisions are healing properly."

We all shook Dr. Simpson's hand. My parents thanked him repeatedly. I turned back to Dr. Simpson when it occurred to me what I couldn't quite place earlier. "That's not really true," I said, "what you said about the arm."

"How's that?"

"The fake arm. It picks up things. A fork, a toothbrush. These things in me. They just sit there."

"You're right about that. But as you get older you'll be glad you have them."

I didn't really know what he was talking about, but I nodded and thanked him like my parents had. We walked out of the office together, my dad between us. He draped an arm around my shoulders. As we walked away from the office, I sensed his body, his strength, shift away from me toward Mother. Gosh, she looked feeble. The way she was walking—staggering really, clutching my father's arm for support—you would have thought she was the one who just spent two nights in the hospital.

4. Questions and Answers

A few feet beyond Dr. Simpson's reception area, I heard the secretary. "Just a moment please. A wheelchair is needed."

We all turned around. Surely I was well enough to walk. Then I thought of mother. Did the secretary think Mother might collapse?

"All discharges need to leave via wheelchair," the woman explained with an apologetic smile.

My father lowered Mother to a narrow bench next to the receptionist's desk. She edged to one side and patted the empty space. I sat. In a couple of minutes a woman rounded the corner at the far end of the hall guiding an empty wheelchair.

When she reached us she looked at me like she was talking to a dog. "James LaPlante, that's you, I'd wager." Her voice was high and friendly. Her cheeks sagged. Her stiff hair glowed yellow.

She locked the wheels and offered to assist me into the chair. I told her I was fine. She watched carefully as I sat, then released the wheel lock, rolled me to the elevators and to the parking lot doors downstairs. Dad told me to sit tight, he'd bring the car to the curb. The parking lot was on a hill and I wondered what would happen if I lifted the breaks and just let this baby fly. Hold on tight, boy, here comes the speed. Like coasting down hills at D. W. Fields Park, wind plastered against your face, tears filling your eyes.

In a moment the car arrived and the wheelchair lady relocked the wheels, moved aside the metal footrests and helped me up. "There you go, sweetie pie." She looked at Mother. "Would you like me to help him into the car?"

"I'm fine," I said. "Thank you."

The ride home was quiet. I rolled down my window.

"I don't want to belabor the point, Jimmy, but it's worth repeating that what happened was an accident," my father said. "Obviously, Cliff wouldn't want to hurt you, you know that."

A sudden bump caused unexpected pain between my legs.

"You know that, right?"

"Yes, I know."

"Where you going?" Mother asked as my father kept straight on Centre Street.

"I have to pick up my check."

Silence filled the car again before Mother said, "I thought you were getting that thing, where it goes right to the bank."

"Direct deposit, I still have to fill out the forms." He pulled into the city lot next to the post office and shut off the car.

"Well, you should do that. It sounds convenient."

"Next chance I get," he said. "You need anything in here?"

She shook her head. My father kissed her cheek and left. She reached back and touched my knee. "You holding up?"

"I'm fine. The bumps hurt a little."

When my father scooted back into the car Mother said, "Try to avoid the potholes, will you?"

He caught my gaze in the rearview mirror and nodded. "Of course," he said.

**

Dinner was also quiet. Cliff sat across from me sullen and jittery. He ate, though, gobbled up everything. Nothing so silly as sending me to the hospital would ruin his appetite. And after eating the last morsel off he went.

"Not too late," Mother said as he slid into his jacket. "Spend some time with your brother tonight."

He came home plenty early, but all we did was sit down in the playroom and watch *The Six Million Dollar Man*. Fine with me. Mother sat with us. During a commercial she said, "You know, it wouldn't kill you two to talk to each other." We just looked at one another and nodded. I didn't know what she was making such a big deal about. Sometimes it was better not to talk. Sometimes words did more harm than good. I was about to drum up some phony conversation, anything to keep her happy, when Steve Austin burst back onto the tube. Steve Austin, the bionic man, with his bionic legs and arm and eye, loaded up with wires, metal and hi-tech plastics. What if his balls were bionic? What would they be capable of?

**

Sleep did not come easily. The new bandages chafed. I repositioned the gauze to make it less irritating, but it was no use.

I was still awake when my parents went to bed. I heard them talk as they settled in. It was impossible to make out words, but there was something in the strained way they spoke that made the conversation seem ominous.

I got out of bed. I couldn't get too close because they slept with their door open, but at least I'd have a chance to hear. Mother's voice seeped through the darkness, becoming louder as I drew nearer. ". . . so foolish."

"Not at all," my father replied. "You're doing fine."

"I'm supposed to have it all together."

"Says who?" he said in a rush, then changed to a more comforting tone. "Don't do this."

I inched closer.

"How can I expect him to handle this if I can't?" My father didn't answer. Was he rubbing her back? Maybe the sides of her head as he sometimes did when she suffered a headache. Quiet now. Had they fallen asleep? I stepped a little closer to peek inside when Mother said, "I left my cream over on the bureau. Do you mind?"

At the sound of the mattress squeaking I about-faced and hurried back to bed. I played that last part in my head over and over, the bit about her not handling something. Should I have just asked her what she meant instead of scampering away? I remembered how sad she'd looked at the hospital. But it didn't make sense. I was on the mend. Feeling fine now except for the bandages, and those would be gone soon.

I thought back to the hospital, the way Dr. Simpson kept saying sack. Funny word, sack. Sack. Sack sack sack. Sack it to me. Sack a doodle do. Sackalicious. Action Sacktion.

My parents were still talking next door. I heard murmurs, but didn't dare get out of bed again. Because of the bandages I had to sleep on my back. I felt the rough edges of the dressing and wondered what it looked like underneath. I wondered what was in my scrotum now. Fake balls. Were they heavier or lighter than the originals? When I got older, would I need newer larger models? And how were they stored at the hospital? I imagined ping pong balls in hard plastic and cardboard packages like the ones in the sporting goods section of Stuart's at Cary Hill Plaza.

I must have dozed off. I heard a footstep at my door, but when I looked the space was empty. Maybe my dad checking on me. Was it Cliff? Maybe after our silence downstairs tonight, Mom and Dad had told him to make an effort. Maybe he wanted to apologize, sit on the edge of the bed for a heart to heart. Would I have allowed it? Or kicked him out? Or just turned on my side and faced the wall? Either way, the doorway was dark and silent when I closed my eyes.

**

Eight days later the bandages were gone for good. I was finally allowed to shower. Up to now, I washed myself with a soapy washcloth and Mother washed my hair in the sink. I felt my testicles in the shower, pressed against one of them with my thumb and index finger. Could I still refer to them as *my* testicles? Could I still refer to them as testicles? They felt harder, but not rock hard. I felt the slight pain of the pinch against skin, but no pain inside of the testicle itself. Were they hollow? I imagined it as a small Christmas ornament hanging from the branch of our tree; or wrapped in red and green tissue paper and tucked away in the holiday box.

I wanted to see the wound, but the incisions were on the underside of the scrotum. I bent over, twisting the loose skin of my scrotum around with one hand and holding my gut up with the other, but I couldn't catch a peek. Once I toweled off I walked to the front door where Mother kept a hand mirror hung on the coat rack next to the door. Cliff was out, dad was at work and Mother was downstairs. I'd be all right if I did this quickly. I hung my towel on the coat rack and held the mirror between my legs. I stopped adjusting the angle when I spotted the scabs. They were rough to the feel, two small patches of sandpaper.

It became a compulsion, this examination. Every day when no one was around I took out the mirror, angled it just so and watched the scabs shrink.

**

Fat Swim started in September at the high school, but I joined a few weeks late because of the surgery. The pool was divided into several sections. One lane was reserved for laps. In the shallow end, kids tossed a basketball at a floating net. A water polo net had been set up in the deep end, but it wasn't being used because kids were jumping off the diving board. Kickboards lay scattered around the deck. Swimmers tossed weighted discs and rings and plunged to the pool floor to retrieve them.

There were only a handful of fat kids, both boys and girls. Some were even fatter than me. Others were extremely skinny, with jutting bones that poked at tight papery skin. Burn scars covered one girl's left arm and chest in thick ropy scrawls.

As I struggled out of the pool after about a half hour of taking shots at the basketball net, hoisting my upper body over the edge, I notice the dye from a boy's bathing suit dripping down the back of his leg. He was walking toward the diving board. It seemed strange that the dye was running down only one leg. "Excuse me." He was at the opposite side of the pool so I had to raise my voice. "Your bathing suit is dripping down your leg." He turned to face me. For some reason the front of the leg wasn't blue. "The back's all blue," I said.

Most of the other kids along the deck heard and stared at the boy. He reached down and touched the dye, but it stuck to his skin, like a crust. "It's a birthmark," he said.

"Uh. I'm sorry. I didn't mean . . ." It wasn't my fault! The birthmark was the same color as the suit. I just hung there, my torso flat against the deck, my legs still submerged.

"Don't worry about it." He seemed cool, but who knew what he was thinking. He walked over to the diving board and waited in line at the ladder.

After the session we all took showers. It was a gang shower, a dozen showerheads sticking out of the tiled walls, everyone exposed. I was fine at first, but then I noticed the swirl of lather on one of the boys across from me, the way it cascaded down his chest over his belly and down between his legs. For some reason I couldn't look away from his penis and the tiny pouch. I couldn't stop thinking how I was different from him, different from all of them. I thought of my ping pong balls, just hanging out down there doing nothing. I imagined them bored and lazy, restless.

I didn't know how long I was staring, but I stopped when the kid turned his body around and shut off the water. He looked at me strangely. It wasn't until they had all paraded past me, looking at me like I had a third arm growing out of my chest, that I realized I was cupping my penis with both my hands. I dressed quickly, not even looking at the other kids, bolted from the locker room and scrambled into my father's waiting car. I told him that I didn't want to return, that I felt uncomfortable starting weeks after all the others.

"You have to," he said. "It'll get better."

I shrugged my shoulders.

"You can't stop doing something just because it's hard at first. Go back next week, make friends."

I wondered if the kids would think I was too weird to befriend, standing still under the falling water and holding my pecker. But my father stared at me as though I'd be letting him down if I didn't give it another shot. "Okay."

He started the engine. I noticed the kid with the blue birthmark walking along the sidewalk toward Belmont.

"I met that kid today," I said. "Can we give him a ride?" I still felt bad for what I'd said.

"Sure."

My father slowed and I rolled down the window. "Hey," I said. "Are you walking home?"

"Bus." He nodded to the sign on the corner.

"Where do you live?"

He lived out in Dexter Flats, deep into the east side. We lived east too, but not that far east. He practically lived in Cranmore, off Jackson Drive. I'd never been out that way. I relayed the neighborhood to my father. Dad shook his head, no problem.

"We can give you a ride."

"The bus is okay."

My father leaned over to the passenger's side. "Get in," he said. "It's cold. Your hair's wet. Your mother will have a fit."

Finally he gave in and climbed into the back seat. After a moment he said, "My mother's not around."

My father looked into the rearview mirror. I turned back. "Hm?"

"My mother won't have a fit. She's not around."

"Around today?" I said. "Or like . . . like long term?"

He shifted his gaze out the window and watched the old storefronts as we rolled beyond downtown. Jackson Drive was a desolate strip that snaked its way through Canary Woods. He told my father to take a right and after a few hundred yards we passed a settlement of tiny houses shaped like trailers. A minute later he directed us to a dilapidated house. Green—maybe gray—paint had been chipped away in large gashes. Dark smoke wafted out of a chimney in need of repair. The only vehicle was a motorcycle, its back wheel propped up on a block of cement.

He hopped out, saying thanks, and took the porch stairs by stepping on the side of the boards along the broken railing, as though if he walked in the center they would bust.

"What's that boy's name?" my father said.

"No idea."

I wondered if his mother died. Maybe he never even knew her. Maybe his parents were divorced. Somebody was in there, though, needing a fire to keep warm.

Back in Cary Hill my thoughts returned to the shower, the looks from the kids as they left. I wondered about the blue-legged boy's reaction. Did he think I was a weirdo? Was that why he hesitated before getting into the car? Had he even been in the shower when I freaked?

I promised my father I'd go back the next week, and I did. I stuck with it, even made friends with a few of the kids, like he said. I knew I'd never shower again, though, not in that room, that chamber.

**

The library showed movies for kids on Sundays. There was no theater or anything fancy like that, just a portable white screen and a couple of room dividers that Mrs. Kaplan arranged in the corner of the children's room. Sometimes my father watched with me, sometimes we met afterwards. Today we agreed to meet. Halloween was Wednesday so they were showing *Abbott and Costello Meet Frankenstein.*

I watched for a while, but I grew restless. I'd already seen the movie, but that wasn't it. Dr. Simpson had recently proclaimed my scrotum fully healed. In fact, it was probably the last time I would see him. He mentioned again the endocrinologist I would eventually meet and said something about "future battles" with a pumped fist and spoke the words in a triumphant tone, as though they would be adventures to embark on.

That's what I was thinking about while the other kids gasped at the appearance of Dracula. I had at least an hour before I needed to meet my father. The main librarian's desk was downstairs behind a broad circular counter.

"Do you have a medical section?" I asked one of the three female aides, who snapped a wad of bright pink gum.

She looked up from a math book and some figures she was making on scratch paper. "Huh?"

"Medical section?"

She pushed black-rimmed glasses up the ridge of her nose with her index finger as she approached the counter. "Can you be more specific?"

I knew that Dr. Simpson was a urologist, but I was more focused on those future battles. "Endocrinology."

"What's that?" she said with a scowl.

"Hormones, I think."

"Come on, Doc, let's check the card catalogue."

I followed her to the massive drawers that took up a large center section of the floor. She stopped in front of the SUBJECT drawers. Her fingers danced along the cards in the *End-Eng* drawer.

"Sorry I interrupted."

"Please. You're doing me a favor."

"Math is hard."

"You said it, Doc. Why don't you check under hormones."

After a few minutes she took a slip of scrap paper from a tray atop the card catalogue and a mini yellow pencil from another tray and wrote down some numbers and titles. I pointed out my cards and she scribbled some more. "All right, here we go." Using the scraps of paper as her guide, she scanned the shelves in an area of the library I'd never been. "I don't know about this," she said as she stepped onto a footstool to scan higher shelves. She looked at the papers again. "*Hormone Replacement Therapy In . . .*" "*Treatments of Menopause . . .*" "A lot of these pamphlets, I think, are doctors' publications. We're not going to have them."

"But they're on the cards."

"Because we share information with other libraries. Southern Mass. Community College has a medical library. I can check and have them sent over if you want."

"That's okay. No big deal."

"Don't be bummed," she said, stepping down. "You gonna be a doctor or something?"

"I don't know. You?"

"No way." she said. "Too much math." As she walked away she said, "You know where to find me."

One of the books on the shelf at eye level was *Human Physiology.* It was a heavy thick schoolbook-looking thing, obviously for high school or maybe even college, but it had tons of pictures so I brought it to a table. Some of the pictures were identical to the ones in Dr. Simpson's office, others focused on close-ups of kidneys and lungs and the brain. I thumbed to the front of the book and checked out the preface: *Human physiology is the science of the mechanical, physical, and biochemical functions of humans—their organs, and the cells of which they are composed.* Good grief.

I turned back to the table of contents. The chapters were divided into the body's systems: nervous, musculoskeletal, circulatory, gastrointestinal, respiratory, urinary, immune, endocrine, reproductive and integumentary. Urinary started on page 298. It mentioned the kidney, the bladder and the urethra. But what about the scrotum, the testicles?

"You have a visitor, Doc."

My father waited for the librarian to leave before he sat down and held my wrist. "Are you out of your mind? You scared the crap out of me."

"I'm sorry. I was going to go back up there."

He noticed the book. He turned it to face him. "You're curious about this, huh?"

I didn't say anything.

"You can just ask me, you know," he said.

I wasn't sure if I should say what I was thinking. I didn't want to make him feel worse, as though any of this was his fault. But out it came. "You can just *tell* me."

I wasn't sure if he wanted to hug me or scold me. The yellow lights from above made his face look sallow. He took the book and turned some pages. "This is new territory, not only for you, Jimmy, but for me too, and your mother. I'll tell you anything you want to know, but I don't always know the best time. I don't know what you're thinking every minute. So I need your help. You tell me what's on your mind and I'll tell you everything I know. Sound fair?"

I nodded.

He stood up and said, "Hug?"

I practically jumped across the table to feel his arms around my back, to smell that old gardening jacket, years of soil ground into the elbows. He took the book with him as we left the table.

"I'll put it back," I said.

"Let's check it out," he said. "If I'm gonna tell you everything I know, I gotta know something."

Outside on the front steps my father pointed to a food cart on the corner of White Avenue. "You've been doing good, right?" He was referring to the diet my pediatrician had started me on about three weeks ago. If that didn't do the trick, the doctor had said I'd have to get a nutritionist. No way did I want that. No more doctors. No more lab coats.

"Pretty good, yeah."

My father ordered "two dogs all around" and we sat on a bench on the plaza across from the library. The heavy book lay on his lap like a cinder block while he gobbled the last of his hot dog. When he looked up at me he laughed and wiped a smear of mustard from the side of my mouth with his napkin.

"So . . ." he said, his eyes on the book. "You want to . . . um . . . dive right in?" He mashed the yellow-stained napkin in his fist.

I nodded.

"All right. This will be good. Okay." He cleared his throat and lifted the cover. "Here we go . . ."

**

When Ben started junior high I was in sixth grade. I pumped him for information. I wanted to know what the classes were like, who his teachers were. I had heard they offered all kinds of after-school activities and it was true. It seemed there was a club for every class. Math Club. History Club. Social Studies Club. Ben shook his head as if he'd bitten into a lemon. "If you have to go to Science *class*," he said, "why would you want to join Science *club*? French class *and* French club? I don't think so."

It was a weekday, around 5:00. Ben had already been to practice and supper was about an hour away. We sat at his kitchen table on opposite sides of a chess board. He had just finished arranging his pieces and was now lining up my little guys he called pawns.

"So it's like a fancy version of checkers?"

"No." He was unfolding some papers that came in the box. "In checkers all the pieces do the same thing. These things move in different directions. Check it out." One of the pages diagrammed the moves each piece could make.

"Looks complicated," I said. "Hey, this thing's cool. What is it, a tower?"

"It's a rook."

"Why's it a rook?"

"That's what they call it."

"How's that a rook?"

"It's not a rook?

"A rook's a bird."

"A bird? How'd you know that?

"My uncle. He takes us bird watching. He's got a book, with pictures."

Ben flattened out the folds in the directions, as though it would somehow change the words. "You think this is wrong? What do ya call it, a misprint?"

"I don't know."

"Well, this one's called a knight. But it's really a horse."

"At least a knight rides a horse," I said. "There's a connection. I don't see a connection between a tower and a bird."

"A bird can fly into a tower."

"I guess."

"I don't know."

"I don't like this game," I said.

"Come on, you want to learn, don't you? It's supposed to be fun. Mr. Miller says there are tournaments."

"Why couldn't you join the TV Club? We could be downstairs watching *Candlepins for Cash*."

"My mother said I had to join something and this only meets once a week so it doesn't interfere with swimming. Gotta keep everybody happy. Besides . . ." He stopped abruptly.

I didn't like this. Ben had something to say, but was deciding whether or not to speak. Was he holding something back? From me? "What?"

"There's a girl."

"A what?"

"A girl. You know what a girl is, don't you?"

"Yeah, I do."

"Well, you said '*a what*' like it was disgusting or something."

"No. It just seemed like . . . I don't know, like you weren't going to tell me."

"I'm telling you, aren't I?"

But he hesitated. Maybe that would drive us apart someday—girls. I'd never relate to them the way Ben would. Or any normal boy. I knew by now that I'd never have kids, it was one of the first things I learned from my father. And since all wives wanted kids I'd probably never get married. And since I'd never marry, what was the point of having a girlfriend?

"Her name's Ann. Everybody was going down the list of clubs. She kept elbowing me, like, *hey let's do this one, let's do this one.*"

So Ben's plan was to use me to become a better chess player so he could impress his new friend. This was starting to resemble an episode of *The Brady Bunch.* With me as Bobby getting sore at cool big brother Greg for falling for a girl. The thing was, though, I liked girls too. There were plenty of girls in sixth grade. This one girl Mindy got on the bus two stops after mine and I always squished against the side to make room in case she wanted to sit next to me. She never did.

The thought of that half-empty grammar school bus seat led to a vision of a half-empty junior high bus seat, which led to a half-empty high school bus seat. Empty bus seats swelled in my head as Ben blabbed on about the chess girl, how she lived near Oak Gardens, where they built the new go cart track and her older brother worked there every summer and let her and her friends ride for free.

I kept returning to his hesitation. That brief reluctance to share, which indicated that this chess-playing, go cart-riding wedge that was being driven into our friendship was so dear to him that any mention of her to me would somehow lessen her importance. And that wasn't fair. He was supposed to tell me everything!

And as I fought the urge to push away from the kitchen table and run from the house I remembered what I'd been keeping secret for over a year. He had asked me about the injury my first day home from the hospital. I told him it was a hernia because that's what I heard Mother tell his mother, not to mention a lot of other mothers.

I couldn't tell him the truth. It was too freaky. No way could I tell him that I was going to need medicine in order to grow up normal, to be a man like he was going to be a man, like our friends were going to be men, that if I didn't get the medicine I would practically grow up to be a woman, without the ability to grow hair, with soft unformed muscles and a high girlish voice. I would actually develop tits! I couldn't let Ben know that without a doctor's needle in my body I'd grow up to become a laughingstock, a twisted prissy sideshow attraction.

**

Sixth grade was almost done so homework meant long division and fractions. Cliff was out and Mother was downstairs with the stereo on. A half an hour ago I had asked my father about the differences between me and normal kids, but he put it off, saying homework first. Now that we finished the final math problem, I put my pencil down and neatened the stack of grey worksheet paper.

I could tell he wanted none of the medical talk tonight. Work had kept him an extra two hours and his eyes looked droopy.

"We can talk tomorrow," I said.

"Tonight's fine." A damp toothpick danced from side to side in his mouth. "What's on your mind?"

"At school. My friends. I still think of myself . . . I don't know, different. Like there's them. And then there's me."

"You should focus on the similarities, if you're going to focus on anything. There's very little difference between you and your friends."

This was his usual response, and that's why I brought it up again. It was comforting to hear him say that I was like everyone else.

"We've talked about the fact that you can't have children. Of your own. That's the only major difference. But that's not something you have to worry about for a long long time."

"Ben and I were talking a while ago. There's this girl. And, you know, they could grow up and, well, make a baby. They'd have a family, like us, like all the families around here. And, and there I'd be, maybe living on the same street. Sometimes I picture . . . you know . . . their house filled with chatter and activities. Then there's my house, all dark and quiet."

"Stop it," my father said, taking the toothpick out of his mouth. "You can't think this way. You should be thinking about homework. It's May, you should be thinking of the Red Sox. Fun stuff."

"Okay. But, but I can't help what comes into my head."

"One day you're gonna meet a girl and fall in love and get married. And the two of you will talk about it. Maybe you'll adopt."

"But girls want to get pregnant. It was on one of those talk shows. This guy talked about adoption, but the woman, every time she was on screen she was crying about how she wanted to be pregnant."

"Women can still get pregnant."

"How?"

"There's . . ."

"Intercourse with another guy?"

"No, no."

"I was gonna say!"

"But another guy's sperm could get paired with a woman's egg. She could get pregnant that way."

"Who's the other guy?"

"You wouldn't know the other guy. It would just be his sperm. A donor."

"Like a transplant?"

"Yes!" my father said, standing up, as though my questions were over.

"How's that work?"

"Huh?"

"The sperm..." I touched the tips of my index fingers. "...and the egg."

Instead of sitting back down he walked to the fridge and grabbed a beer. "You want anything?"

I shook my head.

He returned to his seat and said, "Jimmy, I'm no expert at this. I got a vague idea. I think sperm can be injected into a woman when she's . . . Hey, you know what? Honey?" he shouted downstairs.

"Yeah?"

"You got a sec?"

She walked to the top of the stairs, repeatedly clicking the head of her pen. "What's up?"

"Jimmy was wondering. We were both wondering really . . ."

I never spoke to Mother about the medical stuff. Maybe they spoke about it all the time. It didn't seem likely, though, not the way my father phrased his words so carefully, as though now that she was standing over him at the top of the stairs, hands on hips, waiting, he wished he hadn't called her in the first place.

He continued, " . . . if Jimmy here were to get married. And he and his wife wanted to . . . have a baby. How would that, that happen exactly?"

Her eyes shifted to mine before returning to my father's. "He's eleven years old."

"We were just talking," my father said. "One question leads to another."

"It seems a little beyond where we need to be, doesn't it?" she said. "Jimmy, when you and your wife want to have a baby, there will be plenty of opportunity to discuss the alternatives. Okay?"

"Okay," I said.

"Can I go downstairs now?" she said to my father.

"Okay," he smiled. But it was a mask, I could tell right away. A dark fire fluttered behind his eyes as he watched Mother descend the stairs. But wasn't she saying the same thing dad had said just a few minutes ago, that I shouldn't be thinking about these things now, that there would be time enough to deal with adult problems?

He finished the rest of his beer in one swallow, then walked toward the refrigerator again. I thought he was going to take another beer, but he opened the cupboard next to the fridge where he kept drinks for company. He removed a bottle of brown liquid, filled a glass with ice then poured a small amount. He watched the dark liquid flow over the cubes.

I wanted to ask more questions, but I got the feeling I'd put him through enough. "Guess I'll go upstairs and read."

"All right." I left him leaning against the counter, contemplating his glass.

I had no intention of reading. As soon as I heard my father walk down the stairs into the playroom I crept down into the kitchen. I didn't look down the staircase, fearing they might be standing at the bottom.

"I'm not avoiding anything," Mother was saying, "but come on, he's eleven years old, what do you say we let him stay a kid for a few more years?"

"Normally that would be great, but the circumstances—"

"For Christ's sake, he's a little boy."

"Yes, I know he's little. But he's curious. You think he's not going to find out what he wants to know at the library or somewhere else?"

"I'm supposed to talk to him about sperm donors and fertilization? He's only eleven years old."

"Stop saying he's eleven as though it's an excuse not to have to deal with him."

Mother didn't respond. After a couple of minutes of silence I climbed the stairs to my bedroom. I was deep into the novelization of *Star Wars*, but kept drifting away from the story, thinking how I had started a fight. I tossed the book aside and walked downstairs into the playroom. If they were still fighting, I would interrupt them; if they weren't fighting, even better.

They were sitting next to each other on the sofa watching Tony Orlando & Dawn. A skit was taking place in an office. The audience was in hysterics.

"Come sit," Mother said and they made room as I sat between them.

After the skit, Tony Orlando & Dawn sang an upbeat song and he ended up in the audience shaking hands and kissing ladies on their cheeks.

Mother rested her hand on my leg.

"When you and your father asked me earlier about getting pregnant and that whole situation, I didn't mean to ignore you or . . ." I kept my eyes on Tony greeting his fans. "Well, all that matters is, like your father has said in the past, we'll answer any question you have. Um, this question, though, getting pregnant . . . We've been lucky. So we'll have to look into . . ."

My father stirred. "Let us worry about this. You worry about finishing up sixth grade with a bang, reading your books, being with your friends."

Our attention was back on the TV. Tony Orlando had rejoined Dawn on stage for the end of the song. The audience exploded with applause. They stood and cheered. Everyone was happy.

**

About a week later I got the pregnancy lecture. I was less interested, though; my questions had moved to other topics. We sat at the kitchen table. I listened to what they had to say, Mother doing most of the talking. She talked about sperm donors and sperm banks and artificial insemination, even something called test tube babies, like from a science fiction story.

"That's not all there is to it, though, right?"

"All there is to what?" my father said.

"Intercourse."

Mother turned toward my father.

"We talk about having babies," I said. "But the way some people talk about intercourse, the older kids . . . it's about, like . . . like it's a hobby. And there's this one thing I read about testosterone, how it drives urges that . . . that lead to intercourse."

My father said, "Look, when the time comes you'll have the same urges everyone else your age has. You'll want to be with a girl. At some point you'll kiss her, you'll have a relationship."

"Will I have sex?"

Mother made a noise, a gasp.

"Want me to handle this?" my father said.

Her chair scraped the floor as she pushed away from the table. Instead of leaving, she said, "No, I'll stay."

"Yes, you'll have sex if you want," my father said when I stared at him.

"I'll get an erection?"

Mother's chair scraped again. "Maybe I'll just . . . downstairs . . . finish up some things . . . I'm glad we talked, sweetie." Her fingers lightly scratched my back as she walked behind me toward the stairs.

When Mother reached the playroom and turned on the radio, my father said, "Anything you read about normal sexual development also applies to you. The only difference, other than the baby thing, is your hormones will be administered manually. Once you get past that, everything else is routine."

In the library I had read pamphlets about sexual desires and erections. They also talked about orgasm and ejaculation. They were written in black and white, offered by the library, so I knew they were true. But I still wanted to hear from my father that the facts in those pamphlets were also true for me.

"I'll be able to do an orgasm?"

My father's earlobes turned pink. He nodded, unable to speak.

I wanted to be clear of the order of events. "So first it's the erection. Then the ejaculation. Then the orgasm."

He must've known that his face was becoming a different color because he looked down, hiding it. When he looked up I saw that he was holding in laughter.

I laughed too. "This is funny, right?"

My laughter seemed to release his. His hands squeezed mine as our laughter topped each other's. When I opened my eyes I saw that he was wiping away tears. As the laughs faded, he said, "The erection definitely comes first. The others . . . ah, they're interchangeable, I guess you'd say. But trust me, please, you don't have to worry about that for a while."

"Can I ask one more question?"

"May as well."

"If I don't have sperm, why will I need to ejaculate?"

"You don't *need* to. It's just something the body does. When you're with a girl, sometime in the distant future, and you're fooling around, everything that we just talked about will happen. Some things just take care of themselves."

"Yeah but, since I can't make sperm the body won't have anything to ejaculate."

"Um. Okay. The actual sperm, the little guys with the tails, we've seen them before, right? Well, they're just a tiny part of what gets . . . ejaculated. You also got all this other stuff, the semen that carries the sperm where it needs to go. Like when we watched *Wide World of Sports* last weekend—"

"*The thrill of victory, the agony of defeat.*" Whenever we mentioned the show one of us always quoted Jim McKay from the opening sequence.

"Exactly."

"I think Evel Knievel's gonna be jumping buses on the next one!"

"Okay, we'll watch it, but last week's episode, that surfing competition from Hawaii, remember?"

I nodded.

"The big waves in the ocean are like the semen. And the surfers trying to get to shore, those guys are the little spermy fellas. And you saw what those waves did, they just brought them surfers home easy as pie."

5. The Testosterone Effect

It was toward the end of September. My first weeks of junior high. Mother picked me up after school, then we got Dad at the post office and off we went to the clinic in Braintree. We'd already been there a bunch of times for tests and talks. Dr. Young and Joanne were so nice I'd only really been nervous the very first visit. Sometimes, while waiting to see the doctor, I talked to Joanne about school and sports. Today would be different, though. Today was my first injection.

Joanne waved enthusiastically from behind the glass. She slid the partition open and asked us to have a seat. I sat between my parents on a couch and took *The Time Machine* out of my book bag. A woman about Mother's age sat on a couch across the room. She wasn't reading a book or magazine; just stared at the wall in front of her, then at the carpet, then at the ceiling as she slumped backward.

A teenage girl wearing a baseball cap emerged from the inner door. The woman on the couch had just removed a small mirror and lipstick from her pocketbook and now quickly stashed them and joined the girl at the glass. What's wrong with her? I thought as they left. What hormone does she have too little or too much of?

Joanne asked us to pass through the inner door, which buzzed as we approached. She showed us into the examination room just as Dr. Young stepped out of his office. He spread his arms expansively and smiled. "LaPlante family. All right." Dad called him the sweater doctor because he wore sweaters all year around. Today's was a rust-colored job, what Mother called cable knit. It kind of matched the brown and reddish hairs of his beard and moustache.

He led us into the tiny room where he asked me to remove my pants and hop up on the examination table. When I slung the pants over the back of a chair the "Husky" label showed. I picked them up, rolled them tight like they did in the army and set them back on the chair. Once on the table, I leaned forward to cover as much of my bare thighs as possible. I had grown a few inches, and the pediatrician's diet and Fat Swim had helped, but I was still uncomfortable the way the fat of my thighs spread so easily across the table.

Dr. Young took a seat at a small metal desk and thumbed through my file. Inside were forms and some x-rays of my left hand that had been taken over the summer. Joanne was gone. My parents stood by the closed door.

"So I'm going to give you a little shot. It won't hurt, just a pinch is all."

"Testosterone, right? Like we talked about last time?"

"That's right. Testosterone enanthate, to be precise."

"Are there lots of kinds?"

"Not really. Two common types. I'm going with enanthate, if that's okay with you."

"Yeah, yeah, sure. Is it a lot? What if it's too much? Will I get all hairy? I don't want to look like a gorilla."

He smiled as he looked down at the x-rays. "Pace of progression," he said as he slid one out of the folder. "Several factors go into the prescription dosage. We look at your age. You turned twelve last month. We look at your size. Are you a big kid, a little kid? We look at bone age." He held up the x-ray. "By looking at these growth plates we're able to see how much growth is possible. Typically, we start at fifty milligrams a shot per month and work our way up to two hundred every two weeks."

He talked to me like I was a real adult. But there was lightness in his manner too, the way his face brightened when he smiled at the end of his sentences.

"Where do you get it, the hospital?"

"A drug store, like any prescription."

"For how long?"

"How long?" the doctor said.

"Yeah, for how long do I have to take it?"

"This is forever, kid."

I knew that already. It had been mentioned at the last appointment. Just hoping for a different answer. Forever was a long time.

He stood up. "Your parents will always be there for you. And you got me around the clock if you need anything. So, you ready?"

My fingers gripped the edge of the table. Dad gave me a double thumbs-up from the door. Mother's thumbs went up too.

"You a thigh man or a butt man?" Dr. Young asked as he removed a needle and small glass vial from the pocket of his smock.

He walked toward the door and held the vial and syringe in front of my parents. The liquid inside was brownish, like watered down tea. "I know you've been over this with Jo but it doesn't hurt to see it again." He withdrew the needle, walked toward me and said, "All right Jimmy, let's make you a thigh man."

"It's not dirty, is it?"

"Is what not dirty?"

"It looks brown."

"Ah, a nifty observation. You're right, most medications are clear, but this is suspended in sesame oil."

"Why sesame oil?"

"Well, sesame doesn't leave much of a residual, also it's not allergenic. Testosterone is an oily molecule and needs to be kept in an oil to form what's called the depot pool, from which it will be absorbed over time. Long story short, it aids in the administering of the medicine. Are you good with that?"

"Sure, okay."

"So what do you say?"

I looked at the floor and closed my eyes.

And there it was, the pinch. On the outside of my thigh. It wasn't very painful, not like that tetanus shot last year, but my fingernails dug deep into the table padding anyway.

"That wasn't too bad, was it?"

"No." I rubbed my leg while he demonstrated for my parents depositing the syringe into a red plastic safety cartridge for disposal. "Are we coming back soon?" I said as I slipped on my pants.

Doctor Young said that my parents would be giving the shots from now on, that I wouldn't need to return to the clinic until next year for new x-rays. He stressed a couple of times, though, that if I had any questions, I shouldn't hesitate to call.

On the way home we stopped at the Shaw's across from Brockton High. As we passed the athletic fields Mother craned her neck. "I wonder if we can see Cliff."

"Practice is probably over by now," my father said.

Cliff was on the junior varsity football team. His love of high school sports had started as soon as he walked through the doors of Brockton High a few weeks after he sent me to the hospital. He'd tried out for everything and ended up settling on football (which lasted until the end of November) and wrestling (which picked up where football left off and lasted through February).

Baseball occupied March to May, but that only lasted his freshman year. With baseball, you needed to be on your toes even when there was no action in your immediate vicinity. No way would he have had the patience; it must've bored him to death. He dabbled in swimming and basketball, but thrived more on sports where he could level as much viciousness as possible on his fellow students.

With practice every day, Cliff arrived home in time for supper, but on nights that he had games or matches, which was often, he ate near the high school at Friendly's or Angelo's. The kid was never home. Mother said a whole world of opportunities was opening up and he was smart to take advantage. But I couldn't help think of these newfound interests as opportunities to avoid me.

"Maybe you'll play sports when you go to high school, Jimmy," Mother said as we found a parking spot. "I still say you should have played in Little League this year. You love baseball."

Both Mom and Dad, not to mention Ben, had encouraged me to attend tryouts in May. But I just couldn't do it; I was still too fat. The thought of trying out had led to images of my jiggling belly hurtling toward first base trying to beat out a grounder. Maybe next year when I've dropped a few more pounds.

So Cliff had football and wrestling. I had Fat Swim.

**

I opened the vanity door beneath the bathroom sink. Just the usual items—a basket of mother's hairclips, jars of lotion, a few hairbrushes and a can of hairspray. Where would they stash the goods? I thought. Would they hide them from me, as though I would grab the syringes and start shooting myself willy-nilly? No, but they would probably keep them from the eyes of curious neighbors. I slid open the linen closet just outside the bathroom. A utility bag sat on the top shelf. I used a footstool to reach the bag. I grabbed it and sat down. Inside were the vials, the syringes and the mini safety containers. My parents were watching TV in the playroom. I removed one of the glass vials from the cardboard box. I wanted to see it up close, check out its weird oily texture, its tea-like color. I felt the ridges of the measurement lines against my fingers—100mg, 200mg, 300mg. It was covered with a rubberized top. The whole process seemed easy enough for me to do; stick the syringe in the top, withdraw the right amount, then inject it into my thigh. Well, that last part wouldn't be easy. I couldn't imagine stabbing myself. But someday, I thought, when I'm old, I would have to do it. My parents wouldn't be with me forever and I shouldn't have to depend on a doctor or nurse. I ran my fingers along the packets of syringes and thought: Someday I'll be on my own.

**

I was old enough by now to take the city bus to the high school for Fat Swim. The school's tennis courts lay out behind the pool building. Alongside them stood a massive cement wall for people without partners to whack a tennis ball against. I always arrived an hour early to play with my India rubber ball. On the Saturday after the injection I played against the wall as usual. I threw some at the bottom of the wall for grounders then at the tar near the base to get fly balls.

My mind kept wandering to the injection. What was really inside those vials? It looked thin and watery, but Dr. Young had said it contained oil. So was it watery, or oily? I pictured it inside me, coursing through with the rest of my fluids, the blood, the pus, whatever swished around in there. This new stuff was different, I imagined. It pulsed with a life all its own, separate from my heartbeat. I knew it was yellowish brown, but I pictured it turning neon green and radioactive once it entered my bloodstream. I imagined myself transforming into The Incredible Hulk. *Don't make me angry. You wouldn't like me when I'm angry.*

One ball that I whipped really hard arced way over my head toward the roadway that led from Belmont Street to the school's main parking lot. I'd never thrown one that hard before. Was it from the injections? Was I stronger already? I sped to get under the ball, but hearing a car draw near, stopped at the edge of the curb. A station wagon stopped. A stocky man with sandy curly hair and a bushy mustache got out of the car and retrieved the ball. He threw a dart from where he stood. The ball landed in my glove like a missile.

"You gotta be careful, son." He walked toward his car and rested his arms on the roof.

"Sorry."

"You on a team?"

"Me, no. I don't usually get picked for teams."

"You like to play, though. I see you here a lot."

"It's baseball," I said.

He opened the door and settled in behind the wheel. "Trust me," he said through the passenger window. "It's more fun with others."

The car rolled away and parked near the gym entrance. He opened the back of the wagon and removed a huge bag, out of which extended the handles of a dozen or so aluminum baseball bats. I watched him lug the bag into the gym.

I thought about following him, but it was time for Fat Swim. Four of us played basketball. I dove for sunken treasure for a while. Mr. Clancy, who normally wasn't there but stopped by to pick something up from his office, made me swim four laps before leaving. Hardass.

I finished in time to leave with the rest of the kids. I bypassed the showers and headed straight for the locker room, a practice I never altered since that first day. I couldn't even dress in front of them. I brought my clothes into one of the stalls. It made no sense; on the outside I was the same as everyone else. I looked no different. But I was different, and that's all that mattered.

**

Before bed, in the bathroom, I checked myself out in the mirror. If the drugs were making me throw harder then it shouldn't be long before my body started to change. I lifted my arm and examined my armpit. Not a single hair. I moved my face right up to the mirror, looking for something on my upper lip. No change. I felt my chest, my arms, my legs. Nothing. I lowered my underwear. Bald down there too. Bald everywhere, except the top of my head.

**

The only good thing about gym was that Ben had the eighth grade class that followed mine. We talked by the gym door right up until the bell rang. Some days they were the only moments we saw each other. Being in different grades we had no classes together and Ben swam after school.

In the locker room, I found my favorite locker, farthest away in the back corner, and changed into my shorts and tee shirt. I pulled the shorts down to cover as much thigh as possible. Class started by separating the boys from the girls. The girls were to perform calisthenics for the first half of the class on the far side of the gym near the double-doors while the boys played basketball. At the halfway point we'd switch. All the boys lined up along the front row of the bleachers and counted off by twos—one, two; one, two; one, two—all the way down the line. I was a two.

The instructions were bellowed matter-of-factly by the gym teacher, Mr. Callahan, with a metal whistle around his neck and a basketball tucked up underneath his armpit. His face was tanned reddish brown and topped with a full head of white hair combed backward like a foamy wave.

"All right," Mr. Callahan shouted after a blast from the whistle. He was tall, over six feet. You could tell he sucked his stomach in, but he must have lost concentration once in a while because sometimes it expanded outward in a tight tee shirt-encased ball. "Shirts and skins. Ones are shirts, twos are skins. Decide who's gonna start and get into position."

Shirts and skins? I thought I'd misheard him. But as I looked around I saw that the twos were removing their shirts. Some were doing it against their wills, perhaps as stunned as I. But a few kids, their bodies mature and as defined as high school kids, cast their shirts aside with pride, as though they were born to expose their bodies to an admiring public. As though they were moving in slow motion so the girls twenty or so yards away could soak it all in.

I kept my shirt on and wandered over to the shirts side of the court. Mr. Callahan wouldn't care. I was nervous that the shirts might notice and banish me back to the skins once they realized I couldn't dribble without looking at the ball.

Even after the game, as I was struggling through a sit-up, I still couldn't believe the whole shirts versus skins debacle. Would it kill someone to go to the store and pick up a couple dozen red and blue tee shirts? I thought. Isn't red versus blue a lot less barbaric than shirts versus skins?

I didn't shower after gym class, of course, but I wasn't alone in that so I didn't feel too self-conscious. Although the boys who did shower made a point of singling out those who did not. I was trying to improve my fastest-dresser-in-East-Junior-High routine when Brian Haskins cornered me in the rear section of the lockers. I was already sitting on the bench with my socks on, about to beat my best time. This was supposed to be a safe place to change, away from the more crowded areas, but I realized that what made it safe also made it dangerous. It was far away from Mr. Callahan's office and the hampers where janitors store the towels for laundry. I realized now that it was also darker than the other areas. One of the overhead fluorescents was less lit than the others. Another one in the corner was completely dead.

Brian stood a few feet away, staring, his still-wet body wrapped in a white towel over narrow hips. You could see one of his hipbones just over the towel. Water dripped from his legs and pooled on the floor. He was the kind of kid you wanted to disappear around, just seep into the space between lockers.

"Time to shower."

All right, I thought, come on, get it over with so I can get the hell out of here and meet Ben. A few other kids, some also wrapped in towels, shuffled behind him, and for some reason it wasn't until this motion that I noticed the other towel dangling to the floor from Brian's hand. I reached for my shoe, but Brian glided forward, quick and agile, and kicked both shoes away, causing them to spin wildly to the other side of the floor. He moved like a predator.

"You're stinkin' up the hallways, tubs."

He spun the towel until it coiled like a snake then snapped it in the air, the sharp pop of a firecracker. As he drew closer his friends gathered behind him. The commotion brought kids from other lockers, spectators, gawkers.

"Come on, Bri, let's go—" someone said.

I wanted to grab my shoes and make a run for it, barrel right through them like Sam Bam Cunningham, but remained seated, afraid it might give Brian reason to attack. It didn't matter, though; he attacked anyway. He lunged forward like a fencer and snapped the towel at my chest. I staggered back into the corner of the lockers, shocked, and rubbed with both hands where the towel struck.

In previous classes he only humiliated kids. But now he wanted to harm. Weeks of doing it uncontested, class after class, had made him brazen. "Easy there, tubs," he said, coiling the towel for another strike, "we're just having a little fun."

And as the towel coiled into a spring and shot out from his hand like a whip, I became energized. What's the worst that could happen? I'd been brutalized by older, tougher kids than him. Hell, Cliff had already crushed my balls.

I pictured the testosterone inside of me, brimming just beneath my skin, wrapping around my muscles, engorging them with strength. My biceps and triceps grew beneath my skin, rose against the fabric of my shirt. Was it possible I was turning Hulk green? I felt enormous and powerful. I was my own superhero.

The towel snapped toward my chest and I found myself reaching for it, grabbing it, yanking it forward. Brian staggered and tripped over the bench, falling to one knee. I was shocked that I caused him to stumble, but suddenly wondered if I'd live to see next period. He quickly stood and looked around. I braced myself for another attack, but instead he looked perplexed, as though he'd never fallen before.

"Hasky, we're gonna be late."

"It's just LaPlante, let it go," someone said.

Brian walked away without a word, just a shrug and a fake smile.

"Wow, you're a tough guy," Ben said on the gym floor when I

told him what had happened.

"Yeah, that's me." I tried to play it off, all cool-like, but the picture of Haskins stumbling to the floor flashed in my head and I couldn't stop smiling.

"We meeting at your house or mine tonight?"

"I don't care," I said. "Yours, I guess."

"You're still gonna help me with that Poe paper, right? It's due Monday."

"There's time."

"It's supposed to be three pages." Ben's face tensed.

"No sweat," I said, tapping my head. "It's already up here."

**

Mother's car wasn't in the driveway. She should have been home from work. The door was unlocked. From the kitchen I heard a girl giggle downstairs in the playroom. Not Mother, a real girl. I kicked off my shoes and stepped quietly down the stairs. She lay on the floor alongside Cliff. They faced each other on their sides, one of his arms draped over her shoulders, pulling her close. The row of her shirt buttons were twisted to the side; his shirt was completely untucked. Her brown hair was long and tangled and covered most of her face. They lay at the rear of the room so I was able to watch unnoticed from the bottom of the stairs.

Their mouths never separated. He slid one of his legs between hers and grinded his knee up as far as it would go. She reached for his leg. To push it away, I thought. But no. She spread her legs and pulled his knee up harder against her. He maneuvered his hips, angling on top of her, and she rolled to her back. His hips covered hers, spreading her knees wide.

I wanted to scream to prevent this . . . this thing from gathering more steam. Was he really going to screw this girl right here in the playroom? My playroom? Go out and screw her in the woods, I thought. Why should I have to watch TV where he boinked his girlfriend? I wanted to retrace my steps then slam the door as though I just got home. Throw my bag noisily to the floor.

But I didn't. I watched. I watched greedily. I wanted to see what this was all about. What *she* was all about. Would her pants come off? That wrinkly shirt? I'd seen naked limbs on the beach and at pools, but this was different. This was what Cliff and his friends –what everybody—always talked about. This was sex!

He settled his upper body down onto hers. Their bodies remained completely still for a couple of seconds. Finally he rolled off. They lay on their backs side by side, their fingers interlocked.

"You okay?" she murmured.

"Sure."

"You mad?"

He shook his head.

"You want to do more?"

He laughed and said, "Duh."

She shifted to her side and looked down at him, brushed hair from his forehead. "I'm sorry."

His fingers disappeared into her hair. He played with the strands. "You don't have to say that every time."

"I don't want you to hate me."

"Not a chance." He sat up and crossed his legs. "You thirsty?" he said, hopping to his feet. "We have Kool-Aid, I think."

I was so busy trying to figure out everything they were talking about I almost got caught. I leaped up the stairs as gingerly as I could and ran to the door. They saw me when they reached the top of the stairs.

"How long you been home?"

Wouldn't you like to know? "Just walked in."

"I didn't hear you."

"I'm stealthy." I watched him take a second to digest the word, or at least my use of it, then said, "Where's Mom?"

"She's gonna be late. She left supper in the fridge. I'll heat it up when Dad gets home. She didn't have time to make yours. You'll have to eat what we eat."

I looked at the girl. She stood almost as tall as Cliff, slightly stoop-shouldered and plain. Definitely more homely standing up than lying down, with an odd-shaped chin, sharp, like an arrowhead pointing down. What did she think about Cliff's last comment? Why does he need a separate dinner? she must've thought. What's wrong with him?

"I'm on a diet."

"Really?" she said. "You don't need to be on a diet."

Marry her! I thought. She's a keeper. But she was just being polite.

"My name's Candace."

"I'm Jimmy."

Cliff poured the Kool-Aid, even a glass for me. After we drank Candace asked if I wanted to join them downstairs to watch TV. I declined. I didn't want Cliff making nice to me to impress a girl. I read the sports section at the kitchen table. The Celtics were on a roll. McAdoo was out and some rookie from Indiana State was in. After last year no one had much hope for the Celtics, but Red Auerbach swore this rookie would make a difference.

Cliff asked Candace to stay for supper. When Dad got home Cliff made the introductions and put a large pot filled with shells and meat sauce on the stove. My father and I made a salad while Candace and Cliff made garlic bread. He added his own touch by sprinkling the bread with grated cheese and oregano. Once seated and served, Dad bombarded her with questions, excited with a stranger at the table. Where did she live? What did she like about school? Was she going to go to college? Might he know her father?

The sauce was rich. I took a small helping. Candace offered a piece of garlic bread; I took half. After supper, she said she would do the dishes. Cliff offered to help, something he never did when Mother washed the dishes. They stood at the sink looking at each other and giggling. I gathered my books to take to Ben's.

Upstairs at Ben's, he complained about having to write his English paper, not to mention having to read the story. How could you resent having to read *The Fall of the House of Usher*? How could you *not* want to read it? It was scary as hell, a page-turner, you could read it in one sitting. We were talking about the things he could write about—the personification of the house, Poe's use of foreshadowing—when the phone rang and his mother called him to pick it up.

I looked at his sports souvenirs. I never tired of them. A bunch of posters. Bobby Orr and Terry O'Reilly, Fred Lynn, Dave Cowens.

Nicer items. Baseballs signed by Jerry Remy and Rick Burleson. Framed autographed pictures of George Scott and Dennis Eckersley. My favorite had a place of distinction on a dresser apart from all the others: An autographed picture of Carlton Fisk where he's waving the ball fair in Game Six.

"My mom made hot chocolate," he said, handing over a mug when he returned.

"What's this?" I said, referring to a brown powder that dusted the whipped cream.

"She grated nutmeg."

"Wow. Smells like Christmas."

"That was Cheryl Kramer on the phone. You know her?"

"No."

"You've probably seen her. She's incredible. Something about eighth grade girls. Big difference from seventh. Something happens, they . . . I don't know, they . . ."

"Blossom."

"Yes. They blossom, all right."

I imagined him with girls. Just wait until he reaches high school and breaks all the swim team records his freshman year, I thought. The girls would flock and flutter. I imagined us on a double date. Then myself on a regular date, alone with a girl. But even if I was as handsome and thin as Ben, it was hard to picture myself down in the playroom with a girl, lying down with her, my shirt untucked. Would a girl even want a boy with fake balls? Would she be able to tell the difference?

We tried again with *Usher*. I asked him why he hated it so much.

"Come on," he said. "How many sentences do you need to describe a house?"

"Was there anything you liked? What about when it turns out his sister's not really dead?"

His face stared outward, blank and stupid.

"You didn't even read this."

"I read some."

"How much?"

"Enough to know it's boring."

"When you help me with math at least I do the lessons."

"You always get half of them wrong."

"At least I try!"

"Hey, I started it." He had nothing else to say. The only thoughts in his head were of Cheryl Kramer.

"It's not that long. Read the rest. Then we'll write the paper."

He gave it a few minutes then said, "How are your allergies?"

I still hadn't told Ben about the injections. When I first started seeing Dr. Young I had to come up with something to explain the repeat visits. My cousin Bo had allergies that caused a purple rash all over his arms and neck and he had to keep going back to the doctor for shots. So that's what I went with. Allergies. Not a rash, though; Ben might have asked to see. I told him it was internal, stomach cramps and nausea, things like that.

If I were going to tell him the truth I probably would have spilled the beans by now. Maybe when we got older, really older, like our parents' age. Maybe I would tell him then. For now, though, the secret was mine.

**

My parents were watching television downstairs when I got home, which left Cliff to the small kitchen TV. From what little I could tell while pouring a glass of Tab, McGarrett was circling up with Danno, Ben and Kono to prepare for a showdown with Wo Fat.

Cliff stood up and lowered the volume. "Did you like her?"

"Candace?"

"Who else?"

What did he care? "Sure."

He turned the volume higher. That was it. He had nothing else to say to me and I had nothing to say to him. I tried: "Is she your girlfriend?"

His shoulders lifted. "To be determined."

"She's pretty," I said.

His head twisted to me. "You think?"

"Yeah."

Just as quickly his eyes returned to the set, as if my opinion didn't mean a thing.

**

The library in grammar school was just a jumble of books in a cramped basement. East's library was the real deal, shelf after shelf of books. I usually went after school, what with Ben at practice most days, and I didn't want to sit at home with the refrigerator and cupboards beckoning.

The librarian spent a few minutes with me the first day to show me the different areas, but the fiction section was easy since all the books were in alphabetical order by author. I could have used the card catalogue more, but I enjoyed just walking up and down the aisles, what the librarian called stacks, scanning the titles, running my fingers along the smooth plastic-covered bindings. I was into H.G. Wells and had already read *The Time Machine* and *The Invisible Man*. Next up was *The Island of Dr. Moreau*. It was toward the back near the stairwell.

On my way there, my eye caught a series of tall books on the bottom shelf, their bindings brightly colored. I sat on the floor and slid one out. The cover was a picture of a large elderly ghost on the ramparts of a castle, its arms outstretched toward a boy dressed in black. Others on the castle roof, soldiers or guards, kept their distance, urging the boy to stay back. I couldn't look away. Each character's expression had his own tale to tell.

It was a play. *Hamlet*. By William Shakespeare. The first half of the volume was a series of elaborate pictures like the one on the cover; on the opposite page a synopsis described a scene in the play. The second section contained the full text of the play. I brought it to a table near a window that overlooked the school's baseball and soccer fields.

The first picture in *Hamlet* was the same one from the cover. Under it read the words: *Something is rotten in the state of Denmark.*

"Excuse me," the librarian said from her chair behind the counter. "Four o' clock, we're closing. Would you like to check anything out?"

I brought the book to the counter where she stamped the card and slid it in the back envelope. During a later visit to the library, I cracked open the next book in the Shakespeare series, *Romeo & Juliet*. Its cover showed the picture of a boy hanging from the ledge of a balcony, shouting at a girl who was overlooking it. It reminded me of *Repunzel*. It was easier to follow than *Hamlet*, even though I spent most of the time flipping to the "notes" section at the back of the book.

At one point, while Juliet's father was giving her a hard time for not wanting to go steady with a family friend, I looked out the window and noticed students playing softball on the diamond below. Mr. Callahan was down there too, hitting balls out of his hand. Some kids played catch in foul territory. After a couple of minutes a game started. Bases were overrun. Kids struck out and were given an extra swing. Balls fell between infielders and outfielders. Callahan didn't seem to mind any of it. He showed them how to field and hit, but it obviously wasn't a serious team.

I jammed my books into my bookbag, flew to the locker room to change into gym clothes and rushed for the door. Once outside, though, in the cold, with the softball game only a hundred feet away and the players' voices audible, I stopped. Could I really compete with these kids? Did I even have a prayer? But as I doubted myself I found that, without fully realizing it, my feet started moving again. And in seconds I was facing Mr. Callahan, who stood at home plate helping a batter with his swing.

"You want to play?" he said when he saw me.

"We have a softball team?" I said.

"Intramurals. Grab a mitt." He nodded to a pile of ancient, worn-out gloves that lay scattered near a bench along the first base line.

I picked up a glove and jogged toward the outfield.

"Shouldn't we stick him behind the plate?" said the first baseman.

I jogged toward a gap between left and center.

I knew the importance of a catcher. Carlton Fisk was my all-time favorite player, although some days it was Dwight Evans. But in a game like this all the catcher did was toss the ball back to the pitcher. I hadn't thrown all those balls against the house and tennis wall just to play catch. After a few swings a fly ball came my way but, seeing that another kid had a better angle, I yielded and backed him up.

"Smart move," the kid said after the ball popped into his glove.

With one out and a runner on third, a sinking line drive hurtled toward me. I loped forward clumsily, but got my glove down in time to make the catch.

"Good catch," Mr. Callahan said from home plate.

"Play's at third," a teammate shouted.

"He's off the bag."

"Get back, get back," the other team screamed.

I uncorked a bullet that the third baseman caught at his knee. Out by plenty. The inning ended with a roar from my teammates. As we all jogged in to bat, the kid that suggested I play catcher punched my shoulder with his glove and said, "Nice play."

I spent years working on defense but not a lick on offense and it showed. My first plate appearance resulted in a pop up to the right side. Next at bat I ended up on second, only because the shortstop chucked the ball ten feet up the first base line. The run was agony. By the time I stopped I could barely stand. Cramps twisted inside my shoulders and gut. I bent over to ease the pain.

"You okay, slugger?" Mr. Callahan said.

I stood up and waved, unable to respond verbally. When the next batter approached the plate I half hoped he'd strike out so I wouldn't have to run.

After the game, Mr. Callahan handed out schedules. Practices were to take place a few days a week and games against the other junior highs once a week. As the practices continued the team dwindled, leaving us a core of thirteen. It didn't take long for me to become comfortable with the guys. The outfielder who'd suggested I stay out of his way turned out to be a good kid. And a really good player. He played Little League and was always coming up with tips to play the field—being at the ready position, assuming that every ball would be hit to you, locking the ball into the glove. The whole team got along. We chatted each other up, we ranked on each other. I was surprised how good I got, how at ease, especially in the field.

Before the first game, against North Junior High, Mr. Callahan gathered us all in the parking lot before getting into the van. He gave a speech about how hard we'd been working the past few weeks, how we'd meshed from a bunch of strangers to a cohesive team that worked well together and helped each other. It turned out he took intramurals a lot more seriously than I had first thought when I spotted the team from the library window. So did all the kids. So did I. I wanted to do well. I wanted to win.

**

Frigid temperatures and an early November snowstorm prevented the last three games. After school, I retrieved my glove from my gym locker and was walking out of the locker room when I heard Mr. Callahan shout, "Hey."

I had just passed his office. I poked my head in. He sat at his desk, the sports section of the *Globe* open on top. Grey filing cabinets lined one of the walls. Beyond his desk lay a storage cage packed with basketballs, kickballs, soccer balls, orange cones, bases and bats. "Why so glum?" he said. He wore dungarees and a collared jersey. It was odd to see him out of his red shorts and white tee shirt.

"No more games."

"Ah, this was just a preview." He stood up, his voice filling with enthusiasm. "We'll really get going when the weather improves. Play from April straight through June."

"That's next year!"

"You really have a good time out there, that's for sure. Well, the basketball team plays over the winter, you can always—"

I didn't even hear the rest, his words eclipsed by a mental picture of me running up and down the court. Please! I still had trouble running from first to third without dropping dead. "I don't know, you know. All that running…"

He opened one of the cabinets and rummaged through some hanging files before pulling out some paper. "If you want, something like this might help."

I took one of the pages. The top read, "1800 Calories A Day." It listed foods that should be eaten for all meals and snacks. "I already got one of these. Worse, 1600." I tossed the pages onto the open drawer.

"Do you follow it?"

"Mostly."

"Mostly yes or mostly no?"

"Mostly yes, but . . ."

"But what?" he said.

I didn't want to start blabbing to Mr. Callahan. It wasn't like he was my father.

"Come here, sit down." He pushed out his chair for me, then sat on a large equipment box next to the desk. "Talk to me."

"Nothing. I used to be bigger. But it doesn't matter. Mr. Jeffries talks about this DNA stuff. It's a code that tells you what you're going to look like. I mean, what's the point of all this dieting if your DNA says you're going to be a fat guy anyway?"

Mr. Callahan looked down at his paper for a couple of seconds. "Hey, I'm not a Science teacher, but I think DNA is a little more complicated than that. If you don't eat crap and keep playing ball like you do you're bound to lose weight. Plus you're going to get taller. How tall's your father?"

"He's a regular-sized guy, kind of tall, I guess."

"There, you see? It's just a matter of time." He stood up, patted his stomach and said, "Besides, look at me. I should practice what I preach." He lifted his shirt to reveal a hairy belly hanging over his jeans. I laughed. He grabbed it in both his hands and shook. "Look at this mush-mush." He took the papers from the drawer. "You know what? You have your diet. I have mine. We'll do this together."

I followed him to the back of the locker room where the doctor's scale stood. He stepped on and moved the dials. "Two forty-one," he said. "Christ, when did that happen?" He stepped down and motioned for me to take his place. I hesitated. "Hey, I should be more embarrassed than you." I stepped on the scale. I weighed a hundred and seventy-two pounds. "We can do this once a week," he said, "say every Monday after school." He held out his hand as I stepped off the scale. I shook it.

**

For the first time in Brockton, an in-depth sex education curriculum was planned for junior high. Articles had sprung up in the *Enterprise* about it, columns and letters to the editors. Subject matter was altered dozens of times, but in the end lesson plans were agreed to by the School Board.

First up was a slideshow called *From Youth to Adolescence*, which compared an eleven year old named John to his fifteen year old brother Barry. Slides showed how the older brother's muscles were more defined. They showed the brothers standing next to each other, one hairless and the other sprouting patches under his arms and between his legs. It followed the same track with two sisters, Sally and Monica—muscle development, body hair, breast and hip size. A few kids in the class giggled. The narrator talked about how Barry's interest in girls had increased over the past couple of years. One picture showed them sharing a milkshake at the counter of a drugstore. Another showed them kissing. One revealed Barry in profile with a limp penis; in the next one his penis shot straight out like a pencil.

"Pinocchio dick," someone whispered.

More laughter. This time it seemed from the whole class. Except me. I shifted in my seat. I wanted out. Especially when the narrator started talking about hormones and sexual urges, about semen and ejaculation. This was different than reading about sex in the library or talking about it with my father. Seeing everything blown up on the big white screen was nerve-wracking. I could feel the other students looking at me, waiting for me to flinch. At any moment they all might stand up and shout: "Jimmy LaPlante isn't like the rest of us. Ha ha ha. Jimmy LaPlante has plastic balls."

Sex. I was inundated with it: Conversations with my father; studying books and pamphlets. I thought about Cliff and Candace going at it in the playroom. Sure, boys and girls had sex all the time; and it supposedly felt amazing. But there was something safe talking about it with your father or reading about it in a book. There was nothing safe about watching this filmstrip in the middle of a classroom. This wasn't about Cliff and Candace. Or Barry and Monica. This was about me. This *was* me.

Even though I was assured everything would be normal in the *being with girls* department, I had doubts. Hey, I had fake testicles and fake hormones. Imagine plastic ball boy approaching a girl at a party. I pictured myself in a couple of years home alone reading or watching TV while the rest of the world was out holding hands, cuddling, kissing, out there ejaculating, semen spewing left and right.

I watched my classmates. Their faces shimmered with silent energy, curiosity and embarrassment, as though Barry and Monica might leap naked from the screen and start going at it on Mrs. Snow's desk.

The following week we learned more about orgasms and condoms, sex for pleasure and reproduction. Wet dreams. Alternative forms of birth control, family planning.

Mrs. Snow talked about masturbation, "when both boys and girls, adults too, play with their genitals until orgasm is achieved." Holy crap, I thought. They got a name for that? Other kids did that? Adults too? My father and I never covered this. I sat there smiling at my desk. Maybe I wasn't so different. I thought about the times I'd sat on the toilet and stroked myself long enough to feel a rush of pleasure between my legs.

When I rubbed myself these days, though, I thought of Jennifer Montrose. Jennifer and I had been partners assigned to work on an outline of events leading to the *Declaration of Independence*. She had wavy long hair and large boobs compared to most of the girls in school, even the eighth graders. She was pretty, with a narrow face and light pinkish skin, and I definitely thought about kissing her. I wondered what her breasts looked like in her bra. And what would happen if the bra were removed. I imagined touching her nipples and the skin around them. Did a girl's nipple feel different from a boy's? It would be rougher, like mine, but maybe less so, and the actual breast smooth and squishy, like a marshmallow.

**

I sat on the edge of my bed with my pants down. As always, Mother looked away guiltily as the needle pierced my skin. I hated when it was her turn. My father probably didn't like injecting me either, but he was better at hiding it. Maybe I should have suggested that Dad give all the shots. Maybe not, though. It might make her feel bad, like I didn't trust her.

At first I thought her guilt came from the jab of the needle. But she'd been doing this for seven months; she must have realized by now the needle wasn't painful. I imagined the testosterone piercing my skin and muscle, swimming different strokes through my body, the backstroke down my legs, the butterfly to my fingers, hardening muscles as it flowed past, pushing out wiry black masculine hairs through every follicle.

"You don't have to do it anymore if you don't want to."

"Hm?" She was depositing the needle into the plastic safety sheath.

"Maybe Dad will take over." Her face twitched.

I truly thought I was being helpful. "Or I can do it." I should have listened to my instincts and kept my lips zipped. "It's just…if you don't like doing it. I, I can help, that's all."

"Obviously I don't like doing it," she said, twirling the plastic case in her fingers. "Who would? It's just . . . just . . ." She started to speak several times then stopped. She sat next to me on the bed as I buttoned my pants. The harsh light from the bedside lamp accentuated the gray shadows beneath her eyes and in the hollows of her cheeks. "Yes, these shots are hard for me. They remind me of everything you went through when you got hurt. Also of what you're going through now."

I wanted to say I'm sorry, not to worry about all that, but was afraid of another backfire.

"I know it's easier for you with your Dad. You two talk. That's important. And I understand why you'd want him to do this . . ." Her eyes filled with tears. She turned her head away. " . . . some days I just feel so damn helpless. You know, I just want to, I just want to fix it." She snapped her fingers, once, then again. "Boom. And it's fixed. Just like that."

"I'm sorry." I had to say something.

"No, no," she said. "Don't *you* apologize. It's me, it's stupid me. There's so little I can do about this whole . . . this business. I'm just . . . just sitting on the sidelines. The least I can do, the one concrete thing I can do is, is this." She held up the cartridge.

"Don't feel helpless," I said.

"Thanks." She leaned forward until her forehead rested against mine. I felt the moist layer of perspiration on her skin. I felt her breath on my mouth.

I remembered the day of my first injection at the clinic. Dr. Young had said that I   should never worry because my parents would always be there for me. As Mother struggled to hold back tears, I couldn't help but wonder if she was there for me or I was there for her.

6. Watching from the Sidelines

It was April and intramurals would be starting soon. I barreled through the front door after school. "Ma!"

"Down here." The laundry room, if you could call it a room. More like an alcove off the playroom. "You know I don't like shouting."

"Sorry," I said from the doorway. "Do you have an old blanket? A heavy one? I want to hang it over the clothesline and throw balls against it. Mr. Callahan said it would make my arm strong."

"You don't want to play against the house?"

"I'm gonna use a baseball!" I only had so much time to play before homework and supper.

"All right, calm down. We'll take a look in the crawlspace after we fold the laundry."

"Fold laundry?"

She toed a basket of whites toward me and we folded the underwear, socks and tee shirts. Next came the colored socks. I sped through them. "What's that?" She nodded at my stack. "They're mixed up." I had folded some of the navy socks in with the black. "That's a redo," she said. I refolded. Then we folded the towels and washcloths. Finally, we pulled a couple of boxes out of the crawlspace. The blankets inside were too small. We opened another box.

"What's this?" I said.

"It's filthy," she said, trying to contain the dustballs that swirled on the floor. "Don't trail these all over the house."

It was a massive tarp, with grommets every couple of feet around the perimeter. The box also contained several rusty stakes. I was outside in a minute hanging the tarp over the clothesline and staking it to the ground.

"You'll have to take that down when you're done," Mother said from the screen door. "I'll need the line for sheets."

"All right." I only had a few baseballs and softballs so I had to run back and forth to shag the balls. Tomorrow I'd buy more balls. More balls, I thought. I need more balls. Very funny. Hardy har-har.

I started close to the tarp and after a couple of minutes took a few steps back, then a few more until I was ninety feet away, the length of a major league base path. I must have been throwing for a half hour when my father got home.

"Ingenious," he said as he walked down the side yard. "You know, we could play catch."

"This way I can play whenever I want."

"Let's go for a ride," my father said.

Child World was the biggest store at Westgate Mall! It was a castle, with turrets and battlements along the roof. Colored pennants and streamers hung above the entrance. A panda in blue overalls greeted people with circulars as they emerged from their cars. "Peter Panda" was written across his overalls. As we approached the glass doors they opened automatically. We didn't even have to touch them!

Inside was massive, like one of those garages for airplanes. We were greeted by hundreds of Atari games and mountainous displays of *Star Wars* and *Superman* action figures. Store clerks in blue smocks pointed shoppers in the right direction. Kids from toddlers to teenagers shouted at their friends and parents, while an endless line of registers clanked and rang with purchase after purchase.

I could have wandered around all night, but my father was on a mission. When it came to shopping, he was a get-'em-in, get-'em-out kind of guy. He shot up one of the aisles toward the back of the store. We passed hundreds of coloring books and different types

of crayons and markers and paint by number sets. I wanted to stop
and look at all the yoyos—dozens of them—but I would have fallen
behind.

The aisle opened up to the sporting goods department. Tents
had been erected, sleeping bags had been laid out. A hundred bikes
hung overhead from wires—three-speeds, ten-speeds, trail bikes,
little girl bikes with pink tassels hanging from the handle bars. The
baseball section contained more gloves and bats than I'd ever seen in
one place. You could smell the leather and wood. "Hm," my father
said to no one in particular. "Maybe they don't carry them."

"What are we looking for?"

My father's mission didn't allow for my intrusions. Off he went
down another aisle and stopped midway. He squatted to get a better
look at some large flattish boxes on the bottom shelf. A picture on
the top box showed a pitchback.

"We have one assembled," a female clerk said from behind. She
led us to the display area on the other side of the tents. It stood
about five feet high and four wide with bright orange piping and
white netting with a red square in the middle for the strike zone.

"What do you think?" my father said.

"It's great!"

At home, mother came out into the backyard while we were
sorting the tubes and wing nuts. "One second you're pulling up in
front of the house. The next you're gone. My son's gone."

"We bought a pitchback," my father said, standing amidst metal
pipes, netting and discarded box.

"A pitchback," I said. She held her rigid gaze on my father. I
wanted to defend him. "You throw a baseball at it and it comes right
back to you."

"Yes, Jim, I know how it works," she said. Then to my father:
"Try to keep me informed of the comings and goings, okay?" She
marched back toward the house and stopped at the tarp. "What
about this?" she said, turning to me.

"It's still early." Had she expected me to put it away before
going off with Dad? It took forever to fold that thing. "I was
hoping to still use it."

She opened the screen door with a jerk and strode into the

house.

"She's mad," I said.

"Maybe we'll go out for pizza."

It's not on my diet, I thought. I didn't say anything, though. Why should my diet prevent others from eating what they wanted? If it meant Dad getting back in Mother's good graces, I'd go. I'd eat a salad. Besides, I was usually allowed a slice when we went to Home Café. You couldn't go on a family outing to the pizza joint and not allow a kid one measly slice.

The pitchback was assembled in twenty minutes. Dad set the box aside then said, "Go on, I'll toss some." He threw the balls into the netting at different angles causing me to run from one side of the yard to the other. After throwing me a few ground balls he broke down the box and went inside. Playing on my own, I discovered it was hard to judge the throws. I threw too hard at first and all the balls sailed over my head. I still liked it, though; I'd get used to the angles.

It turned out Mother had already made macaroni and cheese. I got lean beef cooked with onions, peppers, broccoli and cauliflower. Mother placed a tiny serving of macaroni on my plate, like she always did when the rest of the family was served a dish she knew I liked. And, as usual, my father always asked for some of whatever I ate.

I talked the whole time about the pitchback. How fast the ball flew back at you. How tough it was to judge where it would sail off to. "I can't wait to get back out."

"You haven't done your homework," Mother said.

"It's Friday."

"What difference does that make?"

"I have all weekend."

"Homework's done the same day," she said. "You know that."

"I'll be sure to leave enough time."

My father said, "Homework first."

"So I can play after?"

"It'll be too dark." Mother again.

"There's a light at the back door."

"That little thing? You'll kill yourself."

"Maybe we can get a light for the backyard," I said. "One of those big bright ones that light up everything, what do you call 'em?"

"Flood lights," Cliff said.

"Yeah, right. Flood lights."

Before bed that night I snuck some leftover macaroni. Not too much. I wanted to gobble it up like I used to, but I thought of Mr. Callahan's scale—the way the needle hovered between the numbers and lines—and covered the baking dish after a couple of bites.

The next day I was out there bright and early with the new toy. No, not a toy; a tool. I stood close to the net and threw it hard so the ball would soar over my head and I'd have to make a running catch. I noticed a figure out of the corner of my eye.

Cliff. He wore a glove and had settled under the ball where it descended near the base of the house. He tossed the ball back to me then nodded to the pitchback for me to throw another. I threw about ten before he took over. I wanted to hate him, every inch of him. The way part of his hair fell over his face, covering an eye, as though he was trying to be Tom Petty. But I remembered what my father had repeated about how he hadn't hurt me on purpose, and the way Mother so desperately wanted us to get along.

After a few throws from Cliff, a car sounded from the driveway. Todd McAfee had rumbled along in his broken down pickup. The thing must have been fifty years old. The passenger door barely closed. The front bumper would surely fall off at the slightest thud. It seemed strange to see Todd behind the wheel, like a real grownup.

"Gotta go," Cliff said.

The passenger door squeaked louder than a haunted house. I watched the old Sanford & Sonmobile limp away down Miller Avenue. I started playing again, but it was a letdown. Just wasn't the same alone. That guy in the station wagon all those months ago had been right: it was definitely more fun when you played with others.

**

Little League tryouts were the second Sunday in May. I woke up early so I could practice with the pitchback shielding the sun with my

glove. After a while I hung the tarp. I gathered all my baseballs—
I had dozens by now—in a large beach pail and started throwing.
When the pail emptied I did it again. I wanted to be as ready as
possible; I needed every advantage because I was still fat and slow.

It had been about six months since I started my diet with Mr.
Callahan. It worked better for him. He only lost twelve pounds
but it looked like a lot more. "It's my height," he said. "I carry my
weight well." I lost more weight than Mr. Callahan, but I barely grew
an inch. It felt good to drop sixteen pounds, but anyone seeing me
for the first time would see a fat kid who carried his weight like a
Weeble.

Near the end of my fourth pail Ben arrived on his bike. He
watched me throw for a minute then said, "You're really bustin' it,
huh?"

"I want to make a team."

"Jimmy, it's Little League. You can show up with one leg and
make a team."

I kept throwing. "I want to make a good team. Then I want to
make the All-Star Team." The regular season was to finish at the end
of June, after which all the coaches selected the best in the league
to represent Brockton, Massachusetts in the Little League World
Series.

"If we don't leave now you're gonna miss it altogether."

"You're coming?"

"I'll check it out."

"I'm nervous," I said as we rode along North Quincy Street
toward Brookfield Park.

"What are you nervous about?" Ben said. "Keep your eye on
the ball. Nothing to it."

"Yeah, nothing to it."

The park consisted of four diamonds but everyone was packed
into the one closest to the parking area. Ben climbed up to the
farthest row of the bleachers, extended his legs down a couple of
rows and leaned back on his elbows. Kids dressed in shorts and
sweatpants and tee shirts, carrying gloves and bats, filled the infield,
outfield and foul ground. I was surprised how little most of them
were and realized that this was the last year I'd be eligible for Little

League. I was an old-timer.

At least I was stronger than these pipsqueaks. But what if I flopped? What if these kids who could barely lift a bat off their shoulders were faster and stronger than they looked? Any one of them could probably beat me in a race from first base to second. Beat by a midget. In front of Ben. This was a big mistake. I had to get out of there. I started to wave Ben down from the bleachers when I heard my name called.

It was Steve, the first baseman of the intramurals team. I was about to tell him I had to get going, but he said, "I'll do your arms," and, grabbing my palms, pulled my arms toward each other behind my back. I returned the favor. As I waited for him to say *when*, I noticed Ben on the bleachers looking toward the playground, where a few girls played on the swingset.

Ten coaches holding clipboards huddled near first base. Steve started windmill stretches and I followed along. I guess I decided to stick around. He pointed to the fence behind home plate. Mr. Callahan stood there holding a toddler in his arms.

"You coaching Little League, Mr. Callahan?" Steve said.

"Just out for a walk with Alice here. She wants to be a big leaguer some day, don't you, honey?" He lowered her to a stroller at his side and strapped her in. "Figured since I'm out I'd see how my guys do."

"Listen up. Gather at the bases," one of the coaches bellowed from the middle of the infield. By the time I turned around, another coach was shouting out names and pointing to positions. "Come on, let's move," another one yelled.

Every kid got tried at every base, plus shortstop, by the coaches hitting out of their hands. Ten chances at every position. There must have been a hundred of us. Four coaches hit, the others kept score. Four kids up at each position, four down. Four up, four down.

As I took my position at second, a shout rose from the bleachers: "Keep your eye on the ball, little buddy." Ben was cracking up from his perch in the top row. He pointed two fingers at his eyes then made the shape of a ball with his hands. "Eye on the ball."

I started to laugh, but contained it and focused on the batter. I wasn't sure how they kept score, but I fielded everything cleanly at first and second, seven for ten at short and six for ten at third. They held a break after infield tryouts, except for fifty or so kids who needed to be retried for their throw from third to first. I wasn't among them.

During the break, I noticed that the girls from the swings had made their way over to the fence near the bleachers. Two of them tugged at a third, probably to go back to the swingset, but she didn't budge. She leaned on the fence and watched the field as coaches instructed players where to go next. From across the diamond I noticed that she sucked on a strand of her long brown hair.

I aced the outfield, caught everything, pop flies, line drives, short hops, so I was one of about forty to show the coaches my arm from the outfield. When I caught the ball deep, a coach yelled "cut-off" and I heaved it to the cut-off man at short. When I caught a shallow fly, he yelled "plate" and I did what I always did at intramurals: held up a few feet so I could catch the ball with momentum. My release was quick and I pumped my fist when the ball reached the catcher waist high on the third base side of the plate—a strike.

During the break before batting practice the coaches gave me a few balls and asked me to stand behind third base and throw to first. I threw accurately each time, hitting the same spot.

"You ever pitch?" one of the coaches said.

"Underhand."

"Underhand?" He was a tall lanky guy with bushy black hair and sideburns.

"Softball intramurals at East Junior High."

"You ever play baseball?"

"Not for real."

"Well, I'll be." He looked at the man who had caught my throws at first base. A little heavyset guy with a face all scrunched up like he was looking into the sun. "We gotta get you practiced up, kid, see what you're made of."

So I was the first to pitch batting tryouts. The first two slid out of the strike zone about shoulder high. "Easy, Jimmy." Mr. Callahan was still around. A woman nearby played with Alice. "Don't worry about the velocity. Just get it over. Nice and easy, like you're playing catch." The next two pitches were slower and they got clobbered.

I increased the speed as I continued and managed to keep decent control. My last three pitches were strikes, two swinging.

Everyone got ten swings. Ten only, no excuses. Strikes, fouls, everything. I'd never faced live pitching before, not with a baseball, not competitively. We batted alphabetically, so I had time to study a bunch of pitches from the outfield. When on deck I stood as close to the plate as possible to gauge the trajectory and get a feel for the speed of the pitches.

The brown haired girl had moved again, close to where I stood on deck. I could see how her light brown hair was just about the same color as her skin. It was hard to focus.

"You should try out," I said. I'd never seen a girl play Little League, but I didn't think it was against the rules. Maybe we'd make the same team.

She just shrugged, then walked casually to the bleaches and sat on the bottom row.

"LaPlante," a coach shouted. "Pay attention."

I jumped back at the first pitch. I must have looked ridiculous. It wasn't *that* inside. The next pitch was just as far outside. The next was high, but I swung anyway. Missed by a mile.

"Wait for your pitch," the guy with the scrunched up face said. He had long stringy hair that hung down past the back of his neck. "We ain't going anywhere."

I took my time; at least I thought I did. Didn't do much good, though. Two swinging strikes, three infield grounders, a called strike, two singles to left, a fly ball to right and a dribbler up the first base line that stopped in foul territory. Had the girl distracted me? So much preparation for this day and I let some girl interfere? No, I told myself in the end, it wasn't the girl. I just stunk.

**

I dreamed I was the kid from that health class filmstrip. Naked. The kids in the classroom looked at me on the screen as my dick grew. The boys raised their arms in the air, thumbs up.

'At a boy, Jimmy.

Get a load of that thing.

But girls screamed, fled the room. My penis kept growing like

one of those retractable pointers teachers sometimes used. I tried
to stop it. I tried to leap from the screen, but its edges contained
me like a prison cell. My dick, though, pushed through into the
classroom. I hollered, but all of a sudden the room was empty. My
fists banged hard against the screen, which felt like Plexiglas. My
penis now extended over the first row of desks. For some reason, I
noticed things I never really noticed before: the American flag that
hung by the door; the loud ticking from the wall-mounted clock; the
blunt stumps of chalk on the blackboard tray.

Then I saw her. Sitting in the back. The brown-haired girl with
the golden skin. She watched me scream and bang with the same
casual curiosity she had watched the tryouts. I stopped shouting. I
waved. She slowly made her way to the desk where my penis rested.
She sat and cautiously touched it.

I couldn't feel her finger. Just a dull lifeless pressure. She started
to stroke it, gently at first then more vigorously. She stood and put
her whole body into it, her arms, her back, heaving back and forth,
pushing and pulling.

My dick changed into a humongous long baseball bat. And she
was sanding it down, like a pro on the on-deck circle. Her hair now
snarls, heavy and dark with sweat. She stopped and looked up at me,
her whole body drenched in sweat. I shook my head, turned up my
palms, useless. She shrugged like she'd shrugged at tryouts, pushed
her hair back from her face and wandered out of the classroom.

My penis disappeared. I tore open my fly. Nothing there but a
ragged patch of tiny pubic hairs. My heart raced. I kicked off my
pants, my underwear. Then blood. Right between my legs, where
my dick should have been. A round drop about the size of a quarter.
Matting the pubes. Another drop, then more.

Boys weren't supposed to bleed down there. Was I given the
wrong prescription? Blood pooled on the desk. Should I call Dr.
Young? Oh no, I thought, no, no, no. Am I becoming a girl? Oh
God, I'm turning into a . . .

"Jimmy. Jimmy."

I startled awake, felt my body jump.

Mother's hands held my arms. "You were screaming."

"I was?"

"Your face, it's sopping."

"Oh, I . . . I . . ."

"You're burning up."

"No, I'm fine."

She left. Water ran in the bathroom. A flutter of images flashed in my head. The girl sanding my penis. The ticking clock. Then the blood; I found myself lifting the sheet, checking the bed. Mother returned and pressed a cold washcloth against my forehead, cheeks, neck.

"Just a dream is all," she said. "Just a dream."

When she left for the night I couldn't help pulling down my underwear. Make sure the little guy was still there.

**

Twelve of us made up the Korkin Hardware team. The first day of practice was the Saturday after tryouts. We gathered at home plate. The coach was the dumpy guy with the stringy hair who had told me to take my time at the plate. Coach Wicker. The younger guy with the black hair and sideburns was Mr. O'Rourke, but he said to call him Mitch. I looked for the girl, but didn't see her.

"Confidence is bred by experience," Coach Wicker was saying. As his voice rose in enthusiasm, it became nasal and shrill. "The more you do the more you know. The better you get. If we don't have practice one day, practice on your own. Remember. The goal is to win baseball games. To win."

The practice was structured like the tryouts. Everyone got ten chances at each position. Coach Wicker and Mitch evaluated each performance on clipboards. Wicker wasn't much physically—in fact, I hadn't noticed it before, but he walked with a limp—but when he hit the ball out of his hand it left the bat like a bullet. And every ball ended up exactly where it was aimed.

Afterwards, we were given position assignments for batting practice. I got right field. Not center, but I was playing baseball so I didn't complain. Hitting was still a bit of a mystery to me, but I felt more at ease today than last week and hit a few line shots and hard grounders. We played live ball on the final pitch, meaning the batter ran the bases and the fielders tried to throw him out.

Some parents had started to trickle in to drive kids home. As we gathered our equipment, Coach Wicker shouted, "Time to run. Three perimeters of the park. If you stop I tack on another. This is how we end every practice. Get used to it."

The whole park? I thought. It must be a mile! But kids started running. I tossed my glove and followed, passing Coach Wicker and Mitch as they consulted each other's clipboards. I immediately fell behind. After the first lap my sneakers felt like cement blocks. My throat hurt, like I was breathing shards of glass. Finally, I stopped running, but kept walking as fast as I could.

Coach Wicker sidled up next to me. "You're gonna have to run an extra lap."

"Huh?"

"You stopped."

"I did not. I'm still going."

"You stopped running."

"I'm still moving." God, I couldn't run another step, never mind another lap. "You said an extra lap if we stopped. I'm still moving."

He stopped walking, but I kept my legs in motion, jogging in place. I wouldn't let him trick me. He stuck his angry red nose in my face. "Are you a lawyer?"

"No, sir."

"I didn't think so. Start running right now, not walking, not jogging. Good hard running. Once more around the park. And on the third time around when you get halfway, you're gonna break into a sprint. You do all those things and maybe I won't make you run a fourth. And maybe I won't kick you off this team."

He slapped my butt as I started off. I ran the second and third laps as slow as the first. By the time I crawled back to get my glove everyone was gone. Coach Wicker was collecting balls, bats and bases into a huge equipment bag he held over his shoulder. His limp worse under all that weight. "Gotta get in shape, kid," he said.

That night in bed a baseball was coming at me and I swung. I woke up with my arms flailing. And when I dozed again there was the ball again, only this time I was in the field and I awoke with my feet bunching up the covers at the bottom of the bed. Batting, fielding, twisting, turning, all night.

A week later I was taking infield practice when a ball skidded on the ground and took a funny hop. I lunged for it, but there was no play. Coach Wicker raced over from the plate. You knew he was mad when his forearms moved back and forth like little pistons when he walked. He looked like those midget wrestlers they showed on Channel 56 on Friday nights.

"Keep your whole body behind the glove. Don't be afraid of it. You got enough padding there." He grabbed my chest flab between two knuckles and squeezed.

"Ow," I said as he walked away. I rubbed my chest. "What the fuck," I said to myself.

Wicker spun around. "What did you say?"

"Nothing."

"You say a bad word?" The guy had dog hearing.

"No."

"I don't want you saying a bad word."

Then don't squeeze my tit, I thought.

Outfield drills were spent calling for balls, blocking the sun, getting breaks on the ball, hitting the cutoff man. After practice, Wicker ran beside me on the final lap. When I slowed, he placed his hand on my lower back and pushed. With about fifty yards to go he sped in front of me and said, "keep up." He ran backwards, facing me, screaming, "Come on, strong finish."

I collapsed when I reached the infield and rested my head on my glove. Wicker leaned against the fence, just as beat. He struggled for breath. "How can you stand?" I said.

"Hurts too much to get back up."

"You should run when you don't have practice too." His face was red, he breathed hard. "A little every day. Build up your endurance. You'll be faster in the field. On the bases. Swinging the bat."

Coach Wicker offered to throw my bike in his back seat and give me a lift home, but I figured I'd burn a few more calories. Riding up Miller Avenue had never been so hard. Near the top, I had to get off the bike and walk the damn thing up the hill. At the table after supper, I announced, "I'm gonna start running after school."

"You have softball," mother said.

"After softball. Coach Wicker wants us to run."

My father said, "Jackie Wicker?"

"Just goes by Coach."

"Korkin, that's your team. Must be the same." My father bought his gardening supplies and paint there, and nails and screws, things like that, so he knew Coach Wicker's father pretty well since he was always at the store. "How long has he been back now?" my father said to Mother.

"Are you kidding?" she said. "It's been years."

"But remember they couldn't move him. He stayed there for a while, then even longer at the hospital in Seattle."

"Funny, I saw him when I picked up those fixtures for the bathroom. He must work there part time."

"Back from where?" I said.

"Hm?"

"You asked how long he's been back."

"Oh," my father said. "Vietnam."

All I knew about Vietnam was that it was fought far enough away that we didn't have to worry about it in Brockton. I checked the school library, but the only war books were on World War Two and Korea.

The first Little League game was against Smithtone. I pitched, but it wasn't a big deal because everybody pitched, but only for two innings and never in consecutive games. Little League rules. On deck for my second at bat I noticed Cliff skulking around the border of the woods that lined the park.

I wondered what it would be like if he were a regular brother, standing on the bleachers as I approached the plate, cheering me on, talking me up. *Way to go, Jimmy boy, let's make a little bingo here, little bingo.* I reached first on a walk and when I looked for him he was standing near the ice cream truck eating an ice cream sandwich.

As the days and weeks continued, running became a little easier. Some of the kids could run for miles and never tire. Not me. I still ran last and pellets of pain ricocheted into every part of my body. At least I was no longer getting lapped. Running meant one thing— playing better ball and making the all-star team. Maybe even playing in a league where the bases were actually fastened to the ground and players wore metal cleats instead of plastic. Real spikes! I imagined Cliff watching me stand at the plate, the Red Sox uniform a perfect fit over my slim muscular body. Jimmy LaPlante at the plate, nothing left of Tanker 10.

I lost thirteen more pounds by the end of the regular season. I was faster in the field and at bat. The last game I got three hits. I remembered Wicker's comments about how running would improve my at-bats. Confidence swelled as the coaches spent three days selecting the all-star team.

I was crushed. I cried. I slammed the door. Shoved my face into the pillow. Dad was talking before he even opened the door. "You can't take it personally," he said. "There's over a hundred kids. They can't choose them all. It doesn't mean you're not good." He sat on my desk chair.

"I don't care about that," I said. "I just want to play. Softball's over soon, now no more baseball."

"The parks are full of kids playing ball."

"But it's not organized. There's no coaches. No umpires." I sat up on the bed.

"Come downstairs. We'll watch some of the game." I followed him down. "This was your first year, Jimmy. Consider how far you've come, how hard you've worked. That's not for nothing."

I tried to conjure those words on my way to the park to watch the first all-star practice. I hoped that some of the kids would hang around for a pick-up game. I saw Coach Wicker near the on deck circle talking to someone I recognized immediately. The burly guy with the station wagon who had lugged the bag of bats into the high school. Coach Wicker nodded and waved me over. Maybe a player dropped out, I thought. I'd be a replacement.

"Sorry we couldn't pick ya, Jimmy," he said as I walked through the gate. His hair was tied back with a cord of gimp. "We needed bigger bats out of the outfield."

"Good luck," I said. "Thanks for, for . . ." I remembered his hand on my back while I ran. "Coaching, I guess."

Coach Wicker's attention was suddenly drawn to the plate, which left me alone with the stranger. "No more playing against the wall?"

he said.

"It's more fun with others." I had no idea if he remembered that he'd said those words to me so long ago, but I enjoyed saying them back to him.

"Yeah, it's more fun playing a game, but that don't make you better." He chewed a straw as he spoke. He wore a flannel shirt, despite the heat, sleeves rolled up to his elbows, showing hairy muscled forearms. Dark glasses covered his eyes. "That arm of yours didn't come from playing games, no sir. How many chances do outfielders get to throw a ball during a game? Maybe six?"

"How do you know about my arm?"

"I know everything baseball around here."

"You go to the games?"

"I go to enough. What I don't see firsthand they tell me."

"Who are you?"

"I'm Mike Walsh. I coach the high school team."

"I'm—"

"I know who you are. Eighth grade, East Junior High. Put this team out of your head, Jim LaPlante. You go home and the first chance you get, you get yourself a tee."

"A tee?"

"That's right. A pole from the ground yea high." He held his hand at hip level. "You put a ball on it. Then swing."

"How many swings?"

"Don't think in terms of how many swings. More like how many hours." He smiled, the straw completely frayed. "You swing till you can't swing no more."

"Sounds like a lot of swings."

"You got something better to do?"

"Not really." I envisioned my days split between the pitchback and the tee. "How do I make it?"

"Make what?"

"The tee."

"You're gonna make it?"

"No?"

"I guess, if you're good with your hands. Most people just buy 'em, though. At Herman's, say." He chuckled to himself and shook his head, saying softly, "Make a tee. That's funny."

I waited around on the bleachers to see if a game would start, but it no longer seemed important. All that mattered was getting that tee. I pictured myself playing for the high school team. Why else would Coach Walsh have spent all that time talking to me if he didn't want me on his team? I sat there thinking, Why did I wait so long? I could have been playing Little League for years and been that much more prepared for high school.

Time lost. Wasted. My parents and Ben had been right. I should have tried out sooner. I was an idiot, sitting around, sorry for myself because I didn't think I was good enough. Afraid to even try. Well, no more. I leaned back on the row behind me, my glove as a pillow. I closed my eyes. The sun warmed my face. I might have dozed off if not for the sounds of the practice, kids cheering, balls hitting bats, gloves and earth.

**

Herman's had to order the tee. I took baseball books out of the library. I gobbled up the hitting chapters, I memorized every instruction. I took the books outside and swung along with the pictures and charts, mimicking everything the experts said about gripping the bat, proper alignment, the swing itself, its extension and follow-through.

When the tee arrived I set it up in front of the tarp. The base was flat and shaped like home plate, the pole adjusted by height. As I used the tee, I applied everything I had learned. At first it was awkward; I swung too low, hitting the plastic pole and feeling it smart my hands. Then I swung too high, missing the darn thing altogether, the momentum spinning me around. When I got sweaty and achy from swinging, I tossed the bat down and threw, first into the pitchback to field the returns then into the tarp to throw with all my strength. When I got tired and wanted to stop, I heard Coach Walsh's voice in my ear: *Swing till you can't swing no more.*

I'd been at it for at least an hour and I was beat. I was tugging at one of the tarp stakes when I heard a voice from behind.

"What's that?" Cliff's friend Todd had grown every year, like some kind of magical giant. His heavy black work shoes made him seem even taller. He carried around some bulk too. His oversized corduroy shirt couldn't disguise the softness at his belly and back.

"It's a tee."

"I've heard of a golf tee. But . . ."

"It's to practice your swing."

Todd looked at it for a couple of seconds. Dozens of balls lay scattered along the tarp and at the foot of the tee. "Can I try?"

I lifted the tee higher so the ball was at his belt. He hit the pole on the first swing, just as I had, but he swung so wildly the whole thing toppled over. I reset the tee and he slammed it again in the same place. And again.

"Swing higher," I said. "The ball's up here."

His mighty swing flailed north of the ball by a good six inches. The force almost brought him to his knees. "Hey, hey," he laughed, straightening himself. "Just like The Boomer."

"Yeah, just like." I didn't admit I had just done the same thing.

He stood there for a moment, apparently done, but for some reason not relinquishing the bat. Without warning, he swung the bat out in front of him at shoulder level, first to the left then to the right. He repeated the movement several times, lunging deeply with each swing. He looked like a ninja. I reached up on my tippy toes to remove the tarp from the line. He circled back to the tee, dropped the bat and said, "I got that, I'm taller." He pulled at the tarp. "How often do you play out here?"

"Every day."

"Then why are we taking it down?"

"My mother makes me."

"Wow. That blows."

"You looking for Cliff?"

"Yeah. Figured I'd see what's up." He finished removing the tarp, then grabbed an end and helped lay it flat on the ground.

"He's at practice."

"Oh, that's right. I lose track, you know, with me at a different school now."

"You moved?"

"Na, I transferred to Southeastern Tech." We folded the tarp into a narrow column and walked toward each other, like folding a sheet. "In a couple of years I'll be helping my dad with his air conditioning and heating. They call it climate control."

This was our first real conversation. Strange. He was talking to me like we were in the same grade. I knew in that moment that he would never tease me again.

"Tell Cliff I stopped by, all right?"

"I will." I held the tarp in my arms and watched him lumber around the front of my house.

**

We arrived at the hospital a little before noon. Today was my third physical and stress test since the operation. It followed the same agenda: the usual poking and prodding by the pediatrician then the short drive to Dr. Aranofsky at the hospital for the stress test. I stood on the treadmill in a room only slightly larger than the treadmill itself, my feet astride the black running belt. Red and white lead cables hung from the familiar round electrodes glued to my chest and torso. They were bound by a cord, draped over the railing of the treadmill and plugged into the EKG console. A thin female technician bent over the machine running a test print while a man in a lab coat leaned against the open doorway writing on a clipboard. My father sat on a bright orange plastic chairs behind the treadmill.

"You ready, Jimmy?" the woman said.

"Sure." Let 'er rip, I thought.

She pressed a button on the treadmill's panel and the thing rumbled to life. It was a clunker from another era, twice the size of a modern treadmill. I walked as the belt slowly moved. The speed and incline increased every three minutes until, after a while, I was forced to jog. My physical had gone well. The weight loss was no surprise, but I still smiled when the nurse noted it in my file. Down to 151 pounds. Still heavy, yes, even fat, but I had lost 23 pounds since I'd first weighed myself with Mr. Callahan. And grown two inches.

At 21 minutes I was running pretty hard. Sweat dripped down my face and sides. The mood in the room suddenly changed. The technicians huddled intently over the EKG. They spoke, but

I couldn't hear them over the rumble of the treadmill. My father stood when the woman reached for the wall phone.

My father stood in front of me and asked if I was okay.

"What's wrong?" I asked. *Some*thing was wrong. I was aware of the pounding in my chest, but from the running or the sudden commotion I wasn't sure.

Before my father had a chance to respond Dr. Aranofsky walked calmly into the room. He didn't even look at me; his eyes dove straight for the EKG needle. After studying it for ten seconds he stood beside my father. He didn't look much different than last year; actually, he didn't look much different from that night I discovered him hovering over my hospital bed. He had lost weight, though. His nose seemed more hawk-like than before.

"How do you feel?" he said.

"I'm good." He was so calm and pleasant my anxiety instantly disappeared.

"You can keep going?"

My father gave the doctor one of his looks.

"Yeah."

"Are you sure?" my father said.

I nodded.

"Short of breath?" the doctor said.

"No," I said between gasps. "I mean, except, you know, that I'm running."

What was Dr. Aranofsky doing here? Usually we just checked in with him before leaving. Something weird on the EKG. But he didn't seem alarmed. He and my father remained at the front of the treadmill until Aranofsky signaled to slow the treadmill's pace. Once the belt stopped, the male technician guided me to one of the plastic chairs while Dr. Aranofsky bent over the EKG.

"You made it up into the twenties," my father said, his hand on my knee. "Farther than last year, I think."

"Definitely," the male technician said. "Fourteen thirty-two last year. Twenty-three fifty-six today." He then unclipped the wires from the electrodes, coiled them into a circle and slid them onto a shelf under the EKG machine. The woman pulled the electrodes from my skin in several quick painless tugs then handed me a towel to wipe off the glue and sweat.

"Another for your face," the male technician said and tossed me a matching towel from a tall storage cabinet in the corner.

From the doorway Dr. Aranofsky said, "Why don't you wash up and get dressed. I'll see you in my office in a few minutes."

His door was open so we didn't have to knock. My file lay on his desk. He asked us to sit on the two plain wood chairs. "Well you gave us new data, young Jimmy. It's the first time we've seen your arrhythmia since your operation."

I looked at my father. He seemed about to say something, then stopped.

"Is that bad?" I said.

"I don't really know." He leaned forward with his elbows on the desk and rubbed his mouth. "I think maybe it's not good or bad. It just is."

Huh? Jesus, was I the only one asking questions here? Come on, Dad, step up!

"When this type of tacchycardia occurs, that's what it's called, tacchycardia, patients usually complain about it," the doctor continued. "It feels like a, like a marble bouncing around in your chest. You didn't feel it at all, you just kept on going. That's pretty unusual. Then again most of our patients are fifty years older than you and walk a forty minute mile, so . . . "

He smiled and allowed a few seconds to pass.

"Is this something . . ." my father suddenly stopped, still grasping for words. "Something we need to worry about?" Maybe he felt leery about asking that question in front of me.

"Well, I'd like to prescribe Inderal, a minimal dose, just to even the heartbeat."

"A needle?" I said.

"No, no, a small tablet, it's really nothing."

"Is it really necessary, though?" my father said. "If this only happens once every few years, I don't want him taking pills every day for God knows how long."

"Because he can't feel the tacchycardia we don't really know how often it occurs. I'd like to have Jimmy wear a Holter Monitor for a twenty-four hour period." He looked at me. "A simple device that monitors your heartbeat as you go about your day." His glance shifted back to my father. "We can schedule that at your convenience."

Why couldn't I feel it? What the hell was wrong with me? Would it strike me down with no warning? A vague memory of a relative of Ben floated in my head. An old man collapsing in the bathroom in the middle of the night. Would that be me, but decades younger? Alive one second, dead the next?

"The sooner the better," my father said. "May as well get answers."

"In the meantime, I think he should take the Inderal." He leaned back in his office chair and folded his arms over his chest.

"I . . ." My father shifted.

"You're uneasy."

"He's already got the shots."

"They're not mutually exclusive." He waited for my father's response. "What I mean by that is the two prescriptions won't adversely affect—"

"Yes, I know what mutually exclusive means." He sat up rigidly in his chair. "It's just . . . You see, he's got the shots. Now these pills. It takes a toll. A kid just wants to be a kid."

"Maybe a trial period," the doctor suggested. "See how it goes."

It was only a matter of time before my father would agree. I couldn't picture him defying a doctor, not after everything he'd told me about how important it was to follow doctors' orders. But I didn't want Dr. Aranofsky to think my father was caving. The doctor was a nice guy, but he was pompous too; he shouldn't have the satisfaction of feeling superior over my father.

"I don't mind," I said, looking at my dad. "You know, a trial period."

"Why don't you give us a moment alone, Jimmy, all right?"

I left the door open on purpose and stood just outside. He was crazy if he thought I wasn't going to listen.

"First thing. The shots. Is it possible they have anything to do with this heartbeat thing?"

"I wouldn't think so. The arrhythmia was initially detected before the shots were ever administered."

"But they couldn't exacerbate it?"

"Very unlikely. I'll raise your concerns with Doctor Young. I promise. But I don't think that's a factor here."

There was a long pause before I heard my father. "I wonder if you did the right thing by keeping Jimmy running after his heartbeat accelerated. What if something happened? He's not your guinea pig, he's my son."

"Mr. LaPlante, please—"

"Your data should come second. I think you got it the other way around."

"Mr. LaPlante, I understand your concern, but Jimmy was in no danger. If I thought he was I would have stopped that treadmill like that." He snapped his fingers. "You're Jimmy's father, what you say goes. The truth is I think Jimmy is a perfectly healthy thirteen year old whose heart, for some reason, once in a while speeds up. Would I like to see him on Inderal? Sure. Why? Because over the years I've seen it help people."

As we said our goodbyes I imagined myself tearing around third base about to score the winning run in extra innings. A few strides from the plate I'm stricken by a ripping sensation in the center of my chest. My knees hit the base path. I fight to rise, but it's no use. The pain pulls me to the ground. I'm flat on my stomach. Can't move. I extend my arms toward home plate. My fingertips. They're inches away. Less. My eyes close. Victory denied.

**

I measured every day, week and month in terms of softball and baseball. The calendar on my desk was filled with intramural practice dates and the names of teams we played against. Each night I crossed off the day with an X, looking forward to the next practice, the next game. When the first session of intramurals ended, I counted six months on the calendar until Pony League tryouts. To bridge the gap I went to the park for pick-up games when the weather allowed. I continued to make use of the tarp, the pitchback and the tee.

Ben stopped by one morning while I was playing in the yard and suggested we head over to Brookfield. "I'll pitch some to you."

At the park, Ben stood to my side and flipped baseballs in front of me, one every few seconds, as I slapped them into one of the backstops. I offered to flip some to him, but he said, "Na, my dad doesn't want me playing other sports. Could strain something."

Sports-wise, Ben was confined to the pool, the weight room and the track. His first high school meet was still a couple of weeks away, but the team had been practicing for several weeks and Mr. Clancy had been training Ben alone before that. "He even wants me to be careful about what gym classes I choose."

"You get to choose?"

"Yeah, there's tons. Gymnastics, field hockey, ultimate Frisbee, golf."

"Golf?"

"Yeah," he said, "they got a driving range and a putting green. Tennis, too. And they got tons of teams after school. Not just baseball and basketball. They got rugby, ice hockey, lacrosse."

By now, he was fully immersed in the culture of Brockton High and whenever he talked about it, my head buzzed with questions. But what really got me jazzed was the baseball team. What would those tryouts be like? Would Coach Walsh even look in my direction?

"Hey," Ben said, "we should get going."

We were invited to Sonny Cabrera's family pool party. I knew Sonny from Little League and Ben's father knew Mrs. Cabrera because she worked at Brockton High. It seemed strange to have a pool party in April, but it was being held at the country club on Wentworth Avenue, which had an indoor pool.

It had been a warm April and today was the warmest day yet. Warm enough that the sliding glass doors along the pool had been opened. Guests used the expansive wooden deck that connected the pool to an outdoor patio and elaborate gardens. Food was arranged on long tables on the deck and nearby grounds. The adults headed straight to one of the tables where the hosts greeted arrivals. Ben and I hit the locker rooms, changed quickly into our suits and walked the tiled hallway into the pool area.

Sonny shouted and waved from the deep end where he was playing volleyball with a few kids I didn't recognize. I waved back.

"Wanna play?" I said to Ben, who watched the guests mingling outside.

He shrugged. Obviously not.

"What's wrong?"

"Any more chlorine and I'm gonna gag."

"You know it's a pool party, right?"

"Let's eat," Ben said.

He grabbed one of the many sweat suits the club had stacked on metal shelves near the sliding doors and slipped it on, then handed me a set. We scoped all the tables and settled on the chili bar. Small glass bowls of the stuff topped with shredded cheddar and chopped onions.

"Hi, Ben." Two girls had joined the line behind us.

"Hey, Joanna," Ben said.

They knew each other from Brockton High. The other girl was Sonny's sister, Adriana. I didn't even know he had a sister. She went to Brockton High, too. They were both pretty, Adriana more than Joanna, even though Adriana wore braces. Their hair styles were similar, shoulder length and feathered back. They wore bikini tops with loose-fitting shorts over their bottoms. We carried our bowls to a deck table. They complained about their teachers and homework, about the classes they would have to take next year, like Geometry, Algebra, maybe even Chemistry.

I had nothing to say. I just listened. Ate my chili. Watched Adriana. She didn't seem at all self-conscious about her braces; she laughed the whole time Joanna told a story about a teacher hassling her for wearing a skirt he considered inappropriate.

I imagined kissing her, the feel of her braces against my tongue. Would it hurt? Would I care? Not likely. Forget her mouth, though, check out the boobs! They were small, but pushed up by her suit. And every inch of her skin was mocha brown. And not a single tan line! Made me wonder if she sunbathed nude. Where?! I pictured her laying on a lounge chair rubbing tanning oil into her body, her hands sliding along her inner thigh, her thumb brushing the small mound of her pubic hair.

"Do you go to Brockton High?" she asked me when the laughter stopped.

"Next year."

"You look familiar, though."

"I, um...I play ball with . . ." I gestured toward the pool. " . . . Sonny."

"Oh, okay."

Joanna clanked her bowl on the table. "Well, are we going for a swim, Ad?"

"Sounds good to me."

"You should really wait thirty minutes," I said.

Joanna looked at me strangely.

I tried to laugh. "Just a joke. People always say, you know, you should wait thirty . . ." I shook my head. "No?"

They nodded kindly. Or maybe cruelly. I couldn't tell. The girls walked toward the pool.

"Leave the jokes to me," Ben said.

"You're not funny."

"I'm funnier than you. This chair is funnier than you."

"Ben," Joanna said from the sliding doors not far away. "Are you going to come demonstrate the butterfly?"

"Sure." Ben started to stand, but his knee struck the table, rattling the empty bowls. "Ow." He returned to his seat as the girls disappeared into the pool area.

"I thought you were sick of the chlorine."

"Forget that. And forget the butterfly," he said. "I'm gonna teach her the *breast stroke*." He spoke the two words slowly, exaggerating the enunciation.

I ran into the Clancys when I brought the empty bowls back to the chili table. They introduced me to another couple and we chatted for a few minutes. By the time I passed through the doors into the pool the volleyball game had broken up. A few kids were tossing around a red kickball in the deep end. Ben had an arm across Joanna's torso as he swam, carrying her across the shallow end. "That's all there is to it," he said. "Cross-chest carry. Learned it last week in Junior Lifesaving."

Real subtle, I thought. At least he wasn't cupping her tit. She shrieked that she wanted to carry him. "My turn, my turn." My thoughts drifted ahead to several months from now when I'd be at Brockton High. Not the difficult classes and homework that Ben and the girls had covered. What struck me as Ben and Joanna splashed around, their limbs entwining, were the parties, the dances. Girls.

Joanna finally gave up. Ben was just too heavy. They stood in the shallow end, smiling, water dripping down their chests, their hips practically touching. I backpedaled until I was out of sight. They watched the kids from the deep end hop out of the pool and disappear into the locker rooms. They stood completely still looking at each other. She touched his sternum with her index finger. Kept it there. They glanced to the sliding doors, then the locker room doors, then snuck a quick kiss on the lips.

A group of people, kids and adults, walked onto the pool deck from outside. I left, not wanting Ben and Joanna to see me. I walked toward the food. Dove straight into the pasta table. Piled a plate with lasagna. What if they hadn't been interrupted? What would they have done? How far would they have gone?

My thoughts roamed again to high school. Would I be as smooth with girls as Ben? Probably not. What if I didn't find a girlfriend? I'd be some kind of freakish misfit. My fear was that everyone would be expected to pair off and if you were discovered sitting alone in the cafeteria you'd be ostracized, shipped off to some dank corner of the school. The Loser Wing.

I brought my plate to a chair near the gazebo. Enjoying not only the taste, but the texture, the smell. Savoring it the way I used to. I stopped halfway through and tossed the leftovers into a barrel where the lawn bordered a large stand of woods. A sign welcomed visitors to walk the 23 acres of hiking trails.

I followed one of the paths that eventually split into several smaller paths. After strolling for five minutes I heard shrill gasps off to my right. I ducked under some low leafy branches and crept into a tiny clearing. A naked guy, a teenager, lay on top of Adriana pumping his hips urgently between her legs. Her brown breasts— her whole body—shook under the kid's thrusts. Her dark hands, practically black against the glaring blue-whiteness of his bare ass, pulled him toward her, *into* her, as if the guy's force wasn't enough. I bent to one knee behind the branches.

The guy panted loudly, but Adriana was louder: "Yes. Oh, Hank, yes." Her neck and back arched under Hank's weight. "Oh, God," she grunted fiercely. "Oh. Oh."

I remembered when I spied on Cliff and his girlfriend. There was something sweet about them holding each other on the playroom floor. There was nothing sweet here. This was two hogs fucking. They even sounded like hogs, with their grunting and groaning and snorting.

I knew I was supposed to run, but I couldn't turn away from this. From the bikini bottoms coiled around her ankles. From the flesh of her hips being mashed into the dirt and twigs. Her eyes squeezed shut in some kind of strange grimace.

They stopped. Hank lowered his lips to Adriana's neck shiny with sweat. She spun from under him and pulled up her bottoms. Hank started to say something while struggling with his own pants, but she looked away, not listening. Had she sensed me, hunched behind the shrubbery? Hank plopped to his butt, arms around his knees. Just staring at her while she arranged her breasts in the pockets of her bikini.

There was only one path out. And I was in the way. As I scurried quietly from the trails and out into the open lawn, I thought of where I'd stood while watching Ben and Joanna in the pool. Off to the side. Would this be my destiny when it came to sex? Five, ten years from now, would I get my jollies by watching instead of doing? I imagined myself even further into the future, the creepy neighborhood old man, peering into windows, a sinister smile spreading across my face.

**

Pony League tryouts were structured the same as Little League's. Twenty minutes in I knew I would make a team. At thirteen (fourteen in August), I was on the young side and still twenty-three pounds north of my target weight, but I was better than most of the others. Their form at the plate was wrong—sloppy pivots, swings out of the strike zone, hips out of whack, heads flailing.

We went nine and three for the regular season and by the end I was batting third. Our final game was against Buckland Auto. Here I am, I thought while taking practice swings before the game, my first year of Pony League, playing my favorite position. This might not happen next year. Might not happen ever again. I thought of the weird heartbeat in my chest, the little pill I took every day. Who knew how long a person would live? This—my last summer before high school—could be the best summer of my life.

In centerfield, I set myself for the pitch, ready to explode left or right, run in or out, leap headfirst if needed. The final out of the inning was made by our left fielder, Jake Campbell, a running catch on the foul line. I tapped his glove as we jogged toward the infield. In the dugout everyone tapped his glove, celebrating no runs allowed. I loved the way we congratulated each other after a good play. I loved how we hooted and hollered with every at bat. I loved that I was sitting in the dugout surrounded by friends.

I made the all-star team in July. It was only my first year in the league, so there was no guaranty I'd play every game, but at least I was in. We had a week of practices before the Sectionals. Eight local teams. Round robin, double elimination; the last team standing advanced. Our coaches held a practice the day before the final game of the first round. It was after this practice, while gathering our gear that I heard that Evan Banner, by far our best player, wasn't going to play. I found myself running toward him as he slid his glove over the handle of his aluminum bat and pushed it down the barrel.

"You're not gonna play?" I said.

"I can't."

"But a win tomorrow and we're in the Regionals."

"Jimmy, I'm going to Disney World."

"But it's the playoffs."

"So what. I make the playoffs every year."

"Not me."

"It's Disney World. Don't you go on vacations?"

"Yeah, every April we visit my uncle in Pennsylvania. We . . ." I was about to tell him how I spent the week. Seeking bookstores on the cobble-stoned streets of State College; rowing boats through the narrow waterways of Penn's Caves, eating an ice cream cone at the Davenport Dairy. But it would have sounded lame compared to Disney World.

We ended up beating Whitman in a tight one, 4-3 without Evan. The first game of the next round was a home game against Saugus. We lost 13-3, which would keep the pressure on us for the rest of the Regionals. Game two was against Jacksonbury. My first game where I'd have to drive more than fifteen minutes. A real away game. Under the lights no less; a 7:00 start, just like in the Majors. The only bad thing was that my father had to work middle shift at the post office and it was Mother's day to volunteer at the Skyler Project, a commitment she couldn't break. Cliff worked at Ponderosa Steakhouse that summer and I wouldn't ask him anyway.

I drove to Jacksonbury with the Banners. Evan spent most of the time talking about the Magic Kingdom. We were down two guys and I was scheduled to play, so I just nodded and wondered about the level of pitching I'd have to face.

Our caravan arrived as another game was ending. The Jacksonbury field was like Fenway Park compared to Brookfield. The outfield fence was six feet tall and made of wood, not chain link. It was painted blue and signs hung on it advertising local businesses. Even the bleachers were bigger and better. And along the third base line I saw a mini press box. A manual scoreboard stood in center field, the numbers ready for the new game. Visitors 0; Jacksonbury 0. A grounds crew chalked the lines.

At about ten minutes of seven the lights came on. I stared up into the banks of lights and became mesmerized by the glow that floated down to the grass, the way it accentuated the fluttering moths and countless particles of air.

The bleachers were filled by the time the game started. There must have been a couple hundred people and many more watching along the fence. These people came to watch their team win. I didn't even see an ice cream truck.

We had first ups. Edward Glaston pounded the donut off his bat and left the on-deck circle. As he approached the batter's box, the deep voice of God broke through the clouds. "Batting first for Brockton and playing second base…Edward Glaston." Speakers hung halfway up each of the infield light poles. Then I remembered the press box. Holy shit, I thought. This is the real deal.

I led off the second inning. Halfway to the batter's box from the dugout the announcer started to speak. I stopped. I wanted to hear this. I wanted to soak it in, enjoy it. Then it came: "Batting sixth, playing left field . . . Jimmy LaPlante." This was fantastic! I imagined myself in the Big Leagues—the lights, the PA system, the electric crowd. The umpire had lifted his mask and was staring at me when I reached the plate. He was a grumpy-looking guy, with a layer of swinging fat under his chin. I must have still been smiling.

"Having a good time?" he said.

"It's fun."

"Glad you're enjoying it. We like to keep things moving is all."

"Sorry," I said.

I was distracted, and it only took me four pitches to strike out. I flew out to right field my second time up, then lined softly to the first baseman. By the time I got up the fourth time in the seventh and final inning, we were losing seven to five with one out. Bases loaded. Don't hit into a double play, I said to myself. No double play, no double play. Don't make the final out of the season.

The pitcher, an Ichabod-looking kid with straight black hair, held the ball. His next pitch was a strike I let sail by. Two-one count. While the pitcher eyed the base runners from the mound, I yelled at myself for the way I was thinking. I was so busy telling myself what not to do, I forgot what I needed to do—get a hit!

The next pitch was a ball. With a three-one count I was ready to swing at anything. I hadn't hit the ball hard all night so hopefully the pitcher would feed me a fat one. I swung. The connection was sweet. The ball sliced through the air between right and center. As I raced toward first, the rightfielder dove, but the ball skidded under his glove and rolled toward the wall. I rounded first, tapping the inside corner of the bag, and barreled toward second. This would score three for sure. We'd be ahead. Could I score too? A home run? Me? Tagging second, I looked to pick up the third base coach. But instead I saw someone else.

Cliff screamed, with his arms in the air, his hands balled into fists, his whole body jumping up and down on the bleachers. I was so surprised to see him that I overran third base and got tagged out. No fucking way! I stood on the bag, mortified. Sonofabitch! I couldn't believe it, even though I had seen the umpire's arm rise toward the sky. I kicked the ground; dirt sprayed over the bag.

It was Cliff's fault. What the hell was he doing here? I wanted to tug the base out of the ground and hurl it into his face. Jogging to the dugout, I braced myself for my teammate's jeers. I'd seen kids on other teams "baa" like goats when players made mistakes.

But I was wrong. They gave me high fives, pats on the back. We were back in the game! I basked in their praise. Suddenly I remembered Cliff. I looked into the bleachers where I'd seen him, but couldn't distinguish him from the rest of the crowd. We scored two more runs that inning and lived to play another game.

"That was fantastic," Cliff said in the car on the way home. "What a win."

"When did you get there?"

"I picked up Dad's car at the post office. Got to Jacksonbury around quarter of eight." After a while, he said, "So, who you guys play next?"

"Walpole, I think."

"They any good?"

"Oh yeah." It was weird, talking back and forth like this, like friends. Like brothers.

At home, Mother had heated up chicken wings and sweet and sour meatballs. "Jimmy played great," Cliff blurted to our folks before I even had a chance to tell them the score. He told them about my game-winning hit, like he was talking about a real athlete. "Drove in the winning run," he reported. "Like a hero."

7. Eye on the Ball

I had received a reading list in the mail for Accelerated English. I was near the end of *To Kill A Mockingbird*, where Scout and Jem are on their way home from the Halloween pageant. I couldn't put it down, even through the sounds of Cliff packing in the next room. Tomorrow Dad was driving him to UMass.

It was the masking tape that finally forced my book down. I walked down the hallway and leaned against his door jam.

"Hey," he said without looking up. He was kneeling over a large box, trying to keep the lid down and tape it closed.

I wanted to say, Pipe down. But who was I to tell him not to pack. I kneeled on the other side of the box and held down the cardboard flaps. May as well go the extra mile, I thought. It'll be months before we see each other again.

Once secure, he grabbed a black magic marker and wrote "Records + Books" on the top of the box. He sat back on his haunches and surveyed the room. Everything was packed, labeled and ready to be brought downstairs.

I sat on the edge of his bed as he stacked the box on top of some others. "You scared?"

He plopped down on his desk chair. It was a real antique office chair, made of wood; it swiveled and had wheels. He'd seen it at a rummage sale and paid for it with some of his own money. "Not scared really. Maybe . . ."

"Nervous?"

"A little." He eyed his stacks of boxes and suitcases, then looked about the rest of the room.

"By the way," I said, "I talked to Mom. She said it was okay to break down the wall, make it one big room. *My* room."

He laughed. "You're taking over, huh?"

"Yep."

"Where will I sleep when I come home for breaks?"

I liked that he was still playing along. I shrugged. "Outside?"

"I guess that's what I deserve." He wasn't laughing now. No mirth whatsoever.

I didn't know how to respond. He wanted to talk, have a little chit-chat. He may have even wanted forgiveness. That would have been a gift. And I wasn't about to give him a gift—not that one. I felt myself standing, walking toward the door. Then I felt bad for leaving.

"You need anything else?" I said.

"Na, I got it." He hopped out of his chair, gathered the tape, scissors and other supplies and zippered them up in a clear plastic bag

"I can carry boxes down."

"I said I got it." He consulted a piece of paper on the bureau, then made a check mark on the page. When he saw that I was still standing at the door, he said, "Seriously, I'm fine."

The next morning, after Mother and I watched them turn onto Miller Avenue, I walked into my bedroom and discovered he had replaced my desk chair with his.

**

New school. No brother. Everything was different. Brockton High was huge. Four separate buildings (Yellow, Green, Red and Blue) and the Core, which housed the Science Department. Each building had its own library and cafeteria. The school held over six thousand students. Each day I had one free period to go wherever I wanted –library, study hall, cafeteria. If the gym was free, I could even shoot hoops or throw the ball around.

Third day there I was still getting lost. I was almost at Y214 for a freshman elective called Current Events when I realized I was supposed to be at R214. Every freshman received a packet which included a floor plan. I kept turning it this way and that to figure out where I was, but got more confused the longer I looked. Finally, I asked a teacher. I had to race through the Core, past the science labs and planetarium. Then back up two flights of stairs.

The door was closed when I got there. I opened it. The teacher was already addressing the class. He turned to me and pointed to the seats. The desks were arranged in a semi-circle. One sat empty near the center, wedged between a boy and a girl. Some maneuvering would be necessary. The boy wasn't helpful. The girl, though, edged her seat back enough for me to sit down.

"Got enough room?" she said.

"Fine, thanks." But when I sat up straight my elbow swept the edge of her desk and her pen clattered to the floor. The teacher stopped talking. I squeezed out of my chair to retrieve the pen.

When I finally got settled, I sensed that the girl was looking at me. I snuck a peek at her profile: a slight bump on the bridge of her nose, tiny stud earrings and a long neck. I'd never seen her before. I listened to the teacher talk about how we'd be responsible for the class's subject matter. I looked over again, real nonchalant-like. Her hair was reddish blonde. It fell to the nape of her neck. She turned her head and caught me looking. Before I could turn away, she gave a quick smile and faced the teacher. Maybe she liked me. Maybe a couple months from now I'd be walking her to class hand in hand. Maybe in April she'd be watching me play centerfield.

Could this be one of those love-at-first-sight relationships? I thought. High school sweethearts, together forever. JL + CG (cute girl), TLA, true love always.

It's dumb to think about, I told myself. But I couldn't help it. I glimpsed another look at her from the corner of my eye. *You see, my brother crushed my balls when I was ten, but don't worry, I'm a normal guy, as long as I get shot with a jolt of testosterone every once in a while. That's me, yessirree…Completely normal.*

It's not like I thought about this stuff all the time. There were too many classes, hard classes. And I worked out and played ball as much as possible. But no matter what I did, it all rushed back at me when I sat down for my shot. *It's that time again, Jimmy,* the needle said, *here I am, a poor little needle looking for some lovin', a little bit of skin to pierce. Why do you think I'm called a needle, 'cause I got needs, Jimmy. I need to give you a little prick. You follow what I'm saying, right? A little prick.*

**

A month into high school I still hadn't run into Coach Walsh. I was afraid that if he didn't see me until baseball started in March he wouldn't remember me. Brockton High had six gym teachers and they all shared a large office above the gymnasium. I walked by a few days in a row during my free period, but he was never around.

During one visit I stepped inside. A handful of class schedules were tacked to a bulletin board on the far wall. I wasn't sure if kids were allowed in here, but I stepped in anyway and took a peek. It was period five now; "tennis" was scribbled in Coach Walsh's "P5" box. He taught "v-ball" in the gym "P7." No good for me, I had geometry. Maybe I could see him between classes and be a little late for geometry. I knew it was kiss-assy, but I had to let him know I was gung-ho.

He stood sturdily at the post of a volleyball net when I arrived at the gym. He nodded at the kids as they ambled into his class from the locker rooms. I must have stuck out since I was the only one not in gym clothes.

"Look at you," he said as I got closer. "Slimming down."

"Yeah, been working at it."

"Good." Coach Walsh looked over his class, which was almost assembled.

What an idiot, I thought. I concocted this elaborate plan, but I hadn't the smarts to think of something to say.

"You have gym this period?"

"No, I . . ."

Then why the hell are you here? he was probably thinking.

"I had gym earlier and I think I, I think I forgot something in a locker."

"Line up and start the count," he called to the group milling around.

I had to think of something to say. It would have been too awkward to leave like this, too weak.

"Tryouts aren't until March. I was just thinking, wondering what I could do, you know, until then . . ."

"What are you doing now?"

"Running. Playing games, when we can get enough kids together."

"Still using the tee?"

"Oh, yeah."

"Well, keep doing what you're doing. Use the freshman weight room a few days a week. Don't go crazy with the weights. Keep it light, plenty of reps. And I'll see you in March."

Fantastic! A personal invitation. Then again, maybe he said *I'll see you in March* to everyone. I needed to know.

"So come March then . . . I mean, you want me there? At tryouts?"

"What difference does it make what I want?"

So it wasn't that he didn't want me on the team. He simply didn't care one way or the other. How could I have been so stupid? The school was massive, with thousands of students. In March, he would have his pick of the best players in the city.

Or did he mean that he would have been disappointed if my decision to try out depended on whether he wanted me there or not? You want something bad enough, you go for it no matter what other people want. I didn't have a chance to get clarification. By the time I thought of something to say, he had turned away and was walking toward the sidelines of the volleyball court.

"What are you waiting for?" he yelled while he clapped his powerful hands. "Someone serve the ball. Let's play."

**

For many years Christmas morning began with me storming into the living room and practically crashing into the pile of presents surrounding the tree. Since I stopped believing in Santa Claus, Christmas morning started with a big breakfast. Dad made scrambled eggs. Mother let me flip pancakes. Cliff made a racket using the juicer. Mother had bought something called turkey bacon.

Hopefully it would taste as good as regular. It sure smelled good sizzling in the pan. We passed the food around. Dad looked at the bacon suspiciously, but ate six pieces. I ate four.

I sat across from Cliff. Where we always sat when we shared the kitchen table. That horrible food fight came into my head, the night I threw ground beef and shells at his face. I must have laughed.

"What's up?" Cliff said.

I shook my head. "Nothing."

"Good, huh?" he said, his mouth full of food.

His skin was dark with stubble, his sideburns longer and more unruly than when he left. Even though my daily inspections showed strange solitary hairs sprouting randomly on my cheek, upper lip and chin, I still hadn't started shaving yet. But Dad would have to give a lesson soon. Mother had brought it up to him a couple of times. For a second, I thought that, since Cliff was home, he could show me. But the image of us in front of the bathroom mirror, him holding the razor to my skin, struck me with panic. He'd probably be in such a hurry to finish he'd slice my cheek.

"Working tomorrow?" my father said.

Cliff nodded. His former boss let him work his old job while he was home.

"Why the need to work so much?" Mother said, nibbling the bacon. "That campus restaurant over Thanksgiving. Now Ponderosa every day."

Cliff shrugged. "Pocket money."

My father leaned across the table and said in a mischievous whisper, "A girl, more like."

Cliff rolled his eyes and continued eating, the trace of a smile curling his lips.

As my parents and I stacked dishes in the sink, Cliff called me to the tree to open his gift. We all made our way into the living room. Cliff handed me a small box and watched from the edge of the sofa. Inside was a baseball encased in glass.

"It's autographed," he said.

The name was easy to make out, with the large swooping D and E. Dwight Evans. I pictured it in the center my bookcase. Maybe

I'd get more, start a collection like Ben's.

"Wow," I said. "It's great." Must've cost a bundle.

"A friend at school, his uncle owns a memorabilia shop. I'll bring a catalogue home."

So maybe it wasn't expensive, since he got a deal from his friend. Still, to think ahead, order it, whatever he had to do to get in time for Christmas. It was better than what I got him. A shirt. Like one of those kinds with the crocodile on the chest. But without the crocodile; that would have cost three times as much.

He opened the gift. After pulling it from the box he held it up to himself in front of the mantelpiece mirror. "Look at me," he said. "Mr. Fashionable." Dad laughed from the kitchen archway. Cliff flung off his tee shirt. I could see the lines of his arms and stomach muscles. He had chest hair like a man. I had pubic hair and armpit hair and hair on my legs. But nothing on my chest.

There was something forced in the way he was playing Mr. Nice Guy, as though putting up a front for Mother's sake. *Hey Ma, look how much I've matured. I'm all grown up now, able to move on.* Mr. Fashionable. Please.

Mother watched as he slipped on the shirt. "Oh, that's a nice fit. And green is a good color on you." She caught my eye in the mirror. "Excellent choice, Jimmy."

She stood between me and Cliff and extended her arms. Her fingers held our wrists. Literally, a link that bound us. Despite the fact that I doubted his sincerity, as I watched Cliff in his new shirt I couldn't shake the notion that his hair was my hair, his muscles my muscles, his blood my blood.

**

Although it was called Freshman Dance and was designed to welcome new students to the school, all grades could attend. I didn't really want to go, but Ben kept bugging me.

"I ain't going."

"Why not?"

I was squeezing in some library time before hitting the track. Ben hung with me doing homework, to the extent that he did homework. "I don't know . . ." I mumbled. "You know."

"I went last year. It's fun. Music. Food. Highjinks."

"High jinks, huh?" I said.

"Not really. I just felt like saying it. It's a funny word."

"It's actually two words. High. Jinks."

"I think I've seen it as one." He watched me closely as I read. "So, the dance."

"I don't know . . ."

"You nervous?"

"No."

"Nothing to be nervous about."

"Yeah, that's why I said I'm not nervous."

"You went to the eighth grade dance, right?"

"Yes." They made everyone go, took attendance like it was a field trip. "Wasn't so hot. Just stood around while some guy played records."

"This'll be better. There's a band. Real dancing. Maybe you'll make out."

I took notes in my notebook, unsure of what I was writing.

"What's the matter, you don't want to make out?" He leaned forward and puckered his lips, making obnoxious kissing sounds.

"Pipe down, will ya?"

He stopped after a couple of seconds, but when he realized I wasn't going to answer his question, he started up again.

"Will ya stop it? Of course I want to make out. Who doesn't want to make out?"

"It's not like you've never kissed a girl."

Sure, I'd kissed a girl or two. There was that cousin who visited from California last year. Our lips touched when we said goodbye.

"Have you?" he said, insistently.

I didn't feel like defending myself to my best friend. Or lying.

"So you haven't? For real, I mean?"

"I don't know . . ."

"It's not an I-don't-know question." He watched me as I wrote.

I kept my head down, eyes shifting from textbook to notebook. "So you've never kissed—"

"What the fuck, Ben?" I said, too loudly. "Not everyone looks like you."

He closed my notebook with force. "You can what-the-fuck-Ben me all you want. But you're not fat anymore. And high school ain't no place for shy."

"Whatever that means."

"It means you're going to that dance, if I have to drag you."

After a second, I said, "Can I open my notebook please? You see, I actually do my homework."

"I do homework." He leaned back in his chair with a smile and, after a moment, flipped open the cover of a textbook. "Occasionally."

**

My parents drove us to the high school. Their plan was to catch a movie and pick us up afterward. While we walked from the curb to the gym door, Ben talked about how last year there had been places, like the back stairwell that led down to the pool, where you could smell pot. He checked out a couple of pretty girls as they walked in front of us. Then, as we entered the door, another girl came out and Ben watched her ass all the way down the cement path to the curb.

"You sure do stare."

"Hmm, what?"

"Your head snaps whenever a girl walks by."

"It's a reflex."

"A reflex. Okay."

"What are you, a homo?"

"Yeah, I'm a homo."

He pushed me through the door. Several round tables were scattered around the outskirts of the dance floor. A small stage had been set up along the far wall. Five old guys, all wearing black vests, milled around the stage turning knobs on amplifiers, closing instrument cases and tuning guitars. Music blared from speakers arranged around the gym. Air Supply belted out *Making Love Out of*

Nothing at All.

"Food," Ben said.

Snacks had been set up on the tables, chips, cheese curls and large bottles of soda with plastic cups. We grabbed an empty table. Turns out I knew a lot of kids from junior high and baseball, not to mention my classes at Brockton High. Some of them stayed at our table and I introduced them to Ben. I was psyched; I introduced more of my friends to Ben than he did to me. The band started. A familiar song, but I couldn't name it. A bunch of girls trickled onto the dance floor. After a couple more songs it was packed.

Some boys and girls partnered up on the dance floor, but for the most part it was a mishmash of swaying and shaking bodies. The band started a slow song—*Loving You*—and the dancers scattered like ants. A woman had joined the band. She was doing the Stevie Nicks thing, layers of flowing black lace and frills and long frosted blonde hair.

I hadn't noticed until now, maybe because the lights were low, but apparently it was close enough to Valentine's Day to decorate the gym with heart-shaped balloons and a vast assortment of papier-mâché cupids. Like there wasn't enough pressure with a room full of girls and a band playing slow songs.

Celebration came next. When the music was at its loudest our table joined the floor. I was nervous at first, but we all looked like dorks. My moves couldn't really be called dancing. An inarticulate jangling of arms and legs; a clueless shaking of head, nodding of chin. I mouthed the words to the song. Maybe that would make me look cool. Mr. Rock Star. I tried to mimic the girls, who were more loose-limbed and carefree. As the song continued, the jumble of bodies broke off into couples. I found myself alone. Panic froze me to the floor, more and more alone as the couples drifted further away. Then I was rescued.

"What's up?" The girl was older than me and fashion model gorgeous, her dark blond hair wavy to the middle of her back. She bounced around to the music in snug blue jeans and a tight-fitting Lycra top. Why was this bombshell dancing with me? I looked around; maybe her friends had put her up to it. But nobody was staring, not overtly anyway. She clapped her hands over her head. *Celebrate good times, come on!* That's when I noticed the red button on her shirt. She was on the Dance Committee. Ugh. A pity dance. I wanted to crawl away.

"You don't have to," I said.

"Have to what?" she shouted over the music.

"We can stop."

"You don't want to dance?"

The song was ending, so I let her off the hook and drifted over to an empty table. When I sat I was surprised to see her taking the seat next to me.

"Boys don't usually walk away from me."

"Come on," I said. I could have sat there and looked at her all night, but part of me was getting annoyed. "Get real."

"What's your problem?" Her cheeks were flush from the dancing. Or perhaps anger. Either way, it made her even prettier, if that was possible.

"You *had* to dance with me." I pointed to her button. "It's an obligation."

She stood up. "I came up to you because you were out there having a good time instead of sitting around waiting for something to happen."

I didn't care that she was pissed. Hell, it was worth it if one kid saw us together.

"The next time a girl wants to dance don't question it. Just shut up and dance."

I sulked as she walked away. The next song was slow. It was toward the end of the night, so the floor was more crowded with hook-ups. From my seat at the table, I noticed Ben. His partner was a brunette almost as tall as him. Her long smooth arms disappeared behind Ben's neck. You could tell she was into it by the way she lifted her head from his shoulder to look into his face. I felt like I was watching an old movie—a love story on the deck a of ship, moonlight beaming down. I wondered if they would have started kissing if chaperones weren't watching.

Beyond the dancers I noticed my bombshell chatting with three friends. A couple of them were pointing at ceiling decorations, probably discussing how to take them down. The song was almost over. I would need to move fast. I stood up and walked. My best friend was dancing with a beautiful girl. Why couldn't I? Ben said I wasn't fat. He said the time for being bashful was over. I moved within range. They were still looking at the decorations. Good thing: she might have worked up an excuse if she saw me coming.

This was going to be a gargantuan failure. Toni Tennille was moaning *Do that to me one more time; once is never enough from a man like you.*

"Hi," I said.

The four button-wearers turned as one. They were all several inches taller than me and very good looking, even the boys. Like being attractive was a prerequisite to join the Dance Committee. I didn't talk. I was afraid my voice might crack or something stupid would come out. I offered her my hand. It hung out there for seconds, like one of the sagging heart-shaped balloons.

"I know how you love to dance," I said.

She stepped forward and slipped her fingers into my palm. We held hands to the dance floor, then joined the other couples in slow dance mode, hips a few inches apart, swaying to the music. I looked for Ben, but he was lost in the sea of couples. I wondered if I should say something witty to make her laugh. No. I just wanted to breathe her in, absorb the fact that I was dancing with the prettiest girl in the room. My hands around her waist. The pressure of her wrists on the back of my neck. The slippery feel of her blouse against my chin.

The song ended abruptly. Not fair. We'd only been out there for thirty seconds.

"I'm sorry for what I said." I wanted to get it in before she left. "Nothing against you." I wanted to say more, that I hoped I'd see her again, if not officially, then maybe just passing in the hall. I thought of asking for her name, but this girl breathed air from a different stratosphere than me.

"Thanks for the dance. It was nice." She leaned forward and kissed the side of my mouth.

My dick startled like it had been awakened by a trumpet blast. I watched her walk toward her friends and wondered if people could see my erection through my pants, but when I looked down all was cool.

A new song started. I floated to the edge of the floor. I spotted Ben laughing it up at the brunette's table while polishing off the rest of the orange soda and a bowl of pretzel sticks. He saw me and waved me over. A chair wasn't free, so he stood up as I drew near.

"Glad you came?" he said.

"Yeah, it's fun. I danced and everything."

"All right."

"A slow one even." I wanted to tell him all about it.

"How about that," he said in a dead-on Mel Allen impersonation.

I pointed to the clock on the wall. "My folks are probably waiting. I'm going to split."

"Hold on. I'll just be a second."

"You don't have to—"

But he was already saying goodbye to his friends, taking an extra moment with the girl.

"You don't mind leaving?" I said as we started for the door.

"No."

"But that girl you were dancing with. Maybe you had a chance. She's pretty."

"Smokin' body, too."

"I'll say. So why don't you want to stay?"

"You said your parents are here."

"So. You could get a ride home with someone else."

"Doesn't matter. Her father's picking her up any minute. Besides . . ." His blonde hair glowed under the parking lot lights as he removed a small piece of paper from his pocket. "I got her number."

**

My days were repetitive. School all day, then the track or the weight room and drills at home until dark. Homework at night. At some point I bought a squeeze grip and used it all the time. When I got bored with the grip I used a tennis ball.

A few inches of snow coated the ground in late February, but I continued to practice. Throwing in the cold was hard. It took twice as long to get loose. Pain settled in the shoulder and elbow, but eventually eased. I shoveled a patch for the tee and swung away. By now I was taking a couple hundred cuts a session. Placing the ball on the tee. Taking a swing. Bending down for another ball. Over and over. The monotony was excruciating. It was like running; at one point you hit a wall, then you break through and it seems you can go forever. I liked the sound of bat against ball. The loud sweet *crack* of wood and the high *ping* of aluminum. They used both in high school so I switched up to see which one I liked better. To quell the tedium I imagined myself at tryouts next month lighting up unfortunate pitchers.

"You know what to do when someone actually pitches it?" Ben was home from practice early. It wasn't even 4:30 yet.

"I'll let you know in a few weeks." We laughed. "Practice get cancelled?"

"Na, they're still there." An odd grin crept over his face, as though he'd done something wrong. "Swimming lap after lap. Flipping turn after turn."

"What's going on?"

"Nothing." He tossed his knapsack to the ground and sat on the mound of snow I'd shoveled. "Keep swinging." His knit hat was pulled down over his ears. He wore a puffy down coat that made his body and arms look twice their size.

"I'm done. What's the deal?"

He stared at the tarp. I leaned on my bat looking at him. The grin was gone, his expression blank, impossible to read.

"I don't want to swim anymore."

"Really."

"Not on this team." He hadn't looked at me since he started talking. His fingers kept busy with the cloth handles of his bag. His pants were soaking in the snow, but he didn't seem to notice. "They have this thing where the upperclassmen initiate the freshmen. Toss them into the shower after they're dressed. Give them a pink belly, things like that." He grabbed a ball from the ground and tossed it in the air. He caught it, then tossed it again. "You know Lance Durphy?"

"No. Should I?"

"Real scrawny kid. Greasy brown hair. Teeth all fucked up. I think he went to South. You'd know him if you saw him. Anyway, he's geektown to the core and he's not that fast a swimmer." He continued to flip the ball skyward as he spoke. "Today was his turn."

"And?"

"They beat the shit out of him." He dropped his hands to his lap. The ball fell from the sky and thudded onto the snow.

"Did you know it was going to happen?"

"You kidding? They know I think it's moronic. They're a bunch of goons. Hey, I took my licks last year. No big deal. And it's been pretty innocent. But this Lance kid. He's an easy target and they went after him."

"What did they do?"

"They were pushing him around the locker room. He tripped over one of the benches and smacked his face on the floor. When he stood up his nose was bleeding. I figured . . . you know, it's over. Well, these guys were just getting warm. They carried him into the showers. They forced his face right up to the nozzle. The kid couldn't breathe."

"What did you do?"

He lifted himself from the mound and walked along the length of the tarp. His feet crunched the icy snow. "That's just it . . ." He walked to the fence and leaned his weight against it. "I didn't do anything. I saw this kid's face turned up into the shower, the water coughing out of his mouth."

"If you did something they would have turned on you."

"So what! They wouldn't have smashed my face in, tried to drown me. I'm the fastest swimmer they've ever seen. I'm the coach's son. All they would have done was shove me around a little, give me a wedgie. And still I didn't do anything."

I'd never seen him so riled. "You mind helping me with these balls?" We grabbed two pails and filled them with the baseballs that littered the yard.

"Something like that happens . . ." He was bent over a ball. He stood, slow to fully straighten. "And you realize. This is the kind of person I am. Right? The person I've become."

"Jesus Christ, Ben, you make it sound like they killed him. They didn't kill him, did they?"

"It's not funny." He set down his bucket and faced me full. "I did the wrong thing."

"*You* didn't trip him. *You* didn't force him in the shower."

"They tied his pants around his ankles and shoved him outside. That door by the stairs stays locked. They knew he couldn't get back in."

"How did it end up?"

"They just waltzed in to practice. They didn't care. When I let him back in he was shivering, crying."

"So you helped him. You should feel good about that."

"All I know is I don't want to go back there. I don't think." His eyes looked confused. "Tell me what to do."•

"If your dad knows that's why you're not swimming he'll put an end to it."

"He should be home soon. I gotta come up with something to tell him." He hoisted his knapsack over his shoulder. "Hey, I may have some free time so I'll pitch to ya if you want. One of us should be on a team."

"You're gonna go back. Fuck those other kids."

**

The next day, Saturday, I was in the yard first thing. I needed to get the drills in early because we were going to Faneuil Hall in the afternoon, then to a friend of my parents in Brookline.

"Hey." A loud shout from up the street. "Hey." It was Ben's voice, probably from his back yard, which I couldn't see from where I swung. I walked to my backyard. Ben's head sat atop the tall wooden fence that lined his yard. "I can hear you whacking that thing from here."

"What's going on?"

"Come on over. Bring your baseball crap."

He met me in his front yard.

"You tell your father?"

"I told him I got sick. Nurse sent me home."

"What are you going to say on Monday?"

"I got the weekend to come up with something."

Ben's back yard opened up to what used to be a stand of trees where Ben and I had long ago played hide and seek and pirates. Most of the woods had been cleared in recent months, though, for a house to be built at the corner of Clydemore and Holmes. The vacant lot was perfect for ball.

"All right," Ben said, "Let's see if you can hit my curve."

"Yeah, like you have a curve."

I struck a couple near Ben, but most of them scattered all over the yard and field. It wasn't fun. Besides, we risked hitting a window. "Want to just play catch?"

"Why don't you hit 'em out of your hand? At least you'll be swinging."

We played for a while. I needed to get home soon for our ride to Boston. Just a few more. I swung hard at one, but got underneath the ball and it soared into the air toward the Clancy's front yard.

"I got this mother in the air!" Ben bolted toward the house.

"Keep your eye on the ball," I laughed. "Eye on the ball."

I leaned over to pick up another ball. That last one hurt my hands. Real shitty feeling when a swing hurts your hands. You want the connection to feel smooth, like swinging through a soft stick of butter.

At first it sounded like a human shriek, straight from the throat. But no. The screeching of tires. I ran across the front lawn. The first thing I saw was the ancient red pick-up. Half on the road, half off. Then Ben. Oh fuck! Ben! I flew to where he lay and stood over him. His legs and arms extended from his torso at ghastly impossible angles. Like pickup sticks dumped from the box. He looked dead. Couldn't be. His eyes were open. But as I fell to my knees to see if he was okay I realized that they weren't moving. Even his pupils remained still.

I felt for a vein on his wrist. No pulse. But it could have been the wrong vein. There were so many. My fingers scrambled over his wrist. But what did I know about checking other people's pulses? I checked my own. There it was, on the side of my wrist. I searched Ben's again. Still nothing. What about the neck? I felt both sides of Ben's neck. No pulse. I lowered my head to his face hoping for the sound of breathing. Or to see the rise and fall of his chest. That's what they did on TV.

I looked at the truck. Todd stood against the open door, completely still, his gaze straight ahead. Then, as if rattled from a trance, he ran across the lawn of the closest house and banged on the front door. Calling for an ambulance. Good move, Todd, good thinking.

One of Ben's sneakers was barely on his foot. As though it had been kicked off, hanging by the toe. The other was gone. Ben always wore the latest sneakers. His father would be pissed if it were lost. His mother would be angry too if he showed up with only one shoe, especially in the winter. I needed to find it. I looked around his body, then on the street. There it was, near the pick-up truck. I ran for it and brought it back. I tried to put it on his foot, but it wasn't easy.

"Come on, Ben, a little help."

Something moved. I scampered to his head. Those eyes again. That permanent look of surprise. His mouth wasn't open before, I could have sworn. Maybe he had tried to say something.

"Can you hear me?" I shouted into his face. "Say what you were gonna say."

Maybe he hadn't tried to speak. Maybe the jaw just dropped. None of that shit mattered anyway because I saw something move again, maybe a finger, maybe he moved his head. "I think you're all right," I screamed. "I saw something move." A gust of wind blew the sleeve of Ben's coat and locks of his hair.

Soft cries from the truck. Todd was on his ass, his back against the front tire. Weeping. Shoulders convulsing up and down. The dumb fuck. Why the hell was he driving on Clydemore anyway? It wasn't a major street, it didn't even *lead* to a major street.

I heard the squeak of a screen door. Mrs. Clancy. I thought of Ben's eyes, cold and still. She shouldn't see them. Maybe I could close them. I'd seen it done in war movies. I could do it. I placed two fingertips on his lids and lowered. They closed easily. Like the eyes of a doll. I'd done a good thing. In an instant, though, they lifted. And he was staring into my eyes. So maybe he was okay. Maybe he was fighting it, struggling to stay alive. Anything was possible.

She shoved me aside and kneeled over Ben . "Benji," she screamed into his face. "BEN."

"You're going to be okay, Ben," I said, standing over Mrs. Clancy. "Keep fighting."

She kissed him all over, his cheeks and lips, his forehead. Then she held her arms over his body, as if to shield him from something unseen.

As I looked in the direction of the sirens I saw the baseball on the far side of the road, just a few yards away. I wanted that ball. When this was over, I'd be able to show it to him. Check it out, I'd say, all this hubbub over a measly little baseball. I slid the ball in my pocket, and when I started back toward Ben I saw that Mrs. Clancy was no longer kneeling. Instead, she had nestled herself to Ben's side, her knees curled up like a fetus, and arms draped over his chest.

**

My first wake. The funeral parlor was no bigger than a small house. My parents and I stood aside as a handful of downcast, grey-faced mourners stepped through the door on their way out. Dad signed a guest book, then led us down a narrow hallway. It was slow-moving because of the crowd. Nothing to do but stand and look at all the strangers. And the photographs of downtown Brockton at the turn of the century that adorned the walls.

Eventually we passed through an archway to the right and entered the rear of the main viewing room. Ten rows of folding chairs filled the small space. I didn't realize until now that I was in a procession, all of us moving toward the open casket. After which each person was to kneel for a moment, then get up and say a few words to Mr. and Mrs. Clancy.

I forced myself to stay in line. I could do this. Then I drew near enough to see inside the coffin. From my angle I looked over the back of his head. I couldn't see his face, thank God. But I saw his hands. His fingers intertwined, resting on his sternum. They were too perfect. Mannequin hands. No lines where the fingers bent. No wrinkles at the knuckles. And those fingernails. What had these morons done? I'd known his ragged-ass fingernails all my life and now they were straight and polished and glossy. He would have hated that. And a three piece suit? Ben never wore a three piece suit. Had they bought it for the funeral? What a waste. The whole fucking operation was a sham. This thing in the casket was an imposter. Where's my Ben? I screamed inside my head. I want my Ben!

I can't do it, I thought. Not me. I loved him. I still love him, but I can't get any closer. I left the line and stood in the back of the room. "Terrible accident," someone said. Other voices: "Such a shame." "Just a boy." What the fuck did they know? They didn't know Ben. I knew Ben.

I recognized some kids and teachers from school and nodded, shook hands. No one spoke more than a couple sentences at a time. "They did a nice job, don't you think?" I heard someone whisper. Nice job? I wanted to say. Did they bring him back to life? Then no, they didn't do a nice job, not at all. Idiots.

My parents were talking to the Clancys. Mother dabbed her eyes with a Kleenex. After a moment they weaved their way toward the back. Mother said, "Why don't you head up there now, Jimmy?"

I looked at the line leading toward the coffin, but stayed put.

"It will mean a lot to them," my father said.

As I knelt at the casket, my eyes fell on his hands. They were far less perfect close up. Like they were molded from chalk dust and paste. I wanted to touch them. Touch *him*. It would be my last time. I could do it quickly, without anyone seeing. My finger brushed his finger. And it was gross.

Not only did it look like a mannequin's finger, it felt like one too. Hard and unyielding, like cement. I glimpsed the side of his head. A thin fold of skin pleated the length of his temple, like a tiny patch of creased wallpaper. Jesus Christ, Ben, what did they do to you? Where are you, buddy? I just hope you're okay, that's all. I'm sorry I haven't cried. I don't know what's wrong with me. I think about it continuously. I picture the truck bearing down, slamming your bones, sending your body in the air, but my eyes stay dry. Did you even see the truck, try to get out of the way at the last second? Did it hurt, Ben? I hope not. What did you think at that last moment, what filled your head? Were you scared? I wonder all the time if you

died when the truck hit you. Or when your body hit the street. Or
somewhere in between. God, I miss you. Seeing you on the street
like that. The ambulance guys tearing your mother away from you.
Seeing it every time I close my eyes. No sleep that night. Not much
since.

The whole stinking thing was my fault. The ball came from my
bat, from my hand. And those words: *Keep your eye on the ball.* What
was I thinking? Encouraging you to blow off the oldest rule in the
book—look both ways before crossing the street.

It would have been better if we both got hit by the truck. The
damage could have been split between us. Yeah, we both would have
been hurt, maybe even crippled for life. But we'd have been crippled
together, and you'd be alive.

I didn't know how long I kneeled there. I wanted to be done,
get away from the thing in the coffin, but it was the last time I'd see
him. Besides, I wanted to kneel long enough to be respectful. I rose
and faced Mr. and Mrs. Clancy. They were exhausted. Mrs. Clancy
barely sat up straight; her body leaned heavily into her husband's.

"He admired you so much, Jimmy," she said, mustering the
strength to lean forward. Her eyes were glassy. She licked her lips
between words. "Your perseverance, your smarts. Really."

I didn't know what to say. So I did what everyone had done. I
leaned forward and kissed her cheek. Mr. Clancy took my hand in
both of his, but there was no strength in them, no grip.

My parents kept me out of school for the funeral. Relatives of
the Clancys, along with Mother and other neighbors, had made all
the arrangements for the gathering after the funeral. Although it
was at the Clancys' home, they didn't have to lift a finger. We set up
tables and chairs in the dining room and downstairs in the den. Food
and drinks had been brought in. I noticed a couple of ladies on
clean-up detail. Every time something littered the floor one of them
swooped in with a broom or dustpan or sponge to whisk it away.

Some of Ben's teammates stood uncertainly near the door. They
nodded respectfully as adults walked by. They spoke quietly amongst
themselves. One of them I'd never seen before, but I knew him
right away. I couldn't understand why he'd be hanging out with the
very people who days ago had pounded him to a pulp. The corner
of his mouth was still swollen. I said hello to a couple of the kids I

knew and was introduced to the rest, including Lance.

He separated himself from the team to pour a cup of soda.

"Ben was really upset about what happened," I said, joining him at the table. "The initiation thing."

"He told you about that?"

I wondered if I should have kept my mouth shut. "We told each other everything. It's not like he told anyone else. We were best friends."

"Ben was a . . . He made it easy. To be friends with, I mean."

"I just thought you'd want to know. That it bothered him"

He looked toward the swimmers at the door. "They've been pretty cool since. Included me in coming here. I almost feel like one of the team now."

"You're still on the team?"

"Sure."

"I think Ben was under the impression you quit."

He shook his head while sipping. "Nope. I went into practice the day it happened. What were they gonna do, kill me?"

"Right." Pretty ballsy, I thought. The kid takes the beating of his life and a few minutes later hops in the pool with the goons who beat him. "Damn, I wish Ben knew that."

A little later, a couple of the other swimmers meandered over and asked Lance if he was leaving with them. He set down his cup, shook my hand and left with his teammates.

After a while I left too. I stood outside on the street where Ben was killed. I looked up the street to where the truck had veered off the road. Todd. I hadn't seen him since the accident. Mother said he had attended one of the wakes with his family. I walked up Clydemore and all the way down Holmes until it hit Upton Street. My dress shoes were new and pinched my toes. The shiny black company van sat in the driveway, "McAfee Air Conditioning & Heating" written on the side, along with a phone number. The pick-up was nowhere to be seen.

Todd and his father appeared from their backyard carrying a couple of boxes. Mr. McAfee set his load down to open the side door. Todd nodded when he saw me, then lowered the boxes into the van. I walked to the driveway.

Mr. McAfee waved and said, "Hello Jimmy, it's been a while."

"Hi, Mr. McAfee."

"I can't tell you how sorry we all are." He lifted his hand to his boy's shoulder, kept it there. "He was a fine young man, from what I hear. I'm sorry I didn't know him well."

"You want me?" Todd said. No hostility.

I shrugged. Mr. McAfee retreated to the back yard, maybe to get more boxes, maybe to leave me and Todd alone.

"What's up?"

"I don't know." It was the truth. I wasn't sure what the hell I was doing there. I didn't blame him. I didn't hate him. I didn't want to scream at him. At the same time I didn't want to get all lovey-dovey with him either. "Just say hey, I guess."

"Yeah."

It wasn't until I saw he was wearing gloves that I realized how cold I was. I wasn't wearing a jacket. "See ya. Okay?"

"Yeah. Okay."

**

Once home, I changed clothes, hung the tarp and set up the tee. I concentrated on the swings, each one a precious at-bat at a pivotal point. I pulled the ball, inside-outed the ball, even bunted. Images of Ben crept into my thoughts—that crease in his skin, pebbles for eyes. I swung harder, more feverishly, to smash the pictures away. I tried replacing images of Ben with ninth inning, game-saving swings. It didn't last. I couldn't swing hard enough to keep Ben away.

I remembered the ball. I'd put it on the floor of my closet the day he died and hadn't touched it since. I went to my room, grabbed the ball and took it out to the tee. I crushed it. Instead of replacing it with another ball, I retrieved Ben's and teed it up. And crushed it again. I kept it up, each time looking at the marks I'd left. I wanted to kill that fucking ball. But no matter how hard or how often I swung, Ben kept coming back. His busted limbs; his gaping mouth; Mrs. Clancy clinging to his corpse.

I walked to the ball at the base of the tarp. I lifted the bat over my head and swung it like an axe onto the ball. Again. And again. It felt good. I searched my father's stone pile for a rock, then kneeled in front of the ball and slammed it with the boulder. Oh, this felt much better. Not just crushing the baseball, but the whole lousy foolish sport. Why did I want a future in baseball anyway? A bunch of grown men trying to advance ninety feet at a time while another group shagged balls? Didn't they have anything better to do? I was going to smash the ball down to its cork, pound the thing to dust.

My arms and shoulders killed. My face and neck were drenched in sweat. I didn't care. I remembered the bargain I'd made at the funeral, me getting struck along with Ben. But that wasn't enough. I would have taken the full hit. My life for Ben's. Straight up. He had more to live for than me. Think of all the girlfriends he would have had. He would have gotten married, had children. And he was better at swimming than I was at baseball. He might have become famous. It would have been the right thing: Ben alive, Jimmy dead.

I slammed down the rock—again.

**

Afterward, I sat at the dining room table and looked out the large front window. At the bare branches. The dead grass along the street. I was drinking a large glass of ice water and wiping my face with a towel. A low bookcase sat under the window. Mother used it for a couple of plants and porcelain figurines. The bottom shelf contained photo albums. I had hardly paid attention to them, but I remembered that a bunch of pictures had been taken when Ben went with us to Pennsylvania one year. Mother had labeled the binders so it only took a minute to grab the right one.

I slid it from the shelf and held it in my lap as I flipped the pages. Pictures of us climbing rocks, swimming in a lake, paddling a canoe. We were three years younger. I was thirty pounds fatter. I pulled the canoe photo from the album and pressed my hand against the picture. My eyes suddenly overflowed with tears. I'll never play with Ben again. Never seek his advice. Never help him with schoolwork. I had other friends, but Ben and I had history, practically from birth. My best friend was all gone. My crying grew loud and sloppy. Wild breathless gulps of tears.

8. Facing the Cage

We visited the Clancys the night before baseball tryouts. The five of us sat in the den, listening to silence. Mother's Kleenex never left her hand. Mrs. Clancy had poured me a hot chocolate.

Bouquets of flowers still filled the room. They reminded me of the funeral home. Which reminded me of Ben's corpse, his chalk fingers, that seam of skin. On the sofa, Mrs. Clancy leaned into her husband. The skin beneath her eyes sagged in pockets of smudged grey.

A car rolled by outside. Her eyes closed for a fraction of a second. "It's a little easier now. The cars, I mean." She touched the handle of her teacup. "At first I covered my ears. Couldn't bear it."

Mr. Clancy grabbed her hand. A tear ran down the side of his nose. He swiftly wiped it away. His hair was unwashed and his face unshaved. When he moved his feet I noticed that he wore different colored socks. He hadn't been at Brockton High since the accident.

"When I heard the tires," Mrs. Clancy said, "it didn't seem like much of anything. It was loud, but you hear noises like that all the time. I just kept washing the dishes. I passed by the front window and there's Jimmy. Bending over Ben . . ."

Mr. Clancy sighed. Bushes rustled against the window. I couldn't take it anymore. I took my parents' empty cups along with mine into the kitchen.

"Aren't you sweet, Jimmy," Mrs. Clancy said.

With any luck my gesture would help get us out the door. The kitchen table and sideboard were stacked with pies and breads, cakes and pastries. The sink and stove sparkled. The oven was cold. I wondered if they had eaten dinner.

I passed through the den, saying, "Just going to use the bathroom" and climbed the stairs. Ben's door had been closed every visit. Tonight, though, it stood open a few inches. I stepped inside. Nothing had changed. Bobby Orr decorated the wall above his headboard, his arms high in the air and smiling that wide Stanley Cup smile.

The wallpaper was a pattern of athletes—a hockey player stick-handling over the blue line, a quarterback fading back, a baseball player in mid-swing, a basketball player making a jump shot. Years ago Ben and I had written our favorite players' names under the figures. We were just going to do a few, but before we knew it we'd covered a large chunk of the wall. I leaned in to examine the wall; you could still see the marks from when we furiously erased them after realizing what we'd done. I kneeled on Jimmy's bed to get a closer peek.

"He told me about that, you know."

I turned. Mr. Clancy filled the doorway.

"Come here," he said as he walked toward one of Ben's dressers. "He would have wanted you to have this." He lifted the Game Six picture, Fisk waving the ball fair.

I took the picture and said, "Thank you." But did I really want it? Sitting in my bedroom? Would it just keep me awake? Remind me of closing his lids over those frozen pebbly eyes? "I don't . . ."

"You don't want it?"

"Of course I do." I held it in my hands. When I looked up, he was sitting on the edge of the bed.

"You can have it. Some others if you'd like."

"Um . . ." It wasn't that I didn't want them. But to start taking Ben's things. It was as though I was being given a responsibility I wasn't quite ready for. Not to mention it seemed a little ghoulish.

"Not tonight necessarily. You'll be over again. Or I can bring them to you. Whatever you'd like."

I was relieved to set the picture back down on the bureau.

When we got downstairs, Mother was helping Mrs. Clancy tossing out some of the older flowers. "I'll stack the cards on the corner here in case you want to keep them."

Mr. Clancy and I joined my father around the coffee table. He was returning to work tomorrow and Dad asked him his game plan. He listed the things he needed to do to catch up. He also wanted to spend some time writing thank you cards and letters.

Mother washed the dishes; Mrs. Clancy dried and placed them in the cupboard. Mother lifted the stuffed trash bag out of the basket. "We'll dump this on the way out," she said.

"We sure appreciate you coming over," Mr. Clancy said, standing up. "I won't lie, the company helps." He walked from behind the coffee table to say goodbye.

"Mmmm," Mrs. Clancy said when the door opened. "That cool air feels nice."

**

I played with my glove as kids entered the gym, bending it inside out, flipping it in the air from the leather strings. I remembered the night I got it. My tenth birthday. Ben across the kitchen table.

I counted eighty-eight candidates by the time five coaches entered the gym. Coach Walsh brought up the rear. By now I'd heard all the rumors. He seemed like a nice guy, but his surly demeanor was infamous. According to some, his wife ran off with another coach and took their daughter. Others said he'd lost his family in a fire. One rumor claimed he'd gotten his wife so mad she pushed him down the stairs and was now serving time in Acton.

One of the men separated from the rest and stepped in front of the bleachers. "My name is Coach Hannah. I coach the junior varsity squad." He wore blue jeans and a black tee shirt torn at the sleeve. His thin blond hair was parted neatly on the side. He explained how Brockton had three teams—freshman, junior varsity and varsity. "When tryouts are done at the end of the week, we'll have about fifteen to eighteen players per team. Now take your gloves, line up along this line and count."

We lined up along the length of the gym and shouted our number. Some upperclassmen already on the team handed out rolls of masking tape and instructed us to tape our numbers to the backs of our shirts. I was thirty.

Hanna's voice boomed over the commotion: "We're staying inside, boys. Too much snow on the ground. Today we warm up and complete two skill sessions. Tomorrow, you'll start where you left off."

After fifteen minutes of warming up with stretches and playing catch, we separated into three groups. My first skill, along with twenty-three others, was simply to play catch for thirty minutes, from whatever distance the coach demanded. I did well enough that the coach tapped my shoulder and asked my name. My group's next skill was grounders. I lost count of how many grounders we faced, dozens it seemed, but I must have flubbed five. I did not get tapped. Once done, the coach overseeing the skill said, "Sit tight," then checked in across the gym with Coach Walsh.

We had to wait for the group at the batting cage to finish before being dismissed. Bernie Humphries, a kid I knew from East, suggested we sit.

"You think that's allowed?"

"He said sit tight," Bernie said.

"I don't think he meant it literally," I said.

Bernie sat. The rest of us followed.

As we hit the floor, Coach Hannah approached and said, "What's happening, boys?"

"Waiting for them to finish," Bernie said.

A couple of us pointed lamely in the direction of the cage.

"Is this what athletes do while they wait? Come with me." He led us to a vacant area of the gym and formed us into three lines. He stood in front of us, clipboard still in hand, and started doing jumping jacks. Of course, we followed. "Enjoy this," he said. "It will be your activity until everyone else is off the floor. You stop, don't return tomorrow."

"Idiot," someone said to Bernie. Someone else: "Retardo Mantalban."

The next day we renumbered our shirts with the tape, took fifteen minutes to warm up and hit the skills. The batting cage was manned by a four player rotation: one batted, one swung on deck; one swung from the tee, batting balls against a net; the final kid fed the automatic arm, then took cover behind an L-fence that pitchers used for batting practice. The rest of us stood around the cage and watched.

"Don't pay attention to the machine," the batting coach said to the crowd. "Just focus on the ball."

I studied the contraption. It looked like an old-fashioned movie camera, with spinning wheels that extended from the neck of a tripod. The balls were dropped into a vertical shoot and the wheels spat the balls toward the plate. Coach Walsh took a seat near the plate end of the cage and leaned forward, a Brockton cap pulled down close to his eyes. I batted fifth. I must have faced the plate with trepidation because the batting coach said, "It's easier than live pitching. Just keep your eye on the ball."

Keep your eye on the ball.

What did he have to say that for? The pitch was released. A perfect strike. I let it pass.

"You only get ten, Thirty."

I wanted to swing, I really did. But every time I saw the ball—*keep your eye on the ball*—I saw Ben running into the street. I heard the screech of tires. The next pitch came. I swung. Missed it by a mile. Another one. Swing and a miss.

Coach Walsh sat up. "No different than a tee, Jimmy. Ball's right there." The batting coach looked at Coach Walsh as though it was the craziest thing in the world for him to speak.

I nodded. Noises caromed in from other areas—balls popping into gloves, sneakers skidding on the floor, aluminum striking ball, ball striking floor. The pitch. Ben's voice: *I got this mother in the air.* The ball passed my hips without a swing.

Should I ask for a time-out? I thought. It's hard to focus after your best friend gets mowed down in front of your eyes. They would know I was for real because an announcement had been made over the intercom the day after Ben died. There was even a moment of silence throughout the school after the pledge of allegiance. But I couldn't launch into the whole ordeal. No excuses allowed.

"Can I skip a turn?" I asked the batting coach.

"Uh . . ." He looked at Coach Walsh, who said nothing, then shrugged. "I guess. You used four pitches."

"Thank you." I stepped out of the cage and grabbed my glove. "Hey, you want to toss for a minute?" I said to a kid who had already hit.

We played catch. Maybe I just needed to clear my head. I looked at the cage. The hitter was taking good cuts. As I pictured myself in the hitters' place, I found myself walking away.

"Hey," the kid I was tossing the ball with said. "We still playing?"

I didn't answer. Just kept walking. Through the door and down the stairs to the locker rooms. I can't do it, I thought, sitting on the bench in front of my locker. Can't face Ben every day like that. Every at-bat. Every swing. Him running for the ball. No way.

On the bus ride home, I knew I wasn't going back tomorrow. How could I? How could I fail again? Fail in front of Coach Walsh and everyone else? I couldn't go back. Simple as that.

What would be the point anyway? I thought. Look at it realistically. Even if they let me continue my session, I was already 0 for 4. Lots of kids, even freshman, were hitting the ball cleanly six or seven times. And the weather was so crappy we'd never get outside for relay drills and fly balls. What was the point of having a good arm if you couldn't show it off? Didn't matter; Coach Walsh wouldn't let me back anyway.

Instead of going straight home, I wandered around what was left of the woods next to the Clancys'. I walked where Ben and I had walked, sat where we'd sat. I talked to him—not out loud—told him what happened at tryouts. Told him I wasn't going back.

I could hear him say, Are you crazy? What's your problem? Ah God, I missed him. I thought of the day he showed up at my yard wanting to quit the swim team after he felt he hadn't done enough to protect Lance Durphy. I remembered my advice; just get back in the pool; it wasn't your fault. That's what he would have advised now.

The woods emptied out to the vacant lot. I walked to where the truck had spun off the road. The skid marks were gone. I wondered if they just faded. Or had Mr. or Mrs. Clancy scrubbed them away? Farther down the street, I stood where he died and looked at the tar. Stood for a long time. Maybe. I wasn't sure.

At dinner, my father sensed my gloom.

"Nothing makes sense," I said.

Mother was setting plates of food on the table. Broiled chicken in an orange broth, sautéed broccoli with garlic, baked potato.

"They don't let us outside so we can't catch fly balls, we can't throw long distances. We can't even face live pitching. They got this pitching machine."

"Are you doing well?" my father said.

"The hitting . . . Not so good." I thought about not getting into it, but I wanted to talk. "I was hitting out of my hand to Ben when he . . . when he—"

"Yes, I know."

"I'm fine when I play catch and field. When I hit, though . . . I keep seeing him run into the street."

Mother had taken her seat at the table. "Going to school, playing sports, those things help. They occupy our minds, keep us busy."

"Not really," I said. "I'm not going back."

"What?" It took them both by surprise.

"That doesn't make sense, Jimmy," my father said.

"I can't do it. Face him with every pitch. It's like he's with me." I felt my voice rising just thinking about it again, the accident itself and the horror of reliving it every time I swung.

"So you blame Ben?" Mother said.

"No, I blame me."

"This is disappointing." She placed her fork on the table. She looked at my father, who said nothing, just looked at me. "You hit a bump and blame Ben?"

I stood up. "What the fuck, Mother, you're not listening."

"Jimmy!" my father said.

Mother was too surprised to speak. Her head reared back as though she'd been slapped. Finally, she uttered, "How dare . . ."

"Well, you don't get what I'm saying. I said it's my fault. It's. My. Fault. That's the whole point. That's why I'm not going back."

"But you can't just—"

"Because I killed him!" I started to cry. I felt wobbly, needed to sit. I fell back into the chair, but the chair was gone. My back hit against the wall. I didn't give a shit. My weight dragged me down the wall and my ass thumped to the floor.

Suddenly the tears dried up, completely obliterated by fear. Had I just screamed at Mother? I'd never screamed at her before. And I sure as hell had never sworn at her. Even Cliff had never sworn at her.

Mother was on her knees on the floor. I wasn't sure when she got there.

"I'm sorry," I said. "I didn't mean to—"

She clutched my hands in hers and held me against her body. "I'm sorry, Jimmy," she said in my ear. "*I'm* sorry." She wiped my face. "What's best for you. That's all we care about."

"Come on," my father said loudly, as cheerfully as he could, and reached down to grab our arms. "Everyone up. We're supposed to be civilized. Look at ya. Flopping around the floor like animals."

Mother gave me another squeeze before taking her seat across the table. Dad and I sat too.

"Still hungry?" Mother said.

I nodded.

"It makes sense that you think about Ben when you play," Mother said toward the end of the meal. "It's a positive. I mean, what do you suppose Ben wants? Do you think he's looking down from heaven hoping everyone who cared for him suffers because he's gone? Gives up?" She set down her fork, folded her hands on the table and leaned forward. "You said it's like he's with you. That's a good thing. You *should* picture him beside you when you swing. Running the bases alongside you. Cheering you on. Making you better, not worse. More committed, not less."

I almost chuckled, picturing Mother as one of my coaches, screaming instructions from the bench.

"You're laughing at me," she said.

"I'm not laughing." I didn't want to talk about it anymore. "You're right. I know what I should do."

"I just feel—"

"Ma, I get it. No more win-one-for-the-Gipper speeches, okay?"

She cut her chicken in evenly sized cubes.

"It was a good speech, though," my father said.

I wasn't sure she appreciated his attempt to lighten the mood. She pushed the tiny squares of chicken around her plate.

"You okay?" my father said.

She brought her dishes to the sink. "I'll put on some coffee."

"How about you throw in a splash of the good stuff?" my father said as he joined her at the sink. He stood behind her and kissed her shoulder as she scraped the leftovers into a storage container.

"Me too?" I said.

"What do you say?" he said to Mother. "Hot chocolate and Bailey's for the kid?"

"Coming right up."

After supper, my father knocked on my door. Syringe at his side.

I sat on my desk chair and lifted the leg of my shorts.

He spoke as the needle plunged. "It's not a crime to feel sorry for yourself." The needle was out in an instant. He held it carefully. "We've all suffered. Nobody more than the Clancys. But I think they'd agree that you don't give up something you love because you lose someone you love." He bent down and kissed my cheek. Our nightly ritual. "Good luck tomorrow."

I envisioned tryouts. I saw the batting cage, my stance at the plate, my swing. I looked at my clock. 7:45. It wasn't late, but it was dark outside and cold. I didn't care. I went down to the cellar, put on my winter coat and batting gloves and brought everything I needed outside.

I hit the first three cleanly. But it would be harder against the automatic pitcher. I saw it in front of me and felt myself choke. Come on, dickhead, the thing's just a machine. It's throwing at the same place at the same speed every time. Hit one, hit them all. Same place. Same speed. Every time. Same place. Same speed. Every time. That was the litany I would play in my mind. I took dozens of more cuts on the tee. Picturing the ball coming at me. Same place.

Same speed. Every time.

**

First thing in the morning I looked out my window. I wanted the snow to melt. No such luck. Tryouts were indoors again. As we entered, we were told to line up in front of Coach Hannah for skill assignments. As kids gave their names, Hannah told them to report to their respective areas.

My turn. I started to say my name, but Hannah interrupted.

"Mr. LaPlante," he said, loud enough for others to hear. "As far as I'm concerned quitters don't get second chances. But I don't make those decisions. You're starting in the cage."

I wanted to say something, but he was already addressing the player behind me. "Coach Hannah," I interrupted.

His gaze shifted to mine.

"If I was a quitter I wouldn't have come back."

Maybe I shouldn't have said anything. I didn't want him to think I was a smartass. But I didn't want him to think I was a quitter either.

I was fourth to bat. My mental mantra started as I walked into the cage. Same place. Same speed. Every time. When Ben crept into my thoughts, it would be as a spectator, watching with all the others.

"Wait a minute, Thirty," the batting coach said before the first pitch.

I held my stance at the plate and took practice cuts. After a minute, Coach Walsh ambled over and planted himself in his customary seat. Odd, though, several kids had already batted and Coach Walsh wasn't summoned.

The mantra worked. I made contact with every swing but one, some more convincingly than others. Two were fouled off, but I was happy. Coach Walsh stood up and trudged away.

Coach Hannah announced that a list would be posted outside the phys. ed. office tomorrow at noon. If our name was not on that list we should not show up anymore. The stairwell to the office was packed. The page held fifty-seven names, listed alphabetically. Mine was dead center. One step closer. Backs were patted and hands slapped as kids walked down the stairs and into the corridor leading out of the gym. I noticed Steve Kupperman, a kid I'd been playing with since junior high intramurals, walking away dejectedly. I checked the list. His name wasn't there.

After warm-ups the next day, we were told to grab our gloves and report to the football stadium. Masking tape numbers were no longer needed. The coaches knew us; they all held index cards profiling every player. As we approached the stadium, a truck was plowing half of the huge parking lot. Outdoor baseball. Finally.

We shagged fly balls, hit live pitching, threw tandem relays. Most of the kids taking part in the relays and long toss held their shoulders or elbows after only a few minutes. Throwing in the cold took its toll. Me, I was accustomed to it.

"Listen up," Coach Hannah said as we huddled around him putting on our coats. "The final list will be posted tomorrow at noon. The first practice will be Saturday at 10:30 in the gym."

I had late lunch period on Fridays so I couldn't check the list until well after it was posted. The stairwell was empty. There were three lists: Freshman, Junior Varsity and Varsity. "Jimmy LaPlante" appeared midway down the Freshman list.

Would I play every game? What position? Where would I bat in the order? I must have floated down the stairs. I had no recollection of reaching the cafeteria, which corridors I walked, who I saw. It was Friday, though, which meant pizza, and I celebrated with an extra slice.

**

Cliff phoned the following night. I told him I made the team

"Fantastic," he said.

We hadn't talked since the day after Ben died.

"Yeah," I said, "I'm excited."

"Good, good." Dead air for a few seconds. "You should be."

Another moment passed in silence.

"Mom made butterscotch brownies," I finally said.

"Oh man, I miss those."

"I bet . . . So . . . You talk to Todd at all?"

"Na, we haven't really kept in touch. We called each other a couple of times when I got here. Then, you know . . ."

"He was pretty shaken up. Ben and all."

"You think I should call him?"

How was I supposed to know? "I guess. If you want."

"Well, we'll see. Anyway . . . Just wanted to check in. Let me know how you do."

"Thanks."

"I remember when you used to throw that beat-up old tennis ball against the house."

"A long time ago," I said.

"Like a lot of things."

"Right."

There it was again; Cliff reaching out. Part of me liked that, liked the power it gave me over him, the emotional leverage. Ammunition.

**

The first game against Brookline was two weeks away. After a week of practices, we lined up for uniforms. Tad McKenzie, the equipment attendant, chomped gum and nodded to players as they approached the swinging half-door of the equipment closet.

"What's shakin'?" he said as a bubble grew in front of his face. "Freshman?"

"Yes."

"Medium, yeah?" The bubble evaporated into his mouth.

"Sure."

He reached into the racks of jerseys behind him, grabbed number 14 and laid it across the shelf of the door. I saw that the jersey next to it on the rack had a 10 on the back. I remembered the black and gold tee shirt from my tenth birthday. Tanker 10.

"Is the 10 a medium?"

"Yeah, all the numbers beginning with 1."

"Can I have that one?"

He laid it over the door, then handed me the matching pants. I heard the announcer's voice echo over the heads of 30,000 spectators: *Now batting and playing centerfield. Number 10. Jimmy LaPlante.*

**

The showers turned out not to be a big deal after tryouts because most of the kids bolted from the locker room to catch the 5:15 buses. And on weekends everyone showed up to practice in their gear and showered at home. That all changed once the schedule kicked in. After games the shower became a chamber of celebration or complaining, depending on the outcome. If victorious, hooting and hollering caromed off the tiled walls. If we lost, the only sound heard was the splattering of water. I knew this because I could hear the showers from my bank of lockers only a few yards away. My strategy hadn't changed since Fat Swim. Get to my locker as fast as possible, get dressed, then get the hell out.

Couldn't do that on the road, though. Instead of showering, I washed up at the sink and doused my hair, then busied myself in front of my locker until the others came out of the shower. I wanted to appear as though I had taken a shower, but I wasn't fooling anyone. After all these years I had grown used to not showering in front of others. I'd avoided it for so long that the very thought scared the shit out of me.

After a home game one day, as we were making our way into the school, some of the guys asked me if I wanted to join them at Papa Gino's. A few of them were sophomores. I wanted to say yes, but if I did I would have had to shower with them. Either that or wait at my locker until they were ready to leave. What would they think of that? One thing—freakboy.

"My grandparents are visiting," I lied. "But I don't think they're going to stay long. I can join you in a little while." That would allow me to shower quickly at home, then hop a bus to Papa Gino's.

He shook his head. "We're not going to be that long."

After practice one day, the freshman coach said that Coach Walsh wanted me to stop by his office the next morning before classes. My mind raced all night. I was playing well. Errorless in right field with four assists and batting .392. Maybe he wanted to bump me up to JV.

The phys. ed. office was bustling the next morning. Coach Walsh stood up from his desk when I entered and guided me out of the room and down the stairs to the empty gym. He sat on the front row of the bleachers. I joined him. He rested his elbows onto his knees, pushed the tips of his thumbs against each other. Finally, he said, "Cohesion," his eyes fixed on the waxy floor. "Nothing more important than that."

After another second of silence I felt obligated to say, "Sounds right."

He turned toward me, looked me in the eye. "The knock on you is you're arrogant. Standoffish."

"I'm not—"

"Aloof."

"Yeah, I get it." I stood up, flabbergasted.

"I remember when you were a little fat kid throwing a ball against the wall."

"I'm still him."

"Look," he said, "it's a distraction. I don't like distractions."

"Whatever you're hearing, it's because . . ."

Someone finked on me? I thought. Why? Why did they care if I showered with them or not? Maybe some of the players were jealous that Coach Walsh had singled me out at the batting cage during tryouts.

I wasn't sure how much to say. If Coach Walsh thought I was a snob, he was wrong. They were all wrong! I had to say something to set the record straight. "It's the stupid shower. I don't shower because—"

"Look, look," he said, shifting uncomfortably before standing up and stepping toward the stairwell. "Maybe you're shy. Some kids are shy."

"Something happened when I was a kid." I desperately needed him to understand. I wasn't aloof. I wasn't a weirdo. "I had surgery."

"Whoa, whoa, whoa, please, you don't need to tell me anything private."

"It's not private."

I didn't want him to think I was lugging around baggage, that I'd be a drain on the team. "Just a misunderstanding . . ."

"All right, so we're agreed." A smile blossomed to a chuckle. "Unless you got a head of cabbage down there I guess this little problem is behind us." He walked out of the gym. I watched his strong stout legs climb the stairs.

After the next practice, I hung my tattered white towel on the shower hook and stepped in with the others. Naked. No one seemed to care. I instinctively gravitated toward one of the corner showerheads and faced the wall. I knew I couldn't stay like that forever. I turned around. The hot water pounded my skin with an industrial force. I bent forward and twisted my torso from side to side, the water pummeling my back like a scalding massage. A teammate saw that I didn't have soap. He tossed me his bar. So I soaped up with the guys. Toweled off with the guys. I saw their peckers, they saw mine. It turned out to be easy. Well, not easy. But no big deal.

9. Psyched Out

It was October of sophomore year. I walked slowly through the crowded halls, reading information Coach Walsh had given me about American Legion ball. After finishing the season on the JV bench, I had played my final season of Pony League. Next up, AL. Big time, compared to Pony League. And Coach Walsh wanted me on his team.

When I glanced up, I saw a kid staring at me from down the hall. He looked familiar. I flipped through my brain files. Little League, Pony League, East Junior High. I couldn't place him. His hair defied gravity, a tangled black bush, with soft wisps for sideburns.

He was past me when it struck. I turned around and saw that he was turning too. In Fat Swim, his hair had been cropped short and he'd been thin, practically gaunt. Not anymore. He was a little soft around the middle. He wore nicely tailored pleated pants and a white button-down shirt with the cuffs folded up. I was ninety percent sure it was him, but would need to see his leg to make certain.

"I'm sorry," he said as we walked toward each other. "Your name, I don't . . ."

"Jimmy." I don't think I ever knew his name. When I thought of him he was always the blue-legged boy.

"Hey, I'm Vincent. We had that . . ."

"Swim class, yeah."

I remembered that he lived in Dexter Flats, which meant he

should have gone to East, but I'd never seen him there. "You didn't go to East, did you?"

"No, we left Brockton a few years ago. We recently moved back."

Kids swarmed past us to get to class before the bell. I felt the same pressure to move, but Vincent didn't seem to care.

"Man, I can't believe I recognized you. Look at you."

"Yeah."

He stood there staring at me, as though making sure he had the right kid. "Crazy stuff," he said. "Hey listen, I'm having a party Saturday night. You should come."

"Sure."

He opened a notebook and pressed it against the wall, then slid a silver pen from his breast pocket. It was fancy, the kind you turn for the nib to show. As he wrote his address, I remembered his falling-down shack.

I looked at the paper after he sauntered off. A swanky address. A quiet road off West Street, not far from the high school. Jogging to class, I wondered where the blue-legged boy had been all these years.

**

My father turned into the driveway that spanned nearly the full length of the impressive front yard. A stone walkway lit on both sides by ground lights led from the center of the driveway to the door.

"You're sure this is the place?" my father said, looking at the side yard as it rolled beyond our view to the rear of the house. Must have been two acres.

"This is the address." I opened the car door, carrying a brown Purity Supreme shopping bag.

"Well, just give a wave to make sure. And call when it's time to come home."

A handful of other cars were parked along the driveway, mostly clunkers. Vincent's family's vehicles, if this was his house, were probably in the garage. The front door stood dark brown and embedded with six panels of stained glass. As I pressed the bell, I wished I was with a friend. I didn't know who was going to be at this thing. After a moment, a girl about my age with full round cheeks answered the door.

"Hey there," she said in a high cheerful voice. "I'm Colleen." Her mouth burst into a smile. I wondered if she was naturally flirtatious or if she'd been made bold by the Budweiser held in her chubby hand.

"You live here?" I said. "You know Vinnie?"

"Whoa, not so fast." She counted on the fingers of her free hand. "No, I don't live here. And no, I don't know Vinnie."

"Is this his house?" Her face was blank. "Is there a party here? Kids from Brockton High?"

"Oh yes," she said, holding up her beer. "There's definitely a party here."

I stepped outside and waved. My father drove away. When I turned back into the house the girl, wearing tight blue jeans and a baggy grey sweatshirt, was walking across the gleaming black and white tiles of the foyer and through a beamed archway. A set of sofas and armchairs sat off to one side of the room, near the foot of the stairway that led upstairs to a balcony walkway overlooking the foyer.

I followed Colleen's footsteps, which led to a gigantic kitchen. A large island, topped with green granite and surrounded by stools, sat in the middle of the room. Grocery bags and plastic six-pack rings littered the floor. *Flirtin' with Disaster* pounded from somewhere beyond the kitchen.

Colleen was leaning deep into the refrigerator. I could only see her butt and legs, which, though a bit plump, were still worth looking at. She emerged with a bottle in each hand, one brown, one green. "You bring beer?" she said.

"You bet." I couldn't very well have told her I'd brought a bottle of Coke and a family-sized bag of Fritos.

"Gotta love libations," she laughed, holding up her bottles like a game show model. Her light brown hair was parted on the side and fell to her shoulders in loose curls. Reddish freckles dotted her nose. "See you downstairs." She departed through another archway on the opposite side of the kitchen, saying, "That's where all the fun is."

I hung my jacket over a kitchen chair. The refrigerator was so stocked with beer I couldn't find room for the Coke. I managed to wedge it into one of the shelves and grabbed a Bud. I didn't like beer, but I didn't want to stand out by drinking soda. As I was about to head downstairs, a handful of guys stumbled through the archway, laughing and knocking me to the side.

"Sorry, buddy," one of them said.

"Yeah, sorry."

Two of them were big, probably seniors, maybe football players. The heavier of the two held a plastic funnel. "Come on," he said, stepping toward the refrigerator. "Let's be serious."

"Serious? Shut the fuck up and toss that." He caught the funnel from the heavier guy, then removed a black tube from his coat pocket and pushed it over the bottom of the funnel.

He sat at a dinette table, took the free end of the tube into his mouth and held the funnel above his head. While the others gathered around the table, his friend poured two cans of beer into the cone. The gang hooted and grunted for several seconds until the kid with the tube in his mouth signaled to stop.

The sound of Mollie Hatchett led me to a stairwell. Voices rose over the music, laughing, shouting, swearing. As I descended into the dimness of the stairs, Vinnie was making his way up from a cluster of barely visible bodies.

"Hey there," he said. "You seen the place?"

"Na, I just got here."

"Come on, I'll show you around."

In the hallway, I saw that he was wearing a suit with a black tee shirt underneath and untied black Adidas sneakers. He held a tumbler filled with amber liquid and ice cubes. He led me into the kitchen, where he said, "You guys having a good time?" to the funnel drinkers, then through the foyer.

The carpeting up the stairs and along the second floor hallway felt thick and soft beneath my shoes. We passed several closed doors. He stopped at one and ushered me into the room. It was huge, at least six of mine. A bed the size of my parents' lay near the windows on the opposite side of the room. The space had everything: a large color TV in a cabinet; a stereo with turntable and tape deck and speakers three feet high; a small refrigerator; and a massive aquarium, maybe thirty gallons, filled with rainbow colored fish and models of sea wrecks and castles.

"My room," he said, expanding an arm, as though revealing something magical. Several lamps had been left on, but most of the light emanated from the aquarium. He gestured to an elaborately-backed Victorian sofa, which sat in front of the TV.

"It's incredible." I said it because it was true. Also because he wanted me to. I sat as directed. "Wow."

He took a seat in an armchair and sipped slowly from the glass, soaking in the pleasure of showing off the joint. "You should look around. It's quite a house." He crossed his legs, knee over knee, like a grownup, like my father, in fact. He sipped again from the tumbler, an adult glass containing an adult drink. So it seemed; I wondered if the glass was filled with tea. Every gesture he made seemed measured. The sitting, the drinking, his mannered speech. He was playing Gatsby. I thought at any moment he would call me Old Sport.

"Sure is." I wanted to go downstairs, check out the rest of the place and see who else was here, but sensed he wanted to show off some more.

"If only my parents would do something with it. Most of the rooms are empty. A cleaning lady comes once a week, but there's nothing to clean. 'We should take our time with a new place,' my parents say. My goodness, I'll be out of college by the time they make this house a home."

"Hey," I said. "When my father and I dropped you off at that house . . ."

"I remember."

"What happened?" I said, the sheer obviousness of the question causing me to laugh. I leaned forward on the edge of the sofa and placed my beer on a coffee table. He swiftly removed a coaster from a drawer in the table and adjusted the bottle. "I'm sorry."

"Not to worry." He leaned back in the chair and recrossed his legs, even folded his hands on his lap. He looked like a kid version of the old guy who hosted *Masterpiece Theater*. A smile spread across his face. "You really don't know?"

From the way he looked at me, I was the only person in the world who didn't.

"We won the lottery. Four years ago. Seven million dollars."

"Seven million! Holy shit." I recalled a story about a Brockton family winning the lottery.

"Yeah, we moved to New York. My father wouldn't hear of it at first, but finally he agreed to accommodate my stepmother's fantasy. I have to give him credit for holding out as long as he did. Now my stepmother has caved and we're back."

"Are they here?"

"They'll be back tomorrow night. Road trip to Atlantic City. Don't worry, though, they won't blow it all." He laughed as though he'd said something funny. "So. Are you ready to party?"

As we left the room, he said, "Good night fishies" and closed the door. He talked about New York as we made our way downstairs, how he loved to stand in front of the first car of the subway and watch the tunnels fly by. He mentioned Central Park, which was close to his apartment, and his favorite arcade on 42nd Street.

"You ever go to Yankee Stadium?"

"Once, on a school trip," he said. "Never to a game. I'm not into baseball."

Not into baseball?

The funnel drinkers were gone. Vinnie picked up the bags and can liners from the floor and shoved them in the trash, then reached into the refrigerator. I hadn't noticed it before, but the light of the frig revealed that Vinnie had attempted to plaster his hair down with Bryclreem or something.

"You need another?" he asked.

"I'm good."

The music blared even more loudly now. People were screaming "The Nuge" and "Nugity" as Ted Nugent pounded the air with *Cat Scratch Fever*. My nostrils were assaulted by cigarette smoke, beer, sweat and perfume as we reached the cellar. The huge room was carpeted in dark blue shag; the walls were made of stucco; thick wooden beams lined the ceiling like a hunting lodge. The room was dark and packed, but I made out a group of kids in front of a large TV. Other groups surrounded a ping pong table and a pinball machine. Guests sat on couches and chairs talking and playing quarters and other drinking games.

"Hey, come on," Vinnie said to a threesome at the bottom of the stairs. "Smoke outside." When they walked toward the doors, he said after them, "And use a cup for the ashes." He shook his head. "What the hell is wrong with people?" He headed toward the TV, so I followed.

I plopped down in a soft comfy chair, grabbed a handful of pretzels from a bowl on a side table and watched the Bruins.

"Hey Jimmy," a kid from my geometry class said as he passed me walking toward the other side of the room.

"Thomas, what's going on?"

"Vinnie," said a heavy kid from a sofa he shared with a few others. "You gonna throw that movie on?"

Vinnie opened the bottom drawer of the TV console and took out a stack of Betamax tapes. "Remind me to return these upstairs."

"Get one in there," the heavy kid insisted.

"Calm down, George," Vinnie shot back. "You horny motherfucker."

"I need me my porn," he said feverishly, like a drug addict. "Gimme porn, gimme porn."

"Stick it in," someone shouted and the group laughed.

"Yeah, stick it in."

With the announcement of porn, kids from the game area drew near and took seats on the remaining chairs surrounding the TV.

"You knew Ben Clancy, didn't you?" It came from a nearby loveseat. His arm was draped around his date's shoulder. If he squeezed any harder her head would've popped off, though she didn't seem to mind. I recognized him as one of the funnel drinkers. "I'm on the swim team. I used to see you guys together."

It was easy to picture this handsome, thickly muscled guy beating up on that Lance kid. "Yeah, we were neighbors. Friends."

Several conversations were going on around us. Vinnie was being pressured to insert the porniest of all the porn movies.

"He was a good kid," he said.

"Yes."

"Hell of a swimmer, too . . ."

"Yep."

"Alright, alright, shut up," Vinnie said, sitting near the TV. "Here we go."

"Yeah, be quiet" a girl said. "We don't want to miss the scintillating dialogue."

The movie opened with a couple arguing. The guy stormed out of the house and checked into a motel. In a few seconds, a knock rattled the door. He opened it to reveal a tall blonde woman, her shirt unbuttoned exposing massive boobs.

"Who are *you*?" the guy said.

"Room service."

"But I ordered the steak."

"I'm all the meat you're going to need."

"Eeeew," said one of the girls.

"Wow," Vinnie said. "This *is* scintillating."

Their clothes were off in five seconds. He was on top of her, kissing her neck, tits, abdomen, then between her legs. We didn't see the actual intercourse, but we saw a lingering shot of her vagina, with its dark bush. Then came a shot of the guy's dick. It was fleeting, but make no mistake: the thing was monstrous. A boa constrictor. How do you walk around with something like that?

I wanted to leave. Sure, the blonde was hot and when the guy started fucking her from behind her tits jiggled up and down like crazy, which was also pretty wonderful. I felt a slight stir between my legs, but deep down I knew it was fake. The passion wasn't real. The sex wasn't real. The whole thing was a scam. Besides, I didn't like the idea of getting a chubbie in a room full of people.

When the scene ended, I left my beer by the chair and walked to the curtained French doors that opened to the backyard patio and the sound of shouting voices. I untucked my jersey and ruffled it to let in the cold air. The smell of marijuana floated to my nostrils. On the edge of the patio next to the bulkhead a small group, boys and girls, sat on beach chairs passing around a joint.

The shouting came from five kids playing basketball, where a net had been erected at the far end of the patio. One of them was Thomas, who bounced me the ball and said, "Your shot, Jimmy" when he saw me step outside. I let it fly. It clanged off the rim.

"Come on, man," Thomas said.

"Not my game," I said, laughing, hands in the air.

"You get two," Thomas said and passed me the ball.

"Nice try, Johnny," said a girl's voice from behind. It was Colleen, the girl who had answered the door. Her sweatshirt had been discarded. She wore a wrinkled long-sleeved tee shirt.

"My name's Jimmy."

"Nice try, Jimmy." She took a healthy swallow from her beer.

"Want a shot?" I said, extending the ball.

"Not my game," she said with a grin before spinning away and strolling into the depths of the yard.

I tossed the ball to Thomas and walked in Colleen's direction. If she questioned me, all I had to say was that it was dark and I wanted to make sure she was okay. She stood at the edge of a large garden. Except for a couple of melon vines, it was pretty much overturned for the season. In one corner, near where we stood, lay a large compost heap, like my father's. On the top were pieces of rotten vegetables—cucumbers, carrots, tomatoes, chunks gouged out by animal teeth. Part of a cantaloupe had split open and shrunken in on itself.

If she wanted me to join her, she gave no indication. "We have a garden at home." What else was I supposed to say? What would Ben have said? What would he have *done*? "You guys have a garden?"

"Let's go over there," she said. "More private."

My stomach dipsy-doodled at the possibility of being alone with her. She led me farther into the backyard, behind a large oak tree where the lights from the house couldn't reach. The fingers of her free hand rested on my ribs as she leaned in for a kiss. Her lips were soft and wet. Who was this girl? An angel sent from heaven? A mirage? Her tongue tasted of beer. There was something else, smoky and stale, as though she'd taken a hit from that joint back there. It tasted rank. I was about to pull away when her hand slid down my belly to my crotch. She could have tasted like a tire, I wasn't about to pull away now. My dick expanded like a long balloon pumped with helium.

She maneuvered me against the tree. Bark dug into my back. She deftly unbuttoned my pants, especially considering one hand still clutched a beer. I felt my fly lowered. Her fingers touched my dick. Ah God, it felt amazing. No way is she from heaven, I thought. Not even heaven feels this good. I remembered Lou Gehrig's *I'm the luckiest man on the face of the earth* speech. Bullshit, I thought. *I'm* the luckiest man on the face of the earth.

Her fingers brushed my balls as she stroked up and down. What if she could tell that my nuts were fake? Let's face it, this wasn't the first time for Colleen. Maybe she could tell the difference. Maybe they were too hard or too soft or too heavy or too light.

Just like that, my dick took a nap. The thing went limp! What the hell. The hormones weren't working! I pictured them hiding behind the fake balls, avoiding her touch. Abandoned, just when I needed them most.

"You okay?"

I looked at her worried, pretty face. Felt her hand still stroking my dick. How could this be? I kissed her again. I slid my hands down her back and felt the swell of her ass. Come on, testosterone, do your thing. I wanted to enjoy this moment, to wallow in the fact that this girl wanted me, but I couldn't help wonder if I got stuck with a bad batch. Had the pharmacy bungled? Were there expiration dates? I couldn't ignore the fact that the shit in me wasn't natural. It wasn't organic. It wasn't *mine*.

Colleen stopped kissing, but kept the motion going with her hand. What a gamer. Hey, maybe it wasn't my fault. Shouldn't Colleen take some responsibility? Maybe she should use two hands. God forbid she should put the beer down for a minute.

"What's wrong?"

"What do you mean?"

"Well . . ." She pointed with her chin toward my limp penis, which she still held, and blew a strand of hair out of her eyes. The poor girl was wiped.

What's wrong, she'd said. She was right. Something was wrong. With me. I thought of the garden, the rotten tomatoes and cantaloupes. I pictured gnats and flies hovering around the overripe mess of it all. My balls.

I zippered my fly, buttoned my pants.

"That's all right," she said as I fled toward the house. "I'll give it another whirl."

I ran through the French doors, dodged my way through the crowd to the stairs and grabbed my coat off the kitchen chair. I didn't call my folks; the last thing I wanted to do was linger at the house. I just bolted. I let a bus pass on Pleasant Street. I wanted to walk, to think, to wonder what the fuck was wrong with me. The debacle replayed itself in my head. Everything started out fine. I kissed Colleen. I got hard, just like I got hard when I masturbated.

And boy did I masturbate. All it took for me to get turned on was the cover of one of Mother's *Good Housekeepings*. Models wearing conservative blouses, but open at the neck revealing throat and a smidgen of collarbone. Sometimes they wore sweaters, snug enough to see the rise of their breasts. Mother kept plenty of issues in a wicker basket in the corner of the bathroom. Sometimes I stumbled upon a *Glamour.* SCORE!! With ads in the back for breast enlargements and hair removal and sex therapy guides there was enough material to jerk off twice in one sitting.

I could have asked my father what was wrong. But it would have been another awkward conversation. Like the guy hadn't suffered enough awkward conversations. I could call Cliff. Talk about awkward. Since he was responsible for this whole thing in the first place. But still. I could broach it with him. Ben would have been the best person. Ben, expert on all things girls.

Something occurred to me. I stopped. There was no traffic on the dark street, but even if there were, I wouldn't have noticed. I bent over in panic. Would Colleen tell anyone? Were people already talking about me at the party? I pictured Monday morning. Smirks behind cupped hands from the nice kids; outright laughter from the assholes. One thing I knew for sure. Whacking off would be my soul source of sexual pleasure from now on. I was flat-out, sure-as-shit done with girls. *Adios. Finito. Kaput.*

**

"You're home," Mother said. She sat at the kitchen table reading last week's *Parade*. It took her forever to read the Sunday papers. She read practically every article.

"I caught a bus." She wouldn't have liked that I walked all the way home. It was almost five miles. And through downtown.

"Cliff's coming tomorrow. He's bringing his girlfriend. They should be in time for lunch. We finally get to meet Marie." She sipped from a can of Tab. "They'll probably stay over since Monday's Columbus Day."

What a coincidence. Less than an hour ago I'd decided to give Cliff a call. Even better now. Tomorrow we'd be able to talk in person.

"How was the party?"

"It was fun," I said, starting toward the stairs and the privacy of my room.

"Are you sure?" she said, turning to get a look at my face.

"Of course." Damn, I thought, how does she always know?

Under the covers, I thought more about losing the hard-on. Maybe I was just nervous. It was the first time a girl ever held my penis. I slipped my hand into my underwear. I thought of Colleen's lips on mine and my penis immediately hardened.

**

Marie was a petite stunner. I stood behind my folks as everyone exchanged greetings. When she kissed Mother at the door her exotic almond eyes crinkled at the edges. She bussed cheeks with my father.

"My brother Jimmy," Cliff said.

We exchanged a hug. I smelled shampoo and gum.

"It's so nice to meet you finally," she said.

Mother took her coat. A ribbed green turtleneck jersey clung to her body—a body both boyish and unmistakably feminine. She ran her fingers through her fine shiny hair as we trooped into the kitchen.

"Oh, look at this," she exclaimed.

Marie was Armenian, her last name Kapoian, which had given Mother an opportunity to visit the middle eastern food store that had just opened up next to the barber shop on North Main Street.

The table was filled with containers of food I'd never seen before.

"What do we have here anyway?" my father said.

Marie started to answer, but Mother pointed to the containers as we all took seats around the table. "There's hummus and tabouleh and lavash bread and Syrian bread."

She'd enjoyed laying out the smorgasbord and was having a good time now showing it off. It occurred to me that she'd never have the pleasure of preparing a meal for my girlfriend.

"What's this stuff?" My father picked up one of the containers filled with a purply-brown dip.

"It's called babbaganoush," Mother said.

"Ba ba ba ba ba Barino," I sang. *Welcome Back Kotter* had been off the air for a couple of years, but I still remembered all the episodes. When I saw that Marie was staring at me, smiling, I was sorry I opened my mouth.

"Smells good," Dad said. "It goes on the bread?"

"That's right," Mother said, then took her seat at the table after laying out a tray of olives and cubes of feta cheese.

"So, how'd you meet?" my father said.

"At an event co-sponsored by both our departments," Cliff said, dipping a wedge of Syrian bread into one of the containers.

"What are you studying, Marie?" Mother said.

"HRTA."

Mother looked at her, waiting for more information.

"What's that stand for?" I said.

"Hotel, Restaurant and Travel Administration." Her features were sharp, a little on the bony side—a narrow nose and high defined cheekbones. Her skin wasn't white, not white like ours. Not black either, of course. It fell in between, like silky chocolate milk, heavy on the milk.

"Oh, I declared another major," Cliff said.

"What about Food Science?" Mother said, alarmed.

"A double major."

"Oh," mother said.

"In what?" my father said.

"Business Administration."

"When were you going to tell us?" Mother said.

"I'm telling you now," he said, laughing. "It starts next semester. It'll keep me at school an extra year."

Dad asked about the business program and their classes. We ate as we talked, mostly with our fingers. Tabouleh kept falling out of holes in my Syrian bread. The tastes were new and delicious, grainy, creamy, mild, spicy.

"I'll make up the couch downstairs," Mother said to Marie. "It's plenty comfortable."

"I'll sleep downstairs," Cliff said. "Marie can take my bed. Don't worry, Ma, I won't sneak upstairs for any funny business."

Mother laughed, but obligatorily, I thought.

"No hanky-panky," Cliff went on.

Yeah yeah, we get it. The poor slob was trying to show off for his girl. *Look how funny I am, look how at ease I am with my family.* Stop making a fool of yourself.

Besides, who was he to joke about having sex in the room next to mine after what I'd been through last night? He didn't know what happened, of course, but he wasn't stupid. He knew about my balls. He knew I was a hormone junky for life. He should have known that I'd have some awkwardness in the sex department. But did he care? Oh no, he's just going to joke—boast really—about fucking his laser hot girlfriend while I'm next door.

"So, how you been, bro?" Cliff said.

Bro? I thought. "Um . . ." Well, I can't get an erection. Let's see, what else . . . ?

"Everything good?" he persisted.

"Yes . . ."

"You're from Vermont, isn't that right?" Mother said.

Marie nodded. "That's right." Her black hair was parted in the middle, a straight line to her scalp and she had an adorable tick of tucking it behind her ears.

"Do you ski?" my father asked.

"Absolutely. You ski?"

My father looked surprised. "Ah, no, actually."

"I told Cliff I'd take him to Killington first chance I get."

"You'll be careful, I hope," Mother said.

"Of course," Marie said. "Bunny slope all day, if necessary."

My eyes shifted to Cliff sitting next to her and thought, Man, this kid has everything. He's away from home, doing whatever he wants. And doing it with a gorgeous, obviously intelligent and down to earth knockout. And hey, why not. Yeah, we had our problems. But all told he was a good brother, who even wrote letters from time to time. They were lame and superficial, usually about the weather or a class, but at least he reached out. He was a good son, who called home once a week. So he deserved whatever fortune came his way. Hat's off, douche bag. No hard feelings. No hard nothing.

After lunch Cliff asked me to join him in his bedroom. Marie was downstairs with our folks. "Mom and Dad are going out tonight, right?" he said.

"Dinner with Jack and Nancy, I think."

"You got plans?"

My guess was that he wanted the three of us—me, him and Marie—to do something together. Have the little brother get to know the new girlfriend. Especially considering all we'd been through. Maybe dinner at Tip Top, someplace casual like that. We'd be able to delve a bit; we wouldn't be saddled with the parents.

"With Mom and Dad gone . . ." A nervous edginess took hold of his voice. He pushed the door closed. "We were thinking we might have the house to ourselves."

"You're kicking me out?" I was an idiot not to have seen it coming.

"Don't put it like that."

"How then?" I was feeling it rise. I wasn't sure what *it* was, but it was a dark motherfucker, dark and dense and exploding out of my chest in a hellish blaze. "You're up at UMass all this time, you can fuck her whenever you want."

"Don't say that."

"You can't stay off her for one night? Is that what it's like when you get a girlfriend? Me, I wouldn't know." The blaze kept coiling and rising, fearless. "How can you even bring this shit up after what you did to me? How can you even bring her here at all? Flaunting her. Parading her around me like a, like a model, like a whore."

"Hey." He was mad, but not mad enough. Not yet.

"What if I don't leave? Like that's going to stop you? Probably just be a little quieter, that's all. Keep your hand over her mouth."

"Hey . . ." he said, more calmly now, his palms open in front of him. "I didn't mean anything—"

"You know what I was doing last night while you were getting your dick sucked? I was—"

He reached for the door and opened it to leave, but I slammed it closed.

"No, no, no," I pressed, "you're going to like this. It's hilarious."

"Everything okay up there?" Mother said from below.

"I was standing against a tree while some girl was trying to give me a hand job."

He reached for the door again, but I stood in front of it. He shifted from foot to foot.

"I say *trying* because no matter how hard she yanked, my thing just hung there like a . . . like a . . ." I tried to come up with something disgusting to make him even more uncomfortable, more sickened. But I just stood there silent in front of him, my head all of a sudden empty and tired, its contents overrun by hate and envy.

He stepped gingerly toward me and started to extend his arms. The guy wanted to give me a fucking hug, of all things. My arm flung out before I realized what was happening. My fist landed to the left of his nose. His head snapped back and hit the door. My knuckles burned. Blood sprayed; gushed down his lips and chin, down the front of his shirt.

"HELP," I screamed. "MOM, HELP." I took a tee shirt that he'd hung on the knob and pressed it against his nose.

"Ouch!" Cliff shouted. "Fuck."

"Direct pressure," I shouted back. "That's what they tell ya."

"Fuck," he said again.

Blood dripped on the carpet. Spots dotted the wall. Mother was going to hang me. We all gathered around Cliff as he sat on the toilet seat, the tee shirt still pressed against his face. "It was an accident," he said.

They all looked at me at the same time. My father eyed the ripped skin of my knuckles.

"Sorry," was all I said. It was meant for all of them, but I looked at Marie when I spoke.

"It was an accident," Cliff repeated. "He didn't mean it. I tripped, hit the door."

My parents weren't interested in the details. They were just glad it was over. They studied Cliff's nose closely and determined it wasn't broken. I didn't wait on a course of action from Mother. I hustled downstairs, mixed up some hot soapy water and climbed back up the stairs with the bucket and a scrub brush.

My parents decided the fracas wasn't serious enough to alter their plans. As I scrubbed, I knew I'd have to find something to do away from the house that night. What option did I have? I punched the guy in the nose. I owed him one.

I made calls. The plan was for a bunch of kids from the team to meet at Westgate and walk around the mall, unless we could sneak into *The Evil Dead*. Cliff was waiting when I got home.

"Can you breathe through that thing?" I nodded toward the band-aid that covered his nose.

"It's fine. You get a ride home?"

"Yeah," I said, kicking off my shoes. "You cool that I'm here now? Want me to walk around the block a few times?"

"Shut up," he said. "I just wanted to say I'm sorry, all right? I was wrong to ask you to leave. It's just that . . . being with her alone in a house in a real bed . . . Well, it's not the same as sneaking a few minutes alone in a dorm room. You know?"

"Well, I hope you . . . whatever . . . had fun."

"We didn't do anything. The mood wasn't exactly conducive."

"My fault," I said. "Sorry." I hung my jacket on the coat rack. Cliff started to walk away. "She's really . . . Um . . . I like her. She seems really nice."

"She is. She's great."

I moved to walk past him, but he held his ground in the narrow doorway that led to the kitchen.

"Whatever you're going through . . . If you want to talk . . ."

"What are you talking about?" I said.

"Last night. With that girl . . ."

"Oh," I laughed. I didn't want to say anything now, not with Marie waiting. Maybe some other time. "I was just fucking around. I got so mad I would have said anything to piss you off."

"Really?" he said dubiously, stepping into the kitchen.

"Where's Marie anyway?"

"Downstairs. We're watching a tape if you want to join us."

"Yeah, go ahead, I'm just going to grab a drink."

A gulped a glass of apple juice and climbed down the stairs. They sat together on one of the sofas. Marie waved.

"Hiya," I said. "You know, I'm kind of tired. I'm just going to head up, I think."

"You sure?" Marie said. "We'll rewind it. No prob."

"No, I'm good. And I'm sorry about . . ." I gestured to my nose. "Sorry about everything."

**

Early the next week I visited Dr. Young. I hadn't seen Joanne in months. She hopped up when I stepped through the door and came around the glass partition to give me a hug. Dr. Young was almost ready. She told me to take a seat in his office.

Before she left, I said, "Um...How much is it?"

"What's that?"

"My appointment today." I brought all the money I had.

"Don't worry, silly. Your father's insurance covers it."

"I'd rather my folks didn't know if that's okay."

"You're here for a follow-up?"

"No, just to talk. You know . . . personal stuff."

"I'm sure we'll work it out."

I was nervous. I wasn't sure how to start. So when he sat behind his desk and leaned forward I had nothing to say. He asked about my parents, then after another lengthy pause asked how he could help.

"I'm afraid something might be wrong."

"Wrong how?" He scratched his hairy chin.

"I just want to be normal."

"You don't think you're normal?"

"I want to be . . . You know, like my brother. Be able to, to kiss a girl without feeling like a freak."

He looked surprised. "You feel that way?"

"I was at a party last weekend . . ." I told him about Colleen, the aborted hand job, tried my best to articulate what I was thinking. "A normal kid would have . . . you know."

"Ejaculated."

"Don't you think?"

"First of all, whether you ejaculated or not, you're a normal fifteen-year-old boy."

"You say that, but . . . I mean . . . I know I appear normal . . . but . . ."

The phone rang. He picked it up quickly. "No, not now. And Jo. No interruptions, okay?" He placed down the phone and leaned forward again. "You're going to hear this a lot, but it's true. The most powerful sex organ we have, by far, is the brain. Until it gets out of the way, the body will never respond."

That made sense on some level, I guessed, but realistically, how could the brain get out of the way?

"What were you thinking about while it occurred?"

I thought about the encounter, how great it felt. Then I remembered something else. "I kept imagining the hormones flowing through me. I thought about her too, but the hormone stuff took over."

"Why were you focused on that, you think?"

"I don't know. I can't filter what comes into my head. I can't . . . you know, suppress my thoughts. Once I realized something was wrong, forget it, it was over. I kept wondering, Why isn't anything happening. And the longer nothing happened, the more anxious I got, the more freaked out."

"You have to get out of your own way. Just let your body respond to how it feels. To how attractive she is. The intimacy."

Easier said than done, I thought.

"The most important thing you should know is that you are absolutely fine. You're healthy. And don't worry about being so-called normal. Just be yourself. My advice to you—man to man—is to attend another party, find this girl and give it another go. That's between me and you," he said smiling. "And it may not work out the next time, or the time after that. But it will work out. You just can't be afraid to try."

I nodded, but I knew it wasn't going to happen.

"I should ask, though. Have you recently ejaculated?"

"Yes."

"It feels fine? No pain?"

"No, it feels good. But I think it would feel better if another person were involved."

He laughed out loud, a quick unexpected bark. "I think you'll discover that to be the case." He walked me down the hallway into the empty waiting room. "One last thing," he said. "I'm not an expert, you understand. On the psychology. But I know plenty of people who are. So if you ever want—"

"A psychiatrist?"

"Well . . ." he nodded. "A therapist. Someone to talk to. To help you understand that you're not alone."

I didn't need a therapist. I knew the score. Just like when I was afraid to shower with my teammates. If I could overcome that, I could overcome this.

10. Heartaches

I started sophomore year on the JV team as the right fielder. I hinted to Coach Hannah that I wanted to play center. The first time he said, "Duly noted." The second time he nodded and walked away. Toward the end of the season, Coach Walsh pulled me aside and said Barney Conley, our varsity centerfielder, twisted an ankle and I'd be working out with the Varsity squad.

Something inside me must have leaped through my skin because Coach Walsh said, "Don't get excited, he's day to day. You might not even get in a game."

I played it cool for Coach Walsh, but I was thrilled. When I got home, they were the first words out of my mouth. My folks were ecstatic. The next day I geared up and ran to the Varsity field. After drills, it was time for batting practice and we took our positions. Somebody else was headed toward center. I heard Coach Walsh from the infield.

"LaPlante, you're in right."

"I thought . . ."

Coach Walsh jogged to me in shallow center. "Problem?"

"I thought since Conley was out . . . You know . . . I was in."

"You *are* in. You're in right."

"Got it." I turned promptly and started toward my position.

"Hey."

I turned again. He hadn't budged.

"C'mere."

I walked back. He placed both his hands on my shoulders. "I want you to understand something." Grey whiskers speckled the brown; his mustache needed trimming. "You're never gonna play centerfield. Not on a serious team. You're just not fast enough. Besides, you got a cannon for an arm. And cannons belong in right. That's the law."

Barney's foot would take seven days to heal, which translated to four games. I could tell Coach Walsh was uptight. He didn't like the idea of a sophomore on Varsity, but he had no choice. Our outfield was thin.

In the three days before my first Varsity game, the outfielders—especially Barney with his hobbled ankle—took me under their wings. Most of my time, though, was spent with Coach Walsh on batting and hand-eye coordination drills—handball, suicide style; tapping live pitching by holding the head of the bat out over the plate; tons of soft toss.

"You're gonna be in a little over your head," Coach Walsh said as he studied my soft toss sessions, adjusted my stance over and over. "Some of these kids have already been drafted. You're gonna see true fastballs, breaking balls, sliders."

I caught a quick glimpse at him between swings. He must have seen my fear.

"You'll adjust," he said. "Just stay within yourself. Don't try to do too much. Keep relaxed, focused."

In those four games, I shocked the world, at least myself—a .320 average, seven hits, three RBI and two outfield assists. I'd actually competed with upperclassmen; not only competed, but rocked. Upon Barney's return, Deke Monroe, a senior and the everyday right fielder who had subbed for Barney, was relegated to the fourth outfielder slot. Eight games remained; he didn't start a single one. If Deke resented me for stealing his position he never showed it. I still felt horrible. I didn't want to be a usurper. After practice one day I expressed my concerns to Barney.

"What do you care?" Barney Conley was the skinniest person in the world who could generate enough power to hit a baseball 380 feet. He also ran as fast as a greyhound. He was a senior, B.C.

bound. Full scholarship, so I'd heard.

"Well, he's a teammate. If it happened to me I'd go crazy."

"Deke don't care about baseball. Don't you know about Deke?"

"Not really." I knew he always stayed behind to help clean up the equipment after practices. But he was a couple years older than me so we weren't exactly friends.

"He's some kind of genius. President of the National Science Club, going to MIT. Gonna make newfangled airplanes or something. He'll be richer than all of us combined in a few years."

I wasn't sure what Deke being rich had to do with anything, but it was nice playing right field knowing the guy I booted off the diamond didn't care.

By the end of the season my average rose to .331, with seventeen hits, two homeruns, ten RBI and four outfield assists. I didn't break any records, but I was assured by more than one coach that my future on Varsity would be secure.

**

American Legion games started as the high school season drew to a close. They held a kickoff gathering at the veterans hall on Beaumont Avenue, near Dad's post office. On a standing board at the entrance of the parking lot, white plastic letters read, "Welcome American Legion Baseball." It was a ramshackle little building, like a one room schoolhouse from the old west, except for a rectangular addition with darker, less weathered shingles.

Kids and parents from the team were invited. It was kind of weird to see the Brockton High coaches in a social setting, drinking, goofing off. Coach Walsh even laughed once. Eventually everyone took seats at round tables covered with paper tablecloths. While some guy gave a welcoming speech, staff brought in pizzas and salads and lined them on a buffet table. A banner overhead read, "Donated by Cape Cod Café Pizza."

After we ate, speeches were given. At one point, I walked down a corridor toward the bathroom. Smoke drifted through the doorway of a barroom, completely separate from the function hall. A neon Pabst sign lit up blue and white from behind the bar. The Red Sox game was on a TV suspended at the far end of the room. I waited for Ned Martin or Ken Harrelson to give the score.

A familiar figure sat slumped at the bar. I took a few steps closer. Coach Wicker looked about the same as he did when I played Little League—his hair worn in a ponytail, a paunch bulging over his belt. His feet hung from the stool like a little kid's, not long enough to reach the foot rail. One elbow rested on the bar, with his head in his hand. The other hand held a pilsner. He looked in my direction as I drew nearer.

I hadn't seen him in so long, I was excited to say hello. No, not just hello, but, *Hey, look at me, I'm playing American Legion ball.* Our eyes met, but he shifted his body away so that he faced the dartboards. He leaned on the bar with his elbow again, but it slid off the edge. I thought he was going to fall to the floor, but he caught himself just in time. Two old guys at a table, both wearing trucker caps, looked toward him, then back to the TV.

"Coach Wicker." I was standing right next to him. Maybe he was here for the banquet, but had got caught up in the Sox game. "Are you coaching AL this summer?"

He turned his body toward me. His eyes glanced in my direction, but didn't fix on mine.

"You were my Little League coach. Probably don't remember."

"I remember."

I caught a whiff of his boozy breath.

"Fat kid. We ran together."

I could have done without the *fat kid*, but I recalled with a smile the way he urged me to run harder around the Brookfield diamonds, to keep my feet moving. "That's right. Lost weight, though," I added. "So are you coaching American Legion?"

He took a deep swig. The empty glass thudded against the bar.

"Little League?"

He slowly shook his head. "Nope . . . Not me."

"I'm playing AL. My high school coach's team. The Warriors."

Coach Wicker grimaced into his beer. "Hey Dave, another here, a shot, too."

The bartender brought the two glasses. Coach Wicker downed the shot with a flick of the wrist. "Go get 'em, kid," he said into the pilsner before taking a gulp. "Go be a warrior."

**

"Know your symbols and valences." Mr. Czupowski's words were tinged with a Polish accent. He had boxed for Poland in the 1952 Helsinki Olympics. During lectures he sometimes regaled us with boxing stories. Now, though, all he cared about were his symbols and valences. "Study them. Remember them. If you know your symbols and valences, I'll pass you. Because you will be able to solve chemical equations. If you do this, you win. If you don't, you lose."

Well, it looked like I might lose because I couldn't keep more than three or four symbols and valences in my head. I made cheat sheets and taped them inside my chemistry book, in my locker, on my desk at home. Some of the symbols made sense, like aluminum (Al), carbon (C), silicon (Si). But who came up with making the symbol for potassium K? Or silver Ag? Or Sodium Na?

In the end, though, it didn't matter if the symbols didn't make sense because I needed to maintain a C average to play baseball. Whatever it took, that's what I'd do.

Mr. Czupowski agreed to meet me in the Science office on Wednesdays after school. The extra sessions made the classes easier, but what I liked best was checking out the old faded newspaper clippings and pictures that Mr. Czupowski had tacked to the bulletin board next to his desk. Most of them were in Polish. The pictures, though, were riveting. His body was chiseled, his eyes fierce and angry, his arms up and ready for attack, fists closed tight. It was strange to see the old man sitting next to the ancient photos. I kept looking back and forth. Sure, he was still in good shape for his age and still had a full head of hair, but no one would have recognized the teacher and the boxer as the same man.

After each session, he looked me square in the eye and said, "Do you know your symbols and valences?"

"Getting there," I said.

One day as I was leaving I felt a strange sensation in my chest. In the hallway, my heart raced, as though I'd just run an inside-the-park home run. I felt sweat on my neck. I pushed through a door into the stairwell and sat on the top step. After a moment, I stood up, but immediately felt dizzy and had to sit back down. Should I lay down? I thought. What if I died here and no one noticed until tomorrow?

"Are you all right?"

I lifted my head. Sondra Clarke, a senior in my Algebra class, was climbing the stairs. "Chest feels funny," I said.

"Can you stand?"

She helped me up and by the time we reached the bottom of the stairs I felt better.

"You should go to the nurse," Sondra said.

"Yeah," I said, remembering my stress tests and Dr. Aranofsky.

The medical assistant behind the counter asked me to wait. Sondra sat by my side.

"You don't have to stick around if you have a class."

"Are you kidding? I'd rather sit with you than sit in Mr. Dracut's class." Her small mouth broke into a smile. She had fine, fly-away blond hair and fair skin that looked like it might burn easily in the sun. She was a pipsqueak, a cute pipsqueak.

The nurse called me in. Sondra said bye and started to leave.

"Sondra," I said.

She turned to me in the doorway.

"Hold up," I said. "Dracut's going to want a pass."

I told the medical assistant how Sondra had helped me. She signed a hall pass and handed it over. I gave it to Sondra.

"Thanks," she said.

"Thank *you*."

When I told the nurse my symptoms, she called Mother, who arrived in fifteen minutes. We picked up my father at the post office and drove to Dr. Aranofsky's office. I thought back to my last stress test, which was uneventful. In fact, I hadn't even thought about my heart since Dr. Aranofsky took me off the Inderal.

The three of us sat in front of his desk in the small office. His hair had grown bushy on the sides. I told him what happened. "It was kind of scary. The suddenness of it."

"Yes, it can be scary, especially if you've never felt it before. But it's not dangerous."

"That's definite?" I said.

"You've been my patient a long time. And when we see someone over the course of years, we have the luxury of seeing the big picture. We've talked about it before, the supraventricular tachycardia. It's common. Now, if you feel these palpitations again tomorrow and the next day and they start to last longer, then we'll talk some more. But I don't think that will be the case."

My parents seemed at ease; I got the feeling they had spoken to the doctor while the nurse had taken my blood pressure.

"I read you can die from it," I said.

"Where?"

"Library at school."

"Do you have the article?"

"They don't let you take out reference books."

"My guess is that you were reading about *ventricular* tachycardia . . . But not yours. Not SVT."

**

The next day in Math class before the bell Sondra sat at an empty chair next to mine.

"What happened with the nurse?"

"I got this heart thing—"

Her eyebrows rose, surprised.

"It's nothing, really, but my mother wanted to be safe so we saw the doctor."

She smiled. Even brighter than yesterday's smile. She returned to her seat in the second row. We spent some lunches together in the cafeteria. Occasionally we went to the movies, but usually with other kids. Whenever we were alone together I remembered the girl from Vincent's party. Don't forget the rules, I told myself on every date. Don't get too close. Kissing's okay, but that's it. Everything will be fine as long as your dick doesn't end up in her hand. No way—NO WAY—would that happen again. Of course, thinking like that threw me into a tizzy because in her hand was exactly where

I wanted my dick to be, not to mention her mouth, but God, that was too much to even contemplate.

One night we saw each other at the autumn dance. We kissed, but her lips felt timid against mine, so I thought maybe she wasn't interested. All signs had indicated that she liked me. Maybe it was my lips that were timid, afraid of where the kiss might lead.

I hoped it was hers, though. As sweet as she was, the chief reason I spent time with her was because it was what people expected. I'd been going out with my teammates on Saturday nights and I would have looked ridiculous if I stood there at parties or wherever and just watched my buddies try to hook up.

With Sondra around, I looked like one of the guys. Even if she wasn't around, I could always claim I was being faithful. Sure, I wanted to take her in my arms and give her a long passionate kiss and then some, but rules were rules.

The scariest part of this whole thing was that she'd be graduating in June, which meant no more buffer. I'd have to start over, find someone else. I knew I was being a jerk. She was kind-hearted and adorable; she could have had lots of guys. And here I was using her, stringing her along. She deserved better. Maybe we could just be friends. Would she go for that? But I needed everyone to think we were more than friends. And deep down, of course, I *wanted* to be more than friends. The whole thing was a confusing mess.

On a Saturday night in January we were at a movie at Westgate. She took a gulp from the pail-sized cup of Coke, then rested her hand on my thigh near the knee. I thought of our weak kiss the night of the dance. We hadn't kissed since, so this hand-on-thigh thing was a surprise. This changed everything. Well, maybe it wasn't such a big deal, since her hand was close to the knee. But would she move it toward my upper thigh, or, God forbid, my *inner* thigh?

It moved. Her hand slid slightly upward, I was sure of it. No, not sure, not a hundred percent. I looked down. The hand still seemed the same distance from the knee as before. My mind was playing tricks. Either way, I put my hand on hers to keep the damn thing in place. Which was idiotic because it signaled that I was into touching her as much as she was into touching me.

Jesus, enough with the hand. I didn't even know what was going on in the movie. Why was Paul Newman drinking so much? And why was the mean judge out to get him?

We held hands leaving the theater, all the way to the car. I'd gotten my license a couple of weeks before; it was only the third time I'd driven the car without one of my parents along.

"Want to go to D.W?" she said as I turned onto Westgate Drive.

"The park?" Did she want to neck?

"It's early. The moon's almost full."

Shouldn't we wait until the moon is truly full? I wanted to say. Wouldn't that be more romantic?

"If you don't want too . . " She sounded disappointed.

"No, no . . ."

I didn't want her to be upset. Besides, it wouldn't hurt to sit and park for a while. Maybe we'd kiss a little. Maybe she'd let me feel her boobs. There wasn't much there, but it would still be nice to feel what she had. If things got too hot and heavy, maybe I'd be able to distract her with the ducklings and baby swans.

I took a left into the park at the Oak Street entrance and pulled into an empty parking area that overlooked Upper Porter Pond. I shut the engine off, leaving on the heat. She reached for the window handle.

"What are you doing?"

"My parents always say to crack the window when a car's idling. Because of carbon monoxide."

I nodded. "Good thinking."

She leaned her back against her door and looked at me at the wheel. "You like the movie?"

"Sad."

"It was neat seeing all those Boston landmarks. I've been to some of those places."

"Yeah, that was cool."

She leaned forward and touched my leg with both hands, then leaned closer. I leaned toward her until our lips met. She wasn't timid now. Her hands were on either side of my face, then around the back of my neck. Everything seemed hot—her breath, the air from the vents, her fingertips on my skin, reaching under my collar. Her mouth opened wide. Mine too. My penis bulged painfully against my jeans. I was glad it was hard, that's what was supposed to happen, but I was still afraid it might collapse once it was set free. Remember the rules, I thought. Remember Vincent's party. Don't relive that nightmare.

She yanked my shirt out of the back of my pants. I felt her hands move up my back, on my shoulder blades, then my chest, her thumbs on my nipples, rubbing them in circles. Her hands moved incredibly fast. Suddenly they were tugging at her own shirt.

Fuck it, I thought. Just do it. She wants to. You want to. Nothing else mattered. I thought of what Dr. Young had said, about keeping your brain out of the way, just let your body respond. Exactly. I unhooked my belt and pants button. We kissed devouringly, our tongues battling, as she reached for my fly.

I pulled my hips away, no longer hard. What the fuck? Had I thought of Colleen? Dr. Young appeared in my mind again. What an asshole! How could he know what I was going through? How could anyone? I mean, Jesus Christ, it didn't matter that Sondra Clarke was about to be naked in my car, that tonight she wanted to fuck, or something very close to it. As long as that night with Colleen had happened—it didn't matter how long ago—my dick didn't stand a chance.

This wasn't even my fault. I didn't want her hand on my knee in the theater. I didn't ask for that. I didn't ask to hold hands walking to the parking lot. I certainly didn't want to come to the park and deal with this shit. This was Sondra's bright idea.

Her fingers grappled with my zipper. I grabbed her forearms and pushed her away, harder than I meant. Her back slammed against the passenger door.

"Aw, ouch!" She grabbed her back. "What the hell?"

I hurt her! I reached out to hold her, but she pressed herself against the door. She was afraid. "Please," I panted, "don't be scared." I held out my hands and gently touched her shoulders. Her body softened in my arms as I brought her toward me, her head against my chest. "I'm so sorry, Sondra. I didn't mean to hurt you." I rubbed her back softly up and down.

"I was just surprised."

I continued caressing her back for a long while. I wanted to smooth the pain away, take care of this fragile girl.

Her embrace tightened. "Your heartbeat," she said. "It's still pounding. Sounds neat." She suddenly pulled away, her face filled with concern. "Oh no, it's not your heart, is it? Is that why you got mad?"

"No, no, I wasn't mad, it's just . . ." I didn't know what to say. How could I possibly explain that I didn't want to mess around with this beautiful friendly caring girl? "Maybe we can just sit here a while."

"Let the windows defog," she said, smiling.

"Right, right."

We sat there. I wanted to hold her, but wasn't sure what she wanted. After a few seconds she nestled under my arm and we stared out the windshield. I wasn't sure if she wanted an explanation. I wanted to tell her the truth. *So one day I was in the backyard when my brother grabbed a shovel* . . . I couldn't. Sondra was the nicest girl in Brockton High, but even she might have run screaming from the car if I told that tale.

Maybe we'd overcome this. Maybe we'd become the kind of friends that stay up all night on the phone. One day, I thought, I might even tell her the truth. Sondra Clarke, my new best friend. My new Ben.

When I dropped her off in front of her house we kissed briefly on the lips.

"See you Monday," she said.

I waited until she was inside before pulling away.

We talked the following week at school, but neither of us brought up the subject of another date or even getting together with mutual friends. About a month later, though, we were walking down the hall after Math when she stopped before taking her usual right turn to her Con Law class in the Yellow Building. "Glen and Patty were thinking of getting a group together for a ski trip in a few weeks out to the Berkshires. What do you think?"

We'd be alone. Sharing a room. Maybe even a bed! I couldn't even handle being alone with her in a car, imagine a bed.

"I'll be in practices by then." It was a relief not to have to lie, but she looked hurt.

"Okay, I'll let them know."

She seemed fine with that, but as she turned away her face hardened with anger.

**

With homework done for the night, I spread all the papers out on the kitchen table. Baseball season was around the corner. Time to organize. Get prepared. My father climbed the stairs from the playroom. He bent down in front of the refrigerator and came up biting into a green apple.

"Want one?" he said, mouth full.

I scowled.

"Wha?"

"Too tart."

"Tart's good," he said, ambling over to the table. "What's all this?"

"Baseball stuff. Breakdowns of kids in my conference." I fanned the pages so he could see.

"You keep track of what every player hits? Every at bat?"

"Sort of. I use scorecards, like the coach, but I add notes, like the count, where he hit the ball. If he's an aggressive runner, I'll make a note of that."

"How far back do they go?"

"Two years."

"You guys just don't go out there and play?"

"Most do."

"Do you give your classes this much attention?"

"School's going good."

"Yeah?"

"Yep. Really."

As he walked away, I started the business of sorting and three-hole punching the papers, then slipping them into my black binder.

**

In spring sports like baseball it was critical to excel during junior year in order to be taken seriously by college coaches and scouts. If players peaked senior year, it was too late and too bad. Applications had been due in February. Players had already been scouted. Decisions had already been made.

By the end of the Brockton High season, although my defensive numbers were strong, my offense was mediocre. I sprayed the ball around pretty good and made decent wood, but most of the time the ball held up too long, couldn't find a gap. My RBIs were slightly down from last year, which was horrible considering last year I'd only played half the season on Varsity.

Thank God for American Legion. Something clicked. It was as though the high school season was merely practice for AL. And as I whacked the ball throughout that summer, I thought it might work out for the better, what with colleges freer to send more scouting personnel during the summer months.

During a game, a buddy on the bench nudged me and nodded toward a stranger on the stands. "You think he's one?" Every game, men we'd never seen before appeared on the bleachers and we all thought the same thing: What school is he from? Think he's from the pros? What team?

Sometimes the scouts took away our guesswork by wearing school logos on shirts and hats. It made us jittery at first. Coach Walsh had warned us early on: Yes, we needed to impress them with our individual talents, but under no circumstances should their appearance distract us from the task at hand. How could we not get distracted, though? These people determined our futures, our lives.

In the locker room after a game, a few players started talking about their scholarships, common this time of year.

"I'm gonna get a full boat," Jackson McCallister, a decent infielder, bragged.

"Fuck you," someone responded, "you'll get a partial if you're lucky."

"A mini partial," Duffy Simons said. Duffy was a senior, very talented, but lazy at practices. He was off to New Mexico in August.

Everyone stopped talking when Toby Monroe came into the locker room. He'd finally found out yesterday that Vermont wasn't interested. That was his last hope for a major program. He'd already heard from Dartmouth, Maine, Virginia and Seton Hall. He must have heard what everyone was talking about as he approached because he just peeled off his gear, grabbed his towel and strolled into the shower. If Toby wanted to play baseball in college he'd have to qualify as a walk-on, but everyone knew walk-ons didn't stand a chance.

What would I do at college if I couldn't play baseball? They probably had baseball clubs, but they weren't the same. I'd go to classes, of course, but I wasn't like some of these kids. I admired the way they took notes, the way the numbers and letters on the chalkboard transfixed them, the way they hunkered over their books in the library before and after school. Sure, I could get lost in a novel and I knew I'd like some of my English classes. But what was I going to do with that at the end of four years, be a professional reader? And it wasn't like I was Cliff and would end up with some hot Armenian chick to spend my days with. And nights.

**

Every year the local baseball season ended on Labor Day Weekend, with the invitation-only Brockton Tournament at DeSoto Playground on the west side near the high school. It was a showcase for players heading into their senior year to be seen by as many colleges as possible. Coaches sponsored kids from all over the state. Families hosted kids traveling from far away. Games were played all day long on several fields, culminating in the tournament All-Star game held at noon on Labor Day. If the scouts at Brockton High or AL games made kids nervous, this weekend would make them quake.

I made the All-Star Game. I hit a single up the middle, a double which plated two and a sharp ground ball to short. I played right field cleanly, though had no opportunity for assists.

It was after the game. I had already said so long to my folks, told them I'd be hanging out with some of the guys until suppertime.

I was bringing up the rear because I'd left my glove behind. I heard a voice from behind. "LaPlante, right?"

I turned and faced a roly-poly black man with very short neatly-trimmed black and white hair. "Yes, sir."

"Tommy Robb." He stuck out his hand with a jerk. "University of Maine. You know where that is?"

"Of course. Orono."

"You're familiar with the school?"

"I've looked at a lot of New England programs."

"Good." A stuffed cloth briefcase hung from his fist. "It's important to keep an open mind. Give Maine some thought. I'll be in touch with your coach." He turned to leave.

"It's a big school," I said. "Lots of kids."

"So?" He set his bag on the ground, conveying the impression he'd give me all the time in the world.

"I'd want to play."

"You go to a big school now. One of the biggest I've ever seen. You've done all right."

All my friends were under the trees drinking soda. Some were tossing a Frisbee near the picnic area. I felt unprepared talking to this guy. I needed a counselor. "I'm just saying. Maybe playing for a smaller school gets me in the door quicker."

"It's up to you. You're right. UMaine is a big Division One school and we generate a tremendous amount of interest for only forty slots. I've been there a long time, though, and I see you playing, I really do. Right away, your freshman year? Shit, I don't know. There are no guarantees. Not in baseball. Not in anything." He stared at me for a second just chewing his lower lip. "You know, I have risks too. Say I offer you a scholarship. How do I know you can adjust to college life? The classes are harder. The social pressures are off the charts. Being away from home. The girls, the drugs."

Girls, I thought.

"Hell," he said. "I don't even know if you can hit a curveball."

**

I was working upper body in the weight room after school. It was getting late, almost 4:30. The place was nearly empty. Coach Walsh appeared at the doorway in his street clothes and waved me over.

"You spoke to Coach Robb," he said as we walked across the gym to the stairs that led to the phys. ed. office.

"After the All Star game, yeah."

"Well, it's official now. I got a letter. Maine's interested."

"All right. Will I get a scholarship?"

"To be determined. You have to go through the whole rigmarole of applying first. But at least they're interested." He opened the office door and ushered me in. We were alone. "I've heard from some others too."

"Really?"

"Villanova and Providence College."

He sat behind his desk and gestured for me to take a seat, but I couldn't. People I didn't know were writing letters about me. I was on peoples' radar.

"So I can give them permission to call your home?"

"Yes!" I might have leaped as I spoke.

He laughed. "These are good schools. Good baseball programs. You should be proud."

I floated in the office, picturing my father's reaction when I told him the news, imagining the buzz in the house when the colleges started phoning to discuss campus visits.

"Come here a minute, will ya, Jimmy. Sit down."

I sat next to his desk, but it was difficult to remain still. After this, I was going to go home and swing from the tee a couple hundred times.

"At the tournament on Labor Day. You'd just hit your double, knocked in a pair. A couple guys came up to me. They pointed at you and said, 'Where'd he come from'?"

"Yeah?"

Coach Walsh's face became hard and solemn. "They were with the Dodgers, Jimmy."

"The Los Angeles Dodgers?"

"You know another Dodgers?"

"Did they say anything else?" I was standing again. "Did they contact you?"

He shook his head. "That was it. And I hesitated telling you because I didn't want you to be disappointed. But you should know. Come on, sit down. It was an indication, Jimmy. You see what I'm saying? Something real. For millions of kids, playing sports for a living, it's a pipe dream. But you, you should treat this game like you could be a part of it. For real. And no matter where you end up next year, Maine, Pennsylvania, wherever . . . You work as hard there as you work here . . . then a few years from now I'm gonna be saying I knew that kid. I'm gonna be saying . . ." For an instant it looked like his eyes were misting; if so, it was gone in a flash. "That boy . . . He played for me."

**

A couple weeks later, at Coach Walsh's recommendation, I attended the Johnny Toronto Fall Prospect Camp in Fall River. Drills and games were arranged all day long, two straight weekends. A few guys from Brockton also signed up and lots of faces looked familiar from all the teams I'd played against.

Coach Walsh caught up with me leaving the gym the following week to tell me about a couple of other interested schools, including the University of Massachusetts. He handed the letters over as we headed toward his truck.

"Do you have kids, Coach Walsh?"

"Got two girls, all grown up."

"No ballplayers then, huh?"

"Not baseball, no, but my oldest played Lacrosse for Skidmore and my youngest, Beth, played softball for URI."

"Wow."

"Yeah, actually she settled down in Woonsockett after she graduated. My wife and I are visiting next weekend. A little family reunion." He dug his keys out of his pocket and fumbled with them for a second. "Oh, and if you have any questions about next steps . . . you know, applications, colleges. You know where to find me."

**

I was in the library after school. I always chose the same table if it wasn't occupied, the one where Ben had talked me into going to the freshman dance. Chemical equations danced in my head. Fucking things.

"Hi," Sondra said as she sat across the table.

"Hey, what's going on?"

"Killing time. Got a yearbook meeting." She gestured toward a stack of papers sticking sloppily out of a notebook. "Can I talk to you about something?"

"Sure."

"It's about that night . . . at D.W."

Shit. "Okay." I rather would have been left with the equations.

"I don't want you to be mad at me for bringing it up."

"You're too nice to be mad at." I wanted her to go away. I wanted her to stay.

"You know I'm going to Brown in August . . ."

"Of course."

"Well, I guess I just wanted to say my piece before . . . I'm not sure how many chances we'd get to talk before graduation. And I'm not sure if I'll see you over the summer . . ." She twirled the ripped edges of her note paper.

It seemed she wanted me to fill in the blanks: Would we see more of each other before the end of the school year? Or over the summer? No to both. I didn't mean to be glib, but I couldn't linger on the frustration and sadness of it anymore.

"Let me get this out before . . . I don't know. I've wanted to apologize for a while, but . . . Well, it's not easy. A weird night. I could tell you were nervous even in the theater." She continued to play with the frayed edges of the papers. "Sometimes I think if I hadn't rushed things, who knows. Maybe it'd be different now."

"That night was my fault. You didn't do anything wrong."

She took my hand. "I made up my mind that night. I wanted to . . . Well, it was going to be special. I could tell you weren't that into it at first, but then at the park you were *really* into it and I thought if we just, you know, kept going . . ."

"Barreled through . . ."

"Right. Everything would be okay. I mean, it sucked that it would have happened in a car. But . . . Where it happens isn't as important as who it's with." Her index finger traced the ridges of my knuckles. "I didn't want to go off to college without saying how I felt. You know . . . that, that I wish everything ended . . . better." She arranged her books so that all the bindings lined up evenly.

"Me, too."

"Really?"

"Um, what?"

"Like, how do you wish it ended better?"

"Uh . . ." Shit, I didn't know what to say, I'd just wanted to agree with her. "Better, in that I don't want you to be upset about anything, especially anything to do with me."

"What *I* meant was that . . ." She folded her hands at the edge of the table. "Maybe we could get together over vacation. You know, now that some time has passed."

My palms were slick with sweat. I didn't want to turn her down again. "With baseball and all...The thing is—"

"I love you."

Oh God, why did she say that?

She rubbed her forehead and absently tugged on a strand of hair. "That's really what I wanted to say. Whatever you want to do with that . . ." She stood and started to gather her books. "Call me, don't call me."

"Sondra, shouldn't we talk about this?"

"Not here," she said. "You know my number."

I stood beside her, touched her elbow. "What you said . . ."

She looked at me as she pulled her elbow away. She only came up to my collarbone, but seemed taller as she turned and walked across the carpet toward the door.

That night I touched myself under the covers. Sondra ran through my mind as usual, but whenever I thought of her, no matter how tantalizing the fantasy, I was overcome with sorrow instead of lust. I tried thinking of other girls, even invented a few, but every time I started to stiffen, thoughts reverted to Sondra and the miserable truth that I couldn't allow myself to be with someone who loved me and who maybe I loved too.

**

I visited almost all the campuses throughout the fall of senior year: URI, Villanova, Maine, UMass. The visits were all pretty much the same. Dinners at restaurants with the players, coaches and staff; overnights in one of the players' dorm rooms; tours of the facilities; and one-on-ones with coaches. I was accepted by all the schools, except Stanford.

My folks wanted me to choose UMass. During the drives to and from the campuses, Dad sometimes commented on the hefty tuition of the other schools. Mother came along to a couple of the colleges and did the same thing as she thumbed through the brochures. One time she even whistled and I saw them from the back seat exchange a look. This might have been pre-planned, as in, *Hey, let's drop a few hints to Jimmy that it's UMass or nothing.* I had spoken to Coach Walsh in depth about all the options and, although Maine and Stanford were considered the most successful, he loved UMass's program, especially their head coach, Jack Shields.

I had no real objection to UMass. It was a solid school and only about two and a half hours from home. The only drawback was that Cliff's double major would keep him there an extra year. That might be kind of awkward. The school was massive, but we'd obviously see each other.

I thought about him as we drove to UMass, my last campus visit. He and Marie were still going strong. In fact, they'd opened a gourmet market and deli together with money collected from other interested students. Apparently they drew up the business plans and prepared most of the items.

In the end, UMass won out. The money factor couldn't be argued; with the partial scholarship and in-state tuition, UMass was cheaper than the others by thousands of dollars.

The rest of senior year was spent maintaining grades and baseball shape. I struggled mightily through Physics and Trigonometry, but in the end I got a C in both. I was psyched.

I also caroused with the team. Flirted strategically with girls, kissed a few, but never let it get to the stage where I was alone with one for too long. It seemed like every time I was out I needed to carefully plan the evening—Who would I spend time with tonight? How would I get out of it?

The charade provided a thrill in a way. I became skilled enough—smooth enough—to pull the wool over everyone's eyes. It got me thinking of what life would be like at college. I thought of the campuses I'd recently visited—all the girls running around. I'd have to play the same old avoidance game for another four years. And what about after that? Would the rest of my life be a series of careful maneuvers—seeking out women to play a role, then dodging them before things got serious?

At UMass's general orientation, girls visiting from all over the country—at least the state—wore shorts, halters, even bikini tops, their boobs bouncing up and down. It wouldn't be much different come September when classes started. Except there would be more girls. *And more boobs.* Brockton High had a lot of kids, but nothing compared to UMass, which had over 25,000.

Ben would have loved Amherst. Not just the girls. I thought of him during some free time in the orientation schedule. One of the coaches, a batting instructor about Cliff's age, showed me around the whole phys. ed. complex. The pool was huge, with a separate square pool for divers, and bleachers that sat hundreds. I looked down over the last row and watched some figures swim gracefully from one end of the pool to the other. I pictured Ben in the water, blazing a trail, setting records, a star by the end of his freshman year.

"Ready to move on?" the coach said.

"Yeah, sorry."

As we left the building a couple of girls in shorts and sports bras and carrying tennis rackets walked toward the door, which the coach held open. We blatantly watched as they climbed the stairs. One of the girl's shorts were so high we could see the bottom of her ass. Maybe I should have applied to some all-boys colleges.

I had excellent high school and American Legion seasons. I broke two Brockton High single season records, topping the RBI record by one with a total of 66. The other record was for outfield assists. I blew it out of the water with 13. Coach Walsh said I would have made more if the other coaches hadn't got wise to my arm and held up their runners. I strutted through the summer and into the fast-approaching college Fall Ball season. As summer ended, I thought more about me and Cliff. Living in close proximity for the first time in four years.

**

It was a well-kept secret that the Varsity weight room remained unlocked throughout the summer. It was a Saturday night, desolate.

I would have lifted in the morning as usual, but my folks wanted to go apple picking in New Hampshire. They said I could stay home, but it was my last weekend in Brockton before college and I knew they wanted me along.

I was in between sets of lunges, a palm on either side of a narrow wall mirror as I stretched my calves. Stepping back, I looked at my reflection. I lifted my tee shirt, checked out my abs. I lifted it higher, saw how my torso slanted into a V and disappeared into my shorts. I turned my body, but kept my eye on the mirror to see myself at different angles. Finally, I took the shirt off altogether. My thumbs curled into the waist of my shorts and pushed down. I liked how the flatness of my stomach flowed into my hips, muscle into bone.

As I stood there admiring myself, I remembered what Coach Walsh had said about the Dodgers sniffing around. He'd said he could see me in the pros; that, for me, it could be more than just a dream. A few years from now, I thought, my paychecks might be getting signed by the owner of a baseball team, maybe even Buddy Leroux or Haywood Sullivan.

I ran my fingers over the ridges of my ab muscles. My six-pack. I felt the hairs around my nipples and the thin trail of dark hairs that ran down the center of my torso, into the thick dark bush of my pubic hair.

11. Zoo Mass

Mother held me tightly. I had said bye to Dad earlier; he had to leave for work at seven. Richard Schneider was unlocking the U-Haul trailer attached to his beat-up Datsun. We had met at the recruiting overnight at UMass last year and we'd kept in touch.

"Mom, I gotta help Richard."

"I told Cliff to expect a call," she said, finally releasing me.

"You already told me. I have his number." I started to walk away, but she grabbed me and hugged me again. "Jesus, ma."

"You shut up."

"You're coming to watch a game in three weeks. I'll see ya then."

"So."

Richard had already started loading my luggage into the trailer. I rolled my eyes at him after I pulled away. Hopefully she wouldn't start bawling. She watched as I lifted the bags and boxes and Richard slid them toward the back of the U-Haul. I slipped into the passenger seat before she had a chance to grab me again. Instead, she leaned into Richard's window.

"Drive carefully," she demanded.

I waved as the car pulled away.

"Call me when you get there...Don't forget."

As we moved slowly up Clydemore, mother stepped further into the street to keep the car in sight. We rolled by the Clancy house. I saw Mr. Clancy raking leaves in his side yard. His arm shot up, his hand waved. We were too far gone for me to return the gesture.

Richard was smiling. He faced me and said, "Free at last. Free at last." He then turned on the radio and The Cars' *You Might Think* filled the small space of Richard's two-door.

I smiled back. "Thank God almighty . . ."

**

Hampshire dining commons was kicking. The whole team, at least those of us that lived on campus, sat around a long table. Conversation and laughter bounced off the walls. Food was piled high on plates. We could take as much as we wanted. Same for the soda machines and dessert bar. If I wasn't careful, I'd gain thirty pounds in a month.

"So what's shakin' for tonight?" someone said.

"Baseball House," Knudsen said, chomping a grilled cheese. He was a powerful-looking older kid, completely bald. I noticed the muscles working along his jaw and temples. He didn't just eat his food; he devoured it, inhaled it, the whole sandwich gone in three bites. "They're expecting us after dinner. Red Sox and Blue Jays. So chow down."

Baseball House was a large house off campus on Belchertown Road where several of the upperclassman players lived. Apparently it was a tradition to hang out there and watch the Red Sox whenever possible.

"Why do I have to watch the Red Sox?" someone said.

I didn't know his name, but I remembered he was from Brooklyn. The hardest part so far was getting all the names right. Not just real names, but nicknames too. I had to keep asking my sophomore roommate, Huck, who was sitting next to me, for clarification. "Who's that again?" I said.

"Fat Freddy."

"He's not fat."

"Yeah, but it sounds funny. Fat Freddy." He laughed. "That one over there, his name's Paul Parker, but we call him Peeps 'cause his initials are PP. The kid talking now we call Chicken 'cause his last name is Cacciatore."

"All right," Knudsen said, standing up, a statue, more machine than human. "Let's kick it."

"I haven't even started my cheesecake," one of the guys said.

"Take it with ya, Hairy."

"They don't like it when you sneak food out."

"What are they gonna do?" Knudsen said. "Send you home the first day? Over a shitty slice of cake?"

"But it's *cheese*cake."

"Why do they call you Hairy?" one of the newcomers said. I was curious, too.

"You'll find out in the locker room tomorrow," someone said.

"It ain't pretty."

"My name's Harry," he said to the freshman who'd asked. "Don't forget it."

"He can't help it," Richard joined in. "He's Greek"

"Needless to say," Knudson said, "Hairy is one hairy motherfucker."

"Hey, don't goof on me being Greek," Hairy said to Richard.

"I'm not goofing. I'm just saying you're Greek. How's that goofing?"

"Have you ever been to Greece?" Hairy said.

Richard didn't answer.

"Well, don't mess with it until you've been there."

"Have *you* ever been to Greece?" Knudsen asked Hairy.

He let a second go by before saying, "No."

Everyone cracked up at that.

Richard said, "You've probably never even been to a Greek restaurant."

Someone started talking about a Greek restaurant in his town. This led to other kids talking about their towns and cities. It was a tremendous feeling. To be part of a group of people getting to know each other. By talking, just being in their company.

One of the things Cliff had said after he started college was that it was hard adjusting to not knowing anyone. All of a sudden you're plopped in the middle of nowhere on your own. Not in my case. All baseball players who lived on campus lived within three floors of each other in Washington, one of the high-rises in Southwest, just a stone's throw from Boyden Gym.

Speaking of Cliff. I had promised mother I'd give him a call. It couldn't happen today, though. It was too late. We were headed back to the dorm, then off to watch the game. I'd have more time tomorrow. All I had scheduled was practice. Classes didn't start until the following day.

**

Several of the guys had cars, including my roommate, so we wouldn't have to take the bus. By the time we reached the lobby the others were down there ready to go. As we pushed through the glass doors I saw Cliff walking up the dorm steps. It was dark. He didn't see me among the throng. For a second I thought I'd just keep walking.

"Hey," I said.

"Hey yourself," he said, taking in the crowd. "Just wanted to see how you were settling in."

I got the feeling he thought he would find me sitting alone in my room, homesick. "We're heading out to watch the Sox."

"Oh, okay."

I thought about asking him along, but it wasn't my place. He wouldn't know anyone anyway. "I got your number, though. I'll give you mine. You got a pen?"

"That's all right. I got it."

"Okay . . . So . . . I'll catch up with ya."

He stood there. I felt the whole team hovering behind me.

"Give a shout if you need anything," he said and headed down toward Fearing Street.

We made a packy run, then stopped at a supermarket called Louis Foods to pick up snacks and soda. The caravan pulled up a long thin driveway to the side of a large red-painted house. Inside, several guys and a few girls lay sprawled on the couches and chairs in front of a huge TV. They stood up and made introductions. We handed over the beer and one of the guys I recognized from my recruiting weekend carried them beyond the living room to where carpet gave way to the linoleum-floored kitchen.

One of the girls walked to the TV and turned the knob to channel 38. We all sat on the floor and tore into bags of Cheetos, Cheez-its and Doritos. A handful of us at a time were given a tour of the place, but there wasn't much to see. Just four bedrooms, two bathrooms, the living room and the kitchen.

Toward the end of the game I walked to the kitchen to throw out my soda can. I'd had a beer earlier, but one was enough since practice was at ten in the morning. The trashcan was overflowing.

"Hey," I shouted into the living room. "You want me to empty this?"

One of the guys that lived there said, "Yeah thanks, there're barrels outside."

I lifted the bag from the can, tied it up and carried it out to the back porch. The house overlooked a field. On the far side lay a main road and beyond that the parking lot for Belchertown High School. I heard a girl giggle at the back of the driveway. I walked along the porch railing and saw that one of the girls who had been watching the game was sitting on the hood of a car next to two cans of beer. A guy from the house stood between her knees pushing her sweater up over her bra.

"No," she said, still laughing. "It's cold, Danny."

"So." He reached behind her back to unclasp her bra and pushed both sweater and bra over her breasts

"Danny, we shouldn't . . ." She wasn't laughing anymore, but she didn't seem to mind either as she lowered backward onto her elbows.

I watched his mouth cover her nipple, then work its way down her body toward her pants. Before he reached them, she sat up. I about-faced and walked quietly back to the trash barrels at the foot of the porch.

After seeing that, it was hard to focus on the Red Sox game. I got a good look at her tits. They were nice. Marty Barrett and Wade Boggs just couldn't compete. I imagined myself out there between the girl's legs, my lips running down her body.

When we got back to the dorm, a junior catcher named Eric DiFusco showed everyone his new Commodore. Kids gathered in his room wondering what kind of magic the machine could wield. I wasn't very interested in computers. Besides, I needed a few minutes alone.

"You gonna stay here a bit?" I said to Huck as I left.

"Yeah, then hang in the lounge. Help Eric finish his sixer."

"All right."

"Going to bed?"

"Yeah," I said. "I'm beat."

"Rest up. Big day tomorrow."

In my room, I turned the dead bolt. He probably wouldn't be back for at least a half-hour. I changed into my shorts, grabbed the Kleenex box and brought it to the bed. I sat on the edge. A *Playboy* would have been nice. Not necessary, though, since the girl on the hood was vivid in my mind. I was already half-stiff without even touching the thing. I slipped it through the hole in the boxers and tugged. My eyes closed. She stood at the car, our positions reversed. She was between *my* legs, kissing *my* chest, *my* nipples.

I hadn't jerked off in several days and my dick felt humongous and hard as steel. I thought of her mouth descending toward my crotch and before she even reached it my dick erupted. If I was alone I would have moaned, it always felt better that way, but I kept my lips closed and continued tugging until the orgasm completely ended.

**

We woke with a jolt. Someone was walking up and down the hallway banging the doors with something hard, probably a baseball bat.

"Let's go, assholes. Practice is at 10:00. We have to wash, eat and have everything ready to go in three hours."

"Fucking Knudsen," Huck groaned from the other side of the room.

The banging continued. It was getting louder as he worked his way to our door. "In case you forgot, the banging keeps going until the doors open. Huck," he screamed at our closed door, "set a good example for your freshman."

Huck stumbled to the door, opened it a few inches and fell back onto his bed. I had been asleep by midnight so I was okay. I left the room to wash up and brush my teeth. Twisted Sister roared from Knudsen's room: *Oh, we're not gonna take it, no we ain't gonna take it, oh we're not gonna take it anymore.* When I returned to the room Huck was sitting on his desk chair slowly sticking his legs through his pants.

"How late did you stay up?" I said.

He answered with a dry cough that rattled his thin lanky frame. Then he reached into the mini refrigerator he'd set up between our desks and drank from a two liter bottle of Coke.

Knudsen was still shouting to get people into the corridor and downstairs.

"I'll meet you down there?" I said to Huck as he struggled to find the tag on his tee shirt.

"No, hang on. I'm coming."

"You gonna be okay to play?"

"Oh, yeah. I play better when I'm hung over." He took a moment to grab his cleats, wallet and keys.

Huck and I brought up the rear. He stopped a couple of times to burp, then kept going.

"Is Huck your real name?" I said as we crossed the plaza.

He shook his head. "Darren."

"Why Huck?"

"I was killing time in the locker room one day reading *Huckleberry Finn.* They gave me a hard time. God forbid I should read."

"Good thing you weren't reading *Pudd'nhead Wilson.*"

He laughed. "You read Twain?"

"I read the two biggies."

"But you know *Pudd'nhead Wilson.*"

"Never read it, though."

"You should. You'd like it. I grew up in Hartford, near where Twain lived. There's a museum there. I've been reading his stuff since I was a kid."

He stopped at the Hampden entrance and bent over, resting his hands on his knees.

"You gonna puke?"

"Na, I'll save that for when I'm at bat."

**

Practice was indoors, top floor of Boyden Gym, due to eighty percent threat of rain. Before practice even started, though, we needed to report to the equipment manager. Unlike high school, uniforms were dispersed on the first day of practice. I'd been number 10 since I asked Tad McKenzie for it freshman year of high school. Today I was given 55.

"Anyone have 10?" I asked the attendant, an older man with a blonde mustache going grey and slightly separated front teeth.

"Dirk Benson got 10."

"Do players ever switch numbers?"

"He won't. It's done him well."

"Got it."

"Good news is he's a senior. So if you want it next year it's yours."

"You don't mind?"

"I'll make a note," he said, tapping his head. "LaPlante, right?"

The locker room was carpeted and the lockers themselves twice the width of high school lockers. And we had a TV. Most of the channels didn't come in very well, but even without the TV the place was luxurious. A boom box exploded with, *Come on feel the noise, girls rock your boys; we'll get wild, wild, wild; wild, wild, wild.* Peeps leaped onto a bench, clutching a bat as a microphone and mimed Kevin Dubrow's stage antics while a bunch of the guys cheered.

Between returning players, recruits (like me) and walk-ons, about sixty-five of us walked up the stairs and through the doors of the main gym. I noticed some of the players as they stepped inside, their mouths agape at the gym's size. I'd been a little spoiled by attending one of the largest high schools in the state, but any way you cut it, this facility was massive, the size of six basketball courts.

"There are 68 ballplayers in this gym right now." Coach Shields launched right in. He paced as he addressed the crowd, his round face red and jowled. "By the time the season starts in March half of you will be gone." He spoke calmly and reassuringly. "And it's not about talent alone. It's about attitude and energy and leadership. It's about being selfless teammates."

We started with two laps around the gym, broke off into straight lines for calisthenics, then sweated through agility drills, before separating for position drills. Fundamentally, everything was like high school. The difference was the quality of the players. Even Huck, probably still drunk from last night, played with more intensity and drive than all of the kids from Brockton High.

Voices rose as we showered and dressed. I couldn't figure how I could make this team. A lot of these kids had already proven themselves by playing a year or two or three. Many had played in semi-pro summer leagues. Sure, we were all friends. We played together and lived together. But we were also rivals. Shit, for all I knew next semester some of these same guys might be my enemies.

After practice I called Cliff's apartment from the gym. No one answered. I walked around town to get to know where all the stores were, not to mention the bank and post office, and ended up at Cliff's. He shared a place with Marie and another couple right on Amity Street behind Heritage Bank.

It was a large square white-shingled building. Their apartment, number two, was on the first floor. I knocked. No one answered. I remembered the store. They had said it was behind the town supermarket, which must have been where we'd gone last night for snacks.

Behind Louis Foods stood a row of drab single-story storefronts: a laundromat, an accountant's office and "Campus Gourmet". Although I had spent a few minutes with Cliff during the recruiting event and orientation, I still hadn't seen the store. I pulled open the door, jangling a bell from above. The place bustled with students and adults. It smelled tangy, foreign somehow. I realized I hadn't eaten for hours.

"Yeah, I'll take a small amount of the tortellini," a woman said to Cliff, who stood behind the deli case near the rear of the store.

He filled a small plastic container.

"That's a pesto sauce, right?"

"That's right." Cliff bent into the case and righted a description card that had been jostled out of place. "I think you're really going to like it."

The woman took the tortellini and the rest of her order and joined the line at the cash register, which Marie manned. A student in front of her munched his sandwich while standing in line. The place was so jammed they hadn't even noticed me when I walked in.

I figured I'd hang back in one of the aisles until things slowed down. I'd never seen or even heard of most of the items, different kinds of pastes and oils and sauces. Didn't college students eat in the dining halls and order pizza? Kids were laughing by a cooler filled with juice and sodas. I peeked between the shelves and saw Cliff making a sandwich. The wall behind him was a large blackboard with descriptions of sandwiches and salads. "Picnic Packages" included a side dish, a piece of fruit and a drink.

I almost left. But I couldn't. Maybe it was time to end this conflict. Which wasn't really a conflict anymore. I didn't even have to say anything, just walk over and give him a hug. But I didn't. I liked the sense of power I still lorded over him. I didn't want to let him off the hook. Not yet.

I watched him behind the counter. His full-length white apron was smeared with mustard and brown sauce. He sliced a tomato with the precision of a chef. He took his time building the sandwich, first the condiments, then the meat, then the vegetables. I even liked the way he tore the white butcher paper from the wheel and deftly wrapped the sandwich with a few quick motions.

When the last person moved on to the register, I stepped toward the display case and said loudly, "I want a roast beef and cheddar and I want it now."

"Hey, hey." Cliff wiped his hands on a paper towel and stepped from behind the counter.

I stuck out my hand for a shake, but he pushed through it as though it wasn't there and awkwardly wrapped his arm around my shoulder.

"I'm sorry about last night," I said. "I was with the team. It was . . ."

"Don't be silly."

Marie stepped from behind the register. Smiling and waving, she kissed me on the cheek.

"So how's the dorm? Everything going okay?"

We talked while customers milled around the store; chatted about Southwest, my roommate, practice, class schedule. A customer eventually asked for a sub and Cliff headed behind the counter.

"I like the picnic idea."

"That was mine." She looked at the board. "They go like hotcakes when parents are in town."

"The place was packed when I came in."

"Yeah, you want a job?" she said, laughing. "It'll get easier. We'll be fully staffed starting tomorrow."

"Tell him about the party," Cliff said from behind the counter.

**

It was Saturday night. I didn't want to get there too early. One of the fraternities was sponsoring a showing of *The Graduate* at Campus Center. Show time was 7:30, so I'd probably arrive at Cliff's around 10:00, stick around for an hour, then bolt.

The opening shot of Dustin Hoffman sitting in the airplane filled the screen, but I couldn't focus on the movie. I kept thinking about Cliff's party. I should have brought something. I thought of wine, but I'd probably get carded. Not food, since that was their thing. Flowers? Too girlie. For Marie maybe. Na, the stores would be closed by the time the movie let out.

In the driveway I tried to peek through one of the windows, but the blinds were drawn. I rapped on the door. Lots of voices buzzed, as well as a rousing live version of *Dance, Dance, Dance*. No one answered. I turned the knob and opened the door. The noise grew louder. I stepped into a living room filled with people. The apartment smelled faintly of garlic and onions. A yellow banner hung from wall to wall: "Kickin' Off The School Year."

I saw Marie right away. If the party was an occasion to kick off the school year, it was also a way to plug Campus Gourmet. She stood near the door handing out dollar-off coupons and 8.5x11 posters advertizing the store. On a side table next to her sat a zucchini with an intricate rose carved into its surface.

"You know . . ." she said, shoving a stack of posters into someone's hands, "on bulletin boards, bus stops, telephone poles."

Kind of pushy if you asked me, but she looked so nice I wouldn't have hesitated stapling one to the top of the spire of Old Chapel if that's what she wanted. I approached her with a wave. "Cliff's in the kitchen," she said after a quick hug and peck on the cheek.

Halfway to the kitchen toward the back of the living room I was stopped by a tall bushy-haired blonde man. "What can I get you?" he said, his friendly, beaming eyes and round flushed cheeks a few inches above mine. "Beer? Soda pop? Something harder?"

"A beer sounds good."

He led me to the frig, handed me a bottle of Rolling Rock and said, "The formalities are over. Next time you're on your own. *Mi casa es su casa.*" An Eiffel Tower constructed from different sized carrots stood on top of the frig.

"So your Cliff's roommate." As I spoke to the blonde guy, I noticed Cliff in an alcove off the kitchen carefully slicing a brick of cheese, then stepping out to stir something on the stove in a large industrial size pot.

"I have that honor. And who might you be, my good man?" he said, adopting a British accent.

I pointed to Cliff. "I'm his brother."

His face broke out into a canvas of dimples and lines. "No fuckin' way!" He laughed like I'd just told him a hilarious joke. "Hey Cliffy."

Cliff looked over. I lifted my bottle.

The big blonde man wrapped an arm around my shoulder and squeezed. "Your brother's here."

Cliff introduced me to his roommate, Simon Mercier, then I followed him as he dropped off plates of cheese, crackers and dips around the living room.

Cliff asked how many times I'd gotten lost on campus.

"My campus map hasn't let me down yet."

"Can you stick around?"

"Yeah, I'm good for a while."

"You have to stay for the pasta," Marie said as she appeared from the crowd.

"A dinner party?" I said. "I would have brought something."

"Don't be ridiculous," she said.

"What are you making?"

"Linguini with Bolognese," Cliff said, then left to tend the sauce.

I noticed a whole series of fruit and vegetable carvings on a shelf across the room. Radishes made to look like lilies, more roses, this time carved into watermelons, yellow squash and rutabagas. Carved into one of the watermelons was a detailed picture of a couple dancing the tango.

"What's with all the fruit and vegetables?" I said.

"Oh, Cliff was feeling extra creative."

"Cliff made those?"

She must have sensed that I was impressed. "This is nothing. You should see his animals."

I looked at the watermelon again, taking in the precision of the knife marks. My mind spiraled back to the day of the accident. Cliff standing at the fence carving the T and the A.

"I love this song," a girl shouted from across the room.

Styx's *Mr. Roboto* blared over the speakers.

One of the guests, a burly guy with bushy black hair standing nearby, rolled his eyes. "I hate this song," he complained. "These lyrics are so stupid. They go through all this trouble to say thank you very much in Japanese, then they ruin the whole thing by throwing in a mister. I mean, if you say *domo arigoto*, you have to say *Roboto-san*, not Mr. Roboto. You can't have it both ways."

"*Domo arigoto, Roboto-san?*" I said. "Are you serious?"

"Yeah, I'm fucking-A serious."

"That doesn't sound as good," someone said. "It doesn't rhyme."

"I know it doesn't rhyme, but that's their problem. They have to make it sound good *and* have it make sense. That's their job as songwriters."

"Maybe they're just being whimsical," the other kid said. "I don't think it's one of their more serious songs."

"Right," I said. "It's not like it's *Babe.*"

The bushy-haired kid turned on me and said, "You messing with me?"

"No, I—"

But before I had a chance to continue he stomped off toward the kitchen.

Marie leaned into me, laughing.

Small Styrofoam bowls of pasta and sauce were passed around. Garlic bread, too. Everyone ate. People spoke fake Italian. By the time I finished, it was after midnight.

I went into the bedroom where Simon had taken my coat. I could tell from the photographs on one of the shelves that it was Cliff and Marie's room. A picture of them arm in arm by the campus pond, a family shot of all of us from a few years ago at my uncle's in Pennsylvania, Marie with an older couple. One of me. Standing at the plate in my American Legion uniform. He must have taken it from one of Mother's photo albums.

When I reached for my coat on the bed I noticed another watermelon carving. The image carved into its rind and flesh looked exactly like Marie. It was uncanny. It seemed a little creepy at first, but it made sense. If you loved someone, you expressed it any way you could.

**

My parents arrived Friday night at the Campus Center Hotel. When they called I walked up to meet them. Their room was a grey box; it overlooked the pond and beyond that the enormous Fine Arts Center. Mother placed clothes in drawers while my father thumbed through the campus magazines that had been left on the desk.

"What are you doing?" Mother said.

"Cliff mentioned he advertised in one of these magazines."

She seemed more concerned with figuring out how to remove the clothes hangers from the closet, but when my father said, "Hey, here it is," she raced to his side. Dad pointed out the small square advertisement on the bottom of the glossy page.

"Look at that," Mother said.

Dad said, "I can't wait to see what they've done with it."

"I brought you a care package," Mother said, pointing to a Sears shopping bag next to her suitcase.

I took the bag to an armchair in the corner. Inside were two sweaters, sports sections from several editions of the *Globe*, and a Tupperware container filled with brownies. On the bottom lay the framed picture of Carlton Fisk that Mr. Clancy had offered me the night I slipped into Ben's room after his funeral. I lifted it from the bag.

"Your father thought it might inspire you to hit a game-winning homerun."

I stared at it, thinking more about Ben than baseball. "It's great. I should have brought it with me." I slid the photograph between the sweaters.

Once unpacked, we walked downtown to The Pub and met Cliff and Marie for supper. We talked about classes, baseball, Campus Gourmet, the folks caught us up on uncles, aunts and cousins.

The most interesting part of the dinner was trying to convince Mother that tomorrow's game against the University of Vermont was scheduled to last eighteen innings.

"There's only four Fall Ball games. There're lots of kids that have to get rated, sorted out, you know. And there're tons of pitchers. They all need to get their innings."

"What about food?" Mother wanted to know. "Do they provide lunch?"

"We bring our own. PB and J, apple sauce, yogurts, things like that."

Mother looked disappointed when I told her I probably wouldn't play until the tenth inning or later. "The starters play the first nine innings, then replacements play the rest."

"Replacements . . ." she said, the word distasteful.

That night I placed the Fisk picture on my window sill that overlooked Berkshire Dining Hall. It was the last thing I saw before shutting off the lights.

**

My parents sat through the whole game. They'd gone to Campus Gourmet and packed a cooler with sandwiches and drinks. Cliff and Marie showed up after I started playing. I waved from near the dugout. They didn't stay long.

I ended up with two hits, an infield single that the shortstop knocked down ranging to his left, which resulted in several shouts of "Good hustle" from the bench. The other hit was more solid, a line drive over second. I loved stroking liners up the middle; there was something elegant about it, the way the ball sliced through the air over the base, carving the diamond in two. There wasn't too much action in right. I caught a lazy fly ball, then a couple innings later fielded a single and tossed it to second. In the end we won, 14 to 11.

After the game, my parents and I made plans to meet later at Cliff's for a quick bite before they drove back to Brockton. I had just said so long to them when a kid in street clothes started walking with me toward Boyden.

"You're Jimmy LaPlante, right?" He was no more than sixteen and walked closer than necessary.

I nodded.

"My name's Kyle."

He offered his hand and I took it, struggling to balance all my gear.

"I'm visiting my sister and figured I'd catch a game. Get some time with Coach Shields. I hope to play here in a couple of years."

"What year are you?"

"Sophomore, at Reading High."

"Oh, I know Reading."

"Yeah, we played Brockton last year. You gunned down a kid at the plate. It would have been our tying run in the ninth."

"I remember. That was a good game."

"It made me sick, of course. But it was something to see, a throw like that."

We fell silent as we continued along Commonwealth Avenue. He kept sneaking glances at me as though I was supposed to offer some kind of advice. "Thank you," I finally said. "Hope to see you back here."

**

Health Services was located at the northern edge of the Central dorms. A lady at the counter looked up from her work. She smiled, but looked harried.

"Hi," I said. "I have a 2:30 appointment with Randy Richmond."

She said, "I'll let him know you're here" and gestured for me to sit.

Through an arch at the back of the waiting room was a secretarial pool. A middle-aged woman clacked away on a typewriter.

"James?"

He appeared from the other end of the waiting room. I stood up. I had nothing to be nervous about. I'd been injected hundreds of times, by my parents mostly, but by strangers too. I had discussed with my parents the option of self injecting, but the consensus, along with Dr. Young, was that it would be easier to stop by Health Services every couple of weeks. That way I wouldn't have to deal with needles in the room, my roommate stumbling upon them, things like that. No fuss no muss.

"Randy Richmond." His handshake was tight. He was about my height, a fair-skinned guy with long dark hair pushed back on the sides with gel. "I'm one of the RNs. Walk with me?"

"Sure."

"This will only take a sec."

He led me down the main corridor to a small examination room. "Marcy," he said playfully to a woman arranging files outside the room, "what's up, girlie girl?"

"Oh, getting by, Richie Rich."

He closed the door behind us. I saw the familiar needle on a silver tray beside the examination table.

"All right, James, why don't you lower your pants and hop on up there."

I did as I was told.

"So what's your major?" he said as the needle pierced skin.

"English." I felt like saying, No need to distract my attention from the needle going in. I'm an old pro at this.

He asked rote questions as he disposed the needle and jotted a note in my chart: How were my classes? Where did I live? Did I like my roommate? Fine, Southwest, yes. After I put on my coat, he said, "Got something for you" and held out his arm. A three-pack of condoms fell into my hand.

I looked at him.

"Doctor's orders," he said.

"I don't get it."

"There's been a trend . . ." He shifted nervously. I got the feeling he didn't get many of my kind here in Health Services. "Men in your situation, who can have sex without getting girls pregnant, they figure no need for condoms. But there's been a rise in AIDS in that population. Guys like you. So . . ." he pointed to the rubbers. "Don't leave home without 'em."

He started to lead me out of the examination room, but the notion that guys with my condition were out in the world fucking with abandon kept my feet bolted to the floor.

"You okay, James?"

Something debilitating—and brutally unfair—struck me as I stood there looking out into the hallway: It wasn't bad enough that I was different from everyone I knew, from everyone that I would ever know. But even among my own kind I was a freak.

"Yeah, I'm fine."

I stepped out of the building into the bright afternoon sun. A steel trashcan stood outside the entrance. I reached in my pocket to throw the condoms away. But after a second I decided to keep them. Maybe one of the guys would need one in a pinch.

12. Romeo and Juliet

A few weeks into the semester, my pass/fail astronomy class got canceled. My advisor suggested I participate in a colloquium, which carried one or two credits, depending on the selection. I chose Theater 110 because it primarily met at night and wouldn't interfere with afternoon practices and strength and conditioning workouts.

The initial meeting for Theater 110 was for 1:00 on the stage of the Rand Theater, but I was starving and needed to grab some lunch first. I was sitting alone wolfing a tuna sandwich and washing it down with a Diet Coke when a kid sat at my table. I knew him, but I wasn't sure how. His hair was dark brown, a little on the greasy side. Some zits dotted his cheeks and forehead. He was smiling.

"I know you," I said.

"Lance Durphy."

Memories tumbled into place. I remembered the story Ben told about how Lance had been beaten in the locker room.

"We met at Ben's funeral."

"I remember."

"I saw you sitting here," he said, "and figured I'd say hello."

"I'm glad you did. You swim for UMass?"

"Yeah, right," he laughed. "I barely made the Brockton High team." He ripped out a piece of paper from his notebook and scrawled his number. "I gotta scoot. Late for a group study, but let me know if you want to get together."

"Sounds good."

He gathered his books and dashed off.

You couldn't spend much time on campus without seeing the Fine Arts Center. It was a beige cement monstrosity with at least a dozen entrances. The first one I tried led to the Music Department; the second to the Art Department. The secretary gave me directions to the Rand. I finally found it, across from the concert hall. But the lobby doors were locked. I cupped my hands against one of the glass doors and peered inside. The lobby was carpeted entirely in an ugly orange-red and gave way to two sets of staircases going up and down, deeper into the lobby, out of sight. I knocked. No one answered. I consulted my notes to make sure I had the right day.

"Are you looking for the Theater Department?" a voice said.

"Yeah, I'm—" I said, turning, but stopped when I saw her.

"The entrance is this way, through the Curtain Theater." She started to walk away. "I'll take you."

"But I'm . . ." I looked down at my paper. "Says here, the Rand."

"I know, but these doors are kept locked except for performances. You have to enter through the department." She was gorgeous from head to toe.

"I feel stupid," I said, "banging on the door like that."

"Everybody does it the first time. Are you doing the 110?"

"Theater 110, yes. The colloquium."

""You're a Theater major?" she said, leading me down the set of stairs I'd just climbed and up another set leading to the Curtain Theater doors.

"No. English." I didn't like the silence so I said, "Lots of stairs."

"I know, huh." She was quick to smile, had a wide mouth with thick exotic lips. "The Rand is the main stage. This one here, the Curtain, that's our black box."

"Ah."

"Actually, the quickest way to the Rand stage is through the door we passed at the bottom of the stairs, but I'm going up here, see who I run into. The Curtain lobby's kind of a gathering spot."

"I see."

"The 110s are usually for Theater majors. What's your name?"

"Jimmy."

"Hey, I'm Andrea. Anyway, we're required to take three of them. It kinda stinks because if you're an actor you want to do actor things and not be saddled with this technical crap." Her voice rose in pitch the faster she talked. "The thing is you might find something that really interests you. Like I did costumes for my 110 last year and I *loved* it. Not that I'd give up acting, but still."

When she held open the door for me I noticed that she wore a ring on her thumb. On her thumb! I'd never seen that before. Thick silver strands, woven together like braids. It was erotic.

Once inside the lobby, Andrea filed off to speak to someone. A sign that read "Curtain Theater" pointed left; "Department Offices" pointed right. I roamed the floor. Bulletin boards on the walls advertised nearby productions and voice and movement workshops. Another bulletin board was for messages left by students, envelopes and pieces of paper with names on them tacked to the cork. I took a seat on one of many folding chairs outside the Chairman's office. The floor was carpeted in the same red that carpeted the Rand lobby.

I watched Andrea as people strolled through the doors. Her hair was caramel brown and fell to the middle of her back in loose thick curls. Her nose and chin were prominent, Italian if I had to guess, Roman even, her beauty classic and ferocious.

She knew everyone, waving hello with both hands when she saw someone she was particularly happy to see, her voice becoming squeaky with excitement. Her laugh, though, was deep and throaty. She threw her head back, her smooth inviting neck framed by curtains of those caramel curls. A guy with dark brown hair who hadn't shaved in a couple of days greeted her with a wide smile, but when he leaned in with puckered lips, she evaded the kiss. She gave him a dirty look; in less than a second her expression had flashed from joy to irritation.

The lobby resembled a family reunion. I'd never seen that before, people so touchy-feely. Rubbing each others' shoulders, hugging, kissing. Even the guys.

People headed downstairs. I followed. We all walked along a hallway that smelled of sawdust and oil. To our right was a massive wood shop. We filed through a door and onto the stage of a theater. We crossed to the front of the stage to a short set of steps and took seats in the first few rows. The audience area, including little dividers that separated every row, was laid with the same dingy carpet that was used in the other parts of the building. They must have found a good sale.

Andrea shuffled into the row behind me with a bunch of friends.

"Can I have your attention please," a woman onstage said quickly as the stragglers settled in. She told us index cards were coming. We needed to write our contact information, production and crew preferences. She looked at her watch several times.

A man next to her, the Technical Director, spoke about each production and when they'd be mounted. He covered the calendar year, including the spring productions, which I couldn't consider. I needed the latest show possible this semester so it wouldn't interfere with Fall Ball. He also talked about the crews: costume, lights and sets. They all sounded fine to me.

"Hey Andrea," a girl's voice said. "What do you think?"

"I did costumes last year," she responded. "Guess I'll do lights."

I looked back. Sure, to sneak a glance at Andrea, but also to hear their insights. This was a new world.

"Hey you," Andrea said when I turned. "You pick a show?"

"I have to do *Romeo & Juliet*," I said. "It's the only one that fits my schedule."

"You in the CIA?" someone said.

I shook my head, smiling. "Baseball."

"*Romeo & Juliet* it is," Andrea said, writing on her card. "May as well have something to do with it, since I'm not in it."

"Oh, boo hoo," one of her friends said.

"I think I'll try lights," I said. "Always been interested in that."

"Oh, I'm sorry," Andrea said, clicking her pen and slipping it into the front pocket of her knapsack. "This is Dawn, Linda and Barry."

We all exchanged hellos.

People started walking to the stage and handing in their cards. Andrea leaned forward coming out of her chair and I caught a solid glimpse of her breasts as her blouse hung low, even caught the color of her bra. I faced front before I got nailed. We handed our cards over and left the building. Andrea and her friends clung together walking toward the Student Union. They talked about a couple of auditions that were approaching. Linda was thinking of not even showing, she was so unprepared.

My classes were done for the day so I needed to get my workout in before practice. Unfortunately, Boyden was in the opposite direction. I wondered if they'd even notice if I walked away.

"Listen," I said. "Thanks for everything."

Andrea dropped back. "I'll catch up with you guys," she said to her friends. "You taking off?"

"Yeah, gotta head that way."

"Well, I'm sure I'll see you."

I nodded. "*Romeo & Juliet*. Lighting."

"*Romeo & Juliet*," she smiled.

I watched her walk toward her friends. I thought of Nurse Richmond's condoms and wondered if they'd ever see the light of day. If other guys were out there screwing around, I could too. Only a matter of time. College changed everything. No parents around; less structure; tons of free time. Anything was possible here. All I knew was I wanted to kiss those lips.

**

I was with a few of the guys sitting near the campus pond. It was mid-October, but still plenty warm to catch some rays. Ducks and swans floated on the water. We were on the far side of the Fine Arts Center, but I kept my eyes on the Theater Department doors, peeled for Andrea.

"She's hot," Peeps said as a tall, black-haired girl grabbed a patch of grass to our left.

"No way, she looks like Morticia Addams."

"A little louder," Knudsen said. "I don't think she fuckin' heard ya."

"So what, Morticia was hot. And horny. Her and Gomez were always going at it."

"You know who was hot? Natasha."

"Natasha who?"

"You know, from the cartoon."

"Rocky and Bullwinkle?"

"Yeah, yeah."

"How could she be hot? Her head was a rectangle."

"No, I agree," Knudsen interjected. "She was hot. Always wearing those tight dresses."

"Yeah, I guess she had a nice body." The speaker was a freshman, a shortstop hopeful named Roberto. You could tell he wasn't comfortable disagreeing with Knudsen. "Still, though, her head was a little boxy, that's all."

"What I want to know is how an ugly squirt like Boris bagged her. I mean he only came up to her fuckin' knees."

"Hey LaPlante, what are you staring at?"

"Nothing." I shrugged.

"I think he's eyeing that fucking swan."

"Jimmy, are you eyeing that fucking swan?"

"You got me," I confessed. "I'm a swan fucker."

Peeps got to his knees, spread his arms and started singing.

"Swa-nee, how I'll fuck ya, how I'll fuck ya, my dear old Swa-nee. . ."

We laughed our asses off. I had to hand it to him, he sounded like Al Jolsen.

"You know who's hot? The Sun-Maid raisin chick."

"Yeah."

"Absolutely."

"Definitely."

"You're awful quiet over there, Jimmy."

"I was always partial to Minnie Mouse."

The line fell flat. With all the joking about sex, I felt like a wannabe, a sidekick trying to keep pace with the cool guys. I remembered bumping into Lance Durphy in the dining hall and was reminded of how he'd been smacked around because he was an outsider. I wasn't an outsider yet, but I wondered if it was only a matter of time.

After a while we got up and started toward the gym.

"We're playing pool at Charlie's tonight, right?" the freshman said.

"No, I can't," Peeps said. "I have to study for a test."

"But we agreed. We're all going together."

"We can't do everything together, Roberto," Knudsen said. "This ain't the fuckin' *White Shadow*."

**

I entered the theater through the same backstage door as I was shown last month. It was the second meeting of Theater 110—a technical run-through. A few people sat onstage in the midst of a heated discussion. Someone pounced on me as soon as I hit the edge of the stage.

"Can I help you?" whispered a heavyset blonde girl wearing glasses and a black sweater. A headset clung to her neck.

"I was told to watch a rehearsal tonight."

"Please walk down the hall and enter through the green room. This door is off limits."

I felt like I'd done something wrong. "Maybe you should put up a sign."

She nodded curtly. "I'll get right on it."

I was almost at the green room when I heard, "Hey" from behind. I turned and saw the blonde head leaning out the off-limits door. "Sorry I snapped. I appreciate you coming. Seriously."

I nodded and she was gone. The green room was packed. People sat around a long wooden table. They also sat on chairs and sofas that lined the walls, which were decorated with posters from previous productions. In a corner was a dorm-style refrigerator on which sat a half-filled Mister Coffee. A few of the people spoke quietly, others were studying *Romeo & Juliet*. Plenty others were reading something else.

"You lost, brother?" a guy with a thin beard and moustache said, a Mercutio if ever there was one. Maybe Tybalt.

"I don't think so. I'm on a tech crew."

"Marcia," he said and turned away, joining the others at the table.

A thin woman in a black tee shirt and black jeans stood up from a couch. "Can I help?"

"I signed up for the lighting crew. Theater 110."

She pointed to the wall near the door. All the crews were listed on clipboards.

"Put a check next to your name and chill. When they're done rehearsing, they'll call places to start the run-through."

The name "Andrea Carlucci" was three above mine under the lighting crew. There was no check next to it.

A half-hour later I was in the center of the last row scanning the seats for Andrea. A wooden table had been set up in the center of the seats. The director, designers and the grouchy blonde sat around it whispering. Things onstage seemed pretty rough. Most of the actors still held their scripts. The director interrupted periodically to give a brief suggestion or point something out, but for the most part the rehearsal forged ahead. I heard a noise to my left and Andrea took a seat on the aisle of my row. She gave me a two-handed wave.

At intermission, the director leaned into the blonde and whispered something in her ear. She stood up and shouted, "Five minutes, everyone, five minutes."

Andrea scooted toward me in the center.

"How are you? I said."

"Oh my God, frazzled. I am so late." She placed her knapsack and jacket on the seats in front of us. She wore an untucked flannel with the sleeves rolled up and a pair of Levis. Her hair shone under the lights.

"You didn't miss much. A couple kids hit it off at a party. Parents get pissed. You'll figure it out."

"Wish I could laugh. I read the damn thing a hundred times for the audition."

The rehearsal resumed and in ninety minutes all the crews were onstage. The lighting designer, a frail-looking female graduate student named Gwen, urged the lighting crew "downstage." She handed out schedules for the rest of the rehearsal process and performances. Behind her a couple of guys were coiling thick black cables and hanging them on pegs attached to the back wall of the theater. She discussed the "hang and focus," which would be Saturday and insisted we arrive early.

"Shit," I muttered.

After her comments, people ambled around the stage. I could have taken off, but wasn't sure if Andrea wanted me to wait. Maybe I could walk her home. I felt awkward just lingering, waiting for her to finish talking to a kid from one of her Theater classes.

During a break in the conversation, I said, "Well, I have to—"

"I'm heading out too," Andrea said. "See you, Ty."

We left through a door that faced east, the opposite direction of my dorm. I walked with her anyway toward North Pleasant Street. She talked about a scene that she was working on for a class called Period Acting.

"I like that you can take whatever classes you want," I said. "I think I can go through all four years without a single Math or Science class."

"I'm with you there. And if you have to take anything too challenging, there's always pass/fail."

"I know!" I said. "I love pass/fail. It's ingenious."

"It's a blessing is what it is." She giggled.

"You live in Central?" I said.

"Orchard Hill. You live in Central?"

"Southwest."

"Southwest?" She stopped. We were in the empty parking lot next to Franklin Dining Common. "Where you going now?"

I shrugged, feeling like a total moron. Why hadn't I just left right after the rehearsal? "Just walking, I guess."

We looked at each other. Seconds ticked.

Finally, I said, "I'll see you—"

"What's wrong with Saturday?"

"Hm?"

"You swore when Gwen said the hang and focus was Saturday."

"Oh, I usually work out with my teammates on Saturday."

"Teammates?"

"I'm on the baseball team."

"Right, you mentioned that."

"Well, hope to be. Nothing's official till the season starts."

"Are you going to do the hang and focus?"

"Yeah, I'll just work out later."

A wind blew. Andrea tucked her hands into the pockets of her jeans. "Thanks for the escort, Mr. LaPlante," she said, leaning forward in a playful half-bow.

I liked that she knew my last name, remembered it, but I didn't like that she was turning me away. She was probably doing me a favor. What if she invited me to walk her to her dorm? "My pleasure." I returned the bow.

She adjusted the knapsack on her shoulder and walked away.

When I reached my room Huck was on the phone sitting at his desk. He didn't look up when I came in, just focused on the phone.

"Everything okay?" I said when he hung up.

"A girl from high school," he said. "We sort of broke up last year when we knew we'd be going to different schools. She's at UConn. But we've been talking, exchanging letters. Looks like we're gonna give it another shot."

"That's great."

"Yeah. She's got her own room off campus. I'll drive down there on weekends, see how it goes. What about you?"

"What's that?"

"You got a girl?"

"Not now. I dated a girl when I was a junior. We were tight, but she was a year older. She's at Brown now."

"You still in touch with her?"

"We hook up sometimes when we're both home." Poor Sondra, I thought. I'm still using her.

"Brown's not that far. You could come with me to Connecticut some weekend. Take the car to Rhode Island, pick me up on the way back."

I didn't respond. Of course it would never happen.

"Who knows?" he said. "Maybe we'll both rekindle the old flame."

We stayed up late. We jawed about baseball and classes, about my night at the theater. He went on and on about the girl in Connecticut. After a while we shut off the lights. I was nodding off when I heard rustling from Huck's bed. I opened my eyes and saw him sitting bolt upright over the edge of his bed, his hands resting on his knees.

"I miss you," he said. But it wasn't Huck's voice; it was Ben's.

A smell hung in the air—rich, sweet and chocolaty—something from childhood I couldn't quite place.

"Ben . . . Is that you?" I said to the shape on the other side of the room.

His mouth moved, about to say something else, when the refrigerator creaked and buzzed. I looked at it, and when I looked back at the bed Huck was under the covers. It took a while to fall back to sleep.

**

Andrea was already in the green room when I arrived. She was talking to another girl. Both held Styrofoam cups. "Too early for you?" She nodded toward the Mister Coffee.

"Good morning. I'll grab some of this." Two cartons of orange juice sat on the table next to a tower of cups.

"Aren't you healthy," Andrea teased.

I took a sip. "Tastes good too."

Gwen talked as she led the lighting crew, about ten of us, onto the stage. Dozens of stage lights were lined up along the rear of the stage. "I'd like to finish this today. Otherwise, we'll be interfering with other crews' schedules." While she talked, several steel rods the length of the stage lowered from the ceiling.

Gwen split the group in two, A through K to hang stage lights on the rods and L through Z to hang "house lights." Andrea nodded goodbye and headed toward the rows of lights upstage. I felt a tap on my shoulder.

"Hey buddy, you working house lights?" He was a little guy, about five-six, his beard and moustache as long and straggly as his dark hair. His jeans were ripped in several places, but his Neil Young concert tee shirt seemed spanking clean.

"Yeah."

"I'm Lenny, the M.E." He spoke fast. "Can you give me a hand lugging lights upstairs?"

"Sure."

I followed him out a door and down a ramp that led underneath the stage where more lights were stored. The low space was lit by a single bulb. We loaded them onto a flatbed dolly and pushed it back up the ramp into an elevator.

"So what's an M.E.?" I asked after he pressed a button.

"What are you, new?"

I nodded.

"Master Electrician."

"Sounds important."

"Big bucks."

We unloaded a few instruments on every floor, then joined the others hanging lights. Lenny explained that every lighting position was tagged with a slip of paper stating what instrument was needed—fresnel, par can, leko, what have you. Then he showed me how to differentiate one from the other. I heard people talking about batons, twofers, threefers, baffles, louvers, gels. All I knew was that I had to look at the tag, grab the right light and clamp it to the beam.

From where I worked above the balcony I had a clear view of Andrea. She had taken a light and was playfully pointing it at someone on the crew, following him around. The guy who had attempted to kiss her in the lobby tried to join in the fun, but Andrea didn't give him the time of day.

We worked until 12:30, then Gwen called lunch and told everyone to be back by 2:00. We all trooped over to the Newman

Center for sandwiches and brought everything back to the lawn near the pond. It was chilly, mid-November, but everyone agreed it was better than eating in the cramped green room. Some of the gang sat on stone benches along the pond. Others, like Andrea and me, sat on the grass.

A Frisbee game broke out. Andrea joined while I finished my sandwich. Lenny sat nearby and introduced me to people as they joined the picnic. In between chatting with me, he read a beat-up spy novel.

"Man, I'd like to fuck her," a guy sitting near us said.

I turned. It was the guy who had the hots for Andrea. He sat with a couple other guys from the crew. They were referring to a tall athletic-looking girl walking along the path toward the FAC stairs.

One of his friends said, "She's kinda big, ain't she?"

"Yeah," he said, "the kinda big I'd like sitting on my face right about now."

The threesome laughed uproariously. Lenny and I laughed too.

One of the Frisbee players made a circus catch and Andrea jumped up and down and clapped.

"Man, I'd like to screw Andrea straight into tomorrow," her admirer said. His group was gathering their trash and standing up. "What do you think, LaPlante?"

Lenny closed his book. "Just ignore him," he said to me. "He's a jerk."

He knew my name. He must have seen Andrea and me together and asked who I was.

"She's pretty, that's for sure."

"Aw, you're not going to say anything nasty, huh?" His eyes shifted to mine, waiting. He was thin, slightly stooped. Looked like a comma. If I were a director I'd cast him as the villain's henchman, brave while surrounded by cohorts, but quick to turn coward when challenged on his own. "Not about Andrea. You're a good boy, huh?"

If he thought I was going to be bullied by a Theater major he had another thing coming. I wanted to stand up and walk over to him nose to nose, *High Noon* his ass. But he wasn't worth the trouble.

13. The Naked Truth

It was the second week of December, too cold to walk. I stepped off the bus. Wreaths decorated downtown businesses. Holiday lights hung from one side of the street to the other and twinkled green, gold, blue and red. Cliff had invited me to dinner. No party tonight; just the three of us.

As I knocked on the door, a couple of kids walked around from the back of the building. One of them held a Wiffle Ball bat, the other a few Wiffle balls.

"Is Cliff home?" They were both about ten, eleven.

"Yeah, I think so."

Cliff opened the door and was about to welcome me in when he saw the kids. "What's up, boys?"

"You said you'd play this week," one of them said.

"Now? It's cold."

"You get warm when you play."

"I got company tonight, fellas. How about tomorrow?"

They looked disappointed. "You haven't played in a while."

"I don't mind," I said.

"We have to hurry, though," the shorter one said. "The parking lot starts filling up around 5:30."

Cliff stepped into the apartment, said, "Marie, keep an eye on the oven, okay?" and reappeared in his winter coat.

"Is there enough light?" I asked the kids.

"Plenty."

We split into two teams; Cliff took one kid, I took the other. They explained the rules. No bases; just swing and hit. The foundation of the apartment building was a single; first story windows a double; second story windows a triple; roof a home run. We spent about twenty minutes playing. As we headed indoors, I promised the kids I'd play again.

The apartment smelled of rosemary and oregano. Marie took my coat and hung it in the closet.

"What would you like to drink?" Cliff said. "Beer? Coke? You drink wine?"

"Coke's good."

Cliff headed to the kitchen, saying, "Coming right up."

"You got practice tomorrow?" Marie asked.

"No, haven't had real practices since the end of October. We start up again last week of January."

"They give you some time off, huh?"

"We still work out as a team. Three days of strength and conditioning, two days of sprint and agility."

Cliff came back with the Coke and a plate full of little slices of toasted bread topped with chopped tomatoes and herbs. We took seats around a scarred coffee table. I popped one of the toast things into my mouth and tasted an explosion of tomato and garlic and pepper.

"Dang, that's good." I sipped my Coke.

"Starting off with bruschetta."

Cliff and Marie drank white wine. I sat back comfortably on the couch, at ease. Marie still wanted to talk about baseball, whether or not I'd ultimately make the team, the caliber of talent of my teammates, the possible traveling.

Cliff stood up, moving toward the kitchen. "Got a lamb roast coming. It has to cool for a while," he said from the kitchen alcove, then brought the roasting pan to the center of the table and set it on a small towel. The roast was surrounded by sliced carrots and small red potatoes. "Got a few sides too. A spinach soufflé, which sounds gross, I know, but it's really good, and a spicy cabbage thing that's sort of an experiment, so don't be afraid to say it sucks."

"Wow," I said, "real food."

"It's a celebration, after all," Marie said.

"Oh, yeah?" I watched Marie as she stood next to Cliff at the table and wrapped her arms around his waist.

"We're getting married," Cliff said.

"We're getting married," Marie repeated, her bright smile spreading across her face.

"Wow." I kissed Marie on the cheek, shook Cliff's hand and clutched his shoulder. "That's fantastic. When? Where?"

"Next fall in Vermont."

"Do Ma and Dad know?"

"We told them to keep it hush-hush. We wanted to tell you ourselves."

Weren't they too young? Did college students marry? Well, next year they wouldn't be college students. They'd be spouses. My head filled with the notion that this was the closest I'd ever get to a real relationship—a bystander to my brother's.

"I'll check the rest of the food," Cliff said.

"So how did it happen?" I said, hoping to sound upbeat.

"What?" She sat at the table.

"The proposal." I sat too.

"Oh. We were walking along the old rail line in Hadley. It's a beautiful path. The snow was falling. Right out of a postcard."

I found myself nodding. Behind her Cliff was removing baking dishes from the oven. "Sounds great."

A moment passed. Cliff banged away in the kitchen. Then Marie reached across the table and touched my hand. And in that moment I realized she knew everything—my childhood battles with Cliff; the accident; the hormone injections. I pulled my hand away at the shock of the realization, but I could tell from her worried face that she mistook it for anger. She turned away, about to stand, but

I reached and caught her wrist. She stayed put and placed her free hand on mine.

"I'm fine," I said. "I'm happy for you guys. Truly."

Her eyes brimmed with tears. She squeezed my hand and whispered, "He loves you so much."

What could he have told her that brought her to tears? I imagined him confessing to her about the accident, weighed down with the responsibility of it, compounded over years, bloated with guilt.

"Everything okay?" Cliff said, setting down the side dishes.

"I was just telling Jimmy how you proposed." She wiped her eyes. "I get emotional."

"I got down on one knee and everything."

"You know, I never even noticed the ring."

She held it up, a small round diamond set in a gold band.

"It's really nice."

Cliff sliced the roast and served it with the other food. He was right about the cabbage, a little weird, both in taste and texture, but I ate it along with everything else. Marie talked about the wedding plans, how the ceremony was to be held in a park under a ceiling of foliage and the reception in the penthouse of a Burlington hotel. Then we talked about potential honeymoon destinations—Hawaii, Bermuda, a Caribbean cruise.

After dinner, Cliff and I flopped onto the couch and watched MTV while Marie washed dishes. I offered to help, but she wouldn't hear of it.

"Can I ask you something?" Cliff said.

We were watching Don Henley. I looked over. He seemed nervous.

"What's the matter?"

"Nothing. Just, just wondering if you'd be my best man."

The clanking of dishes stopped. I wondered if Marie was listening.

"Hell yeah, of course. Who else you gonna get?" I joked. "It's not like I ever see you with any friends."

"Hey, I got friends," he said, laughing. When the laughs subsided, he said, "I thought . . . you might say no."

"No way," I said. "Mother would kill me."

I couldn't help deflecting his attempts to get serious with smartass remarks. I don't know why, I guess because I felt he wanted to lasso me, have a sappy heartfelt conversation about the accident and its aftermath, a topic we'd never discussed in depth; maybe agree that the past was the past and going forward we'd be the best of friends. But hadn't we accomplished enough for now? We'd just spent the evening together, broke bread, discussed his wedding plans. Hell, I was even going to be his best man.

**

I reached the dorm around 11:00. A few of the guys were tossing a Nerf in the hallway as I walked toward my room. When I inserted my key, Huck came to the door before I could open it all the way. His face was flushed and sweaty, his shirt off.

"What's going on?" I said.

"Hey man, I got an unexpected guest."

"Your girlfriend's here?"

"Sshhh. No, another girl. You think you could find a place to crash tonight?"

I heard rustling from his bed.

"Ah . . ." What was wrong with people? I remembered when Cliff had asked me to leave the house in Brockton so he could be alone with Marie. Hey, I understood that sex was a great, marvelous, wondrous experience, but so much so that it caused people to banish their roommates? Their brothers? I could have stayed at Cliff's, but didn't feel like traipsing all the way back. "We're supposed to give notice when this happens."

"It was unexpected. What can I say?" Huck looked back into the room and whispered something. His face reappeared in the crack. "Tell ya what. Give us an hour. Is that cool?"

The last thing I wanted was for the guys to think I didn't understand the importance of getting laid. I needed them to think I was an active participant in the practice of roommates bargaining for privacy—referred to on our floor as the Fucking Guidelines. "Yeah, that's fine, whatever you need."

I strolled down the hall and sat in the lounge. Johnny Carson was talking to somebody from a zoo while a lizard crawled around his desk. The door was unlocked when I returned. Huck and the girl were sitting fully clothed playing cards on his bed. The air in the tiny room felt heavy and smelled slightly of sweat. When he introduced me she offered a friendly sheepish smile. She deflated any awkwardness by asking me if I wanted to join the game and extending a plate of Saltines and Cheez Whiz that they'd laid out on the bed.

Everything was all right until we hit the hay. She was to spend the night, which was fine, but a few minutes after we turned off the lights I heard a snap, obviously the band of Huck's underwear. I pictured her hand down there, stroking, caressing. They both started giggling. I couldn't take it. I grabbed my pillow and blanket and left. It was around 1:00; the lounge was deserted. I flung my pillow at the end of one of the sofas and tried to grab some shuteye.

**

I snagged a copy of *The Collegian* on my way into the dining hall. The headline stopped me cold: "McBride Collapses, Dies on Court; Irregular Heartbeat Cited."

Reginald McBride wasn't just a UMass story. His Fitchburg High basketball career had been so off-the-charts he made news broadcasts all over Massachusetts. The campus—for those who cared and we were numerous—had been exhilarated since he announced he'd attend UMass.

I didn't even get food. I just sat at a table and read. He hadn't been doing anything strenuous, just shooting the ball around in The Cage with friends. There were no details about the irregular heartbeat, whether it was supraventricular tachycardia, my illness, or ventricular tachycardia, or something else altogether.

I called home, trying not to sound too anxious. Mother was sure that I'd be fine. She said that if I had any concerns I should get a checkup from a cardiologist at Health Services.

"Or," she said, "come home and we'll visit Dr. Aranofsky. But I'm sure you're okay, sweetie."

Just hearing a reasonable voice was calming. My father called when he got home from work, suggesting a call to Dr. Aranofsky would be worthwhile if it would ease my mind. I decided not to call the doctor. I remembered the time I saw him in high school; he thought I was a worrywart. Two days later, Health Services announced that McBride suffered from primary cardiomyopathy, a disease that inflamed the heart muscles and often led to heart failure. The final paragraph of the announcement said: "A university source stated that at some point in the future student athletes may need to undergo more rigorous physicals before joining a team."

Great, I thought. What if I can't play because of my condition? Dr. Aranofsky had said time and again that it wasn't serious. But what if the university needed to be super cautious? Something else to add to my list of problems.

**

That night I arrived at the theater at 6:30. Usually only two or three members of the lighting crew needed to be present during performances, but tonight was closing night and everyone would show up eventually to celebrate the run. I slipped out of the green room to catch my favorite parts—the balcony scene, the scene where Juliet argues with her father, the swordfights, the nurse's bits.

After the play the cast and crew squeezed into the green room and drank champagne from plastic cups. Everyone chatted while crews performed their final tasks and actors removed their costumes and makeup.

We all left for the cast party. It was at the dramaturge's house off campus out behind Southwest. As the lighting crew made its way toward Whitmore, Andrea and I fell behind and talked. She was relieved 110 was over; she'd be able to spend more time studying now that finals were approaching.

"So why baseball?" she said as we crossed Mass. Ave.

"Why?"

"Yeah, what makes it special?"

"I don't know. Hitting the ball. Catching it."

"Oh, come on. Don't be so boring. What makes it special to *you*?" She poked me in the arm.

"To me, huh?" I didn't want to give a throwaway answer. I wanted to be thoughtful. "I like the moment when the ball leaves the pitcher's hand. Hurtling through the air like that, before it reaches the plate. Something's about to happen, but no one knows what.

That anticipation, you know?" I looked at her as we walked. Her eyes were on the sidewalk. "See, boring."

"No. I was just thinking about when you go to a play, there's that instant as the lights go down, before the curtain lifts. Like you were saying. The anticipation, not knowing what's about to happen."

"Hey, there's my dorm," I said, pointing at Washington.

We were cutting through Southwest to get to the party. As we continued through the concourse, a deep voice shouted from above: "Hey, you fucking wussy." Looking up, I saw Knudsen's head hanging out of our lounge window.

"He's looking right at us," Andrea said.

"Don't be offended. I think he's referring to me."

"Party on eight. Bring the hot babe."

"Now he's referring to you," I said

"Fantastic," she laughed. "He's so my type. You know him?"

"Oh yeah. My drill sergeant. You want to go up?"

"Sure, we'll go to the cast party after."

"It might be a little crazy up there," I said as we walked into the building.

"I can do crazy."

The floor was loud. Stereos blared from rooms, all playing different music. The party emanated from the lounge. It was jammed, thirty people at least, all of them in different stages of drunkenness. This thing must have started early. A keg, which was forbidden in dorms, sat in a corner. A guy I didn't know pumped away, then poured a cup.

"You want to catch up?" I said.

"There's not enough booze in all of Amherst for us to catch up."

Outside the lounge, a couple of the guys were kicking a soccer ball up and down the corridor, beers in hand.

"Let's just go to the cast party," I said. "We don't have to stay here."

She stood there, not wanting a beer, apparently not wanting to rush to the other party either. "I didn't eat before the play. Want to order a pizza?"

"I've never said no to pizza."

"Jimmy Boy," the guys screamed as we left the lounge and walked down the hall, trying to evade the soccer ball.

Peeps stuck his head out of his room and sang his special version of *Swanee*, which he did almost every time he saw me. Andrea looked at him like he was crazy.

In the room, I closed the door. We were alone. Her decision. After all, she wasn't eager to go to the cast party. And she wanted pizza, which she knew had to be ordered from my room. I felt excited. I remembered the condoms. In my bureau. Would I need them? I wished they were closer to the bed. Relax Casanova, I thought, you're getting ahead of yourself.

I took our coats and tossed them on Huck's bed. "You want the tour? His side," I said, pointing to where I'd just dumped our coats. "My side."

"Is your roommate in the lounge?"

"Na, he skips town most weekends. Visits his girlfriend in Connecticut. There's a picture of them on the milk crate." I tried to remember if the picture had been there when he was with the other girl.

She looked at the photograph while I opened my desk drawer and picked up the Yellow Pages. Andrea blurted out a phone number.

"You know it by heart?"

"My weakness, if you don't mind Domino's."

"Not at all," I said. "Toppings?"

"Mushroom okay?"

"Sausage too?"

She nodded, then pushed the coats aside and sat on Huck's bed while I ordered.

"So what are you doing during the break?" she said.

"Just going home." I sat across from her on my bed. "Coming back a week early for baseball."

"Really?"

"Yeah, they open the dorm early."

She didn't have much planned. Just visiting high school friends, spending time with her family. "I'm psyched to see my little brother. I love the expression on his face when I walk through the door. Sometimes he waits for me at the end of the street and runs alongside the car until we reach the house."

"Like a dog," I said.

"Exactly. Like a big floppy dog. He keeps bugging me to bring him up to campus."

"How old is he?"

"Eight."

"Does he like baseball?"

"Of course."

"We'll have to play. Maybe I can teach him a thing or two." It occurred to me that tonight was the last night of crew. "We'll stay in touch, right?" I said, hoping I didn't sound desperate.

"Yeah, why wouldn't we?" She nodded toward the picture of Huck and his girlfriend and said, "What about you, you got a girlfriend?"

I shook my head. "Nope."

I was about to ask her if she had a boyfriend when someone slammed repeatedly on the door. When I opened it, one of our catchers, Fred Hickey, stood shirtless in the doorway. He held a beer can in each hand. I couldn't figure out how he'd banged on the door until I saw he was wearing knee pads.

"Come out and play, Jimmy Boy," he said, then noticed Andrea on Huck's bed. "Oops. Look at me . . ." His eyes were half closed; he looked like he was about to topple backward. "I'm interrupting . . . . I'm an interrupter . . . Interrupterer . . . er . . ." He left the doorway and teetered toward the lounge.

When the lobby rang, I took my wallet and ran downstairs. On the way back I grabbed a couple of beers from the keg. In the room, Andrea hadn't moved. I set the pizza on my desk chair, rolled it between us and sat back on my side, near the foot of the bed.

I lifted the box. It smelled oily and delicious. "The biggest slice for you," I said, tearing the piece and handing it over. I talked about the team's spring trip. "It's spring break, the first week of the season.

Schools from the northeast travel to Florida to play teams from all over the country, usually two games a day. Of course you have to make the team first."

"Do you think you'll make it?"

"I don't know. These guys are so good. It's weird, being in competition with them and living with them at the same time. I mean, we're all so close."

She took another slice from the box, but instead of returning to Huck's bed she sat on mine. My heart thumped. She sat pretty far away, near the pillow, but still, she was on my bed.

She talked about the plays she wanted to read during intersession to prepare for next semester's auditions. She was excited about an Ibsen play because it had several strong female characters. *Three Sisters* and *All's Well That Ends Well* were also being performed. Lots of opportunities. She got up to toss her crust into the pizza box, then sat so close to me that our knees touched. "Two's my limit," she said, turning her body to mine and setting her hand on my leg above my knee.

My penis roared in my pants.

"Jimmy, Jimmy," she said, leaning forward.

Her lips touched mine. They were soft and firm at the same time. The rush that I'd felt in my chest rippled through my whole body in glorious warm vibrations. My skin thickened with gooseflesh. Hair bristled behind my neck and under my arms. We kissed in the same sitting position for a while, then she reached for my belt buckle.

Inwardly I flinched. Come on, my man, you can do this, I coached myself. Tonight's all about you. You and the hottest girl on campus. Not a care in the world. All that negative shit is long gone. Another life. Just pick one thing about her and focus on that. Her voice, her hair, her adorable wave, her smooth neck, her throaty laugh. And even if your dick gets soft, it'll still be nice to feel her fingers down there.

Are you crazy? I argued. Once she realizes your dick's soft, she's going to want an explanation. This girl isn't accustomed to limp dicks. Jesus, I wouldn't even be in this predicament if I'd just obeyed the goddamn rules.

Gently moving her hand away from my fly, I guided her down

on the bed and lay alongside her, kissing her the whole time. No big deal that I was pushing her away; we had all night.

I unclasped the button of her jeans and lowered the zipper. I felt the lip of her panties, the softness of her belly. And the prickly thatch of her pubic hair. Her brown eyes opened. She smiled. She lifted her butt and slid her pants and underwear over her hips. My fingers brushed the skin along her pelvic bone. Her knee jerked up wildly toward her chest.

"Ticklish there," she said, giggling.

"Ticklish, aye?" I said in a playful sinister tone and again brushed my fingers just inside her hipbone.

"Ahh!" She flipped onto her belly, screaming and laughing as I tried to tickle her some more. Her pants had been lowered halfway down her ass. I stared at her crack, wanted to kiss it, bury my tongue in it. She moved her hands under the pillow when I stopped tickling, as though readying for a massage. I parted the locks of hair that spilled over her shoulders and kissed the back of her neck.

"Mmm," she breathed, then said, "feels nice," her voice muted by the pillow.

I lowered myself onto my side so that I faced her. "Turn over," I said, no longer playing.

She maneuvered onto her back, pushed down her pants and underwear and kicked them down to her ankles. I couldn't believe how beautiful she was laying there, her mouth parted, her entire body eager. Her pubic hair was thick and coarse, darker than the hair on her head. I moved my hand lower, until my middle finger found the crease of her vagina. My finger slid into its moisture, its warmth, the strange soft ridged texture. She closed her eyes and turned her head into my shoulder.

I moved my finger around in there and after a minute she guided it to the front where she pressed it against a small hard knob of flesh. Her clit. She brought it back deep inside, moving it in and out. Slowly our rhythm increased, my finger always returning to the bump in front. Finally, she let go of my hand and clutched the blanket.

My dick was hard, with no sign of fading. This was the best night of my life!

Her breathing became louder. A tiny high-pitched noise seeped from her mouth. She was wet and slippery as she spread her legs wider and pulled me into the crook of her neck. I felt the pulse of her rhythmic whispering moans. Her back arched, then slowly relaxed. I slowed my hand to a gentle caress. Sweat dripped down her neck where it stained the edge of her blouse.

I stopped.

Her body, her face lay completely still. "Oh God, Jimmy" she muttered and smiled. She reached for my pillow and held it over her face. "I'm embarrassed," she said.

"Why?"

She didn't respond. She just breathed. I watched her chest rise and fall. I watched her naked belly and lowered my gaze to her pubic hair and the curve of her hips. I lifted the pillow slightly and peeked underneath.

She was smiling. "It felt so good."

"Me too. To make you feel good, I mean."

She shifted her body to the side and rubbed my inner thigh up toward my penis. The erection that had been so mighty moments ago had dwindled. I instinctively flinched away.

"Are you okay?" she laughed uncomfortably.

"Sure."

The best plan was to avoid further contact. At least I got her off. That was me, I did that! One step at a time. Maybe if I tried to fuck her my dick would stiffen. But what if it didn't? What if she lowered my underwear and it just hung there like a caterpillar?

She lay on the bed uninhibited, her jeans and panties still gathered at her ankles, her pussy completely exposed. "Come closer," she said, sitting up. "Let me take your shirt off."

I scooted next to her on the bed and lifted my arms. She peeled off my jersey and looked at my body.

"You're amazing, you know that?" she said.

"You think?"

She undid my buckle and slid the belt from the loops. When she reached for the button I took her hands in mine.

"Can we just lay here for a while?"

DO IT! I silently screamed. Take your clothes off and get busy. If you fail, just tell her you're nervous because you've never been with someone so beautiful. She'll eat that shit up.

She smiled oddly, as though I was joshing. "You saying you want to cuddle?" Anyone else on the floor would've been on top of her as soon as they had the chance.

"Do you mind?"

She looked irritated, but after a second, said, "I guess not." She kicked her jeans onto the floor, then reached down and slid on her skimpy panties.

"You can stay over," I said eagerly. "I'll walk you home tomorrow."

She nodded. "I don't have my jammies."

I crossed the room to my dresser and held up a tee shirt.

"That's fine."

I tossed her the shirt.

"I don't normally sleep in my bra."

"Do you want me to turn away?"

"Do you want to turn away?"

"No."

She tossed her shirt onto her pants. She slid the bra straps off her shoulder, then unclipped the hooks and flung the bra on her pile of clothes. She unfolded the tee shirt. Jesus, her breasts. I gawked like an adolescent—they were perfect.

"This is kind of weird, in case you don't know," she said, not unkindly.

"I'm sorry," I said, still staring. "You're gorgeous."

"That makes it even weirder." Socks still on, she pulled down the covers, scooted close to the wall and patted the empty side of the bed.

I took off my pants, then flicked off the lights and joined her in bed. "Are you cold?" I said.

"No, why?"

"Your socks are on."

"I always sleep in my socks."

We faced each other under the covers. Moonlight seeped through the open blind and I was able to see her face. My God, I thought, she's in my bed, here for the taking! Knudsen was right; I was a fucking wussy.

I thought of how her face and body had contorted while I felt her down there and wondered if she'd accept a relationship where I'd please her whenever she wanted and she wouldn't have to worry about pleasing me.

"Are you religious?" she said.

"No."

She looked sad, confused.

"Did I mention you were gorgeous?" I said.

She brought her hand to my cheek and smiled. "Really?"

"Why would I lie?"

"You should have seen yourself when I touched you. You practically cringed."

Maybe I should have told her the truth. I'll tell her tomorrow morning, I promised myself. While walking her home. "I'm sorry," I said.

She traced the line of my neck with her finger.

"Believe me, it's not you," I said. "You're, you're perfect, like out of a dream."

She laughed. Her eyes were becoming heavy, mine too.

Falling asleep, I smelled her on my fingers.

**

I woke up a few hours later; it was still dark outside. She had turned toward the wall, her back to me. She breathed heavily, on the verge of snoring. I touched her shoulder. She didn't stir. I kissed her shoulder. My penis charged with life. I lowered my underwear. The thing needed elbow room. I inched closer, touching the tip of my dick to her ass. I wanted to feel it against her skin—something soft and smooth, womanly.

I maneuvered myself down the mattress and pressed it lightly against the underside of her ass. I was careful not to wake her. I felt her tiny hairs against the taut skin of my erection. Mother of God, it felt so deliriously fucking good. If I rubbed it against her skin a few times I knew I'd come all over the back of her legs.

She moved, started to turn. What an asshole! I thought. It didn't even occur to me until she stirred that this was a violation.

She faced me, apparently not mad at all, just groggy. "What's going on down there?" she said, smiling. "Change of heart?"

She touched my chest, then her fingers descended down my stomach. I flinched away before she reached my penis, pulled the shrunken worm back into my shorts. It defied logic how fast it died.

It just lay there, dormant, sullen. I knew that I wasn't supposed to think, that my brain was supposed to stay out of the way, but how could it stay out of the way if I had to keep telling it to stay out of the way?

"What is it with you?" she said, sitting up, peeved. "What's the problem?"

"I'm sorry." I swung my legs over the edge of the bed and leaned forward on my knees. I couldn't face her.

"This is too much." She flung the covers aside, strode across the bed and retrieved her jeans.

"Don't do that, don't leave. I'll sleep on my roommate's bed. You can stay there."

She didn't bother putting on her bra; just whipped off my shirt and threw on hers.

"You don't want to do this. It's dark out." Hell, you may as well tell her now. Nothing to lose, she's leaving anyway. Tell her you got a medical problem, that you were embarrassed to say something earlier. But you want to tell her now because she's special, because she's funny and she's kind and you want to get to know her better. You want to help her with her lines when she gets cast in a show. You want to play catch with her eight-year-old brother.

She tied her sneakers, grabbed her coat.

I stood in front of the door. "Please don't leave."

"Look," she said, shoving her bra in her coat pocket. "I don't need this." She looked not at my eyes, but at the door behind me.

I stepped aside.

After a second of fumbling with the lock, she was gone.

I couldn't let it end this way. I couldn't let her think I was a pervert; as far as she knew, I wanted to bang her while she slept, a step removed from one of those monsters who fuck dead people.

I should have told her the truth in bed. I threw on some clothes and ran down the hall. She wasn't at the elevators. I leaped down the stairs. She had just passed through the main entranceway as I rushed around the corner into the lobby. I banged through the doors. She looked back at the clanging of metal against concrete.

"Stop," I said. "Give me a chance to explain."

"Why?" She turned, but didn't come closer. At least she wasn't walking away. "It's obvious you want nothing to do with me."

"What? How can you say that after what I did for you?"

"Excuse me?" She stormed toward me. "For *me*? Is that what you think? That this is about making me come?"

I just stood there. Yeah, that's pretty much what I thought.

"Jimmy, it's about . . . it's about feeling connected. Balance. Yeah, it felt good, but there's gotta be . . ." Her hands moved quickly, making a back and forth gesture. ". . . You know, the give and take. It's supposed to be about sharing."

"All right, I'm sorry." I didn't know what she was talking about. "I'm kinda new at this. I don't always know what you're thinking. Shit, I don't even know what I'm thinking half the time. I just don't want you to think I'm a freak."

"I don't think you're a freak," she said, her face inches from mine. "I think you're a jerk."

"Why am I jerk?"

"You think you can do what you did to me, then flinch away like you're too good for my touch?"

"Andrea, I don't think that. I said how beautiful you are."

"Words. Big deal." She was pissed off. "I mean, all your shit works." She pointed to my crotch. "I'm just not allowed to touch it."

I stepped toward her, but she took a step back.

"And, you know, I was willing to let it slide for a night. I figured maybe you're shy, maybe you're a virgin . . ."

"It's true," I shouted, happy to admit I was a virgin if it would smooth things over, give me another chance. "I *am* a virgin."

"Shut the fuck up," someone screamed from several floors up.

"So what. Get over yourself," she shouted, not caring who she woke. "You think you're the only virgin in college?"

"Shhh. Besides, it's not just that . . . When I was a kid, ten years old, my brother and I . . ."

So I told her. I sputtered through it as fast as I could, knowing she was freezing her ass off and wanted nothing to do with me. But I had to get it out. Cliff and the shovel, the pain, the hospital, the surgery. At one point she seemed genuinely concerned. I barreled through: injections, testosterone. "And . . . uh . . . there have been other problems. Like in my head. Messing up when I want to be close with someone. Like tonight with you."

She grabbed her arms, hugged herself.

"This is gross, I know. And I wish I didn't have to blurt it all out like this. I wouldn't for just anybody. I never have before. But for you I—"

"Look," she said impatiently, "I'm sorry for all that, whatever you went through. Maybe someday we can talk about it. But tonight . . . You know, I don't need this psycho drama crap, right now, Jimmy." She walked toward the middle of the concourse. I wanted to follow, but knew she'd have none of it. After a few steps, she turned. "Call me when you grow up. Okay? When you're ready."

I watched her jog across the plaza, her form becoming smaller and smaller as it made its way toward her dorm.

I returned to my room. The tee shirt I'd given her lay twisted on the floor. I opened the drawer to put it away and saw the condoms. What a retard I was for thinking I'd need them.

In bed, after jerking off, I thought about what she'd said. *Call me when you're ready.* It left things wide open. I wondered if I could get away with calling her tomorrow. The semester was practically over. I couldn't imagine not seeing her until next semester. It seemed like years away.

I must have dozed off when I heard a thud against the wall, like someone had tossed a baseball near my head. I looked around. A figure sat on the edge of Huck's bed. Not Huck, though.

"So what's the deal?" Ben said. "You're gonna die a virgin?" He looked exactly like he had when we played together. A boy. I recognized the fancy sneakers.

I didn't know what to say. He sat there. Right there. He stood up and walked over to my bed. I started to get up, but he held out his hand as if I shouldn't bother. The mattress didn't move under his weight.

"Look at you," he said quietly, "all grown up." He extended his hand toward my face, but didn't touch me. "Man," he said, laughing weakly, "she was right. You gotta get over yourself. You gotta get fucking, my man. You gotta do it for both of us." He laughed and I saw that his gums were black.

I pulled away from him, needing as much space between us as possible. "You should be here instead of me." His life would have improved here, grown richer. He rose unsteadily from the bed.

"Where you going?"

"Bedtime." His limbs seemed stiff as he hobbled over to Huck's bed. He moved his arms and shoulders as though he was working out kinks. "I get tired so easily."

He pulled down the covers and crawled under. When I looked carefully, I saw that somehow the body beneath the blanket lay the length of the whole bed. I couldn't see his face, but he suddenly could have been my age. He could have been Huck. He could have been one of the guys.

**

I thought about Ben's creepy little visits the next day, but thoughts of Andrea took over. *Call me when you're ready.* The words taunted me—at the gym, dining hall, library. I must have grabbed the phone a hundred times, but of course I wasn't ready. I wouldn't have to ask myself if I was ready; I'd just know. Right? I needed to ask someone.

Around 9:00 that night I was sitting at my desk. Huck lay on his bed reading *A Connecticut Yankee in King Arthur's Court.*

I reached for the phone and dialed. Cliff answered.

"Hi, it's Jimmy."

"Hey, what's up?"

"You mind if we talk?"

"Shoot."

"Think I could stop by?"

"Are you all right? You sound—"

"I'm fine. I just . . . I just . . ."

"It doesn't matter. Come over."

I caught a bus and was at his place in fifteen minutes. He appeared at the door before I knocked. The house was silent. He looked dressed for bed, in an oversized thermal top and UMass shorts.

"Where is everyone?"

"Simon and Brenda should be back soon. Marie's closing up the store."

I wondered how upset I'd sounded on the phone. Had he told everyone to skedaddle?

"What's up with you?"

I didn't know what to say, how to start.

"You want coffee or tea?"

"Na, I'm good."

"Hot chocolate?"

"Yeah, that sounds good."

I sat on the sofa as he headed to the kitchen. He pulled some envelopes of cocoa from a cupboard.

"Instant?" I said. "I figured you'd make it from scratch."

He laughed. "The whipped cream's fresh. With real vanilla."

After the water boiled, he set the cups on the coffee table, then went back for a plate of chocolate chip cookies. He placed it down and sat next to me on the sofa. He looked tired, his hair mussed, his cheeks and chin dark with a few days of growth.

"I met this girl."

I started from the beginning, how we'd met at the Rand lobby, and ended with last night. The more we talked, the further back in time I traveled. My visits to Dr. Young; Sondra; Colleen. I didn't hold back. I never talked about this to anyone. It gushed.

I delved into the gory details about Saturday night—asking Andrea if we could cuddle, getting hard when she was asleep, shrinking as soon as she woke. Pleading for her to stay. Telling her the whole story out there in the cold.

"I thought as long as I . . . you know . . . I pleased her, then we'd be cool. I mean, *I* would."

"That's how guys think."

"She kept talking about give and take and balance and sharing. Shit, I'm still trying to sort it all out."

"Hey, you're not alone in misunderstanding what girls think. Believe me, Marie and I get in our share of spats."

I suddenly remembered the question that had plagued me all day. "She said, 'Call when you grow up. When you're ready'." I laughed a bit, hoping to mask the self-pity. "You think I should call?"

Cliff slowly shook his head. "I don't know. Maybe give her some time to cool down. You really like this girl, so maybe . . . you know, get some experience first. You don't want to screw up with her again. If it's meant to be, she'll be around next semester. Maybe even a year from now."

"A year!" I let my head fall back on the couch.

"You could always talk to Dr. Young again. Maybe he could prescribe something. Help you relax."

"You think he'd give me a drug to help me get laid?"

Cliff's solutions didn't matter. I was more determined than ever to stay away from girls. I remembered that night in high school when I was on the brink of telling him about Colleen. And here I was in the same scenario. I hadn't matured a single day in three years.

"If it doesn't work out . . ." He shrugged. "Then maybe she's not for you. You're a good kid, star athlete and all. There'll be other girls."

"Yeah, that's me." I took a sip of cocoa. The heat felt good going down.

"I want you to know," he said slowly, ". . . that I'm always here for you. You call me whenever you want." He ran his finger along his teaspoon. "What happened in the past . . ."

"You don't have to say anything."

"Well, it's not fair, you having to go through this shit." He dipped his spoon back into the chocolate and muttered into the cup, "And let's face it, it's my fault."

"It was an accident."

"I'm sure that doesn't make it easier for you. It doesn't for me." He looked at me quickly, then away, unable to hold my gaze. "I just want you to know that I think about it...about you, your life, what it's been like for you. And I'm sorry for it."

"Hey," I said, touching his knee, "I didn't come here for an apology. I came here . . . I told you all this because . . . you know, because you're my brother . . ."

"That's nice," he said, nodding. "You know, the worst part is I feel gipped. All the time we could have been closer. Damn, I don't think I've ever told you how proud I am of you. Of everything you've accomplished. And how sad it makes me that we haven't been friends. I regret I didn't do more to make that happen."

"I could have done more too." I watched him stare off, scratch his cheek. "Maybe we start now," I said.

He said, "I love you."

I couldn't look at him; didn't know what to say. I kept my eyes on the carpet.

"I know that's not something guys say to each other. Not even brothers, but I . . ."

I felt him get off the couch. He gathered the cups and spoons and brought them to the alcove. I followed with the plate of cookies. We bumped into each other a few times as we shifted around in the cramped space, him placing the dishes in the sink and me looking for a cookie container. We faced each other as I was about to open a cupboard, and before I fully realized what was happening his arms were around my shoulders and mine around his back. I felt the sleeve of his thermal against my ear, his rough whiskered cheek against mine. I held him tighter and felt him breathe.

Epilogue: After Party

Cliff, Marie and I hopped a Peter Pan to Brockton. They stayed until Christmas day, then drove to Vermont to spend a few days with her parents. Their plan was to head back to Amherst to keep the store open through intersession.

I worked out at the Brockton Y on Main Street. I checked in with Coach Walsh. We met at the Friendly's near the high school. I did most of the talking.

I stayed up nights thinking of Andrea and wondered if our paths would cross next semester. Or sometime after that. I would definitely be on the lookout. Maybe I'd catch her plays.

Back at school, practices started at the end of January. In late February, leaving the locker room to lift weights upstairs, Coach Shields asked if I had a minute. We stood in the doorway that connected the locker room to his office.

"You like to fly?" he said.

I just stood there, hoping he meant what I thought he meant. "I've never flown."

"Well, you're about to." He extended his hand.

"Thank you," I said. "Really, really."

"You earned it."

We landed in Orlando on March 23rd, scheduled to play nine double-headers against nine different colleges. I sat on the bench for

the first three games. The next game against Florida State I pinch
hit in the sixth inning and belted a single to center. I stayed in the
game to play right and smoked a liner to short for the final out of the
eighth. By the end of the trip, I was platooning in right with a senior
named Connor Douglass, a lefty batter. We shared right field the rest
of the season. We finished in May with a winning record and made
it to the playoffs, but got bumped early on.

I got three calls to play summer ball. In May, I signed a contract
to play with the Chatham Anglers of the Cape Cod Baseball League.
There was no pay and the conditions were a far cry from what you
see on TV, but Cape Cod was a premier league with an endless list
of future major leaguers and I was happy to spend my summer on
a diamond. My host family, the Masons, owned a lumber yard off
Old Queen Anne Road and when I wasn't practicing or at games I
worked there hauling wood for extra money. I only started a handful
of games because the team had depth, but by the end of the season
the coaches made it clear that I'd be invited back.

By Fall Ball sophomore year, Connor Douglass had graduated
and right field was all mine. Dirk Benson was gone too, so I was
back to wearing number 10.

Coach Shields allowed me to miss the second Fall Ball game for
Cliff and Marie's wedding. The weather cooperated and the ceremony
passed without a hitch. The maid of honor was Marie's fourteen-
year-old sister, a caustic kid who had spent most of the rehearsal
dinner the night before insulting guests' outfits with comments like,
"How much did she pay for *that*?" and "She should *not* be wearing
horizontal stripes."

The reception was held on the top floor of a hotel in downtown
Burlington. The floor to ceiling windows overlooked the city on
three sides, with unobstructed views of Lake Champlain to the west
and airplanes ascending and descending at Burlington International
to the east.

The best man's toast. I wish I could brag that I hit it out of
the park. I buckled. I said something perfunctory and ordinary and
predictable. I was nervous. It was my first time speaking in front
of a crowd that size. I said that I had plenty of opportunities to see
Cliff and Marie together up close over the past year and mentioned
how moving it was to see their love flourish. If that wasn't boring
enough, I spent most of it stammering and sweating. I sat down as

quickly as possible.

I was a hit in another regard, though. A girl named Rachel from the wedding party with a habit of glossing her lips every ten minutes asked me to dance. So of course I asked her to dance. And back and forth we went. Like the other bridesmaids, her gown was old-fashioned, like from a forties movie; the bodice clung to her narrow torso and the skirt floated when we danced.

The third dance was a slow number; our hands touched briefly before mine slid around her waist and hers rose to the back of my neck. Her palms were warm and moist. Her perfume was summery, a combination of flowers and grapefruit. At some point in the song, we drew closer. We fit together perfectly.

Steve Perry was pouring it on, a pleading, baleful tune, wondering where it all went wrong. I was thinking of how I'd heard this song just a few days ago on my alarm clock radio. Then suddenly: Bam, hello hardon. It happened so quickly—*Here I am, Jimmy Boy, let's get rockin'*—that I found myself stepping away to avoid embarrassment.

"Are you all right?"

"Fine and dandy." I smiled and she smiled back. I stepped once again into her embrace, careful not to get too close until the erection died down.

"After the reception, a bunch of us are going down to the hotel bar," she said.

"Sounds good," I said, knowing I wouldn't join them. I'd make something up about a disagreeable shrimp or some meat from the carving station. For now, though, this slow gliding dance was just fine. This lovely stranger's breath just under my ear; the feel of her smooth dress against my fingers; and the way she held me, her slender arms over my shoulders, hands clasped tenderly around my neck, as if she didn't want the dance to end.

**

The reception was winding down. Band members coiled wires and loaded instruments and speakers onto dollies. The bartender started packing up too so I ordered a final drink. I'd told him from the start that I wasn't a huge drinker—just a beer or two once in a while, never really acquired the taste—so he set me up with a tasty rum punch concoction that was going down pretty easily.

Cliff and Marie were long gone, as were most of the guests. Some of the wedding party and others, including Rachel, had gathered at the main entrance to the ballroom. She caught my eye and started toward the bar. The only reason I still lingered was because I wasn't convinced I didn't want to join the after-party. As she drew nearer I realized my mind was made up.

"We're going to head down," she said.

"You know, I'm feeling a little . . ."

"What." She touched my elbow.

"I don't know, a little queasy or something."

"Oh no." Her hand slid down until it touched mine.

"Yeah. I'm sorry . . ."

"Oh, that's okay. You'll be at the breakfast tomorrow?"

"Definitely, I'll be there."

"Well . . . come to the bar if you feel better."

We hugged quickly and she disappeared into the crowd of other departing bridesmaids.

My parents were still there, so were Marie's. The men sat together leaning back on their chairs, exhausted. My father's face was red from drink and dancing. Marie's father's legs stretched out in front of him, his hands folded across his wide belly. I said goodnight to them, then to Mother and Marie's mother, who were engaged in conversation by the window that overlooked the water.

In the elevator car, as the doors opened on my floor, I remembered how I had felt when I checked in and sat alone on the bed. I'd hardly ever slept in a hotel room except for the spring trip and even then I shared the room with other players. I didn't want to be alone. I let the doors close, then pressed the button for the lobby.

The doors opened. Music pounded down the hall. I followed it and saw her right away. Dancing with a couple of girlfriends, laughing and shouting over each other. She saw me and waved me over. I danced as ineptly as I had danced at the wedding, but she didn't seem to mind. The other girls broke away.

"What happened?" she said.

I couldn't hear her, but her lips, still glossed and perfect, were easy to read.

"I feel better."

We moved away from the speakers. She grabbed her clutch bag from a nearby chair and we sat on bar stools that overlooked the dance floor. Her last name was Donavan. She knew Marie from a summer high school job and they'd been close ever since. The bar was still serving its late night menu. We split some chicken wings and when the waitress brought them Rachel asked for a tall glass of water.

After the last chicken bone was tossed into the basket, she said, "I'm ready to call it a night."

She reached into her purse and took out some bills.

"I got this."

"You don't have to."

"I haven't spent a dime since I got here. It's no problem."

We said so long to her friends and I mentioned how nice it was to meet everyone. It was several degrees cooler in the lobby, but Rachel still patted her forehead with one of the cocktail napkins from the bar.

At the elevators she said, "You want to make sure I don't lose my way?"

"Hm?" I wasn't sure if I was supposed to drive her home or something. "I thought you were staying at the hotel."

"I am, silly." Her hand on my arm again. "But I've had a few cocktails. I could take a wrong turn." She leaned forward. Her lips brushed my cheek. My inside did some cartwheels. The elevator doors opened and we stepped inside.

Okay, I thought, I'll walk her to her room, thank her for a nice evening and say goodnight. That's all. We reached her door. She removed her key.

"I'd like you to come in," she said. "But I'm rooming with Meg. I'm not sure when she'll be up."

We looked at each other for a couple of seconds. A door opened and closed somewhere down the hall. An ice machine buzzed.

"I'm two floors down."

What did I just do? Stupid move—pure instinct overtaking rational thought. Or maybe the booze had made me bold.

She dropped her key into the purse. "Lead the way."

"Look, I didn't mean to suggest . . ." I needed to correct this mistake. "If you don't want to . . ."

"No, no. I said lead the way."

I was going to say something else in protest, but stopped. If instinct was overtaking rational thought, then just let it. You're feeling loosey-goosey. And look at this girl—she's beautiful, she obviously wants you and she's half in the bag. Plus, you'll never see her again after tomorrow. If you can't get it up for her they may as well have removed your dick back when they removed your balls.

The room was dark when I pushed open the door. I reached for the switch, but she stopped me, placing her fingers over mine. She still smelled like summer. We kissed frantically against the door. She let her bag fall. I rubbed my erection against her thigh, through the frills of her dress. She pulled herself away, then walked to the foot of the bed. The shades were half open and the amber lights from the parking lot lit her from behind. In silhouette, she reached between her shoulder blades and lowered the zipper to the small of her back. With a quick tug at her hips the dress fell to her ankles.

I found myself moving toward her, every fiber of my body coiled with anticipation and lust. For the first time I allowed myself to be drawn in, drawn in by the scent of her skin, and the promise of her touch.

About the Author

Jonathan Curelop is a graduate of the City College of New York's Creative Writing Program. He has studied at Gotham Writer's Workshop and the New York Writers Workshop. His fiction and non-fiction have appeared in various publications, including *Solstice*, *Amarillo Bay*, *Liquid Imagination*, *UMass Amherst Magazine*, *apt*, *Raging Face*, *The Melic Review*, *The American Book Review* and *Aura*. Originally from Massachusetts, where he graduated from the University of Massachusetts/Amherst's Theater department, he now lives in New York City with his wife, Pamela, and works as an editor and as a compliance officer at an international investment bank.

Connect with Jonathan Curelop on Twitter: @JCurelop

Visit www.bookcasetv.com for other titles from Book Case Engine

CPSIA information can be obtained at www.ICGtesting.com
Printed in the USA
BVOW05s1806180914

367437BV00001B/7/P